# November Third

# November Third

Bill Lewers

ISBN-13: 9781974430093
ISBN-10: 197443009X

*November Third* is a work of fiction. Names, characters, places, and incidents are products of the author's imagination or are used fictitiously. Any resemblance to actual events, locales, or persons, living or dead, is entirely coincidental.
Cover Design by Earthly Charms

# Contents


Author's Notes and Acknowledgements · · · · · · xi

**Part One** **The Candidate** · · · · · · · · · · · · · · · · · · · · · · · · · 1

Chapter 1 Monday afternoon, November 2 · · · · · · · · · · · · · · 3

Chapter 2 Tuesday, June 9, several months earlier · · · · · · · · 9

Chapter 3 Tuesday, June 9, 11:30 a.m. · · · · · · · · · · · · · · · · · 15

Chapter 4 Thursday, June 18, 8:30 p.m. · · · · · · · · · · · · · · · · 19

Chapter 5 Tuesday, June 23, 1:30 p.m. · · · · · · · · · · · · · · · · · 22

Chapter 6 Tuesday, June 30, 9:00 a.m. · · · · · · · · · · · · · · · · · 26

Chapter 7 Tuesday evening, 8:00 p.m. · · · · · · · · · · · · · · · · · · 33

Chapter 8 Wednesday, July 1 · · · · · · · · · · · · · · · · · · · · · · · · 37

Chapter 9 Monday, July 6, 5:30 p.m. · · · · · · · · · · · · · · · · · · 39

Chapter 10 Thursday, July 9, 7:30 p.m. · · · · · · · · · · · · · · · · · 47

Chapter 11 Monday, July 13, 8:00 p.m. · · · · · · · · · · · · · · · · · 52

Chapter 12 Tuesday, July 14, 9:00 a.m. · · · · · · · · · · · · · · · · · 55

Chapter 13 Thursday, July 16, 7:30 p.m. · · · · · · · · · · · · · · · · 61

Chapter 14 Sunday, July 26, 5:50 p.m. · · · · · · · · · · · · · · · · · · 66

Chapter 15 Tuesday, July 28, 7:30 p.m. · · · · · · · · · · · · · · · · · 70

Chapter 16 Monday, August 3, 9:00 a.m. · · · · · · · · · · · · · · · · 76

Chapter 17 Monday, August 10, 8:00 p.m. · · · · · · · · · · · · · · · 81

Chapter 18 Friday, August 14, Noon · · · · · · · · · · · · · · · · · · · 84

Chapter 19 Wednesday, August 19, 7:30 p.m. · · · · · · · · · · · · 87

| | | |
|---|---|---|
| **Part Two** | **The Campaign** | 95 |
| Chapter 20 | Monday, August 24, 7:30 p.m. | 97 |
| Chapter 21 | Tuesday, September 1, 7:45 p.m. | 100 |
| Chapter 22 | Monday, September 7, 1:00 p.m. | 104 |
| Chapter 23 | Saturday, September 12, 9:00 a.m. | 108 |
| Chapter 24 | Tuesday, September 15, 9:00 a.m. | 115 |
| Chapter 25 | Wednesday, September 16, 7:00 a.m. | 121 |
| Chapter 26 | Tuesday, September 22 | 129 |
| Chapter 27 | Wednesday, September 23 | 132 |
| Chapter 28 | Saturday, September 26 | 136 |
| Chapter 29 | Monday, September 28, 7:00 a.m. | 139 |
| Chapter 30 | Monday evening, 6:45 p.m. | 149 |
| Chapter 31 | Tuesday, September 29, 5:30 a.m. | 152 |
| Chapter 32 | Tuesday, later in the day | 158 |
| Chapter 33 | Tuesday evening, 6:45 p.m. | 161 |
| Chapter 34 | Wednesday, September 30, 6:30 a.m. | 164 |
| Chapter 35 | Wednesday evening, 6:45 p.m. | 171 |
| Chapter 36 | Thursday, October 1, 2:55 p.m. | 174 |
| Chapter 37 | Friday, October 2, 7:00 a.m. | 176 |
| Chapter 38 | Saturday, October 3, 8:30 a.m. | 181 |
| Chapter 39 | Sunday, October 4, 3:30 p.m. | 188 |
| Chapter 40 | Monday, October 5, 7:00 a.m. | 191 |
| Chapter 41 | Tuesday, October 6, 11:50 p.m. | 193 |
| Chapter 42 | Wednesday, October 7, 6:45 p.m. | 195 |
| Chapter 43 | Wednesday evening, 8:30 p.m. | 201 |
| Chapter 44 | Wednesday evening, 9:35 p.m. | 207 |
| Chapter 45 | Thursday, October 8 | 211 |
| Chapter 46 | Thursday evening, 7:30 p.m. | 214 |
| **Part Three** | **The Rover** | 217 |
| Chapter 47 | Saturday, October 10 | 219 |
| Chapter 48 | Sunday, October 11 | 221 |

Chapter 49 Monday, October 12, 2:00 p.m. 223
Chapter 50 Tuesday, October 13, 7:00 a.m. 227
Chapter 51 Wednesday, October 14, 7:25 p.m. 233
Chapter 52 Wednesday evening, 9:30 p.m. 238
Chapter 53 Monday, October 19, 1:30 p.m. 240
Chapter 54 Friday, October 23, 10:00 a.m. 246
Chapter 55 Sunday, October 25, 3:30 p.m. 251
Chapter 56 Tuesday, October 27, 10:00 a.m. 255
Chapter 57 Wednesday, October 28, 3:50 p.m. 257
Chapter 58 Wednesday evening, 9:00 p.m. 261
Chapter 59 Thursday, October 29 263
Chapter 60 Saturday, October 31, 8:30 a.m. 265
Chapter 61 Sunday, November 1, 6:00 p.m. 272
Chapter 62 Sunday evening, 11:00 p.m. 280
Chapter 63 Monday morning, November 2, 2:30 a.m. 284
Chapter 64 Monday, 2.55 a.m. 286
Chapter 65 Monday, 8:00 a.m. 293
Chapter 66 Monday, 9:00 a.m. 296
Chapter 67 Monday, 9:45 a.m. 298
Chapter 68 Monday, Noon 301
Chapter 69 Monday, 1:20 p.m. 305
Chapter 70 Monday, 3:00 p.m. 310
Chapter 71 Monday, 4:45 p.m. 313

**Part Four November Third** 317
Chapter 72 Tuesday morning, November 3, 3:00 a.m. 319
Chapter 73 Tuesday, 5:00 a.m. 322
Chapter 74 Tuesday, 6:20 a.m. 326
Chapter 75 Tuesday, 7:10 a.m. 332
Chapter 76 Tuesday, 7:45 a.m. 335
Chapter 77 Tuesday, 8:10 a.m. 338
Chapter 78 Tuesday, 9:00 a.m. 342

Chapter 79 Tuesday, 9:55 a.m. · · · 345
Chapter 80 Tuesday, 10:45 a.m. · · · 352
Chapter 81 Tuesday, 11:45 a.m. · · · 356
Chapter 82 Tuesday, 12:15 p.m. · · · 358
Chapter 83 Tuesday, 1:00 p.m. · · · 361
Chapter 84 Tuesday, 1:30 p.m. · · · 364
Chapter 85 Tuesday, 2:15 p.m. · · · 369
Chapter 86 Tuesday, 2:30 p.m. · · · 371
Chapter 87 Tuesday, 3:30 p.m. · · · 378
Chapter 88 Tuesday, 4:30 p.m. · · · 383
Chapter 89 Tuesday, 5:45 p.m. · · · 387
Chapter 90 Tuesday, 6:00 p.m. · · · 389
Chapter 91 Tuesday, 6:30 p.m. · · · 392
Chapter 92 Tuesday, 7:10 p.m. · · · 396
Chapter 93 Tuesday, 7:30 p.m. · · · 398
Chapter 94 Tuesday, 7:35 p.m. · · · 400
Chapter 95 Tuesday, 7:40 p.m. · · · 402
Chapter 96 Tuesday, 8:15 p.m. · · · 405
Chapter 97 Tuesday, 8:30 p.m. · · · 408
Chapter 98 Tuesday, 8:50 p.m. · · · 410
Chapter 99 Tuesday, 9:20 p.m. · · · 412
Chapter 100 Tuesday, 9:30 p.m. · · · 414
Chapter 101 Tuesday, 10:05 p.m. · · · 416
Chapter 102 Tuesday, 10:25 p.m. · · · 418
Chapter 103 Tuesday, 11:30 p.m. · · · 420

Glossary · · · 423
About the Author · · · 431

# Dedication

*On June 24, 2011, I received an invitation to join a group of Fairfax County seasonal employees known as the "rovers." Rovers come in all shapes and sizes: male, female, liberal, conservative, Democrat, Republican, moderate, not-so-moderate. Together we have stocked precinct carts, moved scanners, tested voting machines, examined tapes, packed boxes of ballots, installed flash drives, removed flash drives, stamped test decks, sorted peripherals, counted privacy booths, updated logs, compacted trash, swept the floor, and turned out the lights. Then on Election Day we travel on our "routes," supporting the precincts in any way we can.*

*Then the next election occurs and we do it all again.*

*It is to the rovers of Fairfax County that this book is dedicated.*

# Author's Notes and Acknowledgements

In April, 2016, *The Gatekeepers of Democracy* was published. *Gatekeepers* is a work of fiction. Its people, places, and events exist only in my imagination. It was written to celebrate the woman and men who serve as election officers, those one-day volunteers/employees who run the precincts on Election Day. To the best of my knowledge, it is the only fictional title about election officers. It was a lot of fun to write and was meant to be a stand-alone novel.

In the months after its publication I received a number of inquiries as to whether there would ever be a sequel to *Gatekeepers.* With all the emotion centered on the 2016 national campaign, folks seemed to appreciate a novel which centered on ordinary citizens making their contribution at the local level. A number of individuals wondered if there might be room in the genre of "election officer fiction" for another title. In addition there were others who were less interested in votes and ballots than in what the future might hold for my two protagonists, Carl Marsden and Cindy Phelps. What sort of electoral adventures await them?

Gradually I began to warm to the idea of writing a sequel. I must confess that after the writing of *Gatekeepers,* I wasn't quite ready to say goodbye to my characters. It's one thing however to embrace the concept of writing a sequel and quite another to actually come up with a plot, not to mention a story. What did I want my characters to do? What challenges would they face? Another day at the polls, by itself, would not suffice. A sequel cannot simply be telling the original story all over again.

With nothing else to go on, I just started writing scenes. Scenes that excited my imagination, even though they did not connect with one another or with any overall plot (since at the time, there was no plot). These scenes suggested other scenes. Gradually as I wrote these scenes, a plot began to take shape. Some of my scenes fit into the plot and were retained while other did not and were discarded. I tried to take my characters to places they had not been before while maintaining a focus on the local political/electoral scene.

The result is *November Third.* It is a work of fiction. Its people, places, and events exist only in my imagination. It begins about five months after the conclusion of *Gatekeepers.* While events in the earlier book are referred to where appropriate, *November Third* is essentially a standalone novel which can be read and hopefully enjoyed without having read the earlier book. Once again, a glossary is included to assist with election related terms.

Special mention should be made regarding the chapters that take place at the county warehouse where the voting machines are tested and prepared for Election Day. There is a fair amount of detail in these chapters which result in slowing down the flow of the narrative somewhat. Wherever possible, I have removed unnecessary detail but the complexity of the process can only be simplified so much. Readers should be able to skim these chapters and still be able to follow the flow of the novel.

Much of the narrative was inspired by my experiences as a "rover" for the Fairfax County Office of Elections and I have tried to provide a realistic feel for what that position entails. In other areas of the story, I have been a little more "creative." The professionalism of the county Board of Elections and the sophistication of the county warehouse security systems are things that, as a citizen of Fairfax County, I appreciate, but they don't necessarily lend themselves to a good story. In these, as in other areas, I have given a freer rein to my imagination.

In no way is the county in the story (which is never named) meant to represent Fairfax County or any other actual county. I like to think of it as being some sort of "extra county," overlooked by cartographers, that is nestled between Fairfax County and the Potomac River and which, like the legendary *Brigadoon*, can be entered only on special occasions (such as when an author chooses it as the setting for one of his novels).

Once again I have been blessed by three exceptional beta readers: Catherine Mathews of the Great Falls Writer's Group, Mary Marlow Lewers, and Barbara Lewers. Each one has graciously and carefully reviewed the manuscript and made many constructive suggestions for improving the flow, not to mention uncovering many typos. I am very much in their debt.

I continue to be indebted to the members of the Great Falls Writer's Group and especially its founder and facilitator, Kristin Clark Taylor who both encourages and challenges me to be the best writer that I am able.

I would like to thank Patriot Signage, Inc. for granting me permission to include one of their signs in the author's photo on the back cover.

Finally I must acknowledge my sons, Mark and John, and my wife, Mary Marlow Lewers, who together form the foundation of my life. Their love and encouragement have sustained me throughout my writing efforts.

# Part One

## The Candidate

# 1

## MONDAY AFTERNOON, NOVEMBER 2

THE LAST WORKMAN left at four-thirty.

It was a full hour later than it should have been. There had been that late shipment. All those cartons to be unloaded. And categorized and palletized and shrink wrapped. Didn't they realize that it all took time?

But now it was done. The men gathered up their personal items and one by one left the building. The last man set the lock on the front door and flipped the various light switches, plunging the windowless warehouse into darkness. He then left by the same front door. The door closed with a resounding thud.

The warehouse was now completely dark. And still. And empty.

Except for the lone figure, kneeling in the corner of the far aisle.

The intruder did not move. The plan was to wait. Wait until it was virtually certain that no one would return.

The minutes passed. A half hour. Forty-five minutes. From time to time, the position would change. Kneeling. Standing.

Sitting. But never emerging from the corner. That was not the plan. The plan was to wait.

Outside the rush hour traffic continued its flow. Even though the street was not a major commuter artery, it did attract a certain amount of traffic at this time of day. Better to wait. Wait for the traffic to peter out and the stillness of the night to assert itself.

And assert itself it finally did. At last it was time. A beam of light shone from the far aisle of the warehouse and gradually the intruder left its confines and entered the lane that led to the main area. Slowly down the lane with the solitary beam illuminating the way. There was the welcome desk with the log. A check of the log showed no additional names. Oh well, it couldn't be helped.

A turn to the right to face the vast expanse of the warehouse interior. Now it was time to move forward quickly. There was no longer any point in hiding. Quickness, not stealth, was called for. Straight into the main part of the warehouse. Mountains of supplies all around but that was not the focus. Through the entranceway to the rear of the warehouse. There's the table, just as before. To the left were shelves holding boxes of supplies. A set of keys and a pair of nippers. Exactly as advertised. And to the right was the destination...the massive enclosure surrounded by a rectangular, ten foot tall, chain-link fence.

By the back wall of the warehouse was the entrance to the enclosure. Closed and secured with a padlock. No point in even testing it. Rather, the table was dragged across the floor to the fence. Up on the table, to reduce the climbing somewhat. Now for the tough part. All that earlier bragging wouldn't scale that fence. Work gloves to ease the pain on the hands. Papers and flashlight in the pocket of the hoody. OK, let's do it.

It was tough but that was expected. Don't think about the height. Grab the top of the fence and over you go. Now hold on. Slowly descend. The arms are where it hurts the most. About halfway down let go and land as best you can.

Out comes the flashlight again. A beam of light scans the ceiling. There it is, the surveillance camera, pointing toward the workbenches. Slowly the hood was pulled over the intruder's head.

Now it was time to find the machines. Most of the area inside the enclosure was completely empty. So different from the last time.

And there they were. Against the far wall. One, two, three… seven, eight. Eight machines. There were supposed to be nine.

The intruder approached the first machine and took out the list. Check the tag on the back of the machine. Yes, that's on the list. Fortunately each machine rested on a large black bin which rested on wheels so it was easy to roll it to one of the workbenches.

For the next several minutes each machine was examined in turn and rolled to a different spot in front of the benches. An observer would have noted that they were not placed randomly. Four of them were grouped in front of the benches against the far wall while the other four were spaced fairly evenly along the benches by the back wall.

The lid to each machine was secured with a green seal. One after another, the nippers broke each of the seals. Then back "upstream," with one of the keys unlocking each outer lid and raising it. So easy. Next came the back of the machine. Unlock and open the power cord compartment. Unravel the cord and plug it in. Lots of power strips on the workbenches. Flip the power strip switches to on. Repeat for each machine. At last it was all done. Now to bring it on home. Unlock the inner lid to each machine and lift. One machine after another. Same as before.

Upon returning to the first machine, there was a screen displaying,

"Enter Election Code"

The intruder studied the paper for a moment and then keyed in the code on the keypad.

"Election Code Not Valid"

*Damn.*

Out came the cell phone. Speed dial.

"What is it?"

"The code won't work."

"What did you enter?"

"General113"

A pause.

"Try 'General1103'"

The alternative code was keyed in.

"It works. I'll get back to you when I'm done."

One after another, the alternative code was entered and one after another, the scanners came to life. For each scanner, a configuration report was printed. The intruder then touched "Open Polls" and another, longer report was printed. There were several names on the report and next to each name was the number zero. Once more, the area was scanned for that missing ninth machine. Nothing.

*That's all I can do. Time to get the hell out of here.*

This time there was no table to help with the climb and the adrenaline rush was beginning to wear off. Slowly up the fence. Hands that sting. Arms that ache. Inch upward, ever so slowly. And whatever you do, don't look down. Closer but so far away. Closer. Closer. And at last the top. One more time, up and over.

*Dear Lord. Give me strength.*

And now, ever so slowly, down. Happy landing.

*Should I move the table back? Not much point, I guess. They'll realize pretty quick that someone was here. Still, let's not advertise it.*

The table was dragged back to its original position.

Now it was back through the warehouse, back to the front door. Be careful. Don't want to blow it, right at the end. Fortunately they don't have an alarm system. Slowly the front door was pushed open. No one in sight. The parking lot was completely empty. Good. Quickly, through the front door and across the lot to the sidewalk. A brisk walk down the block to a side street. Halfway down was the car. A reassuring click allowed the intruder to enter.

Again, speed dial.

"It's done. Just one problem."

"Which is?"

"Only eight machines were there."

"Do you remember which one was missing?"

"Yeah, I wrote it down. Let's see, it's the serial ending in 1702."

A pause.

"That's one of the ones we had an eye on. Still this should be sufficient, I would think."

"When will you make the call?"

"Tomorrow morning about eight."

"OK. Well, good luck tomorrow."

"Thanks. You too."

Another pause.

"Am I going to jail for this?"

"If you are, I'll probably be in the next cell. We can pass notes back and forth."

They said their goodbyes and hung up. It was only then that Cindy Phelps realized that she was visibly shaking and covered with perspiration. Opening the glove compartment, she pulled out the pack of cigarettes, a remnant of the habit she had never been quite able to break. She lit up and leaned back in her seat to take a few minutes to compose herself before driving home.

*This has got to be the weirdest thing I've ever done.*

# 2

## Tuesday, June 9, Several Months Earlier

It was 5:30 a.m. and the election gods were not smiling. At least they were not smiling on Carl Marsden. Some of it, he had to admit, was his own fault. Why hadn't he insisted on an alternative phone number, just in case the custodian wasn't there at 5:00 a.m. to open the doors to the Carter Run Elementary School? That was what the manual said needed to be done.

*I must be slipping,* he thought.

From the beginning, he had had a rather uneasy feeling about this election. It was a June primary to select the candidates for U.S. Senate and House of Representatives who would appear on the ballot in November. The contests had been vigorous and turnout was expected to be a bit higher than sometimes occurred in these June primaries.

Part of it was that Carl was still adjusting to being an *assistant* chief election officer. After several years of serving as chief at the Chesterbrook precinct, Carl had been reassigned as assistant chief for the special January election earlier that year. That had been an intense effort as he and the first-time chief, a young lady named Cindy Phelps, had battled through various issues and challenges which paradoxically had both energized and exhausted them.

But now it was June, and Carl didn't even have the advantage of being in his home Chesterbrook precinct. Several weeks ago he had received a call from Rebecca Simpson of the Office of Elections. Would he be willing to serve "out of precinct?" He had done such a great job of breaking in Cindy, they just knew he was the perfect person to be assistant chief at the Carter Run precinct where, for some strange reason, they had experienced a bit of difficulty keeping election officers.

"They serve once or twice but then decide it's not their thing," Rebecca had said. "Very strange."

Well after their Monday meeting at the school, Carl was beginning to understand why. His chief, a fidgety woman of about sixty named Rosemary Pennington, had been unable to secure an appointment with either the principal or the assistant principal.

"They're too busy," explained the secretary. "Everything for the election is in the lobby. That's all you really need."

"May we at least speak to a custodian?" asked Carl.

"Oh no. They're busy, too."

"But we would like to set up for tomorrow. What room will we be in?"

"Room? There is no room. You'll be in the front lobby. I don't know why we have to keep explaining this every year."

This declaration had sent Rosemary, who like Carl was new to Carter Run, into a tizzy, and it had upset Carl as well. He could not imagine an election taking place in a lobby, which was right where the kids were dropped off by the bus.

"In November, when the school is closed, you get the gym," said the secretary. "But when school is in session, all our rooms are being used. We can't have the education of our students compromised just for some silly primary election."

Rosemary and Carl had argued that this was not acceptable, but to no avail. Beaten down they had no choice but to examine the cart (a crate on wheels that contained most of the supplies needed for Election Day) and scanner in the lobby where they had been, according to the secretary, for several days. Fortunately, everything inside the cart had been in order and they filled out the log and resealed it. Still it had been a rather unsettling experience, exasperated by the secretary's reluctance to give a back-up phone number that could be used just in case the custodian failed to appear at 5:00 a.m.

"All our custodians know exactly what to do," she had said, curtly. "There is no need for another number."

Carl had wanted to argue this further but Rosemary clearly didn't have it in her for another confrontation, so he let it slide.

And now they were reaping the consequences. When they had arrived at 5:00 a.m., the parking lot was dark, the school was dark, everything was dark. Rosemary and Carl, each in turn, tried opening the door. It was locked. They knocked on the door. Nothing.

Carl immediately started walking around the school, trying every door. They were all locked. He knocked on each of them. Still nothing. He returned to the front door where Rosemary and the other officers stood.

For a few minutes Rosemary and Carl waited patiently at the door, confident that in just a minute the lights would come on and the door opened. Every few minutes they knocked on the door and tried to open it. As the minutes ticked by with still no sign of life, Carl began to experience an uneasy feeling. Election officers on their team, all people unfamiliar to Carl, started to grumble and ask questions. Questions for which Carl had no answer.

Suddenly Carl remembered something. He shined his flashlight on the door. Just as he remembered, there was a "security phone number" listed on the county decal. Rosemary quickly dialed the number and explained the situation to the county rep on the other end of the line. She looked up at Carl.

"They said they would send someone."

"Any idea when?"

"The person couldn't say. I think she was some sort of switchboard operator."

Carl's mind went into overdrive. What if the person didn't get here before 6:00 a.m.? The ballots and electronic poll books (EPBs) were in the cart, located in the school lobby.

*Ballots and poll books. That's what we need. And pens to mark the ballots and a container to put them in. That's the minimum. With just these things we can improvise for a short time, if we have to.*

"Rosemary, do you have a backup paper poll book in your kit?" he asked, pointing to the suitcase-on-wheels kit next to Rosemary.

"Yes, I'm pretty sure. No, I mean yes, I saw it. It's definite. We have it."

"And there are some pens in your kit as well?"

She nodded.

"And we can empty the kit and use it as an impromptu ballot box. Then all we need are ballots," said Carl, more to himself than Rosemary.

"Rosemary," he said, having finally deduced what was needed. "Who is our rover?"

"Let's see," said Rosemary, opening her manual. "It's Brenda Greenwold. We talked on the phone a few days ago. She seemed very nice."

"Call her right away. Tell her we're locked out. We need her to bring us ballots ASAP. Definitely before 6:00 a.m."

Rosemary quickly placed the call. It took several rings before Brenda answered. From what Carl could tell, it appeared that Brenda was in the process of guiding a new chief through the setup process.

"But we're locked out and we don't know when they're coming," Rosemary kept repeating.

Finally the call ended.

"Brenda said she will definitely be here before 6:00 a.m.," said Rosemary.

"OK, we'll just wait for Brenda. Or security. Or the custodian. Whoever comes first. In the meantime you should probably swear us all in and we can figure out who does what."

Rosemary hunted through her kit, found the oath sheet and swore in the officers. At that point she and Carl started to brainstorm how curbside voting would work. At least light wouldn't be a problem as dawn had already broken through on this mid-June day.

At about 5:45, a car pulled up in front of the school. A booming voice rang out,

"Well isn't this lovely!"

A short, gray haired woman bounded out of the car, went around to the rear, and opened the trunk.

"A pack of one hundred, I would say," Brenda called out. "That should last you until the custodian awakens from his siesta."

She handed the package to Rosemary.

"Here, start counting these while I fill out the paper work that we both have to sign."

"Perhaps I can count those while you and Rosemary attend to the paperwork," said Carl. Counting stacks of ballots quickly was a bit of an art form that Carl had mastered.

The three of them commenced with the necessary tasks that were required whenever a rover brought additional ballots to the precinct. Within a matter of a few minutes, they were done. It was now 5:50 a.m. and early bird voters had begun to arrive, somewhat confused by the curbside gathering before them.

Just then the light illuminating the parking lot came on. The front door opened and a gruff looking custodian peered out.

"Are you all coming in or not?" he grumbled.

Carl, Rosemary, and Brenda exchanged glances.

"It's just going to be one of those days," said Carl.

# 3

## Tuesday, June 9, 11:30 a.m.

"Cindy," said the plump, gray haired woman. "The gentleman over at the check-in table wants to know who the Tea Party candidate is. I think its Anthony Palucci but I wanted to check with you to be sure."

Cindy Phelps looked up from the *Chief's Notes* form she had been working on and gave an inward sigh. Her assistant chief here at the Cooper precinct was a dear, dear lady but once again it was obvious that she had either not read the manual or, even if she had, not assimilated its contents.

"Let's go talk to the gentleman, Nelly," she said with a smile while thinking, *at least, now we have a teachable moment.*

Together they walked over to the check-in table where an intense looking, elderly man stood. He seemed to be having an animated conversation with the election officer, seated on the other side of the table.

"Mr. Gomez, this is our chief election officer. She can help you," said Nelly.

"I want to know which of the Republicans running for the Senate is the Tea Party candidate," the man demanded. "It's a simple question. Why can't anyone answer me?"

"It's not our job to educate you," the seated officer shot back with equal intensity. "You need to take democracy seriously and educate yourself—"

"I think it's Palucci—" Nelly interjected, trying to be helpful.

"But are you sure?" said Mr. Gomez.

"Stop. Everyone. Please," interjected Cindy, in a tone that for the moment at least, silenced the room.

"Sir," began Cindy, slowly and deliberately. "We give you the ballot as it is printed. That's our job. It's all we do. It's all we are allowed to do."

"But how am I supposed to know who the Tea Party candidate is? You're withholding information from me," said an obviously agitated Mr. Gomez.

"You're trying to blame us for your own lack of preparation—" interjected the officer.

"Tom," said Cindy, shifting her gaze to the officer. "I'm handling this. Has Mr. Gomez checked in yet?"

"No, not yet," said Tom. "We never got that far."

"OK. Good," said Cindy, turning her attention back to Mr. Gomez. "Sir, we are strictly prohibited from commenting on the ballot in any way. That's the law and we are bound by it. Now it's not my place to advise you what to do, but the last time I checked, there were folks campaigning outside. You might want to consider going out and talking to one of them. These are partisans but perhaps one of them might tell you what you want to know."

The room became silent. Tom cleared his throat as if preparing to say something. Cindy shot him a stern glance.

At last Mr. Gomez said, "I will go outside. Then I will come back."

"And it will be our pleasure to serve you," said Cindy, with what she hoped was her brightest smile.

As soon as he left, Cindy turned to Nelly.

"Nelly, I know you were trying to be helpful, but we cannot comment on the ballot in any way. Please say you understand."

Even as Nelly nodded her head, Tom interjected with, "That's what I said all along. These voters need to take democracy seriously and prepare themselves—"

"Tom," said Cindy. "Can you come back to the chief's table with me? I need your help on something. Nelly, please take his place at check-in for a few minutes."

Cindy and Tom went back to the table.

"I'm glad we put that guy in his place—" began Tom.

"Stop right there," interrupted Cindy. Tom looked at Cindy with a somewhat startled expression. Apparently he wasn't used to being silenced by someone who was at least thirty years his junior.

"I agree with your sentiments. Really I do," said Cindy. "But it's not our place to be lecturing voters."

"But how are they ever going to learn if we don't bring them to task?"

"That's not our concern. We treat them all with respect and cordiality. The prepared, the unprepared, the gracious, the less than gracious. I should have mentioned this earlier, when you started lecturing that lady who forgot her ID. But I'm telling you now."

Tom's sulky expression suggested that he was less than convinced.

"Is there anything else you want?" he mumbled.

"No, that's all. But please take what I said seriously because if it happens again, you'll be handing out 'I Voted' stickers for the rest of the day."

Tom gave a slight nod and went back to the check-in table.

Even as Cindy prepared to return to her paperwork, she allowed herself a few seconds of reflection.

*So Carl, how am I doing?*

# 4

## Thursday, June 18, 8:30 p.m.

"So then I'll be going into the Government Center next Tuesday to meet with Roger Dellman," said Carl, "and unless I blow the interview entirely, I'll be the county's newest rover."

"Newest and best," declared Cindy. "That's wonderful, Carl."

They were seated in the living room of Cindy's apartment, where Carl, in a burst of enthusiasm, had paid her a spontaneous visit.

"Of course it will be a bit of a pay cut. But my boss at Software Solutions is willing to adjust my workhours to fit the busy season of the election cycle. Eventually though, after those anticipated retirements, I'll be able to apply for a full time position with the Office of Elections. Roger feels that with my technical background, I'll be a good fit."

Cindy was truly happy for Carl. His single-minded dedication to the electoral process had been the thing that had defined him from the moment they had met last January. It was in fact so intense, that it had masked for a while, what a nice person Carl was.

"You certainly have gone to great lengths to avoid having to take orders from me on Election Day," she teased. "You'll actually be ordering me around. That is, if I serve again as chief in November."

Carl turned serious. "Of course, you'll be chief. You were great in January—"

Cindy gave him a raised eyebrow look.

"—once you got the hang of it and you said that being chief at Cooper for the June primary was a snap. There's no way they won't ask you again."

"I suppose you're right," said Cindy. She genuinely enjoyed the work but was not especially happy about using more of her limited vacation time. Still, now was not the time to rain on Carl's parade.

"Even if I am a rover, I might not have your precinct on my route. Milton has had that route for years. Besides, rovers do not boss the chiefs. The chiefs are in charge of the precinct. Rovers simply provide staff support, although we can make suggestions."

Carl continued to describe the various tasks that the rovers performed and how they interacted with the chief's duties. Cindy had heard it all before and simply nodded at what appeared to be the appropriate places. Eventually Carl wound down.

"Anyway, I should be going. Are we still good for Saturday?"

"What? Oh yes, Saturday."

Together they walked over to the door of her apartment.

"I'm sorry again for barging in on you like this. But I just had to tell you."

"I'm glad you did. Congratulations. You work so hard on this stuff. You really earned it."

They exchanged a brief, yet tender kiss and Carl opened the door and left, closing the door behind him.

For the next few seconds, Cindy stood there, staring at the closed door. He was so different from the high octane guys she usually dated. A bit of a nerd except when it came to elections in which case he was the definition of "nerdiness." Certainly not the most exciting person around. She wasn't sure of the long-range potential, but he was kind and reliable and for now, that was sufficient.

# 5

## Tuesday, June 23, 1:30 p.m.

"Most of what we do is in the warehouse," Roger Dellman was saying. "All the voting machines and precinct carts are in our county warehouse in Springdale. Before each election we run a set of ballots through the *ElectionPro* scanner. The printouts need to match the anticipated result or we redo the whole thing again. We also stock the precinct carts for each of the 240 precincts that are in the county, as well as the absentee machines. The whole process takes three to four weeks, depending on how complex the ballot is. This fall will be U.S. Senate, U.S. House of Representatives, and a bond issue, along with filling a vacancy on both the school board and the Soil and Water Conservation Board."

Carl listened attentively. This hardly seemed like an interview. Roger was treating him like the job was already his.

"We'll be starting the serious testing in mid-September for November's election," continued Roger. "But in a week or so, we'll be working for a few days doing cleanup from June's primary. Also there is talk of some additional scanners being purchased. If this happens, we will have to do an acceptance test which should take a few days. We'll let you know."

The discussion continued with Roger describing the warehouse activities in further detail. He gave Carl the two master keys he would need, for the precinct cart and the scanner, along with a lanyard to keep them on. Work in the warehouse could get physical and dirty so the grubbiest of clothing was always the order of the day. He also emphasized the point that Carl already knew, that rovers were there to support the chiefs on their route, but the chief had the ultimate authority. The real surprise came when Roger informed Carl that he would have Milton's old route.

"We've decided to move Milton to a route closer to his home. He's been asking for this for some time and due to another rover's retirement, we are able to accommodate him. He'll brief you on the precincts on your route, one of which, Chesterbrook, is well known to you."

Carl was overjoyed with his luck. This was even better than he hoped for. He couldn't wait to share the news with Cindy.

Roger wrapped it up by discussing the proper way to fill out time sheets. Then he turned him over to Gordon Carruthers, the registrar, who gave Carl a mini-lecture on the need to be strictly non-partisan in both word and deed. This was preaching to the choir as far as Carl was concerned, but he listened attentively nonetheless.

"And now I'll turn you over to our Human Resources person who will take you through the necessary paperwork. Be thankful that you just came on board. All the current rovers will be going through a 'termination-rehire' process that is the result of our need to get our accounting systems up to date. It's been a source of contention among the rovers but at least you'll be spared. Now if you follow me, I'll take you to the HR person."

They left Gordon's cube and walked past several desks until they reached a cube with a big "HR" sign tacked to the side.

"Valerie, this is Carl, our new rover. I'll leave you both to it."

Gordon gave Valerie the personnel folder that Roger had created and turned to leave. Carl, in the meantime, did a double take. It was like he was looking at a slightly altered version of Cindy. Somewhat older and a bit heavier perhaps, but with the same basic look and facial features.

"Hi, I'm Valerie Turner," she said, extending her hand. "Pleased to meet you."

"Carl Marsden," said Carl, as they shook hands.

Now it was Valerie's turn to look startled. Just for a moment, Carl's name seemed to trigger some sort of recognition. The moment, if there was a moment, vanished almost immediately and Valerie began to describe the HR process.

"You need to fill out these forms. Then I'll review them for completeness and accuracy. We don't want all your new found wealth going into the wrong account." She gave Carl a wry smile.

All the while Carl stared at Valerie, mesmerized. Her looks, mannerisms, and even speech reminded him so much of Cindy. Not quite as polished perhaps and a little more subdued but still… Carl just had to ask.

"Excuse me, but are you related to Cindy Phelps?"

"Yes, I'm her sister." The way she said it suggested that she was used to being asked that question.

"Really," said Carl, amazed. "I never know Cindy had a sister."

For the briefest moment, Valerie's face seemed to harden and Carl almost thought he saw her silently mouth the words "how typical," under her breath. Regaining her poise she quickly said,

"Now if you could work on these forms, we'll have you out of here in a jiffy."

Carl began working on the forms while Valerie attended to some unrelated paperwork on her desk. The forms were straightforward and Carl had them filled out in a matter of minutes. Valerie reviewed them and nodded.

"Everything looks in order. You're now officially part of the team. Your final step is to go downstairs and get your photo taken for your ID badge."

"Thank you for your help. I'm really excited about this opportunity," said Carl, who suddenly felt compelled to add. "And I'm sorry for being so abrupt before. You see, Cindy and I have been dating these past few months and I—"

"Yes, I know," said Valerie, crisply. "I'm pleased to have met you. We'll be running into each other at the warehouse, I expect. I'll be there, helping guide the other rovers through the termination-rehire process."

They exchanged a few final pleasantries and then Carl took his leave. *What a small world,* he thought. *I can't wait to mention this to Cindy. I wonder why she never mentioned having a sister.*

In the meantime Valerie inserted all the completed forms into Carl's personnel folder. She then looked up at Carl's retreating figure.

*He seems like a nice guy. I only hope—well that's none of my business.*

# 6

## Tuesday, June 30, 9:00 a.m.

*So this is the famous warehouse.*

Carl got out of his car, which he had parked in a space immediately in front of the warehouse. The address Roger had given him was for a dingy looking building which was linked together with several other dingy looking buildings, along the street which was, appropriately enough, named Warehouse Way. There to his left was a ramp leading up to a metal door. To the side of the door was a picnic bench where some men sat, smoking.

"You can't park there," one of the men called out. "That is for county employees."

"But I am an employee," Carl started to say. "I'm one of the rovers working on the election—"

"Real employees," the man shot back. "None of this part time stuff. You're in the second row back there. That is, if you can find something."

"And if I can't?"

"Well then, you'll think of something," said the man. His companions laughed.

Feeling somewhat chastised, Carl returned to his car and backed out of his parking place. Finding a spot in one of the two back rows was something of a challenge as he had to maneuver around a couple of large county trucks that took up several parking spaces and part of the lane as well. Eventually Carl was able to squeeze his vehicle into a rather tight spot. Making sure his newly minted county ID badge was around his neck, he exited his car. Walking up the ramp, he nodded politely to the men, who had suddenly become indifferent to his presence, and opened the door.

If the outside was unimpressive, the interior evoked an image of industrial grandeur. Piles and piles of neatly stacked boxes could be seen over an expanse that seemed to stretch on forever, both to his left and his right. To his immediate left were platforms, where materials were apparently staged before being put onto trucks. Two big industrial fork lifts were in the center of the floor. To Carl's right were shelves upon shelves holding all sorts of items. Directly in front of him was a desk and a large sign.

*All guests must sign in.*

*I guess that means me,* thought Carl as he approached the desk. There was a log perched there. He could see about seven or eight names, including Roger's, with the word "election" written down as the "reason for visit." Carl quickly did likewise. Looking up at the person behind the desk, he started to speak, but before the words came out, the man said, "Go on back," briefly pointing toward the rear of the warehouse.

Carl followed the man's lead, walking around the desk and forward into the heart of the warehouse. A wide path stretched out before him and he walked briskly past more piles of all sorts of things. One large canvas cart was filled to almost overflowing with what appeared to be old library books. At last he came to an area defined by a large rectangular enclosure. Two sides of the perimeter were brick walls while the other two sides consisted of a ten foot high chain-link fence. Inside this "cage," rammed in every which way, were precinct carts along with scanners, perched on their black bins. He also couldn't help but notice that the air conditioning, that had greeted him when he first entered the building, seemed not to be working back here.

"Hey Carl, you're in the right place."

To the left of the cage was a long table where a group of people were seated. The man who called out to Carl was Milton, who had served as Carl's rover ever since he had become a chief, some five years earlier.

Carl went over to the table where Milton started to introduce him to the various people seated at the table. All were apparently rovers and Carl felt that some of them looked vaguely familiar. Roger was at a different table, conversing on the phone.

"I thought we had about eighteen rovers," said Carl to Milton. There was only six others seated at the table, plus Roger.

"Not every rover shows up for each warehouse session," explained Milton. "Some have conflicts: doctors' appointments, family responsibilities, out-of-town for some reason. And then some of them have 'real jobs.'" He smiled.

For a few minutes everyone sat and chatted amicably. A few exchanged war stories from the recent primary.

"Everything seems to have gone smoothly for Cindy at Cooper," Milton said quietly to Carl. He suspected that the two had developed a "personal interest" in each other. Carl nodded, but said nothing.

Three more rovers walked in from the front.

"Sorry I'm late. I had to walk the dogs," called out a woman who Carl immediately recognized as Brenda, the rover he had encountered at Carter Run, the day of the primary. The matter-of-fact grunts from some of the rovers sitting at the table suggested that Brenda's dogs had been mentioned more than once.

At last Roger completed his phone conversation.

"Good morning," said Roger. "Thank you all for coming out on what promises to be a warm day here at the warehouse. Before we begin, I'd like to introduce our newest rover, Carl Marsden. Carl, why don't you tell us something about yourself?"

Carl had no idea what was expected so he just gave a brief rundown of his election experience and the precincts he had served in.

"So you've become a rover just so you don't have to serve at Carter Run anymore," said Brenda. Murmurs of assent suggested that Carter Run was somewhat legendary as being a difficult precinct.

"For the next few days we will be getting the warehouse back to normal after the recently completed primary," said Roger. "Precinct carts will be emptied of all items that don't belong. Also the backup flash drive needs to be removed from the scanners and the bins examined to make sure there are no voted ballots."

Looking out over the sea of tangled metal that was in the election cage, he continued, "As usual the delivery people just crammed the carts and scanners inside the cage in no particular order. We will start by locating those carts that belong in the first row. Jack, you take the lead in identifying what those cart numbers are. Initially the rest of you just help in clearing those first two rows of carts. Then you form yourselves into two person teams at Station Two. As always, safety first. OK, let's get started."

At that, the rovers all got to their feet and proceeded to file into the cage to start moving carts and scanners. Carl followed, determined to fake it as best he could. The initial thrust seemed to be to remove the carts and scanners from the area that had apparently been designated as rows one and two. In the meantime one of the older rovers, a crusty looking fellow that Carl assumed was Jack, started calling out three digit numbers.

"We need 104, followed by 106, and then 108." He called.

"Carl, why don't you team up with Scott here, at Station Two," said Roger. "There's a cheat sheet at each of the Station Two workbenches that says what needs to be done."

Scott, like most of the rovers, appeared to be at or near retirement age. He motioned to Carl to follow him and they went over to the rear wall of the cage area where a series of workbenches were secured end-to-end.

"Once they get those initial carts picked out," explained Scott, "A sort of assembly line is formed on that side wall. We simply retrieve the next cart and scanner, bring it to our work station, and empty it of all inappropriate items." He held up the cheat sheet. "It's straightforward and a bit dull. In the old days, we'd have it done in a day, but now that we have the scanners as well, it will take a bit longer. Ah, there is the first cart now."

They proceeded to the side wall. Scott took the cart by the handle and pulled it to their work station while Carl pushed the scanner which was fastened on top of a black bin on wheels. Carl noticed that other Station Two teams had formed at the other workbenches.

Carl knelt down, cut the precinct seal with a pair of nippers, unlocked the cart door, and opened it. Immediately a cascade of things tumbled out of the cart, onto the floor.

"Ah, they were in a hurry to get home," commented Scott. Carl sifted through the materials. There were a lot of signs that should have been returned to the Government Center in the blue canvas bag by the chief, on the night of the election. Carl soon learned that all such materials went into a special bin which presumably would find its way back to the Government Center. Of more concern was the brown box of unvoted ballots which likewise should have gone back on Election night.

"They go in a special bin," said Scott. "The chiefs should know better."

Once the inappropriate items were removed, it was necessary to tidy up the contents of the cart. A metal shelf with dividers split the interior into four quadrants and each quadrant held certain things. This particular cart had items every which way and it took Carl a bit of time to get everything back to normal. While he was doing this, Scott examined the bin under the scanner for voted ballots (there were none, thankfully) and removed the backup flash drive (the primary one had been removed by the chief on election night after the tapes had been printed), which was dumped in a box that would be returned to the Government Center. With that, they were done. They then moved the cart and scanner to the Station Three area, which was by the table where they had originally been seated. Other rovers would take over at that point and get the cart/scanner back to the proper row in the cage.

It all seemed so complicated but after a few carts, it became automatic. This was a low pressure way to start, Scott explained. The primary election was "in the books." This was just clean-up. Things would be a lot more intense when they started testing in September, to prepare for the November election.

"Who had Carter Run?" called out Brenda.

"I did," answered Carl. *Why is she asking that? She knows it was me.*

"Well, I'm looking at the cart now," Brenda was saying.

"How is it?" asked Carl, anxiously.

"Well, it's...," said Brenda, pausing for effect. "OK, I guess."

Carl breathed easier. He had supervised the packing of the cart, the night of the primary.

They worked on, breaking for lunch and coming back an hour later. Scott and Carl had developed a pattern. One would take the cart, the other the scanner, alternating with each precinct. It was Carl's turn to take the scanner.

He opened the backup compartment and removed the backup flash drive. As directed he also examined the front compartment, just to make sure the primary flash drive had already been removed. The main compartment of the black bin was empty of any ballots. Everything good, so far. He then opened the auxiliary bin. He reached in and felt around. There was something in there. He grabbed hold and pulled it out. His hand held three ballots. Three voted ballots.

"Scott, I think I've got something. These were in the auxiliary slot."

Scott paused for a moment, and looked at the voted ballots.

"If they were in the auxiliary slot, that means they were not scanned."

"And if they are still here, it means they were never counted by hand either," added Carl.

"Better get those to Roger," said Scott. "I'm not sure what he does with them since it's too late for them be counted but I suspect they go back to the Government Center. Also, tell him the precinct. They are going to want to get in touch with the chief on this. Too bad. Everything else in the cart looks pretty good."

"I'm on it," said Carl. "Which precinct is this?"

"Let's see," said Scott, looking at the stenciled markings on the side of the cart. "Ah yes, it's Cooper."

# 7

## Tuesday Evening, 8:00 P.M.

"Now what is it that just can't wait?" said Cindy, with a somewhat bemused expression, as she ushered Carl into her apartment. She sensed that whatever was on his mind was "important," at least by Carl's standards. He had that determined look, she had learned to recognize.

"Can I get you anything?" she asked, going back to the kitchen. "I'm having a glass of wine, myself."

Carl declined and sat down, waiting for Cindy to return. He wanted to choose his words carefully. Cindy would be receiving a phone call from the Office of Elections and he wanted her to be prepared.

She returned from the kitchen, the glass of wine in her hand, and sat down on the couch, next to Carl.

"How was your first day at the warehouse?" she asked. "Did it live up to your expectations?"

"Yes, it was quite interesting," said Carl. Then, in spite of himself, he started talking with enthusiasm about the physical characteristics of the warehouse, the different rovers he had met, and various tasks he had performed.

Cindy listened indulgently.

At last Carl got to the point.

"One of the carts we worked on was Cooper."

"Really," said Cindy brightly. "And how did it look under your watchful gaze? Did any of my officers leave any half-eaten sandwiches among the tangle of power cords?"

"No, nothing like that," said Carl solemnly. "But we did find something."

Cindy's facial expression changed to match Carl's.

"I'm listening."

"There were three voted ballots in the auxiliary compartment."

For a moment there was complete silence.

"Shit," said Cindy, barely above a whisper.

There was another pause of several seconds. At last Cindy began to speak.

"I know what happened. We had this lady on the team. Gladys something or other. She seemed a bit vague. I started her out as greeter but there wasn't a whole lot for her to do. Anyway around 10:00 a.m., I moved her to the scanner. It turned out she didn't know how it worked. She had voters put the ballots in the auxiliary bin by mistake. There were three of them before we realized what was happening. I made a mental note to count them by hand at the end of the day but obviously I forgot."

"Didn't you pick up on that at the end of the day, when you compared the count of checked-in voters with the machine tally?"

"I just told you, I forgot all about it. We were off by just three. I wrote 'human error' as an explanation on the SOR and left it with that."

"So those three people lost their vote."

There was silence for a few seconds as Cindy digested Carl's words. When she spoke her tone had a biting edge.

"Thank you, Carl. I realize that."

"You also realize the Office of Elections is going to call you about this," said Carl.

"Well, OK," said Cindy, who getting a bit annoyed. "And I'll tell them what I told you. Mistakes happen. Lesson learned. It's not as if any of the contests were close."

"That's not the point—"

"And just what is the point?" said Cindy, getting to her feet. "You come over here on a weekday night and you know I have that big meeting tomorrow. But you just couldn't wait. Couldn't wait to tell me that I screwed up."

"I just thought you'd want to know—"

"Know what?" Cindy was practically shouting. "That I made a mistake? I make them every day. I suspect you do too. Then again, maybe you don't."

Cindy paused. When she resumed, it was in a calmer voice.

"Carl, I am sorry about what happened. I really am. I do take this seriously but…not as seriously as you. I'm not going to lose sleep over this and if they decide they don't want me to serve again, I'll live with that. That's the best I can do and if it's not enough…then maybe we shouldn't be hanging around with each other as much as we do."

There, she said it. It was something that had been on her mind for a few weeks. She liked Carl, she really did, and he had helped her to appreciate things she never had before. But he just got so intense about this election stuff.

The silence in the room reflected the impact that Cindy's words had on Carl. All at once, the fight seemed to have gone out of him.

He got to his feet. “I guess I better go,” he said.

“I think it would be best,” said Cindy. “I have that meeting tomorrow that I’m prepping for and…look, I’m glad you had a full day at the warehouse. But really…just think about the things I said.”

They reached the door together. They exchanged a perfunctory kiss and Carl left.

# 8

## Wednesday, July 1

The work at the warehouse lasted three more days with each day starting at 7:00 a.m. and ending at 3:00 p.m. Carl teamed up with a different rover each day at Station Two and gradually began to learn their names. Each day there would be a half hour break at 9:30 and a full hour off for lunch at noon. Some of the rovers went out to a local deli for lunch while others "brown bagged" it.

The procession of precinct carts and scanners passed through Station Two with assembly line precision. Carl took a special interest in the cart for the Chesterbrook precinct. Chesterbrook had been "his" precinct, where he had been chief for several years. Inspecting the interior of the cart was sort of a bittersweet experience and he noted that while the interior seemed to be in order, it was perhaps not quite as neat as he normally left it.

While many of the precinct carts that passed through his station were perfectly packed, there were a number with contents mixed up in every which way. There were signs that had to be put into the bin going back to the Government Center. On a more serious note, two more carts had boxes of unvoted ballots which were immediately turned over to Roger. None of the scanners Carl inspected had voted ballots in either the main or auxiliary compartment. Cooper had been the only one.

Carl also found himself reflecting on the things that Cindy had said. Most of the time he enjoyed her bright, breezy personality but every once in a while he found the causal way that she shrugged off her mistakes a bit annoying. Perhaps they weren't the best match. Nonetheless her strongly worded suggestion that they spend less time together had been a blow. He realized that for him at least, an emotional bond had developed, a bond that he did not want to see severed. Time would tell in the end.

On the last day in the warehouse, Roger had some interesting news. The county had secured thirty additional scanners from nearby Braxton County. It seemed that Braxton had overbought a few years earlier and these had been declared surplus. They would be doing an acceptance test on the machines at the beginning of August to make sure they were in perfect order. Carl added that to his calendar. He was working on a couple of projects for Software Solutions but this extra time at the warehouse should not be a problem. This "job sharing" that he was doing was working out well and for the moment at least, his contract work was netting him roughly the same amount he had been earning as a salaried employee.

# 9

## MONDAY, JULY 6, 5:30 P.M.

THE BRONZE PLATE on the door read *Harris, Logan, and Marzetta, LLC, Attorneys at Law.* For a moment Cindy hesitated, not sure if she should knock or just enter. She had never been to a law office before. In her right hand she held the printout of the e-mail she had received a few days earlier.

*I would be obliged if we could meet at our office, 1200 Carter Street at your earliest convenience.*

*Brian Logan, Attorney at Law*

*What could we possibly have to talk about?* was the question that Cindy had been asking herself. Brian "Biff" Logan was the chairman of the county Democratic Party committee. Their only interaction had occurred on that cold day in January when Cindy had served as chief election officer during the special election. Biff had challenged Cindy on a number of fronts and although they had eventually parted on amicable terms, he remained, in Cindy's eyes at least, something of a bully who was used to imposing his will on others.

*Well, I'll soon find out,* she thought as she turned the door knob and entered the office.

The reception area had an elaborate, almost palatial, decor, obviously meant to awe would-be clients. Suitably impressed, Cindy walked forward to the reception desk.

"I'm Cynthia Phelps. I have a five-thirty appointment with Mr. Logan."

"Of course, Ms. Phelps," the secretary said, with a big smile. "Mr. Logan is expecting you. Please follow me."

She led Cindy down a hallway, which was lined with paintings that looked like they belonged in a museum. Everything about this place resonated with success. At the end of the hall, the secretary turned the handle of a door that had a brass plate reading "conference room" and motioned for Cindy to enter.

"Ah, here she is," came a booming voice that Cindy remembered all too well. Biff Logan had risen from his seat and strode over to Cindy with an expression that suggested that this was a reunion of two dear friends who had been separated for far too long. Cindy extended her hand which was engulfed in the hearty embrace of Biff's two beefy paws.

"Please sit down. Can my secretary get you anything? Water? A soft drink? Perhaps something stronger?"

"Water would be fine," said Cindy.

Biff motioned to a seat at the near end of the conference table and Cindy obediently sat down. She then became aware that she and Biff were not alone. Seated opposite her was a rather plain looking, gray haired woman of about sixty years of age and a much younger man with an earnest face.

Cindy recognized Emily Weston at once. The environmental activist had been the Democratic candidate for State Senate in that January special election, losing by the narrowest of margins. Cindy also had the feeling that she had met the young man, but she just couldn't recall the time or place.

Biff sat down next to Emily as the secretary brought Cindy a bottled water.

"I trust you know Emily Weston and Howard Morgenstein," said Biff motioning to the pair. "They have both spoken quite highly of you."

"So good to see you again," said Emily. "I enjoyed our little chat back on that 'interesting' day in January."

"As did I", said Cindy, with sincerity. "I was so sorry that you lost. You certainly had my vote. Of course, I could not say so at the time—"

Suddenly Cindy remembered.

"You were the poll worker I talked to just before the polls closed," she said, turning to Howard. "You were soaked to the bone but you hung in there to the bitter end. I remember being rather impressed."

"Yeah, that was me," said Howard, with a shy smile, a bit embarrassed by the compliment Cindy had given him.

An uneasy silence took over the room. At last Biff cleared his throat and began.

"You, of course, are aware of the tragic death of Norman Purvis."

Cindy was about to say, *"Who the hell is Norman Purvis?"* but a quick glance at the solemn expressions on the faces of Emily and Howard held her back. Realizing that she had to say something, she came out with the first thing that came to mind.

"I'm so sorry for your loss."

"He was a giant. A true giant," said Emily.

"I don't think we can ever replace him," said Howard.

"I know, I know," said Cindy in her most soothing voice, trying to get into the flow of the conversation.

"But yet we must try," said Biff, as Cindy took a sip of water from her bottle.

"And you, my dear, are just the person to do it," he continued, with an expansive gesture that suggested that he was simply stating the obvious.

Cindy didn't mean to spit the water out of her mouth onto the table but the shock of Biff's pronouncement came at exactly the wrong moment. Her swallow went down the wrong way, and she started gasping and coughing.

"Are you all right," asked Emily, with concern.

Red faced with embarrassment, Cindy nodded. "May I have a tissue or something?" she gasped even as she reached into her handbag, hoping to extract something to help clean up the small mess she had made.

In a flash, Biff provided a box of tissues and Cindy quickly dried her face and attended to the area of the table that had received the spray. Once this bit of necessary grooming had been completed, she took stock of the situation.

*I can fake it with the best of them, but this is beyond me. I need to come clean.*

"I have a confession to make," said Cindy, suddenly feeling rather inadequate. "I haven't the slightest idea who Norman Purvis is, or rather was. I'm sure he was a marvelous fellow because—well because you all seem to be taken by him, but I can hardly take the place of someone I have never heard of."

"Such modesty," said Biff. "But please let us be the judge—"

"Brian, let me," interrupted Emily.

"Norman Purvis," she began, "served on the county Soil and Water Commission for the past fourteen years. During this time, he provided invaluable leadership in a variety of conservation efforts. He recently passed away, leaving a vacancy on the commission. The members of the Soil and Water Commission are elected every four years, as we're sure you know."

"I am aware of that," said Cindy, "although I think I skipped that office on my ballot the last time I voted."

Biff and Emily exchanged glances.

"No one need ever know," said Biff.

Emily nodded and then continued. "This November, the ballot will include a contest to fill the remainder of Norman's term. Technically the political parties do not nominate candidates for the office, but the reality is that the candidates receive party endorsement. We feel that you would be an excellent candidate for this position."

"I'm sorry. I don't follow," said Cindy, her face reflecting the bewilderment she felt. "I'm hardly a poster child for conservation. I mean, my recycling efforts are halfhearted at best—"

"None of us are perfect, dear," said Emily.

"—and I run the dish washer when it's half empty. And not just sometimes."

Biff started to say something but Cindy held up her hand, an obvious request for silence. For a few moments she just sat there, staring at the table, composing herself.

*Don't be an idiot, Phelps. This is the sort of thing that could give your career a real boost. At least consider it.*

Cindy looked up. Her eyes bore in on Biff.

"Why me?" she asked. "Why not her?" pointing at Emily, "or him?" shifting her finger to Howard. "They're both infinitely more knowledgeable on the subject—"

"And they will be tutoring you so that—"

"That's not what I asked," interrupted Cindy.

Biff looked at his companions.

"Perhaps if Ms. Phelps and I can have a few minutes together?" he suggested.

Emily and Howard took the cue. “We’ll be right outside, if you need anything,” said Emily, reassuringly to Cindy.

Cindy felt anything but reassured but nodded her head, nonetheless.

Emily and Howard exited the room, leaving Cindy and Biff on either end of the table, each looking intently at the other. At last Biff spoke.

“My job as Democratic chair is to ensure, to the fullest extent possible, that the Democratic Party chooses candidates who will win in November. I’m not interested in worthy efforts by worthy people. I want results.”

Biff paused for a few moments to let the message sink in. Then he continued,

“The Democrats had a five-point voter registration advantage over the Republicans in the $48^{th}$ State Senate District. And yet in that January election, the one in which you so distinguished yourself,” Biff said, with what appeared to be a slight sneer, “Emily Weston was defeated by Jennifer Haley. Now why do you suppose that happened?”

Cindy considered.

“Well the weather was a factor. The roads were a mess and that probably hurt the turnout and perhaps—”

“The reason was,” said Biff, completely ignoring Cindy’s observation, “is that Emily Weston, as worthy a person as she may be, is a dowdy spinster who could not compete with her younger, more personable, and *more attractive* opponent.”

Cindy said nothing.

*Damn it, he’s right,* she thought, hating at the same time the direction the conversation was taking.

"You, on the other hand," declared Biff, "and please don't waste our time with protestations of false modesty, are young, attractive, personable *when you choose to be*, and also, my sources tell me, very ambitious. Once Emily and Howard bring you up to speed on the issues, you will be more than a match for any opponent the Republicans throw against us."

Almost against her will, Cindy was beginning to feel excited at the prospect of being a candidate. It was not as though she was indifferent to the concept of conservation. Everyone knew that conservation was a "good thing," saving the penguins and the like. She was confident that she would be able to support the things that Emily and Howard primed her on. Still she had to be careful.

"I have a full time job with MarketPro. I have to be sure that—"

"All the Commission's meetings are at night. And my sources tell me that your supervisors would be most supportive of your candidacy."

With that declaration, all kinds of warning signals went off in Cindy's head. Biff had obviously done a fair amount of research on her, even apparently talking to her supervisor. Intriguing as this whole candidacy thing was, she resented Biff's apparent intrusion into her professional and, for all she knew, private life.

Silence engulfed the room. Biff started to say something.

"Be quiet," snapped Cindy.

At that point, Biff had the sense to remain quiet. Silence continued.

At last, Cindy spoke.

"I need to think this over. How much time do I have?"

"The party can give you to the end of the week. If you say 'yes,' the party will fill out the paper work and submit the filing fee to get you on the ballot. Also there will be a certain amount of money later on for posters and fliers. But all this takes time so if you can't commit by this Friday, we will have to explore other options."

Cindy considered.

"That's fair," she finally said. "On or before Friday, one way or another, you'll be hearing from me."

# 10

## Thursday, July 9, 7:30 p.m.

"May I come in?"

"Why, err, sure," said a surprised Carl, opening the door to let Cindy in. They both passed into the living room of Carl's townhouse. The room had a somewhat cluttered look as books and papers seemed to be everywhere. Carl didn't do much entertaining and it showed.

Before Carl could offer Cindy anything, she immediately began peppering him with questions about his election work. Had he been to the warehouse recently? Would they be doing any work in August? When would they start testing for November?

Carl was always ready to talk about his election activities, especially with Cindy, but he found her sudden burst of enthusiasm puzzling, considering the way they had most recently parted.

"Yes, as a matter of fact, we will be meeting next week at the county courthouse. We will be 'rescuing the bins.'"

Cindy's quizzical expression encouraged him to continue.

"You recall the ballots all go into those blue bins that are located inside the black casing directly under the scanner. If you remember you—"

"Sealed the bin at the end of the day, and drove it to the Government Center," said Cindy, completing Carl's sentence, and adding with a playful grin, "I was there. Remember?"

"Yes. Well anyway, did you ever wonder how we will capture this November's scanned ballots, if all those blue bins are back at the Government Center holding the ballots from the primary?"

"Oh yes," said Cindy, with a deadpan expression "It's been keeping me awake at night, wondering about all those bins."

"Well," said Carl, oblivious to Cindy's sarcasm. "Next Tuesday we go to the courthouse where the bins are stored. We will remove the ballots from the bins and put them in boxes. The boxes remain in the courthouse, to be shredded in two years' time, and the bins go back to the warehouse, ready to be used in November."

"What a relief."

"Then in early August," continued Carl, who was on a roll, "we will be doing an acceptance test on thirty *ElectionPro* scanners that we acquired from Braxton County. They are surplus machines that have never actually been used in an election, but these extra machines will finally enable us to have two scanners in every precinct."

Carl continued on for a bit more about the advantages of each precinct having that second scanner. Cindy listened patiently, waiting for Carl to run out of steam.

Eventually there was a pause in Carl's monologue. Carl sensed from Cindy's demeanor that there was something she wanted to say. He looked at her expectantly.

"Well," began Cindy, suddenly feeling a little bit awkward and shy about the whole thing. "I've got a bit of election news as well."

Now it was Carl's turn to give a quizzical look.

"As you may be aware," continued Cindy. "The November ballot will have a contest for an empty seat on the county Soil and Water Commission. Well I —"

"Oh that," interrupted Carl. "Soil and Water. It's on the ballot every four years. Nobody knows what they do. Most people don't even vote for it. Usually when there's a mid-term vacancy they just appoint the replacement, but for whatever reason they're having it on the ballot this year. Yeah, that will be part of the ballot that we test in September. Assuming they find two people who want to run, that is." Carl gave a derisive laugh.

*Carl, I really like you but sometimes you're such an ass,* thought Cindy.

"Well, they found at least one person to run."

"Really? Who?"

"Me."

"You!?!"

"Don't look so surprised. Biff Logan invited me to his office and said that if I wanted to run, the Democratic Party would endorse me. They even offered to help me fund the campaign. And my boss at MarketPro has approved it. Said it would look good for the company's image."

Carl was completely amazed. He did not know what to say. He just sat there, looking at Cindy.

The seconds ticked by.

"I think you should probably say something," said Cindy quietly. "Some encouraging words might be nice."

"Well, I never thought of you as," stammered Carl. "I mean...I know...look...Cindy, you are an extremely capable person but is this something you really want to do? I've never even heard you talk about the environment—"

"You don't know everything about me," said Cindy, defensively. "I've always felt the environment is important. You know, global warming and everything."

"But are you qualified to do…whatever it is they do?"

"They're going to tutor me. I'm not sure if you remember Howard Morgenstein. He was one of the poll workers for Emily Weston last January. Anyway, he's rather passionate about the environment and he will be bringing me up to speed."

Carl looked at Cindy, dubiously. Something about this just didn't sound right. But to be fair, he also admitted to another conflicting emotion. Jealousy. Ever since they had met, Carl had been the elections expert. In some ways, she had become his protégé. Now suddenly, she had been invited into an area of the election domain that he could only dream of. The fact that the door seemed to have opened so easily for her was a bit annoying.

"Why did they pick you?"

An honest question. It was a question with an unsettling answer, one that Cindy was reluctant to share. But for all his irritating qualities, Carl had become a dear friend and Cindy was compelled to be truthful.

"He thinks I'll make an attractive candidate. He doesn't care about my qualifications. He just wants a win for the Democratic Party."

"So, he's using you," said Carl. It wasn't an accusation. His tone was soft and gentle. He cared about his friend.

"I guess we're using each other."

"And you're OK with that?"

Cindy slowly nodded her head.

"Yes, I am," she said softly.

A pause. Then Carl broke out with big smile. "Well congratulations. If there's anything I can do to help you, just say the word.

Pass out fliers. Put up yard signs. Anything. Except on Election Day itself, of course. I've never worked on a political campaign but I've love to work on yours. That is, if you want me to—"

"Of course, I want you to," exclaimed Cindy, giving Carl a big hug. For the next half hour they talked about the campaign, but only in the most general terms. For all her enthusiasm, Cindy had very little specifics.

"I'll be meeting with Biff at the county Democratic headquarters next week," she explained. "I'll be learning more about the world of campaigning then, I expect."

At last it was time for Cindy to leave. Just then Carl remembered something he had forgotten to mention the last time they were together.

"Oh by the way, I recently met your sister. She works in the personnel division of the county. She processed some of my paperwork."

"Oh. You met Val?"

"Yes, she seemed nice."

A pause.

"Yeah. Well that's good."

For the briefest moment Cindy seemed disconnected but she quickly recovered.

"I'll let you know how that meeting with Biff goes," she said. "And thank you for your support on this, Carl. It means a lot to me."

With a final hug, the two friends parted.

# 11

## Monday, July 13, 8:00 p.m.

"So you're going to make me an expert on environmental policy," said Cindy, brightly.

"We're going to do everything we can," replied Howard. "We need the very best people on the commission."

Somehow, that simple declaration made Cindy feel a bit uneasy.

"Just out of curiosity, are they paying you for this?"

"No, I'm a volunteer. I help out the party, when I can, on matters of environmental policy."

"What do you do in real life?"

"I'm a TA at George Mason, going for a doctorate in Environmental Science and Public Policy. But enough about me. Tell me your environmental background so we can figure out where to start."

"Well I took Earth Science in ninth grade. All about the dinosaurs and stuff."

"I was thinking more about college. Did you have any science courses?" Howard was beginning to have an uneasy feeling about this.

"Not a whole lot. I majored in economics so my schedule was crammed full of econ and business classes."

"I see."

"I did take a year of Biology to satisfy gen ed but I doubt if I've retained much. I just memorized stuff for the tests," said Cindy. Science had always been her least favorite academic area but she sensed that it would be wise not to mention that.

"Let's assume," said Howard slowly, "that we're dealing with a clean slate. Now do you know what the Soil and Water Commission does?"

"It makes regulations concerning the environment?" asked Cindy.

"Not exactly. It doesn't have any legal authority to do that. Rather it supports the county and its citizens in a variety of ways with conservation information, technical services, educational programs, and volunteer opportunities to residents on many aspects of water quality, nonpoint source pollution, and stream health. Here, let me show you some examples."

At that point Howard powered up his laptop and brought up the county website. He then led Cindy through a number of pages covering such topics as stream restoration, problems involving certain soils, drainage and erosion issues, and horse farm management. It was the latter area that seemed especially complex and by the end of the scheduled hour Cindy's head was swimming with all sorts of details.

They sat together in silence for a few minutes.

"I'm not exactly what you were hoping for, am I?"

Howard remained silent, obviously thinking. At last he spoke.

"It's July and the election is not until November. No real campaigning takes place until September, so we have time. For the next few weeks we won't worry about the commission itself. We'll just bring you up to speed on the basics of environmental science. I have an undergraduate survey text I can lend you. We'll meet a couple of evenings a week and I'll indicate which sections you are to read for each session. It will be like taking a crash survey course in environmental science. But don't worry, if you can do college biology, this will be a snap."

Cindy smiled weakly.

"Then after we've finished that, in late August or so, we can get into what the commission actually does."

"Sounds, like a plan," agreed Cindy.

*This isn't going to be as much fun as I had imagined*, she thought as they completed their initial session.

# 12

## Tuesday, July 14, 9:00 A.M.

"There is a rumor," said Scott to Carl, "that Roger might not be with us much longer."

They were at the county courthouse entrance, waiting to be admitted. Today was the day when they were going to "rescue the bins."

"Really?" said Carl, surprised. "I'm sorry to hear that." Although he didn't know Roger very well, Carl had been impressed with the professional way he had handled things during that very challenging January special election.

"Supposedly, he applied for a better position within the county government structure, not with elections. We don't tend to keep machine coordinators very long. It's a full time job, usually handled by younger folks with families to raise so they're always looking for a step up the ladder. Roger has a wife and two small kids so a bigger paycheck would be most welcome."

The door opened and Roger appeared.

"All right, everyone. Pass through the metal detector and follow me," he called to the assembled group of rovers.

One by one they entered the building and went through the metal detector. They then followed Roger down a long hallway to where some tables and piles of flat boxes lined the wall. Roger explained the drill.

"Thank you all for coming out today. We will spend the first hour or so making boxes. Two to a table. There are tape guns along with rolls of tape to secure the flaps. Once all the boxes are made, we will start retrieving the bins from the vault," he said, motioning to a nearby closed door. "Let's get started."

The next hour was spent building boxes. Once Carl got used to handling the tape gun, it went quickly and before long a huge pile of boxes occupied a significant portion of the hallway. Eventually all the boxes were made. It was time to get to the heart of the matter.

"We are not allowed in the vault," Roger explained. "Rolando here, will be lining up bins at the door." Roger pointed to a muscular gentleman who appeared to be one of courthouse employees.

At that point Roger explained the particulars for the day. Rolando would bring the bins to the door of the vault where they would be checked out by a rover named Michael, who by now Carl had deduced to be sort of "second in command." Each rover would take a bin back to his table and empty the voted ballots into one of the cardboard boxes. He would then label the box with the correct precinct and use the tape gun to seal it. The box would be returned to the vault where Rolando and Michael would issue the next bin. While this was going on, one of the other rovers would put the empty bins on a pallet which would eventually be sent back to the warehouse. It promised to be a rather straightforward, if monotonous exercise.

“There is one other thing we need to accomplish today,” said Roger. “As many of you are aware, when you were first hired, the necessary paperwork was not completed. Our leaders have determined that the most efficacious way to rectify this is to do a ‘termination/rehire’ process.”

Moans and grumbles greeted this announcement. The issue had been mentioned before but most had hoped it would “go away.” Carl had already been assured that he would not be affected by this so he allowed his mind to wander.

“As you know, we will be meeting the first week in August to do the acceptance test on those thirty scanners that were purchased from Braxton County. Your termination will begin immediately after that with a rehire date of just after Labor Day, in time for us to do the testing for November. The good news is that most of the necessary paperwork can be filled out today. We will have someone from the personnel staff here to work with you. She should be here soon and then—ah, here she is now—This is Valerie Turner, everyone. Let’s make her feel welcome.”

The “welcome” was less than heartfelt.

*“Do we really need to do this?”*

*“What a waste of time.”*

*“This is so stupid.”*

*“Do we get a going away party?”*

Once the grumbles had died down, Valerie began to speak.

“Thank you so much for your warm welcome,” she said, with a bright smile that reminded Carl a little bit of Cindy. “We will be pulling you out, one by one to do the paperwork. I’ll be here to help you, so hopefully it will be painless. The tax information is the trickiest but I brought with me your original paperwork to help remind you of what you selected when you first hired on. We should be able to have this done for all of you today.”

Valerie's introduction to the process was met with resigned acquiescence. Before anyone else could express any more displeasure, Roger immediately jumped in and announced that it was time to start.

The actual transfer of ballots from the bins to the boxes turned out to be a rather mechanical and not especially stressful process. Unlike the serious pre-election testing, concentration was not really needed. It turned out that one of the rovers was an aficionado of pop music from the '50s and '60s and through his CD player, the rovers got to do their tasks to the sounds of some of the more obscure performers of the period. Progress was swift and by noon, about half of the precincts had been serviced.

Just down the hallway was the courthouse cafeteria and that's where they broke for lunch. Returning from the line with his selections, Carl noticed that Valerie was seated off by herself.

"All alone?" he asked, sitting down.

"I'm not exactly the most popular kid on the block," she said, smiling.

*Well the whole termination/rehire thing is kind of dumb*, thought Carl, keeping his thoughts to himself.

"How's it coming along?"

"It will be done by the time you all leave this afternoon. The interesting thing is that I'll be going through the same thing myself. I'll be taking a leave of absence pretty soon."

"Really?" said Carl, intrigued.

"There's something I've wanted to do for some time and the opportunity has opened," said Valerie. It seemed to Carl that she was being deliberately vague but then again, they were barely acquaintances.

"It will also give me a chance to tutor my oldest," she continued. "He struggled in math this past year, so his father and I enrolled him in summer school."

"I bet he's enjoying that."

"Let's just say I'm not his favorite person right now. It's not all his fault. There were thirty-six kids in his class last year. That's too many. The brainy kids, you know the 'gifted,' get the small classes. As if they need it."

Carl noticed a certain bitterness in Valerie's tone as she continued.

"And a lot of it comes down to money. Everyone says they want good schools but no one has the guts to raise the property taxes. We're losing teachers to the neighboring counties. And the elective programs are getting stripped to the bone, except football of course."

There was no stopping her. For the next twenty minutes she continued on about all the troubles of the school system. So many of the classes were in trailers. All those immigrant kids who needed ESOL classes. Not enough money from Richmond. Along the way, Carl learned that her husband taught middle school English while Valerie was president of the PTA at her sons' grade school. It was obvious that she was both knowledgeable and passionate about the county school system. Carl couldn't help but compare Valerie to her sister. She did not have Cindy's outward charm but what she lacked in sparkle, she more than made up for in sincerity and passion. In a way it mirrored Carl's feelings about election service.

*They must have been an interesting pair growing up, but then again, Valerie appears to be several years older than Cindy so perhaps—*

"OK everyone, back to the salt mines," called Roger.

The afternoon continued just as the morning had. There were no issues, no surprises. By 2:00 p.m., Valerie had finished processing everyone. She said her goodbyes and left. They worked on to about four when Roger called a halt.

“We’ll only need a couple of hours tomorrow to finish this up,” he announced. “Anyone with other things to do should feel free not to come in.”

This suited Carl, as he had a deadline coming up at Software Solutions. The last few bins would have to be rescued without his help.

# 13

## Thursday, July 16, 7:30 p.m.

Cindy pulled her car into a parking lot that appeared to be the first in a series of interconnected lots, which intertwined with some townhouse style condominiums. She was looking for 644B Sunrise Drive.

*Let's see. There's 636, and 638, and 640, and…*

The building ended with 640.

*OK, let's pull around back and…there it is, 644.*

Cindy got out of the car, clutching her notebook. Upon reaching the sidewalk, she checked the shingle on each of the doors. There were staircases, both up and down. Down led to 644A which had a sign labeled "storage," taped to the door.

*So it's up the stairs we go.*

And there it was. "County Democratic Party."

Emboldened by the fact that she had an actual appointment, Cindy opened the door. Before her was a dimly lit, carpeted hallway. She entered and, ever so slowly, proceeded down the hallway, taking in her surroundings. The air was hot and muggy, suggesting that the air conditioner was either not working or nonexistent. Lining the walls were photos of the current Governor and Lieutenant Governor, both Democrats. As she approached the end of the hall, she could see stairs running both up and down.

"Hello, is anyone there?" she called out tentatively. There was no response although she thought she heard some noise coming from the upper floor. She tried again, only louder.

"Hello—"

"Just a minute," came a voice, followed by footsteps coming down the stairs. A pleasant looking man, about Cindy's age, came into view.

"I'm afraid the AC has conked out. I was just on the phone to report it but they won't be here for a few days, at least. Now what can I do for you?"

"I have an appointment with Biff Logan—" began Cindy.

"Oh, you're the Soil and Water lady," said the young man.

"Well, yeah," said Cindy, with a nervous laugh. "I'm supposed to meet Mr. Logan to go over what needs—"

"Sure. Sure. Well he's not going to be here so you're stuck with me, I'm afraid. Why don't we go upstairs and get you started. I'm Steve Winters by the way."

Steve did an immediate about-face and bounded up the stairs. Cindy followed, a bit miffed that the man who had recruited her would not be present.

The upstairs area was well lit and dominated by a large table with piles of papers strewn every which way. Smaller desks and tables, some with laptops and printers lined the walls. A copier machine was in the corner.

"Have a seat," said Steve, motioning to a chair. "May I call you Cindy?"

"Well, sure," said Cindy, feeling a bit reassured that since he knew her name, her appearance had apparently been anticipated.

"Fortunately for you, Soil and Water is not under the Campaign Finance Disclosure Act so your form work is eased considerably. You still need to file some forms however and I'll print them out for you now. Also you need to get a petition signed by twenty-five registered voters. An afternoon in front of a supermarket should take care of that. Just make sure to get some extra signatures. I'd go for at least fifty. That protects you if some of those signatures turn out to be bogus. You know, non-voters and the like."

All the while, Steve was bringing up screens on his laptop and clicking with the mouse. Suddenly the printer in the corner started spewing out paper.

"Biff said that the party would take care of all that," said Cindy.

Steve turned around from his computer screen and looked at her in an appraising sort of way. For a moment Cindy had the impression that he almost pitied her.

"Did he also say the party would give you some seed money?"

"I'm not sure what 'seed money' is but he did say there would be some money for posters and fliers."

For several seconds the room was silent, save for the sound of the printer generating one sheet of paper after another.

At last Steve began to speak. He was obviously choosing his words carefully.

"Cindy, one thing Biff is very good at is picking winners. If he thinks you can win, then you can win. But it is still your campaign. You have to submit the necessary paper work. Once you are on the ballot, the Democratic committee will meet and formally decide to endorse you, but don't expect a whole lot after that. You have to raise the money for your campaigning. The party will share its lists of party faithful and will also publicize any events and fundraisers you organize. But that's pretty much it. You are on your own."

Cindy digested this bit of news. This was going to be more challenging than she had anticipated.

"The first thing you need," continued Steve, "is a campaign treasurer. Trust me, you don't want some well-meaning amateur as your treasurer. The treasurer makes sure all the necessary forms and filings are done. For a contest like this, with a short campaign life for a local office like Soil and Water, you should be able to get someone for maybe $2,000 a month. I can get you someone if you'd like. May I ask how much of your own money you intend to sink into this race?"

Cindy gulped. "I wasn't planning to spend any of my own money."

"I see," said Steve. "Well let me make some calls. I think I can find someone who's willing to wait to be paid until you've done some fundraising. Now, may I ask if you have a campaign manager?"

"No, not really," said Cindy, feeling more inadequate with each passing moment.

"Well I would advise you to get one as soon as you can. At least you won't feel so alone. For some of the more competitive state legislature races, the candidate will get a professional, but I suspect that is not within your budget."

Cindy nodded, thinking *"Right now there is no budget."*

"Do you have anyone who can step up to being your campaign manager? A relative or close friend?"

"My parents aren't local," said Cindy. "I have a sister but…well we're not that close. None my friends are into politics. There is this guy I'm sort of dating who serves as an election officer, but this might be a bit out of his league."

Steve considered. "Look, why don't I help you get started? Just for a couple of weeks until you find someone."

"Well that's nice of you but I really can't pay you."

"That's OK. I do volunteer stuff for the party. It will just be for a couple of weeks and—"

Steve stopped in mid-sentence. He sat, staring at Cindy, as if completely mesmerized. Cindy began to feel a bit uncomfortable.

"What is it?" she asked.

A few more seconds of silence ensued.

At last Steve asked, "Is your sister Valerie Turner?"

That was not the question Cindy had expected. Slowly, she nodded her head. "Yes."

Steve appeared to be considering this information which Cindy found perplexing.

"Yes, she's my sister," she repeated, adding, "And…"

It was an obvious invitation for Steve to finish the sentence.

"You don't know?" asked Steve.

"I've already told you. We're not that close."

"Well close or not, you both will be on the same ticket this November. You sister has expressed an interest in running for the vacant at-large seat on the county school board and the Democratic Party will be endorsing her."

# 14

## SUNDAY, JULY 26, 5:50 P.M.

"NO SIR. SIGNING a petition doesn't obligate you to support or vote for that candidate. It only says that you want to get the candidate on the ballot."

"Well, I don't know. Is she a Republican or Democrat?" the man asked.

"Soil and Water Board is a non-partisan position. She is simply a citizen who cares deeply about our environment," responded Carl, offering the man his pen and petition, mounted on a clipboard.

"Well, I guess that's all right," said the man, tentatively reaching for the clipboard.

"Hector, don't you dare!" shouted a lady, coming out of the supermarket, pushing a shopping cart full of groceries. "We don't get involved with politics."

"But they want to help the environment," said Hector to the woman, presumably his wife.

"No, they don't," bellowed the woman. "They're just trying to sell you magazines or something. Come on. I need help putting all this into the car."

Hector gave Carl an embarrassed shrug and turned around to follow his wife.

Carl looked down at his clipboard. This was harder than it looked. He had been in front of the supermarket for four hours and had exactly five signatures to show for it.

It reminded Carl of one of his summer employment experiences. After his sophomore year in college he had answered a classified ad for a summer job as a "public researcher." It turned out that the job was actually selling magazines as a door-to-door salesman. After eight hours and zero sales, the supervisor declared that this job was obviously not for Carl and let him go.

Now Carl was demonstrating once again that sales was not his thing. He wondered how Cindy was doing at her location. She was at a relatively small grocery store, located closer to where she lived. They had hoped that between the two of them they would get the necessary signatures. They needed twenty-five but Cindy had indicated that someone named Steve, who apparently was her campaign manager, had said that they should get about fifty, just to be safe.

"Excuse me, sir," came a voice from directly behind him. "I was hoping to sign a petition for one of the Soil and Water candidates. Do you know where I can find one?"

Carl turned around and there was Cindy, all smiles, looking like she was having the time of her life.

"I didn't see you drive up—"

"Of course you didn't," she said brightly. "You were too busy trying to reel Hector in. Don't worry about that though. They're plenty of other fish out there. Carl, I am having so much fun."

"I'm glad you're enjoying it," said Carl, genuinely pleased for her sake. "Did you get many signatures?"

"Thirty-six," said Cindy proudly. "A couple of them might not fly though. There were two people who weren't sure if they were registered voters. Still, thirty-six. And some of them said they would vote for me in November. So how many did you get?"

Carl took a deep breath. "Not that many."

"Well, that's OK," said Cindy soothingly. "Every little bit helps and—"

"Five," said Carl.

Cindy looked at Carl in disbelief. She realized that Carl was not exactly a "people person." Still she had expected him to get twenty or so which would put them over the fifty that Steve said they needed. Now she would need to spend another afternoon getting more signatures.

*"What have you been trying to do for the past four hours?"* she thought. *"Piss everyone off?"*

Cindy tried to recover and hide her disappointment. After all, Carl had willingly given up his Sunday afternoon for this.

"OK, we've made a good start. Remember you need to fill out the bottom as the person circulating the petition, and then get it notarized." Cindy tried to sound upbeat but it was difficult to completely hide the frustration she felt at Carl's performance.

"When do you need the signatures?" asked Carl.

"The sooner the better," said Cindy. "Technically they need to be in by August 14. But I wanted to have them by Tuesday night when I'm meeting with Steve to plan strategy. You know, to show him I'm serious. And Monday night I'm meeting with Howard for his environmental science tutorial."

Cindy looked down at her cell. It was 6:00 p.m. She supposed she could stick it out for an hour or two more but she was tired and besides, she had some things to do that night to prepare for her day at work tomorrow.

*Damn. Why couldn't Carl have done better?*

"OK, here's what I need to do," said Cindy, more to herself than Carl. "I'll come back here tomorrow for an hour or two after work, before I meet Howard. I should be able to push it across the finish line."

"I can come and help you," said Carl, eager to redeem himself.

"No, I don't think so," said Cindy dismissively. "I think I can take it from here. Thanks anyway."

"Well, OK," said Carl. "I'll get this notarized tomorrow and get it over to your place."

They said their goodbyes and got into their respective cars.

*I should have tried harder,* thought Carl as he adjusted his seatbelt. *I really need to work on my people skills.*

Cindy for her part was going over the next twenty-four hours in her mind. Talk about being overscheduled! But try as she might, a nagging little memory kept intruding into her mind, a memory of something she had been told more than once.

*You're not the easiest person to like.*

# 15

## Tuesday, July 28, 7:30 P.M.

"Norbert Gilbertson?"

"Yes, Norbert Gilbertson," said Steve. "He is your campaign treasurer. With your approval, of course. He's served as treasurer on a number of local races and is willing to serve on yours for $2000 per month. He will make sure all your forms are filled out correctly. How did you do with your petitions?"

"I have them here," said Cindy, reaching into her handbag. "I've got fifty-two, all together. It took me two days to do it but I think they're all good. Most of them at least."

"You got them all yourself," said Steve, frowning.

"Mostly by myself. My friend Carl, got the five on this sheet here but the rest I managed alone. Is that a problem?"

"Not by itself. But you need to be recruiting a team of volunteers. As much as you can, you want to off-load things to volunteers to leave you free to campaign. Do you know many people who might be willing to help you?"

"Some of my girl friends might. They're not into politics but they probably would be willing to do a little, just as a favor to me. I might be able to get one or two of my work colleagues to help out, but their time is stretched pretty thin as it is. Carl is on board but only to the extent that it doesn't interfere with his work with the Office of Elections."

"That doesn't sound like an especially large stable of potential volunteers. Do I dare ask about potential financial contributors?"

"I called my parents and once they got over the shock of my being a candidate for political office, they offered to contribute $1,000. So that gets me off the mark, right?" said Cindy.

"It's a start. You can now afford to pay your treasurer for two weeks. Do you have any well connected friends?"

"Not really. Most of my friends have pretty good jobs but I'm not sure that translates into extra cash to contribute to a political campaign. A number of them are still paying off student loans. A few might kick in a twenty but that's about it. Carl is older and further along financially, so he might be able to contribute a bit more."

It took a few moments for Steve to fully digest this information. "I think," he said. "I'll approach Norman Purvis' widow. She might be willing to share her late husband's donor list. That is, if we can convince her that you are as committed to the environment as he was. How are your sessions going with Howard?"

"We met last night. He gave me a crash course on matter, energy, and life. You know, producers, consumers, the circle of life, and all that. We meet again later this week to discuss biomes."

"Sounds pretty theoretical. Has he begun to tell you about what the Soil and Water Conservation Board actually does?"

"Not yet. He said I need a strong foundation in environmental science first."

"Well don't let him dwell too long on the academic stuff. Your looks and personality will get you started but eventually you'll have to show some real substance."

Cindy bristled when she heard that. She ran into this occasionally at work when she would meet a new client. People who judged her on her looks and personality and assumed she was all style and no substance. She was about to issue a quick comeback to Steve when that nagging little voice in the back of her head reminded her that,

*Right now, when it comes to the environment, you are all style and no substance.*

"Who am I running against?" She suddenly wanted to know.

"We're not sure," said Steve. "This contest is sort of a last minute thing. Purvis' death came as a shock to everyone. But the Republicans will surely find someone to back. They always do. And occasionally the Green Party runs a candidate if…well if..."

"If what?"

Steve paused. Should he say it? Yes, he decided. She should hear it.

"If they are not that impressed with the Democrat running. But let's not worry about that now. We need to get this paperwork filled out."

For the next half hour they worked on the various forms that needed to be filled out. Once completed, Steve took possession of them. He would pass them on to the Treasurer who would affix his signature and then submit them. In the meantime, Cindy would take the petitions herself, to the Government Center. Steve made a copy of the petitions so he would have the names and contact information of the signers. That way, they could be invited to any fundraiser down the road.

"That last thing we need to discuss is your kickoff event. Soil and Water doesn't normally get much media attention so we need something that will create public interest."

"You mean a gimmick."

"I'm not sure if gimmick is the right word. But we need something to spark the public imagination. Something with human interest."

Steve let the thought hang in the air. He clearly wanted Cindy to perceive the need.

Cindy got the message. She might not know a whole lot about the environment but she could read people like a book.

"Clearly, you have something in mind. What is it?"

Steve paused, apparently in search for the right words. At last he began.

"What would you say to a joint kickoff—?"

"No."

"Hear me out. A joint kickoff with—"

"I said, no."

"And I said, hear me out," said Steve in his most commanding tone of voice. When he was reasonably confident that he had Cindy's silence, if not cooperation, he continued.

"Do you know what your biggest single challenge is?" he asked.

*Other than my complete lack of qualifications, you mean?*

"No. Tell me."

"It's that many, probably most, voters neither know nor care what Soil and Water does. The Democrats have the voter registration edge in the county but since party affiliation for Soil and Water doesn't appear on the ballot, many voters will not even vote for that position. So our initial challenge is simply to introduce you to the voters as a Democrat and introduce you in such a way that they will remember who you are."

Steve paused to let that thought sink in.

"Your sister is running for the school board as a Democrat. School board races get a lot of attention. Also the human interest story is too good to pass up. Two sisters, each passionately devoted to their respective causes, running at the same time. It will get media attention. That's what you need."

*He's right, of course.*

Cindy gave a sigh and slowly nodded her head.

"OK."

"Great," said Steve, visibly relieved. "I believe Stanley, her husband, is serving as her campaign manager. I can meet with him and set up the particulars. Or perhaps all four of us should get together."

"Steve, I'm really backed up timewise," said Cindy. "If you could just take care of this yourself, I would appreciate it."

Steve considered. It wasn't completely what he wanted but it was close enough.

"All right. Consider it done," he said. "Well…I think we've done well tonight."

"So do I," said Cindy, who for the first time that evening allowed herself to relax. "Tell me, are all the candidates you manage as clueless as me?"

"Inexperienced is not the same as clueless," said Steve reassuringly. "Once you start campaigning, you'll be a natural. Wait and see."

"I did enjoy getting those petition signatures," said Cindy. "And I really appreciate you're helping me get started. Once we get all that paperwork in, I'll work on getting myself a proper campaign manager. Then you can go back to doing…whatever it is you do. Come to think of it, what do you do? In real life, I mean."

"I work for a lobbying firm," said Steve. "But what I really want to do is to be a full time political consultant. Volunteering for the party will hopefully get me started."

"So my candidacy may someday be a line on your resume?"

"Something like that. If you win, of course."

"Well then, I guess I better win," said Cindy, breaking out into a bright smile. She liked Steve and sensed that he was smoothing the road out considerably for her.

"So that's it for tonight," said Steve. "I'll get Norbert to submit these forms. You need to run those petitions over to the Government Center by the 14th. I'll let you know when we have that joint kickoff arranged. In the meantime keep working with Howard."

"Yes sir," she said with a mock salute. Gathering up her papers, she nodded to Steve and departed.

Driving home that night, her mind overflowed with images and emotions. Being a political candidate was something she had never even dreamed of, but it was happening. Cindy had always considered herself a "people person" and the idea of "pressing the flesh" appealed to her. Of course that whole fundraising thing seemed daunting but Steve seemed to have a plan for that. And she still needed to educate herself on all that environmental stuff. As well as get through the kickoff event. There was just so much. But she knew Carl would help her. And Steve.

# 16

## Monday, August 3, 9:00 a.m.

"Carl, what's your favorite ice cream?" asked Scott, as Carl took his seat at the rover table in the warehouse. It was Monday, August 3, the day of the anticipated "acceptance test," of the thirty scanners that had recently been obtained from Braxton County.

"I don't know. Chocolate, I guess," said Carl. "Why does it matter?"

"Chocolate. How boring," said Brenda. "Rocky road, for me."

"It's our test ballot for the day," said Scott, showing Carl one of the "test decks" that had been created.

"We don't just cast random votes when we test," Scott explained. "We use a 'test deck' of premarked ballots that have been marked in a specific pattern. The first candidate on the ballot in a race gets the most votes, the second candidate gets one less, and so on down the line. The bottom candidate, usually the 'write in' candidate, gets a single vote. Then we create a specified number of additional votes on the *CreateBallot* device that the handicapped folks use to create their ballot and that is the complete test. So when we run the test we know exactly what the vote total should be, and we simply verify that the numbers in the printout at the end of the test match, and we are done."

"So what does chocolate ice cream have to do with this?" asked Carl.

"We're just doing an acceptance test for these machines. We have no specific election to test them on, so the Command Center created this make-believe ballot."

Carl examined the ballot. Ice cream lovers could choose among vanilla, chocolate, strawberry, butter pecan, and write-in. There were also contests for favorite car, day of the week, movie, and entertainer (vote for no more than three), along with a "yes/no" proposition for making Patrick Henry's birthday a federal holiday.

At that point Roger entered the area, accompanied by a man who appeared to be about Carl's age. Carl wasn't sure but he thought he heard (or sensed) a groan from a few of the occupants at the rover table.

"Good morning, rovers," said Roger enthusiastically. "Thank you all for coming out on what promises to be a 'seasonably warm' summer's day. We have some very important work ahead of us. The Office of Elections had acquired from Braxton County, thirty *ElectionPro* scanners, complete with the outer black bins on which they rest and the inner blue bins where the voted ballots land."

"Today we will be doing an 'acceptance test' for these machines. Our intention is to have two scanners for each of our 240 precincts this November. To reach that goal, twenty-five of these Braxton machines will be needed. The other five will remain in the warehouse as backup. We've been told that while these scanners were given an initial acceptance test by Braxton when they were purchased years ago, none of them have been used in an actual election, so it's critical that we do this acceptance test with our usual thoroughness."

"Now before we begin," continued Roger. "I have an announcement to make. As of September 1, I will be moving over to the tax division of the county. For the rest of the year, I will be on call as a resource, on an 'as needed' basis, but I will no longer serve as 'machine coordinator.' But do not fret. You will not be leaderless. I'd like to introduce you all to Terrence Bucholtz who will be taking my place as of September 1."

Polite but restrained applause greeted the announcement. "I knew something was up," said Scott quietly.

"Thank you, Roger", said Terrence. "I'll be observing today and I look forward to getting to know each of you." He seemed pleasant enough, although a bit ill at ease.

Roger then outlined the mechanics of the day. Michael and a couple of designees would be in charge of Station One where the scanners astride their wheeled bins would be lined up and entered into the county database. Most of the rovers would work at Station Two. Each rover would get the next scanner in the assembly line and wheel it to one of the workbenches. It was then a matter of powering up the scanner and working through the opening sequence where the machines was calibrated, the correct date and time entered, and the zero report produced.

Once that was done, it would be time to insert the test deck, one ballot at a time. Additional ballots would be generated on the *CreateBallot* device and inserted. Then the polls would be closed and the final report printed. Hopefully it would match the anticipated result. Two rovers would be working at each work station, each one confirming his/her partner's results. The final approval sheet for each scanner would hence have two signatures, verifying that it "passed" the acceptance test.

Once the machine was "accepted," it would be powered down and wheeled over to Station Three where Jack would then wheel it into its assigned warehouse position, next to the cart for that precinct.

It was a rather complex assembly line process and Carl realized that he initially needed to just concentrate on his job and hope that the totality of it all would eventually fall into place.

From his days as chief election officer, Carl was quite familiar with many of the scanner operations. Those that were new to him, like calibrating the screen and entering the correct date and time, were not difficult and after the first few scanners were processed, a certain rhythm to the day emerged. He found that the time from when the scanner was powered on to the time it was shut down was usually about forty-five minutes. Sometimes a little less, sometimes a little more. As far as he could tell, the scanners all seemed to be in splendid working condition in spite of their extended shelf life.

"What did you think of Roger's announcement?" asked Scott, when they broke at noon for lunch.

"Well you certainly called it," said Carl, remembering Scott's prediction at the courthouse.

"Rumor has it," said Scott, who seemed to be well connected to the county rumor mill, "that Terrence was a favorite of the previous registrar. They have tried him in a number of positions and apparently he has not excelled in any of them."

"Is machine coordinator the best spot for an underachiever?"

"Not really. There are times the process almost seems to run itself but part of that comes from Roger's leadership. On the other hand, if Roger is still available to consult with, it might not be too bad. Plus Michael pretty much knows the process from front to back. So it should be OK provided Terrence is willing to listen and learn. Hopefully."

The rest of the day went smoothly. The machines all seemed to be in good working order and each one "passed" the acceptance test. By 2:30 p.m., they were done. The next time they would gather would be the second week of September when work would start for the November election. This would leave Carl with lots of free time to help Cindy with her campaign. Up to now however, she hadn't asked him to do a whole lot. Whenever he offered to help, she would usually say "Steve has it covered" or something like that. Carl couldn't help but feel jealous but he realized that Steve had political experience and skills that he lacked. It was only natural that Cindy would lean on him for support. But still…

# 17

## Monday, August 10, 8:00 p.m.

"So how is the world of electoral politics treating you?" asked Carl.

*...and is that why I'm not seeing as much of you as I used to?*

"It's a bit overwhelming," admitted Cindy. "Biff Logan made it sound so easy. 'Just be yourself and they'll all love you,' or words to that effect. But between Steve teaching me about the process and Howard force feeding me environmental science, it's...well it's overwhelming. It really is."

"You sound like you're questioning the whole thing."

"No...I mean...I don't know, maybe. Sometimes I feel like a complete fraud but whenever I say that to Steve, he starts telling me how wonderful I am and how I'm a quick learner and how it will all turn out great."

Carl felt badly for Cindy. It was clear that she was under a lot of pressure. That her situation was brought on by herself and her ambition, seemed for the moment to be beside the point.

"I know this isn't a perfect analogy," he said. "But if you recall last January, you were a bit overwhelmed and yet you rose to the occasion. Of course I realize that a single day at the polls in no way equates to a multimonth political campaign."

The room was silent for a few minutes as Cindy prepared to come to the point of her visit.

"Carl, I need to ask you something," she said. She seemed tentative, even embarrassed.

"Sure. Anything. What is it?" said Carl.

"Well it's…I mean Steve said I need to…"

"What is it?"

Cindy braced herself and continued. "Money. My campaign needs money. Steve says he can get a list of potential donors from the previous office holder, but right now I need to rely on my friends. So is there any chance that you could contribute something to my campaign? Financially, I mean."

"Well sure. Of course," said Carl soothingly. "Is there any amount you have in mind?"

"Not really. Well yes actually…I mean, I feel like such a shit for hitting on you like this. I hate this. Deb gave me twenty and Ginny tried to give me twenty but I gave it back to her. She has student loans to pay and all. Anyway Steve says I should lean on you hard but I don't want to abuse our friendship…" Her voice tailed off.

Carl got to his feet and went to his desk. Pulling out his checkbook, he proceed to tear out a check and fill it in.

"Will this help?" he said, walking over to Cindy and handing her the check. It was for $500.

"Yes", said Cindy, breaking into a wide smile, neglecting to mention that $500 was exactly the amount that Steve suggested Carl would be good for.

"Glad to help out," said Carl. "And look. While I don't have deep pockets I can probably contribute a bit more as you get further down the road."

"I really appreciate it," said Cindy. She wanted to give Carl a hug but somehow it didn't seem right. Like she was giving away her affections in exchange for a campaign donation. "And I hate to run like this but I need to prep for my next environmental science session with Howard. Environmental health and toxicology."

"Sound like fun. Enjoy."

*Oh, what the hell,* thought Cindy, as she gave Carl a big hug and departed into the night.

# 18

## Friday, August 14, Noon

*It's just like you, Cindy. Leaving it to the last minute.*

She had meant to do it sooner. Those petitions had been sitting on the table in her apartment for a couple of weeks. All ready to be delivered to the Government Center. Of course, she'd do it. Real soon. Right away. Tomorrow perhaps.

Well like it or not, tomorrow was today. August 14. Deadline day. And here was Cindy, on her lunch break, driving the twenty miles out on the interstate. She knew she was taking a chance in doing this. She had that 1:00 p.m. conference call scheduled. But what other choice did she have? For reasons she never quite understood, the large building where the county had its administrative offices was in the extreme western part of the county, forcing the majority of its citizens to undertake a long drive whenever they needed to conduct county business in person.

Fortunately traffic was light and Cindy pulled into the parking lot shortly after twelve noon. Grabbing the petitions, she bounded from the car and walked/jogged as quickly as she could to the entrance, sidestepping various people along the way. She entered the building and looked around, hoping to see a large sign reading "Office of Elections, Right Here."

Seeing no such sign, she went up to a uniformed security guard.

"Office of Elections?"

"Third floor," he said, pointing to the bank of elevators.

"Thanks," said Cindy. Ignoring the elevators, she went quickly over to the door marked "stairs." Up the stairs and out into the third floor hallway she went, where she was finally rewarded with the door for the Office of Elections. She opened the door and proceeded to the reception desk. Panting from her exertions, she plopped her petitions on the desk and proclaimed in a loud voice to the room in general,

"These are my petitions to run for office. Who do I give them to?"

"I can take them," said a woman seated at one of the desks, located a couple of rows back from the reception desk. She looked up from her computer screen and froze.

"Oh, it's you."

They stared at each other for a few moments, neither one knowing quite what to say.

"I didn't know you worked the front desk," said Cindy at last, breaking the silence.

"I'm covering for one of the girls on her lunch break," said Valerie as she got up and went to the reception desk.

"Well...here are my papers," said Cindy.

Valerie took the papers and examined them. "Soil and Water?" she said, giving Cindy a raised eyebrow look.

"Yes, Soil and Water," said Cindy, defiantly.

"You were always so passionate on the subject," said Valerie, dryly. Then quickly before Cindy could respond, "No, I'm sorry

Cyn. That was uncalled for." She looked down and studied the petitions. "These papers look in order. I'll make sure the right person gets them."

Cindy took a deep breath and said, "So you're running for the school board?"

"Yes. I'm taking a leave of absence here. Today is my last day in fact."

"And how are the boys?"

"They're fine. Thanks."

"And Stan?"

"He's good."

An awkward silence.

"Well I better get going. It's looks like we'll be having some sort of joint kickoff event."

"Really?" said Valerie. She seemed surprised.

"Yes. My campaign manager was going to get in touch with your campaign manager and set the whole thing up."

Valerie seemed to be pondering what was apparently "new news." "Well that should be interesting," she said at last, with a wry smile.

"Yes, it should," said Cindy, who was suddenly eager to leave. "Got to run. Got this meeting and all," and she hurriedly exited the room.

# 19

## Wednesday, August 19, 7:30 p.m.

"Well, Mr. Gilbertson," asked Cindy. "How does 'Phelps for Soil and Water' stand? Financially, I mean."

"Call me, Norbert," said the fortyish man, sitting at the end of the dining room table in Cindy's apartment. "Taking into account your income so far versus your expenses, which include $2000 to me, thank you very much, your campaign has a net total of $243.62."

"Which means," said Steve, "You need to have a fundraiser now in August. You can't wait for the September kickoff event."

"And why again are we delaying the kickoff to September?" asked Cindy.

"To maximize publicity. No one pays attention to politics before Labor Day. The kickoff is a misnomer anyway. Your campaign has been going on for a couple of weeks now. And let me be the first to congratulate you. The county Democratic committee met last night and voted to officially endorse you for Soil and Water."

Steve paused to allow Cindy to savor the moment.

"Well, hot damn," said Cindy softly, unable to suppress a smile. "This really is happening."

"Yes, it is," said Steve, also smiling. "Now for that fundraiser, I'd suggest an early evening midweek event for your first. A simple meet-and-greet with light hors d'oeuvres would match your limited budget. We need some sort of venue, not your apartment though. Do you know anyone with a house we can use?"

"Carl has a townhouse. Would that be sufficient?" asked Cindy. "The development he lives in has lots of parking."

"Do you think he'd let us run a fundraiser there?"

"I'm sure of it. He pretty much does anything I ask."

That simple statement startled them both. Cindy had not meant to put it so bluntly.

"What I mean is that we're very good friends. I'd do the same for him in a minute."

"I have no doubt," said Steve, dryly. "Well float some midweek dates past Carl and see what works. Invite as many people as you know, even slightly. Friends. Relatives. People from work. People who signed your petition. I'll throw in some of the names from Norman Purvis' old list. The ones who live in this area, at least. Norbert can collect the contributions and make sure they are properly recorded. As for you, just play the gracious hostess. At the right time, I'll introduce you and you make a fifteen minute speech saying how honored you are, the environment is so important, blah, blah, blah. With any kind of luck we should raise enough to order some professionally printed fliers and yard signs. In the meantime, we need to make up a flier on your home computer. Just for something to hand out in the interim."

While Steve was talking, Cindy was scribbling down notes on her pad. So much to do. All this process stuff on top of Howard's environmental science core dump. Sustainable practices in agriculture was their latest "lesson". But at least at the fundraiser she would be interacting with people. That was what she was best at. She would just have to come up with a good speech. And a flier. So much.

"...and a website," Steve was saying. "We need to get one set up ASAP. I can get one set up for you in a day or two but I'll need some additional info from you. Bio, position on the issues, a few quotations, a page where people can volunteer. And another page for 'on the trail' with photos of you campaigning. Here is a questionnaire I've prepared for you. Basic stuff, but I need to have you fill it out right away. Right now, if you can."

For the next hour, Cindy sat by herself, working on the information packet that Steve had given her. Steve and Norbert continued to work on some of the more legalistic aspects of the campaign. Eventually Norbert seemed satisfied that things were under control. He said his goodbyes, and left.

"So how is your paperwork coming?" asked Steve.

"I'm pretty much finished," said Cindy. "I'm not sure my bio is all that interesting."

"Let's take a look," said Steve, taking the packet. "I see your parents are living in California. And your father is actually your stepfather?"

"My dad died when I was in college," said Cindy. "A year later, mom remarried."

"And you have just the one sister, who is nine years older than you?"

"That's right."

Steve paused for a moment, taking it in. Then he continued, reading from the packet.

"Then you graduated University of Virginia. High honors. Phi Beta Kappa. Active in your sorority as well as the drama society. And the rock climbing club?" He gave Cindy a quizzical look.

"Yeah, I can climb practically anything."

Steve considered. "Actually a photo of you scaling whatever might look good on a flier. How about student government? Anything there?"

Cindy shook her head.

"And since entering the work force, your community involvement has been—"

"Three stints as an election officer. Two of those were as chief."

"And that's the extent of your community involvement? Nothing with your church or anything?"

"No."

A pause.

"Do you go to church?"

"Sometimes. Not as often as…Is this really necessary?"

Not answering, Steve turned to the issues portion of the packet.

"You've left a fair amount of this blank," he said, looking up at Cindy.

"Well yeah. I answered the questions dealing with the environment. I didn't bother with the other stuff. I assumed that this was some sort of generic form you've crafted for all sorts of candidates."

"I understand that," said Steve. "Still we need to have the full picture. For example, what's your position on guns?"

"I hate them."

"And that's it?"

"That's it."

"All right," said Steve writing on the page. "We will say that while you respect the second amendment rights of gun owners, you are eager to find creative ways to make sure they don't fall into the hands of the wrong people."

Cindy gave an exasperated look that seemed to say "this is a waste of time" but remained silent.

"How about immigration?"

"I haven't given it much thought but I guess we need to make sure people enter our country legally."

"And the ones who are already here illegally? Should we send them back?"

"Not if they're behaving themselves."

Steve considered. "I think we can live with that. Now can I assume you're pro-choice?"

There was another pause.

"I'm conflicted on that," said Cindy.

"And what does that mean?"

"It means I don't want to talk about it."

Now it was Steve's turn to be exasperated. "Cindy, when you're running for office you can't just decide what issues you want to talk about. You have to be ready for anything—"

"No I don't," interrupted Cindy, her voice rising. "I've been working my ass off with Howard learning about all this environment stuff. He's made me realize so much that I never even cared about before. Global warming. Industrial pollution. Clean Water. And you know what? I'm on board. I may be a flawed apostle but I'm on board. But all that other stuff is completely irrelevant and if anyone asks me about it, that's what I'll say. And if they don't like it, well tough shit."

Silence engulfed the room.

"I mean it, Steve. Don't push me."

Once again, Steve had to choose his words carefully. Managing Cindy was proving to be more difficult than he had imagined.

"Why do you suppose Biff picked you to run for this?"

"Because he thinks I'd make an attractive candidate," said Cindy, reciting from rote in an exaggerated singsong tone. "Biff likes to win. He thinks I can win. He wants the seat on the commission held by a Democrat. We've been through all this."

"That's partially true," said Steve, slowly. He paused, trying to decide how to continue but before he could say anything more, Cindy jumped in.

"What part isn't true?"

"I probably shouldn't be telling you this—" Steve began.

"Yes, you should. Out with it."

"Well you see, Soil and Water really isn't a partisan position. Yes, the parties sometimes endorse the candidates but there's usually not a whole lot of policy differences. We all want clean water."

Cindy looked at Steve with a confused expression on her face. "I don't understand. What are you saying?"

"I'm saying," said Steve, "that if you hadn't agreed to run, I'm not sure the party would have tried to find anyone else. They might even have endorsed the Republican."

"I'm sorry but I am completely lost," said Cindy. "Why is Howard, and for that matter you, going through all this trouble to make me into a viable candidate, if you don't really care if a Democrat sits on the commission?"

"Because you're not running for Soil and Water. Not really, anyway."

Cindy started to say something, but Steve held up his hand for silence.

"A year from now both houses in the Virginia state legislature are up for grabs. State Senate and House of Delegates. Both seats, where you live, are currently held by Republicans and our list of potential Democratic candidates is thin. Now whether you realize it or not, you have impressed quite a few people. People at your marketing firm. Both colleagues and clients. And then the resilience and resourcefulness you displayed during last January's special election. It was featured on the news, how you navigated that icy road to track down that elderly lady."

"You do realize that it was Carl who actually drove the car that night," said Cindy.

"Whatever. Anyway that along with your youthful personality and, you know, your—"

"Yeah, never mind, I get it," said Cindy.

"The challenge is," continued Steve. "That your resume, as you just noted, is not all that exciting. We need something substantial to give you that stamp of legitimacy as a candidate."

"Like a seat on the Soil and Water Commission," said Cindy. "So what you're saying is that what I am really doing is auditioning for a possible nomination for a seat in the state legislature."

Steve nodded his head. "I hope you're not too mad at me."

"Well, I don't appreciate being kept in the dark. How do you know I would even be interested in running for state legislature?"

"We don't, of course. But the feeling was, and is, that a bright, young woman on the rise, like you, would be hard pressed to turn it down. And while there are no guarantees, just think, a state legislator before the age of thirty. There's no telling where all this could lead."

Steve paused, allowing his words to have the desired effect. In spite of herself, Cindy began to imagine all sorts of scenarios.

*Wow! I mean this is...Wow!* thought Cindy.

"Well you certainly have given me something to think about," she said, slowly coming back to earth. "And I will admit, I find it interesting. Very interesting, in fact. But I'm still not answering any of those other policy questions on that questionnaire. Some of them involve issues that I haven't thought about or am not sure of and I'm not about to write something down just to please the party or even to win an election. I've got all I can do to get a handle on the environmental stuff."

Steve realized that it was probably best not to press Cindy any more on the questionnaire. After all he had thrown quite a bit at her that evening and on the whole, she had taken it rather well. Best wait for an opportunity later.

"So, are we done?" asked Cindy, a bright smile returning to her face.

"Yes, we are," said Steve, returning her smile.

Steve gathered up his papers and Cindy walked him to the front door. They said their goodbyes and he left. Cindy sensed that he had wanted to linger. She wasn't sure how she felt about that. She wasn't sure how she felt about a number of things.

Cindy had no idea what the next couple of months would bring but she sensed they would go a long way in defining the life that lay before her.

# Part Two

## The Campaign

# 20

## Monday, August 24, 7:30 p.m.

"So that's the story. Can you imagine that? Me? State legislature."

Carl could see that Cindy was excited by the prospect.

"And who knows what after that?" she exclaimed.

"And the first step to that is winning the race for Soil and Water," said Carl.

"You got it. That's why having this first fundraiser is so important."

"And the next step is actually serving on Soil and Water," said Carl, pointedly.

"What? Yeah. Sure. Anyway, are you OK having that fundraiser here?" asked Cindy, somewhat oblivious to Carl's last observation. "My girl friends all live in apartments and I'd feel a bit strange asking any of my work colleagues..."

"Of course," said Carl smiling. It was hard not to be caught up in her enthusiasm. "It will give me an excuse to clean up the place. How many people do you expect?"

Cindy paused for a moment to consider. "I'm not really sure. There's Deb and Ginny and Sue..." She stated rattling off her friends and work colleagues. "Then we'll examine the names of the people who signed my petition. Anyone who lives close to here, we'll include. And Steve says he'll have some people from Purvis' old donor list. So that's…I don't rightly know."

"I'll plan for about fifty," said Carl. "And if it goes over by a bit, that will be OK."

"Did you ever imagine," said Cindy, suddenly reflecting, "the first time we met that I'd be someday running for political office?"

"The first time we met, I wasn't sure we'd get through the day without clawing each other's eyes out," responded Carl with a wry smile.

Cindy laughed.

"Yeah, that too. So the date for the fundraiser will be—"

"Whatever evening you want," said Carl. "We don't start work at the warehouse until September 15, so I'm working fairly normal hours at Software Solutions. But whatever day you choose, I can be home early, to make sure the place is ready."

The next half hour was spent discussing the specifics of the event. Steve had convinced Cindy that catered refreshments were beyond their budget so Cindy had arranged for some of her friends to bring over some finger food. Carl would supply the coffee and soft drinks. Steve had advised against serving liquor for this type of event. Cindy wasn't sure her friends would like that. She wasn't sure she would like that.

"And how is your environmental science education going?" asked Carl, as they were winding down.

"Great," said Cindy. "Our last session went into all the endangered species. Between Howard's teaching and the things he's giving me to read, I'm learning a lot."

"But are you learning about what the Soil and Water Commission actually does?"

"What are you trying to be? Gloomy Gus?" said Cindy, laughing. "No. Not yet. Howard says I need a strong foundation first. The first debate is October 7. He will have me prepared by then. In the meantime, I can get by with generalities. You know like global warming is bad and the Republicans don't care. That sort of thing."

"That sounds a bit simplistic."

Cindy grimaced and gave a dismissive wave of her hand.

"Yeah, I know. You're right. I'll beef it up a bit."

"Do you know who you will be running against?"

"There are two other candidates. The Republican is someone named Rawlins. He's retired."

"Retired from what?"

"Steve's looking into that. The Independent Green Party is also endorsing a candidate. Steve says I shouldn't worry about that."

"The Independent Green is a state party committed to rail transportation. I would agree with Steve that they shouldn't be a factor."

The room was silent for a few minutes as they both seemed lost in their own thoughts. At last, Cindy spoke.

"There's something you want to say, isn't there?"

Carl hesitated. Should he say it? Should he share his doubts about this whole enterprise? No, he finally concluded. Cindy was making what was obviously a sincere effort. She deserved the benefit of the doubt.

"No, nothing," said Carl, smiling. "Except to say 'thank you' for allowing me to be part of this."

# 21

## Tuesday, September 1, 7:45 P.M.

"We also need to protect the water in our streams to ensure that our water supply is pure and uncontaminated. These are just a few of the concerns that I share with you, concerns that I assure you will be on the top of my mind and heart as I strive to represent you on the Soil and Water Commission. I am truly honored and overwhelmed that you have taken time out of your busy schedules to be with me this evening and I look forward to working with you as we take our campaign forward in the coming weeks."

Enthusiastic applause came from every corner of Carl's living room. For the past hour Cindy had been mixing with the guests, impressing everyone with her charm and graciousness. Carl vividly remembered the first time he had seen Cindy in action. How she could turn on that charm in an instant. At the time he had suspected that it was all an act. A ploy by her to get her own way. He soon realized, however, that much of it was genuine. Yes, she was ambitious and calculating, but she also truly liked people and empathized with them. Right now she was talking to a middle aged couple that Carl had never seen before.

"The erosion on the steep part of the trail was just horrible," the lady was saying. "After each rain storm, it was so slippery you would have to slide down the trail on your backside. So as part of our son's Eagle project, the troop inserted logs to serve as water bars, every fifty feet or so. It was quite an effort, I tell you."

"I wish I could have been there," said Cindy, actually meaning it. "It's so wonderful to see young people involved."

"Exactly," said the husband. "And that's why we signed your petition at the supermarket the other day. We need young people, like yourself, leading the charge on these environmental issues."

"Excuse me, Cindy." It was Steve. "There is someone here that I would like you to meet."

"I'm sorry, I'm being pulled away," said Cindy to the couple. "Thank you again for your support."

"You're doing great," said Steve, steering Cindy in the right direction. "Norbert is in his element, raking in the contributions."

They went over to the side of the room where an elderly lady was seated on the couch.

"Cindy," said Steve. "This is Mildred Purvis. She has so wanted to meet you."

Warning signals went off in Cindy's head. This must be Norman Purvis' widow. She displayed what she hoped was her brightest smile and offered her hand. They shook hands briefly.

"Please, sit down so we can talk," said Mrs. Purvis with a smile. "I've just contributed $250 to your campaign so I hope that gets me at least a brief conversation."

"I'll leave you two to get better acquainted," said Steve. As he left, he flashed a quick look at Cindy that clearly said, *"Don't blow it."*

Cindy sat down next to Mrs. Purvis. She continued to smile as best she could but somehow the scrutiny of Mrs. Purvis' steady gaze made it increasingly difficult. Cindy wanted to say something but no words came.

"Are you enjoying yourself, dear?" asked Mrs. Purvis, with a gentle smile. It was not the question that Cindy was expecting.

"Why, yes I—"

"I bet you are. You're so young and pretty. You should be enjoying yourself."

Cindy didn't know what to say so she remained silent.

"I listened to your little speech just now," Mrs. Purvis continued. "Very well delivered, I must say."

Cindy gave a slight nod. "Thank you," she murmured. Mrs. Purvis' steady gaze was making her feel uneasy.

"The thing is," said Mrs. Purvis, with that gentle smile still in place, "you don't know the first thing about the Soil and Water Commission, do you?"

Cindy tried to come up with a response. To somehow defend herself.

*Think of something fast. Don't blow it.*

No magic words came. She had to say something.

"Is it that obvious?"

"Only to me, dear. They all love you," Mrs. Purvis said, shifting her gaze to the people in the room.

"Now, don't you worry. I'm not going to ask for my donation back. This will be our little secret. And I'll tell you another secret. When Norman started to get involved, he didn't know a whole lot either. But he cared. He had passion. He loved to get dirt under his fingernails. Do you love getting dirt under your fingernails?"

Cindy suddenly became conscious of her manicured hands.

Mrs. Purvis gave a small chuckle.

"Don't begrudge an old lady a bit of fun, dear," she said, taking Cindy's hands into her own and giving them a gentle squeeze.

"But passion is so important." Mrs. Purvis continued, turning serious. "To believe in something that matters. Something beyond yourself. For Norman it was dirt. For you..."

The air hung heavy with the uncompleted sentence. Once again, Cindy found herself speechless.

"But listen to me prattle on. I do believe it's time for me to take my leave," said Mrs. Purvis, getting to her feet.

Cindy also stood up. Steve rushed over with an anxious look on his face.

"Isn't she lovely?" said Mrs. Purvis to Steve, gesturing to Cindy. "I think you have a winner on your hands. Thank you so much for inviting me."

Steve and Cindy both escorted Mrs. Purvis to the door. Once she was safely out of the house. Steve turned to Cindy with a look of triumph in his face.

"Well done, Cindy. You must have really impressed her."

Cindy returned a weak smile.

*Well, an impression was made. That's for sure.*

# 22

## Monday, September 7, 1:00 P.M.

Carl was feeling rather uncomfortable.

For someone so devoted to the electoral process, his views on politics were rather tepid. In college he had briefly flirted with the Democratic Party, moved by the idealistic fervor of some of his classmates. In time however, his temperate nature caused him to drift over to the GOP. Government should be small, or at least smaller than it was, less obtrusive in people's lives. It seemed to him that many of the government programs, although noble in intent, had developed into out of control bureaucracies, spawning waste and inefficiency. This, along with his mostly conservative views on social issues, had placed Carl in the Republican camp for quite some time.

And yet, here he was, at the Labor Day festival, standing behind the table at the county Democratic Party booth, wearing a royal blue shirt with "Cindy Phelps for Soil and Water" in bold white lettering.

*I'm only doing this for Cindy,* he had told himself.

Carl had already decided that he would be voting for the Republican candidates in the U.S. Senate race as well as the contest for House of Representatives from Virginia's twelfth congressional district. He had not yet decided who he would vote for in the school board race. His "back to basics" views on education normally caused him to vote Republican in school board elections but he had been impressed by Valerie Turner's grasp of the county education system and issues. That, along with the fact that she was Cindy's sister, had caused Carl to leave this one open, at least for now. He had hoped that Valerie would be in attendance at the festival as he wanted to hear more of her perspectives on the race but she did not appear to be present. There were some fliers for the Democratic Party that included Valerie's name (as well as Cindy's) but no fliers specific to the school board race. It would appear that her organization was a bit behind Cindy's. Carl realized that this was almost certainly the result of Steve's expertise and guidance.

Carl's job was to hand out fliers with Cindy's campaign bio to anyone who seemed reasonably receptive. They had been printed on Carl's PC using light beige paper. Very appropriate for Soil and Water. More professional fliers were on order and should arrive in time for the kickoff. Her endorsements, listed on the flier, included Mildred Purvis, the county Democratic committee, and the Democratic candidate for the House race (whom she had never met).

Carl's secondary goal was to get people to volunteer to work on the campaign. To that end he had a signup sheet with room for name, address, and phone number. So far Carl had not experienced much action, as most of the attention seemed to be focused further down the table, where the materials for the Senate and House races were. There for the taking, were campaign fliers, buttons, car magnets, pens, notepads, and hard candy. People were clustered around these campaign trinkets, helping themselves.

Suddenly Cindy, accompanied by Steve, appeared out of the crowd.

"We need more fliers," said Cindy, excitedly. "People are taking them, left and right. Of course a lot of them are winding up in the trash but what the hey, it's only paper."

Both Steve and Carl shot surprised looks at Cindy.

"What?" she said. Then, suddenly realizing, "Oh yeah, I forgot. I'm the conservation candidate. My bad. Won't happen again."

In the meantime Steve had looked over at the volunteer sign-up sheet that Carl had been maintaining. "Come on, Cindy," he said. "We haven't hit the midway area yet."

By this time Cindy had grabbed a small pile of fliers and they both departed. Once they were clear of the booth, Steve took Cindy aside.

"We need to talk," he said.

"Sure. What about?"

"It's Carl."

Cindy looked at Steve in surprise. "What about Carl?"

"He's not helping," said Steve solemnly. "Did you see that sign-up sheet? Practically empty. You need to get him out of there."

Cindy let out a sigh.

"Working the crowd is not really his strength," she acknowledged.

"He's dragging you down. I don't think he's making any friends with the other people at the booth either. He's not wearing any of the buttons for the other Democrats."

*Of course not,* thought Cindy. *He's a Republican. But he stood up for me last January when the Electoral Board was preparing to remove me as chief.*

"He's my friend," she said. "And he'll be my friend when this campaign is over."

Something in Cindy's tone told Steve not to push it, at least for now.

"Well at least get one of your girl friends to work the table with Carl."

Cindy considered. Steve was right. She had noticed the same thing, that afternoon when she and Carl had gathered signatures for the petitions.

"OK," said Cindy. "We can have Deb work with him. I saw her down by the funnel cakes, a few minutes ago."

"I'll go get her," said Steve. "You go on to the midway. And don't forget, the parade starts in half an hour."

"Right. I'm in the third grouping, right behind the mariachi dancers and in front of the Tae Kwon Do school. How diverse can you get?"

They split up and Cindy headed for the midway. It was a beautiful sunny day. Wherever she went, people seemed happy to take her fliers, even if most of them didn't seem to know what Soil and Water was. That was OK, Steve had said. Just shake their hands, smile, and say she was running. They would remember her on Election Day. Or at least enough of them would.

Politics was so much fun.

# 23

## Saturday, September 12, 9:00 A.M.

"AFGHANISTAN...ALBANIA...ALGERIA...Argentina..." The directions had said, "Report to Thackeray High School, about nine. Be sure to wear the county shirt that has been issued to you. The ceremony begins at ten."

This was for an "extra opportunity" which the rovers could optionally participate in, if they wanted to earn a bit of cash. Be part of a team of election personal who would be stationed outside the auditorium where new citizens were taking the oath of citizenship. Then as they came out of the door, get as many as were willing, to fill out the voter registration form to become newly registered voters.

Carl hadn't planned to participate. It was optional, after all, and he had promised Cindy he would help with her campaign. A shipment of yard signs had come in and Carl was prepared to go door-to-door in an effort to get people to display the signs on their property. It had all been arranged but when Carl mentioned, in passing, the new citizens event, Cindy had practically insisted that he go.

"You've been so generous with your time Carl, but I can tell you really want to do that new citizens event. Please do it. We'll manage back here."

"...Bolivia...Botswana...Brazil...Bulgaria..."

When Carl arrived, a few minutes before nine, the large parking lot at the school was already completely full, forcing him to park on a neighborhood street several blocks away. Fortunately it was a pleasant, late summer morning, with just the slightest hint of fall in the air. Carl quickly walked to the school where he was greeted by an immense line of diverse humanity, wrapping around the school. All shapes, sizes, ages, and ethnicities. Many were in their Sunday best.

Carl cautiously went toward what appeared to be the school's primary entrance. While he didn't want to be accused of "cutting in," he didn't think he was expected to get in the same line as the soon-to-be citizens. Sure enough, when the official at the door saw his county badge, he motioned for Carl to enter. Upon entering, he saw to one side of the hall, a table with a huge sign that had the county logo and in big letters "Office of Elections." Behind the table, were two elderly ladies, both doing crossword puzzles. One of them looked up as Carl approached.

"You must be one of the rovers," she said, fixing her gaze on Carl. "Betty said we might be getting a few of you today. This is Charlotte. I'm Bertha."

"...Costa Rica...Croatia...Cuba...Czech Republic..." *(strong applause for Costa Rica)*

"How does this work?" asked Carl.

"Did you see all those people in line? They all have to come past us to the check-in tables near the auditorium. Then they enter the auditorium for the ceremony. After the ceremony you and the others work the crowd, getting as many people as you can to register. Charlotte and I man the table here, catching people who elude you."

Carl looked around. "Where are the registration forms they have to fill out?"

"They're not here, yet. Betty brings them about 9:45. That's when most of the others arrive in the carpool from the Government Center. There's a fair amount of waiting time involved. But not to worry. We're all on the clock."

Just then the door opened and the officials barked their commands as the line of soon-to-be-citizens passed by.

"New citizens only. Friends and family come in later. Only new citizens now."

Occasionally one of the people would give a questioning look to the table. Bertha would then call out, "All the way down the hall. Follow the crowd."

"…Ecuador…Egypt…El Salvador…Equatorial Guinea…" *(Thunderous applause for El Salvador)*

"Now friends and family can enter." And a second wave of diverse humanity passed by the table.

Just around 9:45 a.m., as Bertha had predicted, the contingent of personnel from the Government Center arrived. Carl introduced himself to Betty, who was in charge of "outreach" for the Office of Elections. Previously they had only conversed by e-mail.

"Grab a canvas bag, a pile of blank forms, and a couple of boxes of pens," said Betty. "And take one of these boxes to put the completed applications in. Be sure to review each application for completeness. They must enter certain fields. For example, middle name. They have to put in a middle name or check 'none.' And also make sure they check 'yes' for 'Are you a citizen?' Sometimes they forget that."

"...Jordon...Kenya...Kosovo...Kuwait..."

Carl assembled his supplies and positioned himself in a small alcove off the main hall. Others in their group found similar locations. Once the ceremony concluded, the new citizens would leave the auditorium and line up at tables to receive their naturalization certificate. At that point they would go back up the hall toward the front door, where Carl and his colleagues would greet them and get as many as possible to be registered. Now it was just a matter of waiting.

"Carl, why don't you go into the auditorium and watch the ceremony?" said Betty. "When it's winding down, you can come back and alert us. We'll watch your supplies."

Carl left his post and went down the hall to the auditorium. A few small children were running around in the area immediately outside the auditorium, under the watchful eyes of their parents. Apparently the ceremony had been too much for them. Carl entered the auditorium and took an empty seat. He quickly ascertained that he was sitting in the location reserved for "family and friends" of the new citizens.

"...Mexico...Moldovia...Morocco...Mozambique..."

In front of the "family and friends" section were several blank rows. And in front of them were ten or eleven rows of new citizens. Some were still seated while many were standing. The person on stage was reading off a list of countries. When each country was announced, those who had emigrated from that country would stand and join the others. Sometimes it would be just one or two persons who would stand. Other times, a great many more. The reaction from the "family and friends" section would range from polite applause to thunderous ovations complete with whoops and hollers.

"...Netherlands...Nicaragua...Nigeria...Pakistan..."

Both Nicaragua and Pakistan brought fresh waves of energy from the audience. And Carl began to sense it. It was all around him. A feeling of joy. He tried to imagine the paths that these people must have traveled to get to this point in their lives. The list went on and on.

"...Uruguay...Venezuela...Vietnam...Zambia."

And it was done. They were all standing now. It was time for them to raise their right hand and repeat after the person on stage, the oath of citizenship.

*"I hereby declare, on oath, that I absolutely and entirely renounce and abjure all allegiance and fidelity to any foreign prince, potentate, state, or sovereignty, of whom or which I have heretofore been a subject or citizen; that I will support and defend the Constitution and laws of the United States of America...and that I take this obligation freely, without any mental reservation or purpose of evasion; so help me God."*

And that was it. They were now citizens. And now they were all cheering. Celebrating something that Carl had always taken for granted. Once the noise subsided, they were led in the Pledge of Allegiance. This was followed by a video of patriotic music. The new citizens had been issued small American flags which they waved, in time to the music.

Carl gave a start. He had been so wrapped up in the emotion of the ceremony that he forgot his assignment. This must be near the end. Quickly he got up and exited the auditorium. He hurried back to where the others were stationed and gave a wave to Betty.

"OK," Betty called out. "It's showtime. Let's do it."

At first they came by in a trickle.

"New citizen voter registration?" Carl said tentatively to the brown skinned couple walking past. The woman, clutching her naturalization certificate, smiled but indicated she was in a hurry.

"Do I need to do it now?" she asked.

"No, but it's better if you do. Later you might forget. It only takes a couple of minutes."

The lady nodded and accepted the form and pen that Carl gave her.

"When you finish you can give it back to me or anyone else wearing the county shirt," said Carl.

By this time, two other new citizens, both men, had come over to Carl and reached out for the forms. Then another lady. Suddenly Carl was surrounded by people of seemingly every ethnicity, reaching for one of the voter registration forms.

The first lady came back with her completed form. Carl checked it for completeness.

"You need to sign and date it at the bottom," he said and gave the form back to the lady.

More hands were reaching for the forms, even as some were returning completed forms. If the form was completed correctly, Carl would drop it into the box at his feet, offering a receipt and his congratulations at the same time. Otherwise he returned the form to the citizen, showing what needed to be done. Many of the names seemed so foreign. Unpronounceable sequences of letters that seemed to go on and on. Of course up until a few minutes ago these people had been foreigners. Now they were Americans.

The crush of humanity continued. But it was a chaos that was filled with joy. New citizens were taking turns having their photo taken, standing by a large American flag near the front of the lobby. One man even insisted that Carl pose with him.

Gradually the crowd began to dissipate. Some however, seemed reluctant to leave, wanting to savor the moment as long as possible. Carl was reviewing the last form given to him.

"Excuse me ma'am," he said to the lady. "You didn't answer one of the questions."

He showed her the form and she laughed. "Of course. How silly of me."

She took the pen from Carl and where the form asked "Are you a citizen of the United States of America?" she boldly checked "yes."

She returned the form to Carl. There were tears in her eyes.

"I've waited my whole life for this."

# 24

## Tuesday, September 15, 9:00 a.m.

"So the day is finally upon us," said Roger, with a flourish as he looked around the table. Standing beside him were Terrence and Michael. "Or should I say, upon you," he continued, gesturing to Terrence, who gave a nervous smile.

With that, Roger took a seat at the table.

"Thank you Roger, for agreeing to be here for our kickoff," said Terrence. "And thank you all for being here. I'm glad you have been able to come out this morning. Hopefully as we get going, the turnout will improve. Our pattern each day will be the same. We begin at 7:00 a.m. and work till 3:00 p.m. with an hour for lunch. The county generally closes the warehouse down at 3:30 so our schedule is pretty much dictated to us."

Terrence continued. "We may be visited from time to time by representatives of the political parties as well as the candidates. They have the right to observe but not interfere. You may extend to them the normal courtesies and perhaps answer a simple question or two but anything more than that, send them to me."

"Usually they get bored pretty quickly and leave," said Roger.

Carl looked around the table. It was a rather sparse turnout. Milton was there as was Scott and about five or six others.

"The first thing we need to do is finalize the test decks so we can—" Terrence began but halted when he saw Roger hold up a sheet of paper. "Oh, yes. First we need to swear you all in. It's the same oath that the election officers take on Election Day. Please raise your right hand and repeat after me. Afterwards you sign this oath sheet."

*"I do solemnly swear (or affirm) that I will perform the duties for this election according to law and the best of my ability and that I will studiously endeavor to prevent fraud, deceit, and abuse in conducting this election."*

"Now," said Terrence, "we can attend to the test decks. A test deck is a pile of ballots. Each ballot has been "voted" a certain way. When the entire deck is run through the scanner, you will see that each candidate will get a different number of votes. If the vote totals for each candidate matches the expected result, we know the test has been successful and the scanner is in good working order. Fortunately it's a relatively simple ballot this year. Just five things: United States Senate, US House of Representatives, one school board race, one spot on the Soil and Water Commission, and one bond issue. As you know, most of our precincts are in Virginia's 12$^{th}$ congressional district but we still have some precincts in the 10$^{th}$ and 11$^{th}$ districts as well. So that means three different ballot styles to worry about. We will have six test decks for the 12$^{th}$ congressional district and two each for the 10$^{th}$ and 11$^{th}$."

"What about the *CreateBallot* machine?" asked Scott. The *CreateBallot* machine was a ballot creating device used by handicapped people to create a ballot which was then fed into the scanner.

"The ballots we create on the *CreateBallot* machine will supplement those in the test decks." said Terrence. "But we're getting ahead of ourselves. For now, we need to take the preprinted test deck ballots and use our stamp to mark 'test ballot' on each one. Until we do that, we are, theoretically at least, playing with live ammo."

The next hour was spent by the rovers using ink stamps to stamp "test ballot" on each of the ballots in the test decks. It started out as a bit of fun but after a while monotony crept in. At last the task was completed. The decks were then secured with large binder clips and labeled. The six decks for the 12th district were labeled "A" through "F." "G" and "H" were the 11th decks, while "I" and "J" were the 10th.

When that was completed Terrence, with prodding from Roger and Michael, began to explain the testing procedure. The most challenging testing would be right at the beginning because the first machines would be those for the Government Center as well as the in-person absentee sites sprinkled throughout the county. It was rather complicated but Carl followed along as best he could. They would be divided into teams of two, so each tester could have his work checked by a peer. Carl hoped that he would be teamed up with Milton or Scott.

Just as Terrence was winding down and it looked like they would be getting started, Michael motioned for Carl to join him.

"I want you to start on Station One," he said with an air of authority. Carl had more or less figured out that Michael was second in command and his words carried weight.

"Won't I be working with them?" asked Carl, motioning to the rovers who were getting to their feet and proceeding over to the workbenches.

"Eventually," said Michael. "They're working at Station Two, where the actual machine testing takes place. But right now I need you for Station One. It's a critical assignment and I think you'd be the perfect person to do it."

Reluctantly, Carl followed Michael and Jack who were walking in the opposite direction from the others.

"So you drew the short straw," whispered Jack. "Let me guess. He said it was a critical assignment and only you could do it."

Carl smiled weakly and nodded.

"Here we are", announced Michael, cheerfully. They were in the aisle just outside the cage. "Jack will be rolling the carts, in order, into this aisle. Your job is to line them up on the side of the aisle and then make sure they are all properly stocked."

Michael then went through the list of all the things that needed to be in each precinct cart, things like electronic poll books (EPBs), *CreateBallot* machines, adding machines, power cords, earphones, and privacy booths. In many cases those items were already in the cart from previous elections but when they were missing, Michael showed Carl where the replacement items were stored.

Besides the cart, there was also the scanner, mounted on a large black bin on wheels. The acquisition of the extra scanners from Braxton County, would allow them to assign two scanners to each precinct, something that had been a goal for a number of years. As these new scanners were assigned to a precinct, Michael, or Carl under Michael's direction, would enter its serial number into the county database.

While Carl was disappointed that he would not be involved in the actual testing, or at least not for a while, he understood that Station One was a critical part of the operation and he attended to the tasks with his customary zeal. Once a cart and its accompanying scanners were ready, he would roll them through the entrance of the cage, and down the aisle where the Station Two workbenches were located. The testers from Station Two would take it from there. It was the ultimate assembly line process.

Carl soon began to realize that Station One with all its lifting, lugging, stooping, pulling, and pushing was a rather physical experience. It was also a dirty assignment. The extension cords especially, were both grimy and sticky. What had the chiefs done with them to make them that way? Then Carl remembered those times, when as chief, he had secured them to the floor with all kinds of sticky tape.

Probably the most annoying task concerned the wire frames for the so called "real estate" signs that were issued for each precinct. These frames, six in all, had to be secured to the inside door of the cart with a blue painters tape. All precinct chiefs were directed to use this tape as it was guaranteed not to leave any markings on the floors or walls. The problem was that the tape was not very sticky. Carl found that using just a couple of pieces of blue tape would keep the metal frames in place—for about fifteen seconds. Then when he turned his back to get something else, the metal frames would go crashing to the warehouse floor with a loud clang. In order to get the frames to stick, he had to use lots of blue tape, which got everything rather gummy.

Suddenly Carl heard a vibrating sound. He looked up from what he was doing, just in time to see a large forklift coming down the aisle, heading in his direction.

"You need to clear the way," cried Michael.

Carl quickly gathered up the metal frames that had just landed on the floor and closed the doors of the cart that had been protruding into the aisle. In an instant the forklift passed him, its speed undiminished, as it headed to another part of the warehouse.

"He'll be coming back in a few minutes," said Michael. "We are guests of the warehouse and are expected not to get in the way of the full-time workers. This aisle where we stage the carts is outside our cage so we need to clear it, on a moment's notice, when they come on through."

And come back the forklift did. Repeatedly. It seemed that the staging area for the carts was on a major thoroughfare of the warehouse. Clearing the way for the forklift became a normal part of the Station One experience. Still by noon, Carl felt he had acclimated himself to what was expected and Michael seemed satisfied with his progress.

"Don't worry. We'll have you on Station Two in a few days," he assured Carl during their lunch break.

By the end of the workday Carl was both exhausted and filthy. He was also beginning to realize how much he had taken for granted when he was a chief. He had never thought about how those perfectly stocked precinct carts came to be.

# 25

## Wednesday, September 16, 7:00 a.m.

For the next two days, Carl worked diligently at his Station One tasks. Overall progress at the warehouse had been slow, partly because only a relatively small number of rovers were showing up.

"It will pick up next week," said Scott. "It always does."

The other complicating factor was that the initial machines being tested were not actually for the precincts but rather for the locations where in-person absentee voting would take place. The scanners and *CreateBallot* machines had to be programed and tested to process ballots for all three congressional districts which made the Station Two work that much more complex.

Thursday morning, September 17 arrived and with that a brief respite. Carl had told Terrence he would be in late that day as 10:00 a.m. was the time for Cindy's joint "campaign kickoff" with her sister. She had explained to him that it was a bit of a stunt, intended to get some publicity, as she had already been campaigning for the better part of a month.

Carl had no specific duties to perform at the kickoff but he wanted to be there just to show his support. He felt guilty for not doing more to support her candidacy, but in the last couple of weeks she hadn't asked him to do a whole lot.

The event was taking place at a local community center. As Carl pulled into the parking lot, he could see that a small crowd of people were standing on the lawn outside the center. He parked and went over to the crowd. There in the midst of the gathering, a television interview was taking place. Cindy was being interviewed by a reporter who Carl immediately recognized as Tracy Miller from the local TV station.

"So what motivated you to get into this race for the vacant seat on the Soil and Water Commission?"

"So many things," said Cindy. "It's terribly important that our streams stay clear of contamination and that we do everything we can to prevent soil erosion. The environment belongs to all of us and we all have to do our part." She flashed that radiant smile that Carl had learned to recognize.

"How does it feel to be running on the same ticket as your sister? Do you often discuss your respective campaigns?"

"Oh yes. Valerie and I are very close. She encouraged me to make this race, knowing how passionate I am about our environment."

Carl felt a gentle tap on his shoulder.

"Excuse me. Are you Carl Marsden?" He was a rather large man who appeared to be in his forties.

"Why, yes," said Carl.

"I'm Stan Turner, Valerie's husband and I guess, campaign manager." He smiled nervously. "We were scheduled to begin the joint kickoff on the steps of the center a few minutes ago. Each of the sisters is to make a statement. Is there any chance you could get Cindy to wrap up her interview so we can get started?"

Carl immediately understood Stan's predicament. Cindy seemed to be in no mood to quit. At her side was Steve, who also seemed content to let the interview go on.

"I can try," said Carl to Stan, "although I'm not sure how much Cindy is listening to me these days."

Stan smiled appreciatively and Carl began to work his way over to the other side of the crowd where Steve was.

"I think they want to start the kickoff, over by the steps," he said quietly to Steve.

"Sure. She'll be done soon. Isn't she doing great?" said Steve.

Feeling rather helpless, Carl went back over to Stan.

"She should be finished in a minute or two," he said. "I don't know what else to say."

Stan nodded. "Well, I'll be over there." He motioned to top of the front steps where Valerie stood by a makeshift podium. Carl felt the need to pay his respects. They both went over to the podium.

"I don't know if you remember me—" Carl began.

"Of course I do, Carl," said Valerie. "You let me talk your ear off back at the courthouse cafeteria."

"Well I just wanted to wish you well on your campaign. I'd volunteer to work on it but I'm sort of committed," he said, gesturing in Cindy's direction.

Valerie nodded and gave a faint smile. They all stood nervously. There was nothing they could do but wait for Cindy to wrap things up.

At last Cindy finished her interview and came over to the steps with Steve by her side. In addition to the TV cameras, Carl saw some reporters from the local newspapers.

Cindy bounded up the steps and engulfed her sister in a hug. Carl thought he heard Valerie whisper "Glad you could make it," but he wasn't sure.

Steve took the microphone and assumed the master of ceremonies role.

"We're here to kick off the campaigns of two remarkable individuals. Sisters, who each in her own way, has heard the call to public service. We'll start by having Valerie Turner say a few words about the school system."

There was polite applause.

Putting on her reading glasses, Valerie approached the microphone with several pages of notes in her hand.

"Thank you for that warm welcome. Our school system is wonderful but it still needs your support. Let me start by saying, whoever you plan to vote for in the school board race, it is terribly important that you vote 'yes' on the school bond issue that is on the ballot."

For the next few minutes Valerie outlined the renovation projects that the bond issue would fund. From there she went on to explain a number of items in the proposed school budget. She eventually got around to her candidacy and her position on the issues, which for the most part were supportive of the current board.

While Valerie was not a bad public speaker, she lacked Cindy's magnetism. She was earnest, sincere, and obviously well informed but after a few minutes the crowd got somewhat restless. While she was speaking, Cindy had gone off to one side and was talking to one of the reporters. Their whispered conversation, punctuated by laughter, gradually became louder and seemed to distract Valerie to some extent.

"And it's now my pleasure to introduce my sister, Cindy. As you know she is running for Soil and Water Conservation Board and she cares deeply about the environment." Valerie said the correct words but the tone with which they were delivered had a clipped, almost angry quality.

Cindy came forward, took the microphone, and gave her sister a big hug. A robust round of applause and cheers greeted Cindy's introduction. Turning to the audience, she proclaimed,

"Thank you Valerie, for those kind words and more importantly, for being here today as we launch our campaign to promote clean water and prevent soil erosion here in our county. These concerns along with the whole issue of global warming are things that our society desperately needs to address today. My principal opponent, I'm sorry to say, is from a political party that denies the very existence of global warming."

For the next ten minutes Cindy continued, talking about the need to care for the environment and how the Democratic Party had asked her to lead the fight to preserve the county's soil and water. She talked of how as youngsters, she and her sister had played in the streams that ran near their home, and how it broke her heart to imagine them being polluted. Cindy's radiance and skill as a speaker was never in better form and the crowd seemed to be moved by her every utterance.

"She really is a natural," said Stan quietly to Carl as they stood together. "I'm not sure Val is enthralled though."

He paused for a moment, and then added, "They have a somewhat strained relationship. I was hoping this event might ease things between them."

When at last Cindy completed her remarks, there was a sustained ovation from the crowd.

At the request of the photographers, the two sisters posed while pictures were being taken. Afterwards the reporters crowded around them, asking all sorts of questions. Valerie answered the relatively few queries directed at her in a succinct manner while Cindy tended to expound at great length. To Carl, her answers seemed rather general and even, at times, superficial, but the reporters didn't seem inclined to follow up. At last the reporters left and the event concluded.

"Cindy, I need to talk with you about coordinating things," said Valerie, taking hold of her sister's hand and leading her off to one side. Once they were out of earshot, she turned on her.

"That was rude, Cyn. Even by your standards."

"What are you talking about?" asked Cindy.

"I'm talking about everything. That little press conference of yours at the beginning when we were supposed to start. And you joking around with that reporter when I was talking. I lost the crowd's attention when—"

"Come on, Val. No one cared about all those budget numbers. You were putting them to sleep."

"And when the hell did we ever play in streams together? If you're going to tell cute little stories, at least make sure they're true."

"Well at least I'm not a bore."

"Well at least I'm not a fraud."

That hit a nerve. Cindy's expression showed as much. Valerie sensed it as well.

Valerie continued. "Tell me Cindy. What's your position on the Greenway golf course proposal? Do you favor the Reading Run restoration project? Do you support the transfer of the Seneca Woodlands to the park authority?"

"Well I think—I mean—these are all things that need to be studied."

Valerie threw up her hands in exasperation.

"Good God, Cyn. You're the one who's the candidate. I know more about the friggin Soil and Water Commission than you do."

The two sisters glared at each other. Then slowly the anger dissipated, replaced by an air of sadness. At last, Valerie spoke.

"This was our last joint campaign event. If good old boring Valerie is going down to defeat, she'll do it on her own."

Slowly, Cindy nodded her head. "I think that would be best. I do hope you win, Val. I hope you realize that."

"Thank you, Cyn. As always, I want what's best for you. I'm just not sure that includes winning this election."

Cindy started to say something but Valerie continued.

"And just in case some reporter should actually ask you, you know, a substantive question. The Greenway golf proposal is an attempt by a developer to build condos on what today is a 185 acre golf course. I think you're against it. On the other hand the Reading Run project is an attempt to reroute a stream in order to save some trees. My guess is that you're in favor of that one."

Cindy nodded. "Got it. Thanks. And The Seneca Woodlands transfer?"

Valerie smiled. "There is no Seneca Woodlands. I just made it up."

In spite of herself, Cindy laughed.

"I walked into that one," she admitted.

"Take care, Cyn," said Valerie. "And watch out for that campaign manager of yours. I think he's out to get in your pants. That is if he's not there already."

Cindy nodded but said nothing. Turning around, she noticed Carl, in the parking lot, just about to get into his car. She hadn't realized he had been at the event.

"Carl," she called out, giving him a wave. "Wait up."

Quickly, Cindy trotted over to where Carl was.

"Thank you so much for coming. I didn't realize you were here. But don't you have warehouse stuff going on?" she asked.

"I told them, I'd be late this morning. I wanted to see your campaign blast off."

"Well how did I do?" she asked brightly.

There was a brief hesitation.

"The crowd loved you."

"That's not what I asked."

Carl was silent.

"Please, Carl," said Cindy. "You're my friend. Tell me what you think. What you really think. Not just what I want to hear. I have Steve for that."

Carl braced himself to say what had been on his mind for a while.

"What I think is…that…this campaign is not bringing out the best in you."

There. He said it. For a just a moment, Cindy's face registered shock. Then she quickly recovered.

"Well, I didn't ask for this joint kickoff, did I? It was Steve's idea. Bad idea. We can't always be right, can we? Now, don't let me keep you. I've got to move on. I have this noon meeting at work. You know, my real job, the one that pays the bills. Thanks again for coming. We'll be in touch."

Smiling sadly, Carl got into his car.

# 26

## Tuesday, September 22

Carl continued to work at Station One for the rest of the week. This was followed by a quiet weekend. He had deliberately left it open, expecting Cindy to request his help on her campaign but to his surprise, no request came. The awkward nature of their parting at the kickoff event made him reluctant to reach out to her.

The following days at the warehouse were more of the same. Michael assured Carl that he was doing well and that he would have him swap places with one of the Station Two people "soon."

Based on the reports he heard during the breaks, Carl concluded that the testing of the machines for the in-person absentee voting was going slower than they had hoped.

"Part of the problem is with the processing of write-in votes," said Milton, during one of the breaks. "We used to access the names of the people who received write-in votes by pressing an icon on the scanner's screen, near the end of the closing process. The screen would then display the write-ins and the chief would handwrite them onto the SOR. Well people didn't like that so they got the vender, *ElectionPro,* to do a software upgrade to have the printer actually print the images of the write-in votes. The chief just attaches the printout to the SOR and there is no need to write them out. Sounded like a good idea. We installed the change on the machines in the spring, before you joined us. There were no write-ins allowed in the June primary, so this test cycle is the first time we've seen the change in action, with any significant number of write-ins. We are discovering that it takes quite a while to print those write-in votes. Let's hope there won't be many write-ins in November."

Carl was finding that the 3:00 p.m. closing time was fitting his schedule well. This gave him a few hours in the late afternoon and early evening to work on a couple of projects for Software Solutions. It was about 6:00 p.m., Tuesday evening when his phone rang.

"Carl, it's Cindy. Do you have a minute to talk?"

"Of course. How's the campaign going?"

"OK, I guess. Steve got a list of probable Democratic voters and I worked a couple of neighborhoods on Saturday. You know, door-to-door canvassing. It went fairly well. Not too many doors slammed in my face."

"Sounds like fun. How can I help?"

"Do you know what back-to-school night is?"

"Of course. It happens every fall. Parents go to the school and walk through their kid's schedule and meet the teachers."

"Exactly. It's a gold mine for candidates. All those potential voters. For the next couple of weeks, every night, Monday through Thursday, different schools are having them. And I'll be there, handing out my fliers. They just came back from the printer. No more handmade stuff. These are on slick, glossy paper with a photo of me sifting dirt through my fingers like a female version of Johnny Appleseed," said Cindy, with a small giggle at the end.

"Do you want me to help pass them out?"

"Could you? The problem is that with so many schools in the county, there are multiple back-to-school nights going on the same evening. I'm doing the biggies, the high schools and middle schools, which have the greatest number of people, but if you could do some of the grade schools, it would be great. Tomorrow night I'll be at Copper Middle School starting at 7:00 p.m. If you could stop by, I'll give you some fliers for you to take over to distribute at Carter Run Elementary."

"No problem. I'll see you tomorrow at seven."

There was a moment of silence.

"Is there anything else?"

"No. Except to say that I realize the only times I call you these days are when I want you do something for me. I don't like that but right now with all that is happening—"

"Don't worry about it. Tomorrow at seven."

"OK. Bye."

# 27

## Wednesday, September 23

Carl pulled into the Cooper parking lot at 6:45 p.m. He wanted to have an extra time cushion in order to navigate rush hour traffic over to Carter Run. Almost immediately, he spotted Cindy by the curb. She gave him a wave and practically sprinted over to him.

"Thank you so much for coming," she said breathlessly. "There's been a slight change in plans. I'll be doing Carter Run. If you can cover for me here at Cooper, it would be great."

She thrust a fistful of her fliers into Carl's hands. He briefly examined it. It was nicely done with a photo of Cindy, in hiking boots, jeans, and a plaid shirt, kneeling down in front of some bushes.

"It shows you in a whole new light," said Carl, smiling.

"Doesn't it though. Got to run. Thanks a bunch."

With that said, Cindy turned around and quickly went to her car. Within a minute, the car was out of the parking lot, on its way to Carter Run.

While it didn't matter to Carl which school he covered, he did find the abrupt change of plans a bit puzzling. However there was no time for that now, as the first of the early bird parents were beginning to arrive. Carl proceeded to what appeared to be the main entrance.

Almost instinctively, he started to pace off forty feet from the front door. Then with a laugh, he pulled up short. Forty feet was the distance that poll workers, handing out their propaganda, had to be from the entrance of a polling place on Election Day. This of course was not Election Day. He could be as close to the door as he wanted, just so long as he didn't impede anyone's progress.

Carl took his position and contemplated his strategy. In the gathering darkness, it would not be possible to look each person in the eye. But what should he say? He tried repeating "Phelps for Soil and Water" a few times, but it didn't seem to have a good ring to it.

"I wouldn't worry about saying anything. Just give one to anybody who doesn't physically resist."

Carl turned around to see Valerie, holding her own stack of fliers.

"We're well covered tonight," she said. "Biff Logan is around here somewhere, handing out party fliers. They emphasize the Senate and House candidates, but Cindy and I are included, somewhere near the bottom."

"I'm surprised I'm even here," said Carl. "I was supposed to do Carter Run, but that got changed at the last minute."

Valerie smiled. "That's because I'm here. We've agreed not to do the same schools."

"Is that really necessary?"

"Necessary is probably not the right word. But we both think that the 'two sisters' bit has been overplayed. We each have our own campaign and its best if we stay out of each other's way."

Carl didn't say anything but the whole thing sounded a bit strange. All they were doing was handing out fliers and in the dark no one was going to be able to tell who was giving them out.

By this time the trickle of voters had started to increase and Carl turned his attention to giving out his fliers. He followed Valerie's advice of just handing them out with a minimum of words and the strategy seemed to work. Most of the people accepted the fliers, usually with good humor. There were some people who walked by without accepting a flier and Carl soon learned to read the body language of those who had no interest in receiving one.

Occasionally someone would return the flier with a comment like, "I'm sorry but I'm a Republican." Since Carl's role was not as a salesperson but rather just a dispenser of information, he did not take these "rejections" personally and actually found the process to be surprisingly enjoyable. By 8:00 p.m. the influx of parents had ceased and the evening was, for all practical purposes, over.

"I suppose we'll be seeing a fair amount of each other, the next couple of weeks," said Valerie, as she prepared to leave. "That is if you're going to be Cindy's 'designated substitute.'"

"I guess so," replied Carl. "Cindy hasn't exactly told me all her plans but I'm at her disposal."

Valerie nodded. "Well, I'm off."

She paused.

"Carl, just a piece of friendly advice. Don't let my sister take you for granted."

Carl looked at her in surprise.

"Excuse me?"

"You heard me. See you next time."

Valerie's words hit a nerve. There were times when Carl wondered if that was the case. Still, even if that was partly true, the middle of a campaign was not the time to be reexamining things.

On a different note, Carl had taken a liking to Valerie and had finally decided that she would receive his vote. This would be one of those times when he would vote for the person, not the platform. This also meant he would be voting for two Democrats in November. Carl couldn't remember the last time that had happened.

It had been a good night. He had given out a fair number of fliers and finally had the feeling he had helped Cindy's campaign. With a feeling of satisfaction he got into his car for the ride home.

# 28

## Saturday, September 26

It was 10:00 a.m. on the dot when Carl pulled into the parking lot at Cindy's apartment complex. "Can you drop by my place at ten tomorrow to help with the campaign?" the text had said. He wondered if she would have him do door-to-door canvassing. He wasn't sure how effective he would be but was willing to give it a shot for her sake.

He rang the doorbell. The door opened almost immediately. It was Steve.

"Oh, it's you. Come on in."

Cindy's apartment was a beehive of activity. At her dining room table were a number of people who seemed to be sorting campaign materials. Some of them were girl friends of Cindy who Carl knew slightly. The candidate herself did not seem to be around.

"Hi Carl," called Deb. "Are you here to help us with this?"

"I have something else for Carl," said Steve. "These." He pointed to some yard signs that were piled up in the corner.

"These need to be delivered to the following addresses", he said, putting a list in Carl's hands. "These people have all agreed to put up yard signs. Howard here, will work with you. All you need to do is drop them off at their front door. You don't even need to talk to them." Steve's tone suggested that it would be better if Carl didn't.

Carl started to pick up some of the signs while Howard did the same. Carl immediately recognized him as the person who had been tutoring Cindy in environmental science. It took them two round trips to get everything into Carl's car and they were off.

"So we're on the B team," said Howard.

"The B team?"

"Yep, that's us. The first stringers are the ones going door-to-door. That's what the folks at the table were preparing to do. Cindy is already out in one of the neighborhoods."

"Well whatever we can do to help," said Carl. The idea of being on Cindy's "B team" was disconcerting, but he also realized that for him, this was probably a more appropriate assignment.

"How are Cindy's environmental science lessons going?" asked Carl, wishing to change the subject.

For a few moments there was silence. It was as if Howard was trying to find just the right words.

"She's a quick study," he said at last. "Very bright. And a delightful person to work with. The problem is that…there's just so much material…and…" Howard's stream of thought seemed to hang in midair.

"And what?" asked Carl

"Well, she's cancelled a number of our sessions. Says they interfere with her campaigning. You know, back-to-school and door-to-door. It's almost October and we haven't really gotten into what the Soil and Water Commission actually does. If I had realized she would be cancelling these sessions, I would have started telling her about the commission earlier but since I thought I would have the time, I wanted to give her a solid environmental science background." It was apparent that Howard felt badly over what was still to be accomplished.

Carl said nothing so Howard continued.

"The first debate is a week from Wednesday. She needs to buckle down on this. Perhaps you could speak to her."

"I can try," said Carl, "although I'm not sure she'll listen. She loves the campaigning, the interacting with people. That's what truly energizes her. Not so much the—"

Carl caught himself in mid-sentence. He was about to say "Not so much the environmental science."

There was an uneasy silence in the car as they both contemplated the implications of what Carl had almost said.

The task at hand was straightforward. Aided by Carl's GPS, they easily drove through the neighborhood streets, dropping off the signs at the appropriate addresses. By 1:00 p.m. they were finished and headed back to Cindy's apartment. Steve greeted them at the door.

"Finished? Great. Well, that's all for today. Thanks for the hand. We'll be in touch."

Carl accepted this obvious dismissal with as much good grace as he could muster. He did have a number of things he wanted to work on for his project with Software Solutions, so in a way this worked out to his advantage. He also realized that he had a challenging week coming up. Michael had indicated that he would be working Station Two for the first time, and Carl appreciated that there was a lot he would have to learn. Then there was all those back-to-school nights as Cindy's "designated substitute." Yes, it would be a full week.

# 29

## Monday, September 28, 7:00 a.m.

Carl was excited. Monday morning and he would finally get to work at Station Two. At last he had been released from "rover purgatory." Up until now, progress at the warehouse had been slow. They had been at it for two weeks and had finally completed work on the machines to be used at the Government Center and in-person absentee locations. Now they were ready to start testing the machines for the precincts.

"Let's team up," said Scott to Carl, as the Station Two workers headed for the workbenches. "Let's get that first cart."

They proceeded to the staging area, where Carl had spent the past two weeks. Scott took the handle of the first cart and pulled it toward one of the workbenches while Carl took control of the two scanners assigned to that precinct and rolled them behind. They quickly got them into position in front of the workbench. Scott examined the paperwork on top of the cart.

"Precinct 102, Foster, 12th congressional district, two *ElectionPro* scanners, two *CreateBallots*, two EPBs. Looks straightforward. With the extra machines from Braxton we now have two scanners for every precinct with about ten extra, in reserve.

I think they intend to have them programed to give a third scanner to the most populous precincts."

Carl was very familiar with both the scanner and *CreateBallot* although his experience had been that of a user. Now he was going to be a tester. He had done a bit of "testing" back in August when they had accepted the Braxton machines, but that had been with that make-believe ballot. Now he would be testing the actual ballot that would be used in the upcoming election.

"For this first precinct, let me start with the scanners," said Scott. "I'll get them primed and insert the 12th District test deck of ballots. You can power up the two *CreateBallot* machines and create the ballots according to this cheat sheet. When you're done you can insert them into the scanner and we'll print the results."

Carl used his key to unlock the cart. The *CreateBallot* machines were on the bottom shelf of the precinct cart. He took each machine in turn, removed it from its case and lifted it onto the workbench. He then powered them on and went through the opening sequence specified on the cheat sheet. In about fifteen minutes they were ready to perform their function.

Now it was time to create the ballots. Carl had carefully studied the pattern of ballots he needed to produce on the *CreateBallot*. It was quite simple, much simpler than the preprinted test decks that Scott was already feeding into the first scanner.

Carl inserted the first blank ballot card and voted for each of the Democrats along with a "yes" on the bond issue. Out came the ballot, ready to be scanned. Next card. Each of the Republicans and "no" on the Bond issue. The remaining ballots that he created were for various combinations of minor party candidates as well as write-ins.

*There it's done.*

Carl felt pleased with himself. He had internalized the process well. He then executed the same test pattern for the second machine.

"How's it coming?" asked Scott.

"Done," said Carl, proudly.

"Now we will insert them into the scanners. I've already voted the test deck in both machines," said Scott.

One by one, Carl inserted the ballot cards he had created into the first machine. With each card insertion, the counts on the screen increased by one. Once they were all voted, he retrieved them and started inserting them into the second scanner. While he was doing that, Scott pressed the button on scanner number one to close the polls and print the results.

By the time Carl had voted and retrieved the ballots from scanner number two, the first scanner was already printing the results.

"How are we doing?" asked Carl, eagerly.

"Not so well," answered Scott, studying the tapes. The Senate and House candidates are all off by two."

"Too many or too few?"

"Too few. Let me check the test deck. The deck could have been corrupted but that's rare." He studied the test deck. "No, this looks good. Let me see your ballots."

Carl handed him the ballots he had so carefully created on the *CreateBallot* machines. Almost immediately Scott realized. "You don't have any of the *federal only* ballots."

Of course. He had forgotten to create the ballots which would be cast by people who were only eligible to vote for the two federal offices on the ballot. These were citizens who had moved from Virginia to a permanent overseas residence. They were a rarity but they still needed to be tested.

"I'm sorry," said Carl. "I completely forgot about those."

"That's all right," said Scott, smiling. "We'll just take it out of your pay."

A much chagrined Carl, proceeded to create the necessary *federal only* ballots. While he appreciated that Scott had made light of his error, it was still an inauspicious start.

There was a delay as both scanners took an extra five minutes to "think" before printing the write-ins. Once that was done, they zeroed out the numbers so they could reproduce the test. Test deck inserted. *CreateBallot* cards (complete with *federal only* ballots) inserted. Close poll. Print results. Repeat for scanner two.

Scott and Carl examined the tapes. "Looks good," said Scott.

Carl breathed a sigh of relief. He powered down the *CreateBallot* machines, put them back in their cases and shoved them back into the bottom shelf of the cart. They then examined the cart to make sure that all the necessary supplies were there. They were, courtesy of the people at Station One, where Carl had so diligently labored. There was some paperwork to be filled out and placed on top of the cart.

"Now comes the fun part," said Scott. "Why don't you close the cart door and turn the latch?"

Carl closed the door as best he could but it stuck out. He tried turning the latch but it did not turn.

"These carts are old," said Scott, "Sometimes they need a bit of 'creative violence.'"

And with that he gave a well-placed kick on the door. It slammed into place and Scott immediately turned the handle before the door could pop out again.

"One precinct down, 239 to go," said Scott triumphantly. "Let's wheel this sucker to Station Three and we'll tackle the next precinct."

They wheeled the cart and scanners past the other workbenches to the area of the table where the rovers always met at the beginning of the day. There Terrence, aided by one or two others, ran Station Three. Scott explained that Station Three reviewed the work done by Station Two, and performed a few final tasks to prepare the cart for Election Day. They then returned to the staging area for the next precinct to be worked on.

"Precinct 116, Norwood Crossing, 12th congressional district, two *ElectionPro* scanners, two *CreateBallots,* two EPBs," said Scott. "This time you get the scanners up to speed while I'll do the *CreateBallot.* We alternate with each precinct. That, in theory, keeps up sharp."

Carl examined the instruction sheet for each of the scanners. It was more complicated than the *CreateBallot* machine. At one point, an administration password needed to be entered. This allowed the screen to be calibrated and the system clock set.

Next came the entry of the "election" password. Once that was entered, the scanners printed a configuration report verifying the health of the machine and a zero report showing that each of the candidates had zero votes. At that point the screen indicated the poll was open. On each scanner the public count read zero. That was the way it should be. The public count represented the number of people who had voted on this machine for the current election. The protective count was the number of votes cast in the entire history of the machine. Carl noticed that while one of the scanners had a protective count of several thousand, the other had a much smaller number, fifty-six to be exact. He brought that to Scott's attention.

"That's one of the Braxton County machines," said Scott. "My understanding is that Braxton bought them a number of years ago because there was money in the budget they were about to lose. It turned out they never needed to use them. They tested them when they initially got them and we tested them in August. That's why the count says fifty-six, rather than zero but this November will be their first time in an actual election."

"Isn't that risky?"

"Not really. Every machine has a maiden voyage. And don't forget, we are about to test it right now."

Now it was time to get the appropriate test deck. These decks had been created two weeks ago on the first day of testing. There were six identical test decks for the 12th congressional district, labeled "A" through "G." Carl went over to the area where they were kept. The "A" and "B" decks were not there. They were apparently being used by rovers at some of the other workbenches. Carl grabbed the "C" deck and returned to his station.

"Voting" the desk deck was a straightforward and somewhat monotonous process. Once Carl had fed the ballots into the scanner, he opened the bin underneath and retrieved the ballots which were then fed into the other scanner. *I guess this is what they mean by "stuffing the ballot box,"* he thought. He then retrieved the ballots from the second machine and returned them to the test deck area. Common courtesy required that the test decks be returned as soon as possible, so other teams could use them.

Now it was time to insert the *CreateBallot* cards that Scott had created. They were voted, in turn, on each of the machines. Then Carl pressed the screen on each of the scanners where it said, "close polls," and looked on anxiously, as the two scanners printed the results. At last they stopped printing.

"Are they OK?" asked Carl.

"You tell me," said Scott.

Carl read the vote totals for the various candidates, comparing them to the grid that had been provided. He did this for both scanners.

"They look correct," he said.

Scott nodded. They still had to wait while the machines "thought about" and eventually printed the write-in votes. It was printing a photographic image of each write-in ballot which accounted for the delay.

"Fortunately there are no uncontested races this November," said Scott. "It's the uncontested races that result in large numbers of write-ins. If someone doesn't like the only candidate on the ballot, they write-in all kinds of stuff from Mickey Mouse to their next door neighbor."

At last the write-ins were all printed. At that point they needed to enter the "supersede" password so the test votes could be erased and the public count reset to zero. Now the scanners were ready for Election Day. They powered down the machines, completed the paperwork for the precinct, and rolled the cart and machines to Station Three. They then went back to the staging area for the next precinct.

Carl was just beginning to unload the *CreateBallot* machines for Precinct 125, Hopewell, when a loud voice called out, "Who did Precinct 116?"

Carl and Scott exchanged glances.

"I thought we were good," said Carl.

Terrence approached them with one of the tapes in his hand. Looking at the bottom of the tape where testers had put their initials, he asked "Are you CM, and SG?"

"That's us," said Carl.

"The time is wrong on the tape," said Terrence. "You need to correct it and redo the test."

"But I set the time correctly," said Carl. "See it says 8:35 a.m. That was when we started the test."

Terrence rolled his eyes. "What does it say immediately underneath?"

Carl looked. "Oh." It indicated "Central time."

"You need to change it to 'Eastern time,'" said Terrence.

"That was the Braxton machine," said Scott. "The manufacturer is somewhere in the Midwest. If these machines were never used in live combat, they may still have the manufacturer's default."

"Well whatever. You need to be more careful," said Terrence, looking at Carl. Then he noticed the discarded tape in the trash. "What's that?" he asked.

"That was also me," said Carl. "I forgot to create the *federal only* ballots earlier and we had to redo the test."

Terrence said nothing but gave Carl a look that reflected his obvious displeasure. "Retrieve the scanners and cart and set the time correctly. Then redo the test." He turned around and went back to Station Three.

"Don't worry about it," said Scott. "We always make mistakes early in the process."

Carl nodded. He understood what Scott was saying but his confidence was shaken. He always thought of himself as a detail person.

They retrieved the cart and scanner for the Norwood Crossing precinct. Carl corrected the time and they redid the test. The rest of the morning went more smoothly as Carl gradually became more comfortable with the rhythm of the work. He was glad he had an experienced hand like Scott to work with. Noon came and they broke for lunch.

"I won't be here this afternoon. Doctor's appointment," said Scott. "You'll need to team up with someone else."

That "someone else" turned out to be Jack. Jack was an older man, probably in his mid-eighties, who usually was in charge of ensuring the carts were stored in their correct places. He normally didn't do Station Two testing but since Carl needed a partner, they were teamed up. The result was that they worked very slowly which was not altogether a bad thing. Carl wanted to be sure everything was correct. They managed to complete one precinct together with correct results and started to work on a second. Carl was working with the two scanners. He had just run the test deck through the first scanner and was about to do it with the second when Jack called out to him.

"I need help with these *CreateBallot* machines."

The screen on one of them had frozen.

"Let's power down and reboot," said Carl. "That's what we do in the precincts when this happens."

This took some time but eventually they got the machine up and running. Carl went back to the scanner.

"I borrowed your test deck. You didn't seem to be using it," called Brenda from the next station over.

"No problem," said Carl going over to the test deck area. With six decks for the 12th district, there was never any wait. He grabbed another deck and went back to the scanner.

By this time, Jack was well on his way to completing the *CreateBallot* process.

Carl fed the test deck into the second scanner. Now it was just a matter of Jack completing the generation of the *CreateBallot* cards. At last he was done, and they were voted on both machines. The results were then printed. Jack studied the printouts.

"Is this what we should have?" he asked. It was clear that he was not familiar with the grid.

Carl looked at the printout. It was for the 12th congressional district and he had gotten familiar with the pattern. No, it was not. Some of the numbers were off. Carl checked the printout for the other machine. That one looked good.

"It's good for one scanner but not for the other," said Carl. "Let's look at your *CreateBallot* cards."

Carl immediately looked to see if Jack had prepared the *federal only* ballots. He had. Carl studied the ballots that Jack had prepared. They all looked good.

"How about the test deck?" asked Jack.

Carl had already returned the deck to the common area, so he went back to look for it. *There it is. At least I think this was it. Yes, I'm sure that was it.*

He studied the test deck. It looked good. But the printout was bad.

"Terrence, we have a problem."

Together, Jack and Carl walked Terrence through the situation. One of the machines was fine. The test deck was fine. Jack's *CreateBallot* cards were fine. But the printout on the other machine was bad.

"Push the machine into the side aisle," said Terrence. "We may have to replace it. Carl, are you absolutely sure you did everything correctly?"

"Yes. I mean, I think so," said Carl.

"Well tomorrow's a new day," sighed Terrence. "Let's close it down folks. It's 3:00 p.m."

"But I just powered up one of the scanners," complained Brenda.

"It'll keep," said Terrence. "See you all tomorrow."

# 30

## Monday evening, 6:45 p.m.

"Sounds like you had a rough day," said Cindy, as she was counting out some fliers. They were both on the walkway leading up to Burns Elementary School, where yet another back-to-school night was scheduled to happen.

"I don't think Terrence was especially pleased with me," said Carl. "That machine at the end of the day. It may have been just a bad machine—"

"Which is exactly what your mission is. To ferret out the bad apples."

"—but those earlier incidents were clearly my mistakes. Forgetting to create *federal only* ballots and setting the wrong time zone."

Cindy looked up from her fliers. "Yes, they were mistakes. Rookie mistakes. Carl, if you're going to beat yourself up every time you make a mistake, you're going to have a miserable life. If I recall, last January, one of us made quite a few mistakes."

"Yes," Carl recalled. "And I wasn't very supportive of you back then."

"Not exactly," agreed Cindy. "Uh-oh, there's Val. Time for me to do my disappearing act. Here, take these." She handed Carl his portion of the fliers.

"Perhaps I'm the one who should disappear. Force the two of you to work the same school and—"

"Not funny. I'm outta here. We're backed up tonight. Three schools. Steve is at Danby while I'm doing Hagerman. Good luck tomorrow at the warehouse."

Cindy turned and practically sprinted to her car. Carl watched her drive away and then went up the walkway to the front of the school.

"We meet again," said Valerie.

"How many more of these do we have?" asked Carl. He didn't mind handing out the fliers, but between his job at Software Solutions and the warehouse work, he was feeling rather squeezed.

"They're booked for the next two weeks, Monday through Thursday. At least two back-to-school events each night. Sometimes three. We can't cover all of them. We'll do the high schools and middle schools and at least some of the grade schools. It's mostly just Stan and me, but we're doing the best we can."

Carl suddenly had an idea. "You know if you're ever in a bind where you can't cover every school, I'd be happy to hand out some of your fliers as well as Cindy's."

Valerie seemed a bit surprised by Carl's offer. For a few moments she was silent, contemplating what Carl has said.

"That's very generous, Carl. And tempting. But I think you'd piss Cindy off if you did that."

"I don't know why," said Carl. "You're both being supported by the Democratic party, which is not the party I usually side with, but let's not go there. Plus I'm not even sure Cindy needs to know."

"You're really tempting me," said Valerie. "Stan's doing Hagerman Elementary tonight but we have no one at Danby."

"Well Cindy just told me she was doing Hagerman so that would leave Danby open for you, using the criteria that the two of you seem determined to enforce."

This time there was only the slightest hesitation.

"Sold. Here, take these," said Valerie, handing Carl her stack of fliers. "I've got plenty more in my car. Carl, I really appreciate this. Well I'm off to Danby."

"Don't mention it. Good luck."

Carl looked down at Valerie's fliers. There was a photo of her along with Stan and their two small sons in front of a school. A good looking family.

He then considered the best way to hand out two sets of fliers. They were similar in form: glossy, letter sized, folded in such a way that they could be placed in an envelope. Carl considered various ways of handing them out but they all seemed clumsy. You can only do so much with two hands. Finally he decided to merge the stacks so that they would alternate: Cindy, Valerie, Cindy, Valerie, and so forth. Then he would simply hand the top two fliers to each of the parents as they made their way into the school.

This indeed was how he proceeded. Instead of saying "Phelps for Soil and Water," which never had much of a ring to it, Carl found himself saying "Support the local Democratic ticket," when he handed the two fliers to the would-be voter. Inserting the word "local" somehow eased the sense of guilt he felt for betraying his Republican heritage.

# 31

## Tuesday, September 29, 5:30 a.m.

Tuesday morning. Rise at 5:30 a.m. Shower, dress, and a quick breakfast. Out the door at 6:30 for the half hour drive to Springdale and the warehouse. The sun was just beginning to rise as Carl arrived.

"A new day," said Terrence as they all assembled at the table. "No mistakes. All the machines work perfectly. I understand that one or more of the candidates may drop by to watch us in action. Be polite, but don't let them distract you. OK, let's do it."

"Carl, you're with me," said Brenda. "I worked with Tim yesterday, but he's not going to be here this morning. He does volunteer work at the animal shelter on Tuesday mornings."

They approached the workbench that Brenda had been working on.

"Precinct 225. Brandywine. 12th congressional district. One of these scanners was turned on when we left yesterday and is ready for testing. Why don't you get a test deck and feed it into the scanner that's ready. Then you can boot up the other scanner. In the meantime I'll get those *CreateBallot* machines running."

Carl went to the test deck area and grabbed the 12th deck that was on top of the pile. He fed them into the scanner and retrieved them from the bin. Placing them on top of the already completed scanner, he began the process of initializing the other. This took a little while as he still had not committed the steps to memory. By the time it was ready to be voted, the test deck was gone.

"Looks like someone snatched your test deck," said Brenda. "No matter, just get another one. There's lots of decks for the 12th."

Carl went back to the test deck area and retrieved another deck. Brenda finished her work with the *CreateBallot* machines and started to feed them into the first scanner.

"We'll have this precinct done before 8:00 a.m.," she said confidently.

Carl started to insert his test deck into the second scanner. For a few minutes they were silent, each attending to their tasks. Brenda finished first and retrieved her *CreateBallot* cards.

"Here, feed these into your scanner," she said, handing them to Carl, who had just finished voting his test deck. Carl quickly voted the cards Brenda had given him and pressed the "close poll" portion of the screen.

After a few seconds both scanners started to print their results. Carl focused his attention on the second scanner, the one he had recently initialized.

"Let's see," he said. "Date and time are correct. Time zone is correct." Carl gave Brenda a sideways glance. His time zone goof of the day before had made him the butt of a few jokes. Then the vote totals started to come out. First the Senate. Then the House. School board. Soil and Water. Bond issue. All looked good. Now the wait for the write-ins.

"Oh crap," said Brenda who was studying the printout from the first scanner. "The numbers are off."

"The numbers over here are good," said Carl.

"This was the first machine we tested," said Brenda, more to herself than Carl. "I need to examine the test deck we used."

"Who took the test deck we had over here?" she called out to the warehouse at large.

"That would be me," said Milton. "I'll get it back to you in a few minutes."

"We need to look at it as soon as you're done," said Brenda.

There was nothing to do but wait. For a few minutes Carl and Brenda chatted about her favorite subject which was the three dogs that inhabited her home. Carl had grown up with dogs in his house and at various times had considered getting one and he started quizzing her about different breeds.

"So is this how my tax payer dollars are being spent?" came a voice from behind Carl.

Carl turned around. It was Cindy.

"What are you doing here?" he asked in surprise.

"As a candidate in this November's election, I am exercising my prerogative to observe the election preparation process. I showed my authorization paper to the man out front. Do I need to show it to you, too?" she said, in a playfully, mocking tone.

"Don't mind him," said Brenda. "He's just upset because we may have uncovered another bum machine."

Cindy and Carl exchanged quick glances. Realizing that this was not the time for playful banter, she quickly excused herself and went down to one of the other workbenches to observe.

"Here's your deck," said Milton, handing it to Brenda. "Terrence wants me to unload some boxes so I didn't get to run it. But I examined it and it looks fine."

"Well, Carl and I will have a look as well," said Brenda. They carefully went through the deck, ballot-by-ballot.

"It looks good," said Brenda. "We need to bring in Terrence."

Terrence was less than pleased.

"What is going on here?" he said looking at Carl and Brenda, but especially Brenda.

"The test decks look good," said Brenda. "And the ballots we created on *CreateBallot* were good. But the results are off for the first of the two scanners."

Carl suddenly had an idea. "This machine has a low protective number. It was one of the Braxton machines. Could that be an issue?"

"All the Braxton machines were tested back in August," said Terrence. "And we've had a number of them test OK in the last two days."

"That's right. I tested one of them yesterday. It was fine," said Brenda.

"What about that machine that failed yesterday, late in the day? Was that a Braxton machine?" asked Carl, not willing to let go of his theory.

"Let's check," said Terrence. The three of them walked down the aisle where they had temporarily stored the malfunctioning scanner. "Michael, do you have that list of the Braxton serial numbers?" he shouted.

They reached the failed machine. A few moments later Michael arrived with the list. Brenda read off the serial number.

"It's not on the list," said Michael, showing it to everyone. He placed the list on top of the scanner. "This is not a Braxton machine."

"Well, that kills your theory," said Terrence. "Wheel that other bad scanner down here. We'll probably have to replace them both. Fortunately we have those ten precincts that are supposed to get three machines. We can reallocate some of them as we get closer to the end. All right back to work everyone." He gave Carl a long look, as if to say, "How come you're always there when a machine goes bad?"

Returning to their workstation, they completed the paperwork and proceeded to roll the one good scanner as well as the cart to Station Three. Cindy was there, talking to Terrence.

"Thank you so much for allowing me to observe," she was saying, putting on her charm. "I had no idea so much was involved in making an election happen. It's like this incredibly complex, well-oiled machine."

"You are certainly welcome," said Terrence. "Come back any time you wish to visit."

"Thank you. May I ask one of your workers a technical question about one of the things I saw? It won't take more than a minute."

"Of course. We want all the candidates to feel comfortable with our process."

Cindy caught Carl's eye and giving a quick nod, she started back toward the front door. Carl followed.

"What happened?" she asked.

"Another scanner failed. It's my second in a row. They're probably just bad machines. We suspected the test decks but they all look good. Then I thought there might be something wrong with the Braxton machines but that theory fell through. I think Terrence is beginning to question my competency."

"If he is, then he's a fool," said Cindy. She paused for a moment. "Well I'm off to work. Are you ready for some more back-to school tonight?"

"Wouldn't miss it."

There was another pause.

"And just how is all this going to end?" she asked, pensively.

"With you on the Soil and Water Commission, I would imagine."

Cindy gave a wistful smile and nodded. She then turned and went back to the front door of the warehouse.

# 32

## TUESDAY, LATER IN THE DAY

BRANDYWINE'S FAILED SCANNER cast a shadow over Carl for the next few hours which only began to dissipate as he and Brenda successfully tested a number of precincts. Carl was becoming comfortable with the testing process and found it less necessary to consult with the instruction sheets.

"This is normal," said Brenda. "When we begin a test cycle, even the experienced testers have to relearn. It goes slow and we make mistakes. It's simply a matter of correcting the mistakes and moving forward. You were stuck in Station One for two weeks so you didn't have the ramp-up time the rest of us had. You're doing fine."

The last precinct that they tested wrapped up at 2:50 p.m.

"We don't have time to start another one," said Brenda. "It's been a good day. Let's call it quits now."

Carl agreed, even though the failed test of the Brandywine scanner continued to bother him. He proceeded to the gathering table where a number of the rovers were filling out their time sheets. Terrence and Milton were having what appeared to be an intense discussion.

"Again. Another bad test," Terrence was saying. "What's the matter this time?"

"It's precinct 206, Garfield. The numbers are off," said Milton. "Not by a lot but they are off. See here."

"Are you sure you did everything by the book?" asked Terrence.

"Yes," said Milton, without hesitation.

Carl watched the exchange with keen interest. Milton had been his rover during the years he had been chief and as far as Carl was concerned, he was the best.

"Have you examined the test deck?"

"Yes, I have. Its right here," he said, giving it to Terrence.

"We'll have someone else check it, just to be sure," said Terrence. Carl was the closest person to them but Terrence seemed to look right through him.

"Michael," he called. "Come here. I want you to review this test deck."

While they were waiting for Michael to come over from Station One, Carl asked, as casually as he could, "Was this one of the Braxton machines, by any chance."

"I don't know," said Milton. "You can check the serial number. Michael's got the list of Braxton machines somewhere."

Carl knew exactly where the list was. He quickly wrote down the Garfield serial. Then while everyone else was crowding around Michael, reviewing the test deck, Carl went to the aisle where the two failed scanners were stored. Michael's list was on one of the machines. He examined the list. The Garfield serial was on it. It was a Braxton machine.

Carl was sure he had something. He quickly returned to the table. By now the crowd was dissipating and folks were heading for the exit.

"Was the test deck good?" he asked Michael.

"Absolutely. It must be just a bad machine. We're going to wheel it down 'invalid aisle' to join the other two."

"For what it's worth, that's a Braxton machine," said Carl, pointing at the scanner that Milton was wheeling away.

"I hear what you're suggesting," said Michael. "We've had three failed scanners so far. Two of them are Braxton machines. On the other hand about a dozen of the Braxtons have tested fine. We're talking a very small sample size here. It just might be three bad machines. Let's hold any theories in abeyance for the time being and see what the rest of the week brings."

# 33

## Tuesday evening, 6:45 p.m.

"So you had another bad one this afternoon," said Cindy as she handed Carl the evening's supply of fliers. "Is this sort of thing normal?"

"The impression I get from talking to the other rovers is that sometimes the machines fail but when that happens, they simply cease to function. Some internal part goes bad. The screen freezes up or the scanner won't accept a ballot. But that's not what's happening here. These machines are running fine, but they just print out the wrong results."

"Is there any consistency in the types of errors that get printed?"

"They're never large. Just a few off here or there. But that's just with a relatively small test deck. On Election Day when hundreds of ballots are scanned, the gap could be much greater."

"Didn't you have one at the very beginning that was a couple off because of some error you made?" asked Cindy.

"When I forgot to create the *federal only* ballots. But we redid that one and it was fine. That's not one of the ones in sick bay."

"How many machines have been successfully tested?"

"They said we've completed fifty-four precincts so far. Times two equals one hundred eight machines. Plus those done the past two weeks for the in-person absentee."

"That's a lot of machines that are good. Just a few bad ones. They may just be the bad apples which is your job to uncover."

Carl sighed. "You're probably right. At least it was Milton who found this one. I was tired of being the one with the bad news."

"OK, I think you have all the fliers you need," said Cindy, changing the subject.

"Very good," said Carl. "Listen. Can I ask you a question? Two questions, actually."

"Sure. Of course," said Cindy, putting her remaining fliers into a canvas shoulder bag.

"How are the lessons going with Howard?"

"Uh...good...you know...good."

"Howard says you've been cancelling some of the sessions."

Something inside Cindy seemed to snap.

"Well bully for Howard. He doesn't have to cover three solid weeks of back-to-school shit followed by all that door-to-door shit followed by all that other—"

"I'm sorry," said Carl, quickly. "I didn't mean to hit a nerve. The thing is though, that you have this debate coming up next week. If you and Valerie could combine your forces. Have people hand out fliers for both candidates at these events. That would free you to do more prep with Howard."

Cindy's brown eyes bore in on Carl. "Did Valerie ask you to say this?"

"No. Not at all. It's just my idea."

"Well, it's a lousy idea. We are two independent campaigns. Her people support her. My people support me. Totally."

"I do support you. Totally," said Carl. "Do you believe that?"

"Whatever. I have to get going." Cindy turned to leave.

"Do you believe that?" Carl repeated, his voice suddenly hard.

Cindy turned around, an annoyed look on her face.

"Carl, I don't have time for this."

He reached into his shoulder bag and pulled out one of Valerie's fliers.

"I handed these out last night along with yours and I'm handing them out again tonight. Unless you tell me to go home."

"I don't believe this!" cried Cindy, throwing up her hands. "You went behind my back and—"

"Do you want me to go home?"

Cindy looked at Carl in amazement. The seconds ticked by.

"Do you want me to go home?" Carl repeated, looking Cindy straight in the eye.

They stared at each other for a few more seconds. Then Cindy slowly shook her head.

"Don't go home," she said, barely about a whisper.

"Do you believe I support you totally?"

She nodded. "Yes, I do."

"Good," said Carl, as he turned around and walked up the ramp to the school.

# 34

## Wednesday, September 30, 6:30 a.m.

There was a chill in the air as Carl headed out to the warehouse the following morning. He wanted to feel optimistic about the day ahead. About the weeks ahead. About the election. In the past, an election had just meant a few days of excitement occurring in June or November. Now between his work at the warehouse and Cindy's campaign, it seemed like this election had been going on forever.

"Just the man we need to see," said Terrence, as Carl approached the table. Terrence, Michael, and Milton were all hovering over a map of the county.

"We're going over the rover routes for November," said Michael. "Since you've become a rover, Milton can have a route closer to his home. You'll have his old route."

"Sometime before the election, preferably as soon as practicable, you need to drive your route," said Milton. "So you know where everything is, including the side streets and shortcuts. Then map out the most efficient way to cover everything. Of course once Election Day occurs, you run to where the situations are. I've never once driven my route the way it was planned. Still it is important to have a plan."

Carl studied the precinct map. He knew exactly where some of the precincts were. His home precinct of Chesterbrook. And Cooper, where he and Cindy had begun their late night adventure in January. There was Manchester, Seneca Grove, Danby, Wallingford, and Hagerman. All relatively close to his home. Carter Run. He had worked that in the primary. The other three precincts were further away. Their names sounded vaguely familiar but he really didn't know where they were. Tower. Happy Acres. Pikesville.

"I thought Carter Run was on Brenda's route," he said, remembering her from the primary.

"We switched it with Easthampton. Made more sense from a geography standpoint," said Terrence.

"So that's eleven precincts, all together," said Carl, as he continued to study the list.

"Twelve, actually," said Terrence. "They've reconfigured the area around Manchester High School and split it into two precincts. That may be your biggest challenge. Finding a way to squeeze two precincts into that school."

"Don't they have a large gym?"

"They do but we're talking serious numbers here. You may want to put the precincts in different rooms within the school. Your chiefs will make the final determination but you may need to advise them," said Milton.

"Happy Acres. Isn't that the retirement community?"

"Yes," said Milton. "It's a sprawling campus of retirement dwellings. They are usually cooperative but we need a fair amount of extra signage to get the voters to the right building. I'll go over everything with you when we have the pre-election rover meeting, closer to the big day. By then you will have your list of chiefs. I can let you know who you need to watch out for."

"Watch out for?"

"Carl, not every chief is as experienced as you. Or as quick a learner as Cindy. They're all competent in their own way but some require more support than others. We'll discuss this in more detail at the meeting."

"OK, let's move on," said Terrence, addressing the room. "We are going to have a visitor this morning. Our esteemed registrar will be paying us a visit. I'm not sure when he is coming or how long he will stay, but he probably will want to say a few words. So let's get started and knock out a few precincts before he arrives."

The group quickly split up into teams of two for the day's work. Carl found himself teamed with a lady named Jeannette who he had spoken to a couple of times but didn't really know. He was finding that although everyone had the same tasks to perform, each rover had his/her own style.

They rolled the next cart and scanners to their workbench.

"Precinct 322," said Jeannette. "We're in the 300s now. Whitestone. 11th Congressional district. Uh-oh, we may be in for a bit of competition. There are only two test decks for the 11th. They're not that many county precincts in the 11th but if we wind up testing them all at the same time…Let's get the scanners fired up right away so we can run the test deck through both before one of the other workstations needs them."

That sounded like a good idea to Carl. He and Jeannette each took control of a scanner and went through the preparation sequence. It was getting easier now. Flash Drives. Passwords. Calibrate. Set the time. Open polls. Print zero report.

"Done," said Jeannette. "Now let's get the test decks." As his scanner was also ready, Carl followed her to the test deck area. If there were two decks for the 11th, hopefully they could each claim one.

However there was only one. “The other must be in use,” said Jeannette. “No matter. We’ll feed this into both machines and worry about the *CreateBallot* later.”

Jeannette started inserting the ballots into one of the scanners. She was about half finished, when they heard Terrence shouting.

“Attention all rovers. Stop what you are doing. The country registrar is here and he wants to say a few words. I repeat. Stop what you are doing.”

“Go back to the table,” said Jeannette. “I’ll finish putting the ballots in this scanner and then empty the bin. We’ll vote the other scanner after the break.”

Carl nodded and headed to the table where the rovers were taking their seats.

“This should take a while,” whispered Scott. “Our supreme leader likes to talk.”

Terrence cleared his throat to get the group’s attention. “It is my great pleasure to welcome our General Registrar, Gordon Carruthers to our testing facility. He would like to say just a few words.” Carl wasn’t sure, but he thought he saw Brenda roll her eyes.

“Thank you, Terrence,” said Gordon. “I wanted to be with you a couple of weeks ago when you started but there is so much that is happening, that this is the earliest I could get away. I want to let all of you know how much we appreciate all the work and expertise you bring to the process. This is especially important because the media is so fixated on our electoral process…”

He went on and on. How the rovers were wonderful and how the county couldn’t do it without them. The importance of democracy. The sanctity of the vote.

While most of the rovers had heard this before, it was new to Carl and he found much of what Gordon had to say motivating. It reinforced his own admittedly idealistic view of the electoral process. But it did go on for a long time.

At last Gordon paused and asked if there were any questions.

*"Why can't we get into all the polling places the afternoon before the election to set up?"*

*"When are we going to replace those obsolete Electronic Poll Books?"*

*"How come they never listen to my recommendations concerning the selection of chiefs?"*

*"When will we be allocated more space in the warehouse?"*

*"Will we ever get a raise?"*

It was a freewheeling discussion that seemed to cover the electoral process from every angle. Carl was impressed by the poise and expertise that Gordon showed in this obviously unscripted session, a session that ended only when the noon lunch hour arrived.

"Have a good lunch everyone," said Terrence. "We pick up the pieces at 1:00 p.m."

"Carl, I'm out this afternoon," said Jeannette. "You'll need to team up with someone else."

Lunch for the rovers was always a one hour affair. Some went to a nearby deli while others brown bagged it at the table in the warehouse, which is what Carl did this day. After a morning of very little activity, he was anxious for the p.m. shift to begin.

"We've done fifty-six precincts," said Terrence solemnly. "Just about a quarter of the way. We need to step up our game."

"Come on, Carl," said Brenda. "Let's finish up what you and Jeannette started."

They went back to the workstation where the machines had been gathering dust for the past several hours.

"I'll get started on the *CreateBallot,*" said Carl. "You can finish up inserting the test deck in the other machine."

"I can if it's here," said Brenda. She knelt down and opened the black door underneath the machine and pulled out the blue bin.

"Nothing in here. Jeannette must have returned the test deck."

By this time Carl was engrossed in getting the *CreateBallot* machines out of the cart. For the next fifteen minutes he worked on getting them running and the ballots produced. By this time Brenda had retrieved an 11th district test deck and fed it into the other machine. It was then just a matter of Carl voting his *CreateBallot* cards into both of the machines which he did expeditiously.

"Now let's close the polls and hope," said Brenda.

Within a few seconds the printing started. Carl was studying one of the emerging printouts when he heard an exasperated "Oh, come on!" from Brenda.

Carl couldn't say he was surprised. It seemed like they were indeed snakebit. Eventually both scanners stopped printing. Carl examined the printout of one of the scanners.

"This one looks all right," he offered. It was the one that Jeanette had voted before the break.

"Well this one is off," said Brenda. "Not by a lot. Just a few votes. But we need to tell Terence."

Once again, there were the interrogations.

Did you use the correct test deck? *Yes.*

Have you reexamined the test deck to determine if it is correct? *Yes, and it is correct.*

Are the *CreateBallot* cards correct? *Yes.*

Are you sure you inserted each ballot once and only once into each machine? *Yes.*

What the hell is happening? *No idea.*

"OK, just roll it into the bone pile," said an unhappy Terrence.

"Wait," said Carl. He took out the list that Michael had provided the other day. "Just as I thought. It's a Braxton machine."

This time Terrence did not scoff. "We'll see. I'm not saying I buy your theory, but we'll see."

*What am I doing that's wrong?* thought Carl as he and Brenda went to get the next precinct. He was conscious that Terrence was eyeing him very intently.

"Precinct 401. Van Holland, 12th congressional district. At least we're back in the 12th," said Brenda as they wheeled the cart and scanners into position.

"Look Brenda. Maybe I'm being paranoid but let's do this together. Every step we do together. We don't do anything unless we both agree it's the right thing."

"Isn't that a bit extreme?" said Brenda.

"Perhaps. But I want to make sure we get this precinct right. Absolutely sure."

# 35

## Wednesday evening, 6:45 p.m.

"And they both failed," said Cindy incredulously, as she was counting out Carl's fliers for the evening's back-to-school night.

"They both failed," said Carl.

"So that makes—"

"Six machines that have failed. They all run perfectly but then print results that are a few votes off. I tell you Cindy, everyone is on edge. Terrence is a basket case. And I was on the teams that tested five out of the six bad machines. Terrence has been giving me the evil eye."

"But you are confident you're doing all the steps correctly?"

"Yes, at least, I think so. Brenda and I did every step together on the last two. But right now I can believe anything. Maybe I'm just not doing it in the right sequence or something."

"Carl, you are the most detail person I know. I can't believe you're getting the process screwed up."

"And I was so sure that it was the Braxton machines that were the cause, but one of the last two bad ones was an old scanner, not a Braxton."

"So, let's review," said Cindy slowly. "Six scanners down. Four are Braxton, two are not. Are they all from the 12th congressional district?"

"All but one. That one is from the 11th."

"And you've reviewed the test decks?"

"I can't begin to tell you the number of times we have reviewed the test decks. Every time a scanner fails, we go through the same exercise. And they're all good."

They stood silently, each trying to think of some possible explanation.

"Carl," said Cindy slowly. "You don't suppose there's some sort of deliberate sabotage going on. You know, like when you read about the Russians trying to influence our elections."

They looked at each other for a moment and then broke out laughing. It was a sign of how desperate they were that Cindy would have even suggested such a thing.

"Do you really think the Russians care about who gets elected to the Soil and Water Commission?" asked Carl.

"Well they might," said Cindy, trying to keep a straight face. "Anyway, I've got to get to my school. But first I need to ask you something. Are you free this Saturday?"

"I think I'm booked. You see I'm working on this crazy lady's campaign—"

"Well the crazy lady wants to know if you'd like to get some dirt under your fingernails."

"Doing what?"

"Steve has set up a photo op with a local Boy Scout Troop. They're building a trail in one of the parks as part of someone's Eagle project. They need volunteers. People to…I don't know, move dirt. It sounds like fun. And Carl, I am sick of shaking people's hands and telling them how great I am. This will be a chance to actually do something that is related to the high office to which I aspire."

"Sounds good. Count me in."

"Great. I'll make sure Steve sends you the particulars. Now I'm off to my school. It's one of the middle schools so there should be a good harvest. Good luck tonight. And really good luck tomorrow. You'll figure this thing out. I know it."

# 36

## THURSDAY, OCTOBER 1, 2:55 P.M.

"I CANNOT BELIEVE this is happening. I cannot believe it."

"Should I wheel the scanner into 'invalid alley?'" asked Carl.

"I cannot believe—What? Yes. Move it down. Whatever," said Terrence, distractedly. He was almost in a daze. Carl couldn't blame him. This was the fourth scanner that day which had failed.

Carl wheeled the scanner into the row of failed machines. The total was now up to ten and they were nowhere closer to coming up with a reason than they were the first day.

Carl returned to the table. They were almost at the 3:00 p.m. quitting time but no one seemed in a mood to leave. They were all sitting around the table, as if somehow their combined presence could unravel the mystery.

"Perhaps if we look at the test decks again—" began Brenda

"No," shouted Terrence. "We've looked at those damn test decks, over and over again. I'm seeing them in my sleep. And don't start talking to me about those Braxton machines," he added, turning his venom on Carl.

Carl couldn't blame Terrence, as his theory about Braxton had pretty much evaporated. Only one of the four machines that failed that day had been from Braxton. That one had been tested by Milton, first thing in the morning, but that was hours ago. Carl had been vocal at the time but then, one by one, the others had failed, one just before lunch, another immediately after, and now this fourth one. Each one had been tested by a different person. Three had been from the 12th Congressional district, while the one Milton had tested that morning had been from the 11th. It was a headache inducing nightmare.

"What are our numbers?" asked Scott.

"We've tested eighty-seven precincts," said Michael. "Of course, ten of them have just one scanner. We keep getting held up every time a machine fails."

"Has anyone thought about the possibility of deliberate sabotage?" asked Scott.

"I don't know how that would be done," said Michael. "Plus these errors have all been uncovered by different testers. We have to trust each other. Otherwise the whole thing falls apart."

"All right. Everyone get a good night's sleep," said Terrence. "Come back fresh tomorrow. At least it's Friday."

One by one the dejected testers left the warehouse. That night Carl said very little to Cindy. There was nothing to add from the night before. Just more of the same. For her part, Cindy was feeling the squeeze from the campaign that never seemed to end. She would be so glad when it was over.

# 37

## FRIDAY, OCTOBER 2, 7:00 A.M.

"OK, WHO'S GOING to examine the test decks this morning?" asked Brenda. "I did it yesterday. It's someone else's turn."

The rovers all looked around at each other. They had all done it a number of times in the past few days.

"How about Jack?" suggested Milton. Jack was the "senior citizen" of the rovers. He usually managed the moving of the carts to and from the assigned places in the warehouse and only rarely got involved in Station Two testing.

"What do you think?" asked Michael, looking over at Terrence.

Terrence gave a shrug. "Why not?"

"Hey, Jack," called Michael, getting up from his chair and walking past the entrance to the cage, where the scanners and carts were stored. "We have an opportunity for you."

Within a few minutes, they had the pile of test decks in front of Jack.

"Now what am I supposed to do with these?" he asked.

"Make sure they are correct. You know the correct number of votes for each candidate. Here is the grid. Just read off the ballots. Total the results and see if it matches the grid," said Michael.

"And let us know if anything doesn't look right," added Milton. "Anything."

"As you finish reviewing each deck, return it to the test deck area. That way we can continue our testing," added Terrence. "Got it?"

Jack slowly nodded. This was unfamiliar territory for him but he'd give it a go. Anything for the team.

Once Jack had reviewed the first couple of test decks, the rest of the rovers were able to get back to testing. The first couple of hours were relatively smooth. A number of precincts were successfully tested and team moral was slightly improved as they gathered around the table for their 9:30 break.

"The ballots appear as they should," said Jack. "My only question is, 'what are those funny little marks on the outside margin?'"

"It's the code that the scanner reads. So it knows that it's the correct ballot. Sort of like a bar code," said Michael.

Michael paused. For a few moments he seemed deep in thought. Then slowly, but decisively he said, "I would like to see all the test decks back here. Please."

Milton immediately got up and went over to the test deck area while Terrence started bemoaning the futility of it all.

"OK, here they are," said Milton, handing the pile of test decks to Michael.

Michael started going through the ballots slowly, one by one. It was the same thing that each of the rovers had done over the past several days, but somehow Michael's demeanor made them pay attention.

"Do you see anything?" asked Brenda.

Michael did not answer but continued to go through the ballots, reforming the test decks as he went along. Then,

"Why didn't I think of that?" said Michael, holding up a ballot.

In a flash everyone crowded around Michael, straining to see what he apparently had uncovered.

"Looks like a normal ballot," said Tim. "One vote for each of the Democrats and 'yes' on the bond issue."

"But do you see the 'test ballot' stamp?" asked Michael.

"Sure," said Brenda. "We stamped 'test ballot' on each of the test ballots on the first day to make sure it never got confused with an actual—Wait a minute. Part of the word 'ballot' is intersecting with those bar code markings on the side."

"Would that cause the scanner to malfunction?" asked Carl.

"I don't know but let's find out," said Terrence, suddenly energized. "Michael, continue going through those decks. Identify every deck that has at least one ballot where part of 'test ballot' overlaps those bar code symbols."

For the next several minutes everyone had their eyes fixed on Michael as he went through the remainder of the decks. At last, he pronounced his results.

"Two of the six decks for the $12^{th}$ Congressional district, the 'E' and 'F' decks, have at least some ballots with an overlap. Also one of the two decks for the $11^{th}$ district has a couple of 'borderline' cases. It's like they're almost touching."

*So that's it,* thought Carl. *We've been testing with bad test decks. Was it the "E" and "F" decks that I was testing with when those machines failed? I guess it must have been. Usually we have them sorted in order though, and "E" and "F" would be on the bottom and I usually take from the top. But sometimes we don't bother to sort them. That Tuesday morning test. Was that an "A" deck I used? I wish I could remember...*

"OK, here's what we do," said Terrence. "Take those three decks out of circulation. Then we test the ten scanners in sick bay with test decks taken from the remaining good ones. We do it slowly, carefully."

Carl got to his feet immediately. "Let's do it."

"Not you, Carl," said Terrence quickly. "I have something important I need you to do." He then continued, "Michael, team up with Scott. Milton, team up with Brenda. The four of you will do the testing of these machines. You will work through lunch if you have to. We have to resolve this thing. The rest of you continue your normal testing. Let's go."

There was a burst of renewed energy as the rovers headed back to work.

"What about me?" asked Carl.

"What do you mean?" said Terrence.

"You said you had something important for me to do."

"Oh. Oh, yes. You can…uh…oh, yes, there are some power cords back by Station One that are all tangled up. Please straighten them out."

*He's blaming me for testing so many of the bad machines and for my Braxton theory that didn't pan out,* thought Carl grimly, as he headed back to Station One. Nonetheless, there was reason to hope that the worst was behind them.

There were exactly six power cords that had gotten tangled. Nonetheless Carl managed to make himself useful doing some of the Station One tasks that he had become accustomed to performing. Noon came and most of the rovers broke for lunch. When they got back, they gathered around the table, hoping for a status report from the four testers. They all waited. No one was interested in getting back to work until the problem was resolved and Terrence did not push it. Finally at around 1:30, the four returned to the table. Michael was holding a pile of tapes in his hand.

"They tested good," he announced. "All ten."

Everyone was on their feet clapping and cheering, Carl included. He must have been using those bad test decks when those earlier tests had failed. That had to be it.

Terrence was beside himself with relief. "Thank you. Thank you, all," he proclaimed. "Thank you for hanging tough with this. Thank you for putting up with me. Let's get back to testing. We can knock out a few more before we leave and then power through the rest next week. Let's do it."

"Do you still want me to straighten out power cords?" asked Carl.

"Power cords? Whatever for? Find a partner and do some testing."

"Yes, sir," said Carl, heading to the workbench area in search of a partner. It had been a difficult week on so many levels but now things were looking better. So much better.

# 38

## Saturday, October 3, 8:30 a.m.

The sign read "Duncan Hill Nature Preserve." Carl pulled into the parking lot and drove to the far end, away from the Nature Center, to where there was a cluster of teenage boys and a handful of adults. He got out of his car and approached the group. They were breakfasting on doughnuts and orange juice.

"Hi, I'm Carl Marsden," he said to one of the adults. "I'm here to work on the Eagle Project. I believe you have my name."

"Check in with Mark," said the man, pointing to a boy holding a clipboard. "It's his project."

Carl went over to Mark who quickly found his name on the signup sheet.

For a few minutes they all continued to eat their breakfast. A car entered the parking lot and drove down to where they were. Carl saw that Steve was driving with Cindy in the passenger seat. The car stopped and they both got out. Steve was holding what looked like an expensive camera. Cindy gave Carl a smile and a wave as she went over to Mark to check in. Even as Mark was locating Cindy's name on his clipboard, Carl could hear the clicks of Steve's camera.

At last Mark called them to order.

"Thank you all for coming to my project. We will be creating a trail which will connect an already existing trail to a gravel road. We'll be heading into the woods for about a quarter mile, to where the work will be done. Mrs. Jacobs will wait here and direct any latecomers."

With that, one of the adults handed Carl some tools and they all entered the woods via an already existing trail.

It was a cool, crisp morning and Carl felt invigorated as he walked with the scouts. After about ten minutes they came to a gravel road.

"Up this way," said Mark and they all scrambled up a steep embankment, covered with small trees, leaves, roots, and various forms of undergrowth. When they got to the top of the hill, they came to another trail.

"We're going to create a trail, going down to that gravel road, using switchbacks," said Mark. "Right now people are bushwhacking down to the gravel road and it's not safe. This trail will provide a safe means for hikers to get down there and will also provide for runoff in an ecological manner. But before I start, I need to show how you will use some of these tools safely."

Mark then demonstrated the correct way of using a mattock which was a sort of pickaxe, a McLeod which seemed like an industrial version of a rake, and finally, loppers which was a tool used for cutting roots and branches.

This was all new to Carl. He had dropped out of Cub Scouts early and was in no way an outdoorsman. He caught Cindy's eye. She returned his look with a shrug and a grin, shaking her head. She was obviously as clueless about this as he was.

"The kids love to work with these more exotic tools," whispered one of the adults to Carl. "This is how we get them to volunteer for this stuff."

It was now time to start the actual work. "Why don't you rake some of the leaves off the top part of the trail?" said Mark to Carl, handing him what appeared to be a very ordinary rake.

*This must be the scouts' version of untangling power cords,* thought Carl as he accepted the rake, even as the other scouts were being given their assignments.

As Carl started his raking, he could see Steve grab one of the mattocks and give it to Cindy. He then proceeded to take some pictures of her holding the tool in various poses.

"You need to rake harder, mister," said a voice behind him.

Carl looked down to see a small boy, who appeared to be about ten years old. He was holding a rake of his own.

"Hi, I'm Brian," said the boy. "This is my first Eagle project. I just joined the scouts last month. I hope to get Tenderfoot real soon though. Mark said I should work with you. He said we're a good pair."

For the next hour, Carl continued to rake the trail under the watchful eye of Brian who, as it turned out, had very high standards. At one point Carl thought they were done but Brian shook his head and pointed to other parts of the trail which were, in his mind at least, unsatisfactory.

At last Brian was satisfied. "We can go down to Mark and get our next assignment," he announced. By this time the troop was fully engaged, using their tools to cut roots, clear out underbrush, and smooth the ground. Cindy was halfway down the trail, using the loppers to cut out some rather persistent roots. Steve was nowhere to be seen.

"He took his camera back to the car," she explained. "He got some really good shots. He hopes to get them into next week's edition of the local paper."

"No time to chat, mister," said Brian. "We need to find Mark."

Together they approached Mark.

"We raked the top part," said Brian. "We need more to do."

Mark considered. "Brian, join the crew working on the bottom part of the trail. They're trying to figure out the best way around those trees. Jimmy will tell you what to do." Brian went off to find Jimmy. Mark turned back to Carl.

"Mr. Marsden, can you take that case of small plastic water bottles and offer them to the workers? And once they're done, get a trash bag and make sure the empties are appropriately disposed of."

*So now I'm Gunga Din,* thought Carl as he went to get the water bottles and trash bags.

He was handing out water to some of the scouts in the middle section when Steve returned.

"We've got the photos we need and they're great," he said to Cindy. "Now, let's get out of here. We've got a door-to-door route mapped out for you to be followed by a couple of hours in front of a supermarket."

Cindy was on her knees trying to twist an especially difficult root out of the ground with the loppers. "What do you mean? This is going to take a few more hours, at least."

"But we have the pictures. That's what we came for."

"But I'm committed to this until it's done. And it's kind of fun in its own goofy way. I'm actually getting dirt under my fingernails."

"No, you're not. You have work gloves on."

"Well metaphorically, anyway."

Steve's manner changed. "Cindy, we need to get you out of here. Time is everything in a campaign. There is nothing left for you to accomplish here. We have to go. Now."

Cindy got to her feet and dusted off her jeans. She then motioned to the side of the trail where they could speak in relative privacy.

"Steve, I understand what you are saying but I made a commitment to see this through. For the first time in this campaign, I feel like I'm doing something that actually matters. Leave if you must. I'll get a ride home with Carl."

Steve wasn't about to give up. "You know if you're not careful, you're going to blow this whole election. Sometimes you act like this is some big lark, drawn up for your own amusement."

Cindy's face hardened. "I'm not leaving."

Steve threw up his hands in exasperation and started down the hill. As he passed Carl he said, "Talk some sense into her. She listens to you. I don't know why but she does." He got to the bottom of the hill and proceeded down the trail toward the parking lot.

The work lasted for three more hours. About a half hour before the end, Mark signaled to Cindy and Carl. "If you can do one more thing for us, it would be great. We've preordered some pizzas from the Pizza Oven, a few miles down the road. It's already been paid for and is under the name of Troop 825. If you could pick them up for us now, we'll be finished working by the time you get back."

They readily agreed and headed back to the lot for Carl's car. Pulling out of the parking lot, Carl made note of the time. "It's 2:00 p.m. We'll be totally done in a half hour. That should give you some time to do those door-to-doors with Steve."

"So you overheard our little chat," said Cindy. "He's really not a bad guy and I haven't paid him a dime for being my campaign manager."

"Then why is he doing it?—No, I'm sorry. That's none of my business."

"He's very ambitious," said Cindy. "And this win would look good on his resume. The Republican candidate is not especially well known and Democrats have the registration edge in the county, so I really should win. Unless I do something to screw it up."

"Like the debate," said Carl. He half expected Cindy to lash out like she had done earlier in the week.

"Like the debate," agreed Cindy. "You'll be happy to know that your unilateral decision to distribute Valerie's fliers has resulted in Stan offering to distribute mine on Tuesday evening so I can schedule a last minute session with Howard. I suppose I should thank you for that."

"Perhaps this could lead to the two of you mending fences."

Cindy laughed. "Don't push it."

A comfortable silence engulfed the car as they drove along.

"Cindy, I have to ask you something. And again, it's none of my business so if you don't want to…"

Cindy remained silent.

"The times I've talked to Valerie. She seems like a really nice person. Why then…"

Cindy let out a sigh. "She is a nice person. And she has a darling husband and she's a great mom."

Now it was Carl's turn to be silent.

"She's quite a bit older than me and when I was little, she always bossed me around and I hated it. And Dad always favored me but then he got sick just about the time Valerie was supposed to go away to college. So Mom had to work and Val wound up taking care of Dad, going to college locally, and keeping me out of trouble, which wasn't always that easy to do. She was really heroic and sacrificed quite a bit."

The words tumbled out, punctuated by pauses. It was like she was reliving each thought in her mind.

"Then it was my turn to go to college and I really wanted to go to UVa and Dad insisted that I go. So I went and had a great time. I worked hard, I played hard, and …he died. I didn't realize it was that bad. I was so into my own stuff …I missed the signs. I missed…everything. Val never came out and said it but it's the way she's looked at me ever since…Like someone who never measures up… Self-absorbed little bitch who always takes and never gives."

Only then did Carl realize that she was crying.

Gradually Cindy regained her composure. "Sorry about that. Anyway, that's the Reader's Digest version. We just seem to bring out the worst in each other. Better to keep our distance."

Carl didn't know what to say. It was sad but Cindy obviously knew that so he remained silent.

The pizza was ready when they arrived and within a few minutes they were on their way back to the park. When they pulled into the parking lot, they were greeted with a big cheer from the scouts who had apparently finished the project. The pizza was consumed in record time. Cindy and Carl congratulated Mark on his project, said their goodbyes to the adults, and got back on the road.

Cindy pulled out her cell phone. "I better call and see if I still have a campaign manager."

Carl stayed focused on the road, determined not to eavesdrop on Cindy's conversation. It had been a full day. A full week. What the week ahead promised, he could only guess.

# 39

## Sunday, October 4, 3:30 p.m.

"So here we are," said Steve, with a grim expression on his face.

"Yes, we are," said Cindy.

For a moment they were both silent, each taking the measure of the other. At last Cindy spoke.

"Steve, if you're going to dump me, then dump me and be done with it. I'm not the first candidate to defy her campaign manager. I did what I felt was right and I don't apologize for it."

Realizing that she was not going to back down, Steve acquiesced. "Fair enough. You stood your ground and I respect that," he said with a smile. "Now let's move forward. You have this little thing called a debate coming up on Wednesday. Have you scheduled any time with Howard?"

"Yes. He's teaching at the university tomorrow, but we'll squeeze in a bit of time in their cafeteria. Then Tuesday, we'll have the whole evening. I'll stick with it until I drop."

"Good. The two of you then will handle the technical stuff. You and I can talk general strategy. First we'll start with your two opponents."

"Fire away."

"The Independent Green Party is the group that stresses rail transportation. Their candidate's name is Everett Diesel."

"Really, that's his real name? Who is his campaign manager? Sir Topham Hatt?"

"Who?"

"You know, from the—never mind. So what do I need to know about Mr. Diesel?"

"Very little. He will probably stress that increased use of rail transportation will result in fewer cars on the road which will improve the quality of life for everyone."

"The man has a point."

"Perhaps, but his point is not our mission. Be polite to him but don't engage. His support will be negligible. Our real opponent is the Republican. His name is Frederick Rawlins. He is retired from a career as a 'Land Acquisition Manager' which involves advising developers as to what lands they should purchase and dispose of. That suggests that his priorities might historically have been with the developers rather than the environment."

"So are you saying I should go after him on that?"

"I wouldn't advise it unless you are desperate. Going negative is always a risky strategy. I've done a limited amount of opposition research on him and he's respected although his resume is a bit shallow, compared to the other members on the commission."

"But not compared to me."

"That doesn't matter. This is about the candidate, not the resume. Stick as much as possible with generalities. Stress your passion, not your expertise. That story about you and your sister playing in streams was great. She has kids, doesn't she?"

"Yes, two boys."

"Well this is all about the future. Good soil and clean water for the future. For your nephews' future. Put your heart on your sleeve. I've seen you in action. You can do this."

"You don't have to win the debate," he continued. "Just don't do anything to embarrass yourself. This election is yours. Party registration will do it for you. Also don't worry about the audience. Most of them will be there for the school board race. I doubt if many of them will even stick around for you."

They continued on for the next hour but the message remained the same. Learn as much as you can from Howard. Pick up some factoids that you can use if necessary, but as much as possible stay with generalities, passion, and sincerity. Use your assets: your youth, your charm, your attractiveness. The audience will love you.

# 40

## Monday, October 5, 7:00 a.m.

"All Right. We're going to make up for lost time," said Terrence to the group. "All that misery is behind us. What's the count, Michael?"

"One-hundred one. That's our number of precincts fully tested, each with two scanners," said Michael.

Terrence continued, "If we can do twenty-five a day, we'll be done by next Wednesday. Possibly Tuesday. We still need to put the physical ballots into boxes. They should arrive from the printer later this week."

Carl was confused. "But we have the ballots, don't we? That's how we constructed those test decks."

"That was just an advance shipment," explained Michael. "The bulk of them won't come until this week."

"Bottom line," said Terrence, "is that we should be done in the warehouse by the middle of next week. End of next week at the latest. At that point, we will still have two full weeks before the election. I understand they will want many of you to serve at the in-person absentee locations during that time. That's fine with me. Just remember that your primary responsibility is to make sure the chiefs on your route are well prepared and that you're ready for the big day. Any questions? No? OK, let's get started."

There was a renewed sense of optimism among the rovers that Monday morning. Carl teamed up with Scott and by 8:30 a.m., their first precinct was successfully tested. By noon they had completed four. Two more were knocked off in the afternoon, making a total of six for their team, for the day. No errors. Everything perfect.

"We did thirty today," said Michael happily, as they prepared to leave at the 3:00 p.m. closing time. "We keep this up and we might finish by the end of the week."

As he drove home, Carl contemplated the evening schedule for the week. It was the last week that back-to-school nights were scheduled and Carl was slated to distribute fliers Monday, Tuesday, and Wednesday. He would hand them out for both sisters, with Cindy's acquiescence, if not enthusiasm. Wednesday night was tricky because that was the night of the debate. The school board candidates would debate at 7:30 p.m., followed an hour later by Soil and Water. Carl very much wanted to be at the debate but first he would have to cover his assigned back-to-school night at Manchester, the largest high school in the county.

And that was it. Thursday night had just one school and Cindy had insisted that she take that one. Carl had to admit he was looking forward to these evening events coming to an end. Yes, it was all coming together. The warehouse work was looking good. All Cindy needed to do was perform well in the debate.

# 41

## Tuesday, October 6, 11:50 p.m.

"I had no idea," said Cindy. "No friggin idea."

"There is a lot," agreed Howard.

It was close to midnight. For the past five hours she and Howard had been going over the Soil and Water Commission in minute detail: its history, the legalities surrounding it, the efforts it promoted, some of the controversies it dealt with. She was exhausted and feeling a monstrous headache coming on. In less than twenty-four hours she would be facing her two opponents in what would be the first of two debates for this election.

"Howard, I can never thank you enough, but please accept this as a token," said Cindy, handing him an envelope, containing a gift card to a local upscale restaurant. She then added, "You should be the candidate, not me."

"I'm not a politician," said Howard. "I'm just a wonk who cares about the environment."

Cindy suddenly felt the need to ask, "Have I been a disappointment to you?"

"No, not at all," said Howard. "I wish we could have had more sessions but I realize that you're being pulled in a lot of directions. You would only be a disappointment if you got on the board and didn't give it everything you have. You don't need to know everything on day one. But you have to care. And learn. And hopefully be in for the long haul."

"The long haul?"

"This election is just to fill the vacancy for one year. Next November the county elects three members for complete four year terms. You win this November and you'll be a shoe-in for a full term a year from now."

*He doesn't know the plan,* thought Cindy.

"Anyway, we should probably call it quits so you can get some sleep. Are you working your day job tomorrow?"

"I have to. At least in the morning. I'll try and get out a few hours early and review these," she said, pointing to the pages of notes she had taken.

"OK. Well I'll be at the auditorium from 7:00 p.m. on. You can ask me any last minute questions. Otherwise I'll just say good luck."

Filled with emotions that ranged from gratitude to exhaustion to guilt, Cindy gave her mentor a hug as the two ended their session.

# 42

## WEDNESDAY, OCTOBER 7, 6:45 P.M.

"WELL THIS IS certainly interesting," said Carl as he made the four block walk from his parking place on the street to Manchester High School. Fortunately he had seen the backup of cars that snaked back into the street, before it was too late to make adjustments. He was a bit surprised at this. He had been to Manchester High a few times over the years and remembered its parking lot as being rather large.

As he approached the school he began to understand the nature of the problem. Manchester High School was in the midst of what appeared to be a massive renovation program. Bulldozers, dump trucks, and cordoned off piles of dirt occupied major portions of the parking lot. Parts of the school, including what used to be the front entrance were boarded up. Signs that had a homemade quality led pedestrians past the side of the school to what was presumably the interim "front entrance."

This was a rude awakening for Carl. His immediate focus had to be locating that front entrance. As the sole representative for the combined (temporarily at least) Turner-Phelps campaigns, he needed to be in position to hand out as many of the fliers as possible. However, Carl couldn't help but do a fast-forward to November. Two large precincts on his route would be housed here at Manchester High and the two chiefs, whoever they might be, would be severely tested by this landscape that resembled a war zone.

*Well, for the moment, November planning will have to wait,* he thought as he followed the arrows.

It didn't help that many of the parents descending on the school were just as confused as Carl, as they too fell in line. Eventually he came upon a door that was not boarded. As the signs petered out at about this point, it was assumed by most of the parents that this was the front door, although there were a few who continued down the side of the school. Carl chose to side with the majority and started handing out his fliers.

It was a busy and hectic scene. A number of confused parents were in no mood to accept partisan material. Still, Carl had sheer numbers going for him and by 7:50 p.m., when the stream of parents had reduced to a trickle, he had distributed, what was for him, a record number of fliers. Normally he would have waited a few extra minutes to catch some of the stragglers, but he was anxious to get to the East County Civic Auditorium where the candidate forum would be taking place. As a result he found himself trotting, and for the final block running, back to his car.

Fortunately it was a relatively easy drive from Manchester to the auditorium. Carl made it in twenty minutes, without running any red lights, although there was a couple of temptations along the route. The time on the dash read 8:25 p.m. as he pulled into the parking lot. He parked his car, proceeded quickly to the front door, and entered.

A chorus of boos could be heard, coming from the first several rows of the seating area. The two candidates were seated at separate tables on the stage, each with their own microphone. Valerie had her reading glasses on and was referring to some notes that were in front of her.

"...so these numbers show that the needs for the next fiscal year are in line with the projections that the current Board has made... *(More boos from the audience)* ...and in conclusion... *(Derisive cheers)*...I am honored that the county Democratic Party has seen fit to endorse me for a position on the school board. Thank you for your consideration."

There was scattered, but determined, applause from various parts of the audience. Stan was standing in the back of the auditorium, close to where Carl had entered.

"Rough night?" asked Carl.

"It's about what we expected," said Stan. "We knew there would be a vocal presence of naysayers here tonight. Valerie did fine however. She stuck to her talking points and that is what the press will report."

It was now time for the final statement from Valerie's Republican opponent.

"If you want the status quo. If you want more of the same. More wasteful spending. More bloated bureaucracy. More library books that border on pornography. More pie-in-the-sky experimentation from whatever new fad the Ivy League schools come up with. Then by all means vote for my opponent. But if you want a new day. A day where the parents of this county are listened to and respected, then join our movement and vote for Janet Hayes this November." *(Cheers from the audience)*

Ms. Hayes continued to make her points and the crowd roared its approval. Carl had previously studied her positions and he felt some of them had merit. He wondered if he had not formed a bond with Valerie, whether he would be joining in with the crowd. No, he decided. That wasn't his style. Reasoned debate, yes. Vigorous debate, you bet. But always respectful.

"Thank you candidates for a most interesting hour," moderator Tracy Miller was saying. "There will be a five minute break and we will then continue our forum with the three candidates for the open seat on the county Soil and Water Commission."

Valerie immediately got up and went over to her opponent who was only just getting to her feet. She smiled and offered her hand which seemed to take Ms. Hayes aback. After a moment's hesitation, they shook hands. Then they both left the stage.

Ms. Hayes's supporters gathered around her, offering their congratulations on what they no doubt felt was a triumphant debate. Then the Hayes contingent proceeded up the aisle and through the front door, leaving the spacious auditorium with only a relative handful of spectators. Steve was right. Soil and Water was not a marquee event.

Valerie proceeded up the aisle to where Stan and Carl stood. "Well done," said Stan, as he embraced Valerie. "Do you want to stay and watch Cindy's debate?"

"No. She'll be better off without me. Oh hi, Carl."

"I only caught the end but you sounded fine. And the parents at Manchester High now have all the materials they need to make an informed choice."

"And we appreciate that, don't we Stan? But now we have to get back home. We're paying the babysitter by the half hour."

They left and Carl redirected his attention to the front of the auditorium. A third table and microphone had been set up on the stage. On the far right of the seating area, at the foot of the stairs to the stage, Carl could see Cindy talking to Steve, with

Howard off to one side. Also in attendance was Biff Logan, sitting in the first row. Steve seemed to be giving some last minute instructions to Cindy, who was nodding as each one of Steve's points was being made. At last he was finished and she turned to walk up the stairs. As she went up the stairs, she looked out into the audience and spotted Carl. She gave him a bit of a wave and a nervous smile.

At that moment, two men ascended the stairs from the other side of the auditorium. One of them had a mature look about him, Carl would have guessed mid to late sixties, while the other was considerably younger. The three candidates were now on stage but they initially seemed unsure where they were to sit. Then a young man, with place cards in his hands, came walking quickly down the main aisle of the auditorium and mounted the stage. He put a card on each table, Frederick Rawlins on the left, Everett Diesel in the middle, Cynthia Phelps on the right. The three candidates took their seats. As Carl had guessed, Rawlins was the older of the two men.

"Ladies and gentlemen. I am your moderator, Tracy Miller, WMML news. We thank you all for attending what we hope will be an informative forum featuring the three candidates for the open seat on the county Soil and Water Commission. Although these candidates will appear on the ballot without political party designation, each as it so happens, has been endorsed by one of three political parties. They are Frederick Rawlins, who has been endorsed by the Republican Party, Everett Diesel, who has been endorsed by the Independent Green Party, and Cynthia Phelps, who has been endorsed by the Democratic Party. Each candidate will give a three minute opening statement. I will then direct questions to each candidate who will have ninety seconds to respond. The other candidates will then have a chance for a sixty second rebuttal. If in my judgment, there is a productive dialog between the candidates, I will allow it to continue. At the end of the hour, each candidate will give a ninety second closing statement. The order of speakers and the placement on the stage has been determined by lot. We will commence this forum with the opening statement by Cynthia Phelps."

# 43

## Wednesday evening, 8:30 p.m.

Quickly, Carl went down the aisle and took a seat near the front.

"Thank you, Tracy," began Cindy. "I entered this race because I am concerned. Concerned that my small nephews may not grow up in the same wholesome environment that I was privileged to experience. Our environment faces so many challenges today. Challenges that come from the indifference that so many of the leaders of the political party that supports my opponent show toward the sanctity of our environment, a party that denies the very existence of global warming. Our clean water is jeopardized by developers who seek only monetary gain. I look to the future. And I offer a commitment to that future..."

*She's good,* thought Carl. *And I honestly believe she means it, however skimpy her qualifications may seem.*

They were seeing Cindy at her best, where her looks, personality, and sincerity came together. When she completed her opening remarks, there was sustained applause from the auditorium.

"Thank you, Ms. Phelps. Our next candidate is Everett Diesel."

Mr. Diesel, although obviously sincere, was not a polished speaker. He started by giving a brief historical overview of the region's railroads. He then explained how the building of highways was causing a deterioration in the quality of the county's soil and water. This was followed with an impassioned plea for funding to build high speed rail lines similar to what was in Europe. There was scattered applause at the end of his statement.

"Thank you Mr. Diesel. We will now proceed to Frederick Rawlins."

"Thank you Ms. Miller. If I'm elected, these are some things I would push for as a member of the Soil and Water Commission. The landfill at the Millbrook site has been in operation for many years. The Millbrook community has grown over the years and is being negatively impacted by this landfill. I believe we need to actively look for alternative sites and I've listed in my brochure some possibilities. I also believe we need to do a better job of ranking the watersheds in the county so we can focus our efforts on those that are in the worst shape. I also support the proposal by the citizen association of the Vicente Terrace neighborhood to transfer ten acres of county owned land, that is essentially doing nothing today, to the county park authority so it can be transformed into a park that everyone can enjoy. I am also concerned about some of the invasive species that have..."

Mr. Rawlins was the weakest speaker of the three. Reading from his notes he rambled from proposal to proposal, outlining the things he wished to accomplish. Once again there was scattered applause.

"Thank you Mr. Rawlins. My first question is directed to Cynthia Phelps. Ms. Phelps, your opening statement, while moving in many ways, was short of specifics. Could you elaborate more fully on what you intend to accomplish as a member of the Soil and Water Commission?"

"Thank you for that question, Tracy. I want to represent the people, all the people and especially the children, and as a member of the Commission I will dedicate my time and energy to uncover and promote those things that enhance our fertile soil and clean water. I think it is vitally important for new members of the Commission to enter with an open mind to be able to evaluate and promote those endeavors that will preserve our environment for the next generation."

"Thank you Ms. Phelps. Would either of your opponents care to comment?"

"I think she's missing an opportunity by not embracing the high speed rail project," said Mr. Diesel.

"Mr. Rawlins?"

"She didn't really say anything so it's tough to comment."

"Thank you. Our next question is for Mr. Rawlins. Could you discuss more fully some of the alternatives to the Millbrook landfill?"

Mr. Rawlins quickly outlined some of the advantages and disadvantages of the proposed alternatives. He indicated that his preference was for an area in the western part of the county, which had a relatively sparse population.

"Ms. Phelps, would you care to comment?"

"I…er…think that all options need to be evaluated using the strictest standards and it's premature to promote one over the others."

"Mr. Diesel?"

"My website gives a detailed description of how a fast rail line would operate. I would ask all voters to check it out before casting their vote."

The next question was for Mr. Diesel who expanded on his high speed rail proposal. In response Mr. Rawlins expressed skepticism regarding the cost while Cindy said it was an intriguing concept, worthy of study.

And so it continued. From Carl's perspective, Cindy was doing a masterful job, sticking with generalities. It helped that Mr. Rawlins was not an especially aggressive debater.

*She just might make it,* thought Carl, *but it's hanging by a thread.*

"Ms. Phelps. One cannot help but note that your resume of environmental involvement is remarkably thin to the point of bordering on nonexistent. Why should the citizens of our county elect you over an opponent who has obviously had more experience in environmental matters?"

"Tracy, I believe it is critical to look to the future and not the past. I want a county where my small nephews can grow and prosper. And it's true that I may not have my opponent's experience, experience in advising developers on what land to purchase and dispose of without any consideration..."

*Please Cindy, don't go negative.*

"...to the environmental consequences—"

*"How dare you!"* exclaimed Mr. Rawlins.

"I'm not finished—" said Cindy.

But Mr. Rawlins would not be silenced.

"For the better part of an hour, I have listed to your banalities. Do you think you're the only person on this stage who cares about the future? I have five grandchildren and I assure you that I care about them just you care about your nephews. Every purchasing recommendation I have made in my career, and I mean *every one,* has had an accompanying environmental impact study. I would offer to show them to you tomorrow but I suspect you wouldn't comprehend most of what they said."

A deathly silence gripped the auditorium.

"I'm sorry, Miss Miller for speaking out of turn," said Mr. Rawlins. "My opponent is obviously sincere. I apologize for interrupting."

More silence.

"Ms. Phelps?"

Cindy looked stunned.

"I'm sorry… I didn't mean to question my opponent's integrity. Can we move on to a different question?"

"Does that mean you are finished answering my question concerning your qualifications?"

"I think I'm done. Yes."

"Mr. Rawlins?"

He shook his head.

"Mr. Diesel?"

"More rails, less roads."

Cindy was deeply shaken by the exchange and it showed during the remainder of the debate. Gone was her vitality, her focus. She answered the remaining questions in a disconnected and almost incoherent fashion, stumbling frequently.

"Ms. Phelps, what's your position on the Greenway proposal?"

"Why I think that it's…uh…it's good. I mean it will save all those trees, rerouting the stream."

"Mr. Rawlins?"

"I'm not sure what Ms. Phelps is referring to. The Greenway proposal involves that golf course that developers want to---"

"That's right. The golf course. I'm in favor of that."

"Of the proposal?"

"Yes."

"So you want to allow the developers to remove the golf course and put up the condos?"

"No. I mean, save the golf course."

"So you're against the proposal."

"Yes, that's what I said, wasn't it?"

At last they reached the end of the debate. Cindy hurried through her closing statement in a manner that told everyone that she just wanted to get off the stage as quickly as possible.

"I would like to thank our three candidates for appearing with us tonight. I encourage everyone to go to the polls and cast an informed ballot this November. Good evening."

There was scattered applause from the audience. Cindy got up from the table and hurried down the stairs as quickly as she could. Carl considered getting up and meeting her but he saw that Steve was already at the foot of the stairs. Steve started to say something but Cindy cut him off.

"Find a room. We need to talk."

"Look, Cindy," said Steve. "Let's get out of here and we can—"

"No. Find a room. Right here. Right now."

"All right. Come with me," said Steve, as he ushered Cindy out through a side door of the auditorium.

Carl and Howard exchanged looks. Neither spoke. There was nothing to be said.

# 44

## Wednesday Evening, 9:35 P.M.

Steve quickly ushered Cindy into the room and closed the door.

"All right," he said. "You have your private space. Now what is it that can't wait—?"

"Of course it can't wait. You saw what happened out there. I made a complete jackass out of myself!" Cindy was practically screaming.

"It wasn't that bad. You made some very good points on—"

"I stunk to high heaven and you know it."

"Please Cindy, let's calm down," said Steve, in his most soothing voice. He tried grabbing hold of her shoulders to settle her down but Cindy wrestled free and went to the other side of the room and sat down. She reached into her handbag and took out a pack of cigarettes.

"I think this is a no smoking building," said Steve.

Cindy shot Steve a withering look but returned the pack to her handbag.

For a few minutes there was complete silence.

Finally Steve spoke.

"We should have had Howard prep you more. Perhaps he isn't the best person to do it. Maybe someone a little less academic and more down-to-earth—"

"The problem isn't Howard and you know it."

"I'm not so sure about that. He's such a nerdy looking guy that—"

"Oh stop it about Howard," sighed Cindy as she leaned over, resting her head in her hands. "The problem is me."

"Well it certainly didn't help that you went negative."

"Yeah, I screwed that up, didn't I?" agreed Cindy.

The door opened and Biff Logan entered the room.

"OK, we have our first forum under our belt. It could have gone better but we have a week to prepare for the next one."

Cindy looked up and gave a mirthless laugh.

"I don't think there's going to be a next one."

"What do you mean?" said Biff. "It's on the schedule and everything. Steve here can arrange some more sessions with Howard or perhaps someone else—"

"Am I the only one who realizes what that travesty out there meant?" asked Cindy as she looked incredulously, first at Biff, and then at Steve.

"I got blasted out there, not because Howard didn't pump me with the right comeback lines. I lost that debate because I was facing a more qualified candidate. Anyone with half a brain could see it."

"What do qualifications have to do with it?" said Biff. "People saw your sincerity."

"What does sincerity matter if you don't know what the hell you're doing?" said Cindy.

"Biff, why don't you let Cindy and I talk alone for a few minutes," suggested Steve. "I'm sure we can work this out."

Biff looked over at Cindy with an appraising eye. Then with a shrug, he said, "See that you do," and left the room.

"Cindy," spoke Steve in a calm, yet decisive tone. "I know you're upset. I know you're disappointed in your performance—"

Cindy started to say something but Steve held up his hand for silence.

"Believe me. I've seen lots of campaigns and what happened tonight is very, very common with rookie candidates. Trust me, you are a better candidate than you think you are. It just means getting up off the mat and getting back in the game. You can do this. I know you can."

"How did I ever get into this?" asked Cindy, more to herself than to Steve.

"You got into this because you wanted to," said Steve, whose tone had suddenly turned hard. "No one put a gun to your head. You are an ambitious woman and you made a conscious choice."

"I need time to think," said Cindy.

"Of course. Why don't we go back to your place and—"

"Alone," said Cindy.

They glared at each other for a few seconds. Then Steve spoke.

"Very well. Have your 'alone time.' Just remember that some people, including me, have put a lot of effort into your candidacy. You get out now and no one will ever take you seriously again. Your political future will be over."

"Oh my," said Cindy, her voice dripping with sarcasm. "No political future. How will I ever stand it?"

Their unspoken anger continued to pervade the room. At last, Cindy got to her feet.

"Look Steve," she said, her tone softening. "I do appreciate all you've done for me. I really do. And yes, I got into this by my own free will. It's my mess. I own it."

"It doesn't have to be a mess. You can do it. And I will be with you every step of the way."

"I don't know. We'll see. Right now I need to get out of here."

"I'll walk you to your car."

"Sure, if that's what you want."

And together they left the room.

# 45

## Thursday, October 8

Carl left the auditorium, not knowing what to do. There was no way of hiding the fact that Cindy's performance had been a disaster. He wasn't sure if the combined magic of Steve, Biff, and Howard could put her campaign back together again. But that was nothing compared to what he felt for Cindy, as a person. He wanted to reach out to her but for now she was with her handlers and there was nothing he could do. Cindy would contact him, when and if she felt the need.

The following morning found Carl back at the warehouse where thus far they had experienced a good week. A very good week.

"We've tested 181 precincts," announced Terrence. "At this rate we'll be done by the middle of next week. Don't forget that Monday is the Columbus Day holiday and we won't be here."

The day progressed quite smoothly. By the end of the day, they had completed their two hundredth precinct with less than fifty to go. Carl was genuinely excited to see the testing effort come together so well. That excitement was tempered only by the anxiety that he felt for Cindy. As he drove home, he wondered once again if he should try to contact her. But if he did, what would he say?

"Too bad you didn't have what it takes?"

For the first time in a number of days, Carl had no campaign duties staring him in the face and he looked forward to an early night. Even though he was relatively young and in good shape, the warehouse work was something of a physical grind and he was feeling the effects.

He was just settling down to some evening TV when the phone rang.

"Carl, this is Stan Turner. By any chance, is Cindy with you?" There was a bit of anxiety in his voice.

"No. I haven't seen her since the debate. Is there a problem?"

"We're not sure. I'm over at Hopewell Elementary for the back-to-school night. Apparently Cindy was supposed to be working here but she's a no-show. Her campaign manager was here, going ballistic, calling her all sorts of names. I finally settled him down and he's stormed off. I then tried calling her cell but there's no answer."

"I don't know, Stan. As you probably know, the debate did not go well. Maybe she just needs to be alone."

"You might be right. If she shows up, could you let us know?"

"Of course."

After hanging up, Carl reflected on the situation. Should he be doing more to find her? He did have the phone numbers for a few of her girl friends. He also had Steve's number. Steve was probably the one she would most likely be with, if they were trying to resuscitate her campaign. Should he call him? They were not exactly best buds but if Cindy was with him, then at least there would be no need to worry. But then again, he had been at the school where she had failed to show so…

The doorbell rang.

Carl hurried to the door and opened it.

"I need a friend."

"You've got one. Please come in."

# 46

## Thursday evening, 7:30 p.m.

As Cindy came into the light, Carl was struck by the toll that the campaign had taken on her. The shadows under her bloodshot eyes testified to her lack of sleep and her breath smelled of tobacco. But beyond the physical signs was her air of emotional exhaustion. Carl could not recall anyone looking so defeated. He led her over to the couch where they could sit and talk.

"Can I get you anything?"

"I don't know. Maybe a glass of water."

Carl went to the kitchen to draw the water. He also dispatched a text to Stan, "She's here." He returned to the living room with the water.

"You saw it? The debate?"

"Yes. I was there."

"What did you think?"

"I've seen you do better."

Cindy laughed. "No shit, Dick Tracy."

She turned serious again. "So what should I do now?"

"You know I can't answer that."

And so it began. They talked. Mostly it was Cindy. Her ambitions. Hopes. Dreams. Fears. Regrets. And every once in a while, "What should I do now?"

Whatever her choice, there would be consequences that mattered. To people who had invested in her campaign, with money or time or trust. To her recently found dreams of a political career. To a public that deserved to be well represented. To her own sense of self-worth.

It was not Carl's place to nudge her in any one direction. He was simply there to help her discern what was on her mind and in her heart. The minutes became hours. And then gradually, and at times painfully, it came into focus. What she needed to do.

At last, it was time for her to leave. "Are you sure you're all right," he asked as they walked to the door.

"I am now," she said. "And thank you for being here. I'll never forget this, as long as I live."

"Do you want me to come with you?"

"No, I need to do this on my own."

With a parting hug, she left. She got into her car and turned on the engine.

*Is it 10:00 p.m. already? A little late to be making social calls. Still it has to be done.*

As she drove to her destination, she went over the little speech that she had been formulating in her mind. She wanted to do this right. To say the things that had to be said.

It took about twenty minutes to reach her destination, a modest rambler located at the end of a quiet side street. By this time she had her speech memorized.

She went up the walkway to the front door. A light was on in one of the windows. She rang the doorbell.

A good thirty seconds passed. She was about to ring the bell again when the door opened.

"Cindy?"

"Good evening Stan. May I come in?"

"Of course. We were worried about you but then Carl texted us and—"

"Who is it, Stan?"

"It's Cindy," called Stan, turning to one of the bedrooms. Then back to Cindy, "She's just finishing putting the boys to bed. Can I get you anything?"

Cindy shook her head.

*The speech. The speech. The things I need to say.*

"Down at last," said Valerie as she briskly entered the room. She stopped and looked intently at her sister. "Cyn, are you all right?"

She tried to remember the speech, but the lines weren't there. It had all become a jumble of words, feelings, and emotions. Stepping forward, with tears in her eyes and a lump in her throat, she said the first thing that came to mind,

"Val, I would be ever so grateful if you would allow me to work on your campaign."

And in an instant they were together. Hugging and crying and laughing and talking, all at the same time. And the years of distrust, disappointment, pettiness, and envy seemed to melt away as if they had never occurred.

Stan emitted a slight cough.

"I'll be in the next room watching TV, if anyone needs me."

No one did.

# Part Three

## The Rover

# 47

## Saturday, October 10

***Democratic Candidate Quits Race***

*By J.C. Styles, Washington Herald*

*The contest to fill the empty seat on the county Soil and Water Commission took an unexpected turn today as the Democratic Party endorsed candidate, Cynthia Phelps, announced the suspension of her campaign.*

*"I wish to thank all those who invested their time, effort, and money into my race," said Ms. Phelps. "Unfortunately, it has become abundantly clear to me that my continued candidacy would not serve the interests of either the county or myself." When asked by reporters to be more specific, Ms. Phelps declined to elaborate. It is believed, however, that a contributing factor may have been this week's candidate forum where commentators have described her performance as, at best, "uneven."*

*Ms. Phelps declined to endorse either of her rivals, Republican Frederick Rawlins or Independent Green Everett Diesel. "I have great respect for both of them," Ms. Phelps indicated. "They are persons of substance who deserve to be given full consideration." When pressed by reporters, she indicated that she would be casting her own personal vote for the Soil and Water Commission by writing in the name of George Mason doctoral candidate, Howard Morgenstein. "I have had the opportunity to get to know Mr. Morgenstein over the past few months. His encyclopedic knowledge on environmental matters, coupled with his passion for the cause, is remarkable. He would be a tremendous asset to the Soil and Water Commission and I hope that sometime in the future he would agree to be a candidate. In the meantime he has my write-in vote."*

*"Phelps' early exit from the race, while rare, is not unprecedented," said General Registrar Gordon Carruthers. "In terms of election administration, nothing has changed. The deadline for modifying the ballot has long passed. Her name remains on the ballot and any votes she receives will be recorded as such."*

# 48

## Sunday, October 11

***Democratic Party Withdraws Endorsement***

*By J.C. Styles, Washington Herald*

*In a remarkable turnaround, the county Democratic Committee has announced the withdrawal of its endorsement of Cynthia Phelps as a candidate for the open seat on the county Soil and Water Commission. This came as a result of a hastily called meeting of the county Democratic committee.*

*"This was a very unusual situation," remarked county Democratic chairman Brian "Biff" Logan. "The contest for the open seat on the Commission occurred very late in the election cycle, due to the untimely passing of Norman Purvis. Ms. Phelps was the only candidate to request the party endorsement and the committee, possibly in haste, decided to endorse her. Regretfully her campaign has failed to meet the party's high standards and the decision has been made to revoke the endorsement."*

*Actually the question of party endorsement became essentially mute earlier in the day when Phelps announced the suspension of her campaign.*

*Logan indicated that the Democratic Party will not be endorsing either of the two remaining candidates in the race. Nor will it associate itself with any write-in effort that may ensue for Howard Morgenstein, an environmentalist who received Phelps' quasi endorsement as a write-in possibility.*

*"While we have great respect for Mr. Morgenstein, we are not about to issue an endorsement based on the recommendation of a failed candidate. Democrats should vote their conscience in this race, confident in the knowledge that this is a position to be held just for a single year. Next November, all three positions on the Commission will be on the ballot and the Democratic Party will field a full slate of exceptional candidates."*

# 49

## Monday, October 12, 2:00 P.M.

Columbus Day meant different things to different people. For many, it was just another workday. For others it was a day of shopping at the mall. For Carl, it meant a three hour stint at an Octoberfest booth as one of the newest volunteers in the "Valerie Turner for School Board" effort. His assignment was simple. Hand out fliers at the Democratic Party booth and when opportunities presented themselves, talk up her campaign.

He had picked up a fresh supply of fliers from their house and was now parking his car in the open field which was serving as the parking lot for the event. He felt a bit out of place seeing so many people dressed in Bavarian costumes. Polka music could be heard coming over the loudspeakers. He got out of his car and walked over to the area where the booths were all lined up.

"Carl, over here."

He looked in the direction of the sound and there was Cindy waving, standing by the edge of the booth which displayed a banner, "Democratic Party." While they had talked a number of times on the phone over the past few days, this was the first time he had actually seen her since "that night." She was sporting a

"Turner for School Board" shirt and looked like she hadn't a care in the world. What a difference a few days made.

"I'm so glad you're here," she said, taking Carl's fliers. She then added in a whisper, "I don't think they like me," motioning to the other people standing behind the Democratic booth.

"Why ever not?" asked Carl.

"Because I've been defrocked by the party. I had to practically swear that I was only here to promote Valerie's effort and not in any way attempting to resuscitate my moribund campaign. So they grudgingly allowed me space here at the edge of the table. Now that you're here, it will be so much better. They'll like you."

"No, they won't. I'm a Republican, remember?"

"Shhh. They don't know that."

Cindy then introduced Carl to the other folks behind the table. They were polite but guarded. Apparently anyone associated with Cindy was under suspicion.

"Anyway, I need to run," said Cindy. "They're having a strategy session over at the Turner house."

"Are you now one of the lieutenants in the effort?"

"Not really. I'm just babysitting the boys."

"Speaking of which. I understand you were also babysitting them the other night."

"Well, yeah. Who told you that? Val?"

"She mentioned it when I picked up the fliers. Just what did you do with them?"

"Do with them? Nothing. We made popcorn and watched a movie."

"What movie?"

Cindy was looking at the ground, nervously shifting her weight from one leg to another.

"I don't know. One of the movies on one of the channels."

"You're not being very specific."

"All right, it was *The Curse of the Haunted Mansion*," said Cindy, throwing up her hands in a gesture of mock surrender.

Carl gave her a raised eyebrow look.

"Oh, come on. Everyone likes a good scare. The boys loved it. Especially the part where the lady falls into the acid pit."

"You didn't think to clear this—"

*"And only the bones remain,"* said Cindy, in an exaggerated creepy voice.

"Well maybe they loved it at nine-thirty. But that wasn't the case at 3:00 a.m. when their nightmares sent them screaming into their parents' bedroom."

A pause.

"Oh. Is Val pissed?"

"Not really. I think she just wrote it off as 'Cindy being Cindy.' But in your quest to become the 'cool aunt' you might want to make sure the parents are on board. You know, the ones who are actually responsible for raising these kids."

"OK. OK. Point taken. Lesson learned. By the way, how is your warehouse work coming?"

"Excellent. We had a great week last week and—"

"I'm glad one of us did."

"...and did not have a single bad test. We have 226 precincts successfully tested, each with two scanners. There are seventeen precincts to go. We should finish them tomorrow. After that we have to construct boxes to hold the ballots for Election Day. We put the ballots in the boxes, place the boxes in the carts, seal the carts, and we're done. We'll be out of there by the end of the week, which is important because next week is when the county trucks start delivering the carts and scanners to the precincts."

"And all those bad tests from two weeks ago have been resolved?"

"It would seem so. They were caused by the bad test decks."

There was a pause.

"You don't seem a hundred percent satisfied."

"Well I should be. I mean they all tested good after we removed the bad test decks...I'm just not absolutely positive that the decks I used in all my unsuccessful tests were the ones that were bad. The Tuesday morning one especially."

"Are you sure?"

"No, I'm not. To be honest, I don't really remember. And the more I think about it, the more uncertain my memory is."

"And they've all tested good since then? Every one?"

"Every one."

"And all your peers seem satisfied?"

"Yes."

"Have you expressed your doubts to anyone? Milton, perhaps?" Milton had been Cindy's rover, the times she had been chief, and they had formed a bond of mutual respect.

"Not really. And I'm not really sure I would call them doubts."

There was silence for a moment. At last Cindy spoke. "I don't know what to say. It sounds like the train has left the station. If they all tested good, I'm not sure what you can or should do. Sometimes we have nagging doubts. Believe me, I know all about nagging doubts. Just hang in there, Carl. And try to be happy. Gotta' go." She leaned over, gave Carl a kiss on the cheek, and went off to find her car.

# 50

## Tuesday, October 13, 7:00 a.m.

"Today's the day we finish the precincts," said Terrence. "Just seventeen precincts to go. Don't rush it though. We have all day."

Carl started working on a precinct with Scott. Slowly. Deliberately. No mistakes. Normally they would have completed testing it in an hour but it was around 8:45 a.m. when they completed their test. No errors. Perfect.

They rolled the cart and scanners to Station Three and then returned to get the next precinct. Scott proceeded to get out the *CreateBallot* machines while Carl powered up the scanners. He ran the first one successfully though the date/calibration sequence and within a few minutes it was ready to vote. He then turned his attention to the other scanner.

"Uh-oh."

"That doesn't sound good," said Scott.

"It didn't come on," said Carl. "No power light. No screen messages. Nothing."

Scott went over and took a look. It was indeed dead.

"Most sincerely dead."

They called over to Michael. He confirmed that the scanner needed to be replaced.

"Fortunately, we have extras. Ten, to be exact. Originally they were going to give ten of our most populated precincts a third scanner, and they were successfully tested for that purpose. But then Terrence decided to hold them back. In case we ran into situations, just like this one."

Michael then rolled the bad scanner into sick bay and came back with a replacement.

"Michael, we need you up front. A shipment has just arrived," called Terrence.

"OK, I'm coming," Michael called back. Then to Carl and Scott, "You need to retest this with the flash drives from the dead scanner but it should work." He then hurried off to the front of the warehouse.

It did work. Both scanners tested perfectly with the appropriate test deck and the ballots Scott had produced on the *CreateBallot* machine. Still it flashed a warning to Carl.

*You can't take anything for granted.*

"We are done. Bring on the next one," said Carl as he turned his attention to the next precinct in line. "I wonder if we're under 'ten to go' yet."

Carl had just powered up the two scanners when Terrence announced it was time for their morning break. After a brief stop at the restroom, Carl joined the rovers at the table. Terrence was clearly excited.

"The ballots have arrived. We can now put them in boxes, load the boxes into the carts, and seal up the carts. We're going to form teams. Scott, you take three others and start making boxes. Milton, you lead another team to fasten the precinct labels to the boxes, as they are made. These labels were printed at the Government Center and tell how many packs of ballots go into each box. Michael, you supervise to make sure the right ballots, whether they're 10th, 11th, or 12th congressional district, go into the right boxes. Brenda, you will lead a team that will put the boxes into the carts, fill out the log sheet, and seal the carts. We'll have this done before you know it."

When the break ended, they all jumped into the effort with enthusiasm. Carl was initially with the team that made the boxes. The prospect of the testing effort finally reaching its conclusion, transformed what normally would have been a boring, mundane effort into a joyous happening. Piles of boxes all around. Labels on boxes. Ballots into boxes. Boxes into carts. Noon seemed to come in no time.

"Don't forget, that we still have those last few precincts to test," said Michael, as they broke for lunch.

Terrence caught himself, red-faced, "Uh-oh. I hope none of you stopped your testing of those last few precincts to make boxes."

An uneasy silence gripped the warehouse.

"My fault for not making it clear," he said. "Right after lunch, finish up those last few precincts. We'll be here tomorrow for one last day, finishing the packing of boxes and general cleanup."

The lunch hour seemed to fly by and Carl was back in the warehouse, ready to finish testing the precinct that had been started several hours earlier. He had been working with Scott, who was now involved in the ballot packing effort, so Carl needed a new partner. That turned out to be George, one of the less experienced rovers. Together they went over to the workbench where the cart and scanners had been since just before the midmorning break. Other teams were working on precincts in the adjoining workbenches but most of the noise in the warehouse came from the teams tackling the various phases of the ballot packing process.

Carl worked the *CreateBallot* machine. It was all so mechanical now. He could do it in his sleep. In the meantime George fed a test deck into each of the scanners.

"Here are the *CreateBallot* cards," said Carl, handing them to George. In a matter of a few minutes George had fed them into each of the scanners. Carl retrieved the test deck and went to return it to the test deck area while George began the process of closing the polls and printing the results. When Carl got back, both printers were pumping out their tapes.

"This one looks good," said George, examining the tapes from one of the machines. He went over to the next one while Carl verified George's statement. He was right. The first tape was good. George was studying the second tape. What was taking him so long?

"Carl, please look at this," he finally said. Anxiously Carl looked over his shoulder. The counts were off. Not by a lot but they were off.

"You voted every ballot," asked Carl. "Each ballot once and only once."

"Of course," said George, taken somewhat aback that a peer would question him.

"I'm sorry. Of course you did," said Carl quickly. "It's just that —"

"After everything," said George, completing the sentence.

"Yeah. Come on, let's break the news to Terrence."

They found Terrence over by the boxes, talking animatedly to Michael. "Five precincts. We're down to five precincts. And here's George and Carl. What do you have for me, guys? Are we down to four?"

"Well, maybe four and a half," said George.

Terrence didn't quite know how to interpret George's statement.

*This is cruel*, thought Carl. *We need to put him out of his misery.*

"We think one of the scanners printed the wrong results," said Carl.

"What do you mean 'think'?"

Carl handed the tape to Terrence. Michael looked over his shoulder.

"He's right," said Michael. "These are not the correct results."

"Damn," said Terrence.

"You voted every ballot?" asked Michael. "Each ballot once and only once?"

"Damn," Terrence repeated

"Yes, we are sure," said Carl.

"Damn." Terrence seemed to be stuck in the moment.

"We need to move beyond that," said Michael to Terrence. "It's just one machine. We still have ten in reserve." Then to Carl, "Remove the flash drive and roll in one of those ten as a replacement."

"Nine," corrected Carl. "Remember we used one to replace the scanner that never came on."

"You mean another one failed this morning," exclaimed Terrence. "Why wasn't I informed?"

"Terrence, machines do fail," said Michael. "That's why we are testing. This is not the epidemic we had earlier. That was caused by the bad test decks. These are just a couple of bad machines."

Carl suddenly had an idea. "Were the machines that failed from Braxton County?"

"You're not on that again?" exclaimed Terrence.

"Let's take a look," said Michael.

They examined each of the two failed machines. Carl still had the master list of Braxton machines, that he had held on to.

"The one that failed this morning was not Braxton," said Michael. "The one that just failed was."

"And we will take it out of service," declared Terrence. "So it doesn't matter if the machine came from Portugal by way of Shanghai. It is out of service. It will not be used. Nothing about it is an issue." He looked at Carl, almost daring him to object.

"All right," said Carl, admitting defeat. "Can you do me one favor? The machine we use to replace this one. Can we just make sure it's not a Braxton machine?"

Michael and Terrence exchanged glances.

"We do have non-Braxton machines in reserve," said Michael.

Terrence sighed, "All right. It's ridiculous, but I guess, we can indulge you on this one. Michael give them one of the non-Braxton machines for them to test."

Carl wasn't sure why he had insisted. Whatever machine they would get would have to be tested. Nonetheless, this small concession did make him feel better, a feeling that was confirmed thirty minutes later when it's test results were perfect. Now it really was four precincts to go.

# 51

## Wednesday, October 14, 7:25 P.M.

"Turner for school board," said Cindy as she thrust the flier into the hands of the lady who was just about to ascend the stairs to the East County Civic Auditorium.

*Talk about resiliency*, thought Carl, in admiration, as he watched her handing out fliers for her sister's campaign. Here she was, back at the very location where one week ago her own campaign had crashed and burned, acting as though nothing had happened.

He looked down at his cell. It was 7:25 p.m. The school board portion of the evening's local candidate forum was about to begin. It was the second and final forum that had been scheduled.

Cindy crossed over from the other side of the walkway.

"Carl, I'd like to go in and watch the school board debate," she said. "Valerie needs supporters in the audience to counter-balance those obnoxious Hayes people. Can you man the fort out here for the next forty-five minutes or so?"

"You bet," said Carl, taking her supplies. While PR had never been Carl's strong suit, he had become fairly comfortable handing out the fliers, thanks to the time spent at the back-to-school nights. Cindy skipped up the stairs and into the auditorium as Carl turned back to his mission. A few yards from him was a middle aged man, distributing materials for Hayes. They had been intermittently glaring at each other for the past twenty minutes or so.

*We need to be at least civil*, thought Carl.

He walked over to the man. "Could I have one of your brochures?"

The man eyed Carl suspiciously but handed him one. He made no reciprocal request.

"Thank you," said Carl. "Well…uh…have a pleasant evening."

The man smiled faintly and nodded. He then returned to his mission.

Carl continued handing out his fliers. It seemed like more people were walking through those doors than had been here the week before. Most folks accepted the fliers from both campaigns. They wanted to read about both sides. That's why they were here. Most of the Hayes partisans had come earlier, probably so they could get front row seats.

As the minutes passed, the number of people coming up the walkway steadily declined. Carl however remained at his station until he was reasonably certain that there was no one left. He then went up the stairs and entered the auditorium.

There were more people in the auditorium than there had been the previous week and it was also a more animated gathering. People from the audience were shouting at the stage and one another.

"…and I ask you Ms. Hayes, one more time, with a plain 'yes' or 'no', do you support the bond issue that is on the ballot?

The bond issue that will finance the renovations of six different schools. Schools that you claim to care about."

More shouts from different parts of the auditorium. Carl spotted Cindy, sitting in the last row, He took the seat next to her and handed her the unused fliers.

"Val's kicking butt," said Cindy, excitedly.

"I don't think it's that simple—" Ms. Hayes began.

"It's not that simple because the Neanderthal cheapskates who run the Republican Party refuse to acknowledge that quality education costs money."

Staunch Republican that he was, Carl began to slouch lower in his seat.

"There you liberals go. Just throw more money at the problem—"

"Have you been to Schuyler elementary? Have you? What should be an athletic field is littered with trailers. Why? Because five of the classrooms have been designated as unsafe. But you and your Republican friends don't care about that, because it's not in your part of the county."

Cheers from parts of the audience.

"Go get 'em, girl!" shouted Cindy.

"Does she really need to keep saying 'Republican?'" asked Carl, weakly.

The debate continued in a similar way. Carl was seeing a side of Valerie that had been hinted at when they had their discussion in the courthouse cafeteria during the past summer, but had been absent ever since. Ms. Hayes' supporters were still vocal but in the face of Valerie's strong performance, their intensity seemed greatly diminished.

The debate ended at 8:30 and Cindy and Carl went forward to congratulate Valerie on her showing.

"Thank you, Carl," said Valerie, giving him a brief hug. "That was fun."

It was the first time that Carl had seen Valerie when she was really enjoying herself, and at that moment you could tell that she was indeed, Cindy's sister.

"How is the warehouse going," Cindy asked Carl, as they were walking up the aisle to the rear of the auditorium.

"We're done," said Carl. "All precincts tested. Two scanners for each precinct. Nine scanners will remain in the warehouse as back-up. We finished packing all the ballots in boxes today and they are in the carts. Carts are sealed. Next week, the delivery trucks roll."

"And there were no more testing errors?"

A pause.

"Well actually, we did have one yesterday. One of the scanners printed bad results. But it was replaced by another scanner which tested great. So every machine that will be in the field on Election Day has tested good. Everything is OK. Perfect."

Cindy looked intently at Carl, but said nothing.

"I said, everything is fine," Carl repeated. "Stop trying to unnerve me."

Cindy laughed. "I'm not trying to unnerve you. Congratulations. I know you put a lot of yourself into that effort."

"Thanks. And thanks for listening to all my doubts and concerns over the past couple of weeks. Come on, I'll walk you to your car."

Cindy shook her head. "You go on, Carl. I need to stay here."

"You mean for the Soil and Water debate?" asked Carl, incredulously, looking over to the stage where Frederick Rawlins and Everett Diesel were taking their seats. "I would think that would be the last thing you would want to see."

"I can't explain it but I feel like a part of me is still on that stage. Don't worry, I'm fine and I'm at peace with everything, but I just really want to be here. Does that sound strange?"

Carl considered. "No stranger I guess, than me obsessing over a bunch of machines that have all tested good." This was apparently part of her healing process and needed to be respected.

As he left the auditorium, Carl contemplated what was ahead. The warehouse testing was indeed over. He'd be doing a bit of campaigning for Valerie in the next few days and then next Monday he would start a two week stint working at the in-person absentee location at the Center Grove Community Center. Once that wrapped up, it would be only a few days to Election Day when it would all be resolved.

# 52

## Wednesday evening, 9:30 p.m.

Cindy had told only half the story when she opted to stay behind. Yes, she wanted to see the debate. But she had also spotted someone in the audience. Someone she wanted to talk to.

The debate itself was a mannerly affair, quite a bit different from the week before. At one point she caught Frederick Rawlins' eye and gave him a smile and a little wave. He smiled back. But he was not the person she wanted to talk to.

At the conclusion of the debate, she walked over to the side of the auditorium where a group of four or five individuals were talking animatedly. From a respectful distance, she could tell that they were talking politics. Elections: past, current, and future. At last their conversation ran its course and they broke up and headed for the exit. Cindy waited for a few moments and then proceeded to the exit herself.

Once in the parking lot she took note of where her car was, but deliberately went in a different direction. To where a man stood, who had just opened the door of his car.

"So are you going to completely ignore me?"

"Does it matter?" said Steve. He sounded bitter. "You didn't even have the guts to tell me you were dropping out. I had to read it in the damn newspaper."

"I was afraid. Afraid you'd change my mind."

"I put all that effort into your campaign. What a waste. You could have won, you know. No one pays attention to those debates. You could have won if only you would have had the courage to get back off the mat and keep on going. But no, your precious little ego was bruised."

"I did what I felt was right—"

"You keep saying stuff like that. But no, you simply took the coward's way out. You were afraid of losing, so you gave up."

*Yes, Steve. I was afraid. But not of losing. I was afraid of winning. I think Carl may have understood toward the end, and possibly Howard. But you never would.*

"And you would have had such a great future if you had just been willing to hang in there. You would have won. Party registration would have pulled you through just like it will for your sister. She's going to win even though she's the dullest thing on the face of the planet—"

*Whack!* It happened so fast. It was the last thing Cindy thought she would ever do. She looked down at her open palm, amazed by what had just occurred.

"I'm sorry. I don't know what came over me."

"I suppose that made you feel better."

She suddenly felt the need to conclude the encounter.

"I wasted your time, Steve. And for that I am truly sorry. I hope that in time, you won't judge me too harshly."

She turned around and quickly walked away.

# 53

## Monday, October 19, 1:30 p.m.

Monday. A new week. A new assignment.

As he turned onto the street which led to the Center Grove Community Center, Carl was struck by the large number of signs that populated the roadway. Many were signs announcing the time and hours for in-person absentee voting at the center, signs that Carl had helped put up the day before. Others were signs for the various candidates. It was indeed a colorful display.

It was 1:30 p.m. when Carl pulled into the parking lot of the community center. This location was referred to as a "satellite" in-person absentee site, to distinguish it from the county's primary site at the Government Center. This would be the first day of his two week stint at "in-person absentee" voting. Voters with a "good reason" were allowed to vote early. Reasons included being away at college, being a first responder, military deployment, disability or illness, being an election officer, or just being out of the county for any reason whatsoever.

As he proceeded up the walkway toward the front door, he could tell that party and candidate operatives had been hard at work. Additional campaign signs had been pounded into the ground promoting the major party candidates for the U.S. Senate and House of Representatives. The local races were also represented.

*"Turner for School Board"*

*"Hayes for School Board. Time for a Change"*

*"Rawlins for Soil and Water"*

*"All aboard with Diesel"*

Candidate surrogates were also out in mass, trying to interest voters with their brochures and fliers. And in one case, it was the candidate herself.

"Hi Carl," said Valerie. "Can I interest you in wearing my badge?"

"Not today, I'm afraid," said Carl. "I'm in my 'official mode.'"

"Understood. But before you go in, I want to show you something."

Valerie went over to the side and pointed to a homemade sign that had been pounded into the ground, next to the others.

*"Howard Morgenstein. Write-in for Soil & Water"*

"Some George Mason students put this up about twenty minutes ago. They said they would be back, but in the meantime they asked if I'd be willing to give out these fliers, along with my own." She showed Carl some pages that had obviously been run off at a copier store.

"Does this mean he is an active candidate?" asked Carl.

"I don't know," said Valerie. "I called Cindy at work to see if she knew anything, being as this whole thing was her brainchild. She denied any knowledge but I'm a bit skeptical."

"So are you going to distribute his fliers?"

"Sure. Why not? He seems like a well-qualified person."

"You don't think the Democratic Party would object to one of its candidates handing out fliers promoting an unauthorized candidate?"

Valerie laughed. "What can they do? Disown me like they did Cindy? I doubt if they want this to go down as the election where the Democratic Party dumped its entire local ticket. I'll take my chances."

This was all very interesting but Carl had to get into the community center to help get things ready. The supervisor at Center Grove was Scott, one of Carl's fellow rovers, while an elderly lady named Mildred was the assistant. The other eight officers were people who Carl was unfamiliar with. They were all friendly, however. From bits of conversation, Carl soon realized that they all served on Election Day as officers in precincts in the immediate area. Two of the officers were sent outside to post the necessary signs while the remainder worked to turn on the equipment.

Carl's experience as a rover made him especially valuable in setting up the scanner and *CreateBallot* machines and helping Scott record the various counters on the scanner. Within a few minutes of 2:00 p.m., they were ready and Scott went outside to announce the opening of the polls.

The rush of voters coming into the room was immediate. But it was different from Election Day. On Election Day, the first voters were those on their way to work. This was an older group of voters. Many appeared to be retired. Some walked with difficulty or with the aid of a walker.

Carl was stationed at the ballot table. He watched as voters got in line at the check-in table where officers with laptops were ready to check them in on the state database. As they completed the check-in process, the officers would point in Carl's direction. Then one by one the voters would come and hand their completed absentee application to Carl. At the bottom of the application was the correct Congressional district. Carl then filed the application and handed them their ballot with the same official instructions:

"This is your ballot for the 12th congressional district. Be sure to fill in the ovals for your selections in their entirety. Not just a check or an 'x.' Use one of the pens in the booths. The last thing you do is insert it into the scanner."

It was the same statement to each voter. The only modification would be if the voter was in the 10th or 11th district.

There was an initial crush of voters that lasted for about an hour. At that point, things eased up considerably. A couple of hours later Scott rotated assignments and offered people a chance to take a break or to actually vote, if they wanted to. Carl thought, yes, he might as well get it over with.

He filled out his application. His reason for voting absentee was listed as "officer of election." All election officers whether serving "out of precinct" or not were allowed to vote absentee. He went through the steps and received his ballot.

He quickly filled in the ovals for the Republican candidates for Senate and House of Representatives. He then looked down at the bottom of the ballot and saw the school bond issue. As far as he was concerned, Valerie had made the sale. He filled in "yes" on the bond issue.

Now to the local candidates. School board. Carl had read Janet Hayes' brochure and he felt she had made some valid points. But her supporters were so obnoxious. Perhaps some other time he might consider her but this was Valerie's year. He filled in the oval next to her name.

That left the race that had claimed so much. In time. In money. In emotion.

He gazed at the choices:

Everett Diesel

Cynthia Phelps

Frederick Rawlins

Write-in

Who was the best choice? Do you use your vote to help chose a winner or do you use it to "send a message?" Do you go with the candidate you have been committed to for months? Or do you go to where that candidate now points? Or do you return to your own political instincts? Who would have thought that a choice for the Soil and Water Commission would be so complicated? For a moment Carl was tempted to throw them all over and go with something simple and concrete. Like the guy who likes trains.

*Well, I've got to vote for someone. It's not like the fate of the world depends on this.*

Carl finished marking his ballot and took it over to the scanner.

The rest of the afternoon and early evening went smoothly. It was about thirty minutes before closing, when Cindy entered the voting room. From his position by the scanner, Carl could see she was wearing two badges. One was a large professionally made badge that read "Turner for School Board" while the other one was a homemade affair that Carl was unable to make out from a distance.

She went through the process quickly and eventually made it over to one of the booths to mark her ballot. By this time Carl could tell that the homemade badge read "Morgenstein Write-in Soil and Water." She quickly marked her ballot and walked over to the scanner.

Carl was dying to ask where she got the Morgenstein badge. Was it just something she made up or was there an organized effort going on? For the first time he realized that such an effort might have an impact on how quickly the precincts would close the night of the election. They had discovered in the testing that it could take a considerable amount of time for the scanner to print out all the images of the write-in votes. Unfortunately, as he was on duty, he was severely constrained as to what he could ask or say. Cindy seemed to realize this as she inserted her ballot into the scanner.

He offered her an “I Voted” sticker.

“Why thank you, kind sir,” she said with a twinkle in her eye. Then in a whisper, “I think I just cancelled out your vote. At least for the top two races.”

True to his calling, Carl said nothing but just stepped back to allow her to pass.

# 54

## Friday, October 23, 10:00 A.M.

"So in your rover notebook, you will find your precincts as well as the contact information for the chiefs and assistant chiefs," said Terrence.

Eagerly the rovers turned to the appropriate pages.

"Oh no," cried Brenda. "They gave me that same bozo for Golden. I told the office he was no good. I had to do the whole close by myself last time."

A couple of other rovers started to grumble about their chiefs.

"Let's think positively," said Terrence. "And one thing we can all be thankful for is that the schools will be closed both Monday and Tuesday for parent-teacher conferences. So your chiefs should be able to set up in whatever room works best on Monday afternoon. But remember, parents and teachers will be coming and going so it is important that your chiefs claim those voter parking spaces first thing Tuesday morning."

Carl looked down at his precincts.

*Cooper*

*Chesterbrook*

*Wallingford*
*Danby*
*Manchester 1*
*Manchester 2*
*Seneca Grove*
*Hagerman*
*Happy Acres*
*Carter Run*
*Pikesville*
*Tower*

He then surveyed the names of the chiefs. He was glad to see that Nancy Jordan would be at Chesterbrook. Nancy had been his assistant chief for several years, back when Carl had been chief. She was solid. The only other name on the list that he recognized was Rosemary Pennington, who Carl had worked with in June at Carter Run. She was a high strung, fidgety woman, who did not exude confidence, although in the end she had managed to make it work, with Carl's guidance and encouragement.

Carl caught Milton's eye. Milton had this route previously and no doubt knew who some of these people were. Milton nodded. The two would get together after the meeting was over.

Terrence began the meeting by making note of a couple of route modifications. Milton Ayres have been moved to Route 12, replacing another rover who had retired. Carl Marsden would now handle Route 5, Milton's old assignment.

The chiefs meetings would be the first three days of the following week. Chiefs and assistant chiefs were required to attend one of those sessions. Rovers also, were expected to attend one, so they could understand what was being explained to the chiefs. Rovers should start calling their chiefs in the middle of next week, to ensure that they were on top of things. Rovers who were new to their route should drive it sometime this weekend for familiarization.

All rovers would receive a two-way radio which they would use as the primary communications vehicle to the Command Center. Sensitive information however, was to be transmitted by cell phone. Every rover would be issued two *CreateBallot* machines and two Electronic Poll Books (EPBs) as backup. They were not enough unallocated scanners to issue one to each rover. All rovers would have an iPhone which they should plug into their charger so the Command Center would know where everyone was ("Big Brother rides again," grumbled Brenda). While some of these things would be issued today, many of them would not be ready until the day before the election, necessitating another trip to the Government Center.

In addition each rover would receive their own version of the "kit" and canvas bag that were issued to each of the chiefs, which contained many of the forms and signs to be used on Election Day.

It was a lot to take in and by the end of the meeting Carl's head was spinning.

"Let's see who you got," said Milton.

Carl opened his manual to the page with the precincts and chiefs. Milton rattled off his assessment and impressions.

"I see you have Nancy Jordan at Chesterbrook. She's good but you already know that. The chief at Tower is solid, which is good because that's a tough precinct. It's a high rise and many of the voters live inside the building so the precinct has to have two entrances, one from the outside, and one from the inside. It can be challenging."

"The Happy Acres precinct is in a sprawling retirement community complex. You'll need lots of extra signs. The chief is good but rather demanding. The chiefs at Manchester 1 and 2 are both experienced but have only worked in smaller precincts. They are new to Manchester. The Danby chief is competent but headstrong. She will basically ignore anything you suggest. Hagerman has a first-time chief but she has served as an officer there and I think she's well regarded. Cooper and Wallingford also have rookie chiefs but I don't know anything about them."

Carl was feverously scribbling notes, trying to absorb as much of Milton's "institutional knowledge" as possible. Milton kept on going.

"Pikesville is at a new location, a community center, I believe. The chief is OK but he is new to the site. The Carter Run chief is a Nervous Nelly, but more-or-less competent. And finally there is Seneca Grove. The chief there is a bit of a curmudgeon, who in my opinion has outlived his usefulness and is prone to say things that are not politically correct. However it's a small precinct. Not that difficult."

Milton looked up and gave a big smile. "All things considered, it's an interesting route. I will miss it. Or at least some of it."

Carl returned his smile, but weakly. "Any suggestions as to how I plan my route."

Milton considered. "When you call your chiefs, try to assess who needs help the most. Also try to visit as many of the precincts as possible the day before, to see how the various teams are doing in setting up their room and who might need help."

"On Election Day at 5:00 a.m., go to the precinct that you feel most uncertain about. The Carter Run chief will probably ask you to be there for the opening but don't make any promises. Be especially sensitive to the new chiefs at Cooper and Wallingford. If either seems shaky, go there first. After that it doesn't really matter what you plan because you'll get phone calls that will pull you in all kinds of directions."

Having completed his debriefing with Milton, Carl proceeded to take the kit, radio, and canvas bag to his car. The remaining items would be picked up the day before the election. All the information that Milton had given him had been a bit daunting, but it was also exciting. This is what he had signed up for and Carl was full of anticipation.

# 55

## Sunday, October 25, 3:30 P.M.

"What a friggin nightmare," said Cindy in awe, as she stood next to Carl in the parking lot of Manchester High School.

"Isn't it though," agreed Carl, trying to acclimate himself to the site. The last time he had been here had been on back-to-school night, in the gathering dusk. Now in bright sunlight, it seemed even more garish, more bizarre.

Trucks and bulldozers parked every which way. What looked like a "trailer city" in the northern end of the parking lot. And huge piles of dirt, seemingly everywhere.

"Where do you think the voters will enter?" asked Cindy, bringing Carl back to earth. He had chosen this day to "drive his route," to familiarize himself with the various locations, and come up with a navigation plan. Cindy had invited herself along for the ride. It seemed like a fun way to spend a Sunday afternoon.

"On back-to-school night, they entered by that far door," said Carl pointing toward a door, close to where trailer village began.

"Well I guess they have enough parking spaces," said Cindy as they walked toward the door. "But they're going to need a lot of extra signage to get folks to park their cars back here. What is it, Carl?"

Carl had stopped and was staring intently at the front door.

"I'm trying to remember if there was a ramp up to that door on back-to-school night."

"Well there sure isn't one now."

What they saw was three steps that led up to the door. It was completely inaccessible for a person using a walker or wheelchair.

"What do you know about the chief?"

"Two chiefs. They split this precinct in half this past summer. It had grown too large. Milton says that each of the chiefs is experienced but at much smaller precincts. This is their first time working at Manchester."

"And you'll call them when?"

"I'll start calling Wednesday morning, after the Monday/ Tuesday chiefs meetings have been completed. I have twelve precincts and I need to talk to them all."

"Well I would put the Manchester duo at the top of your list. This will be a tough nut to crack."

They returned to the car. Twelve precincts in eleven locations. They had visited all but two that afternoon. The two exceptions, Chesterbrook and Cooper, were well known to both of them.

"So now that you've seen them all, what do you think?" asked Cindy.

"Most of the schools seem straightforward enough. Wallingford, Danby, Seneca Grove, Hagerman, Carter Run," he started checking them off. "Assuming that the folks at Carter Run give us better support than they did in June."

"And the others?"

"That's where it gets dicey. That new community center at Pikesville is probably OK, but I understand that several different constituencies use it, so that could get a bit tricky. Happy Acres is like a little campus. Lots of signs will be needed, especially for voters who don't live within its gates. And there's Tower, which is so different from all the others."

"Because it's a high rise?"

"Partially. But also the entrance. That long, downward sloping, walkway with concrete walls on either side. Definitely strange."

"And then there's this place."

"Right. And then there's this place. And a week from Tuesday, it all has to come together."

Cindy looked fondly at Carl and smiled. "You really love this shit, don't you?"

"Sure. Of course. Who wouldn't? Are you sad to be missing it? Not being an election officer, that is?"

"A little bit," she admitted. "But I'll be busy that day. I'll be handing out brochures for Valerie at a number of locations. And fliers for Howard as well."

"Just out of curiosity. Are you at all involved with this little boomlet that seems to be happening for him?"

"Not really. It's mostly kids from the college. I told them they could use my name if it would do them any good and I've updated my campaign website to reflect that I now support him. Val has done the same thing. Howard of course, has nothing to do with it. He'd be really good on the Commission though. Well, at least he's got two votes."

"Two votes?" asked Carl.

"Yeah me and …" started Cindy. Her eyes narrowed as she surveyed Carl's blank countenance. "You did vote for him. Didn't you?"

Carl hesitated. "You realize that we have a secret ballot in this country?"

"Yeah, I know, 'Four score and seven years ago' and all that. Now tell me, who did you vote for?"

Carl sighed. "I voted for the candidate who I committed to months ago."

"That was a dumb-ass thing to do," said Cindy. "That candidate tanked. She imploded on stage, in living color, before a live audience. You were there. Her candidacy was a complete disaster."

"I don't disagree, but I voted for the person, not the candidate."

Carl started the car and maneuvered it out of the parking lot, making a left turn onto the street. For a few minutes they were silent.

"Thank you for saying that," said Cindy at last, breaking the silence. "Sometimes, I forget."

# 56

## Tuesday, October 27, 10:00 A.M.

"AND WE ARE happy to have two of your rovers here this morning. Milton Ayres and Carl Marsden, please stand and give the folks a wave." The registrar was on the home stretch of the Tuesday morning chiefs meeting, one of several that had been scheduled over the past two days.

"And finally, before we conclude we will have everyone stand and we'll swear you all in. Please rise and repeat after me."

Carl had already taken the oath twice, first at the warehouse, and then at the first day of in-person absentee voting. *Third time's the charm,* he thought as he got to his feet.

"I do solemnly swear (or affirm) that I will perform the duties for this election according to law and the best of my ability and that I will studiously endeavor to prevent fraud, deceit, and abuse in conducting this election."

With that, the meeting broke up as the chiefs proceeded out of the meeting room and up the stairs to the elections suite where they would pick up their "kit" of supplies for the election.

"Excuse me, Mr. Marsden?" It was a middle aged woman with a deferential manner.

"It's Carl. Can I help you?"

"I'm Marianne Tomkins. The chief at the Wallingford precinct. I believe you're my rover?" It was more a question than a statement.

"Yes, I am," said Carl. "And I'm so glad to meet you. This should be a great Election Day."

"Yes, of course. But the thing is…I have never been a chief before. I said I would do it but now I'm not so sure. I've been an officer a few times…" Her voice trailed off.

"And you'll do just fine," said Carl in his most reassuring voice. "Just start by reading the manual. You don't have to memorize it but make sure you understand it and are comfortable with it. Then call your officers in the next couple of days to make sure they can serve and also call your school to arrange the Monday visit. Let me know when you will be setting up on Monday. I'll try and be there."

Marianne listened intently but said nothing.

"Then call me in a few days if any problems come up. Or if you just want to talk. You're not in this alone. Your assistant chief has the same manual that you do. And I'm just a call away."

They continued to talk and gradually Marianne seemed a bit more confident. Yes, she knew where the school was, although it was not where she regularly voted. She would be serving "out of precinct."

Carl remembered the first time he was chief. It had seemed overwhelming but he had made it through the day, albeit with a few rookie mistakes. She would feel better once she made contact with her fellow officers. Milton did not mention this as being a "problem precinct" so Carl was not especially concerned. Marianne was a bit on edge, but that was not necessarily a bad thing. It was the cocky veterans who sometimes ran into trouble.

# 57

## Wednesday, October 28, 3:50 p.m.

Carl was late. Well, not really. Scott had said, "Don't worry about it." Well that was all well and good but Carl did worry about it. He was late.

Up until now he had been able to juggle his time so he could to do his rover work and still fulfill his project assignments with Software Solutions, the company that Carl had to remind himself paid the bulk of his bills. It had involved some very late nights but he had been able to pull it off. Until now.

"You have to get that documentation in today. No more slippage," his boss had told him.

Well, they got their documentation, but it meant that he would be late for in-person absentee voting by a couple of hours. It was just a few minutes shy of 4:00 p.m. when he pulled onto the street which led to the Center Grove Community Center. Almost immediately, he had a sensation that something wasn't quite right. Something was missing. And then he realized.

They were gone. All gone. The official election signs announcing the location and hours of operation of the polling site. Also gone were the signs for Valerie Turner and Janet Hayes. For Frederick Rawlins and Everett Diesel. For the various Senate and House candidates. Vote "yes" on the bond issue. Vote "no" on the bond issue. They were all gone.

Carl drove his vehicle slowly as he approached the entrance to the community center trying to figure out what had happened. Had voting been moved to a different location? They did have procedures for doing that, in the event of a fire or earthquake or whatever. But then there would be some sort of sign directing people where to go. Here there was just…nothing.

He pulled his car into the parking lot and scanned the area by the front door. The usual signs that he had become used to seeing were in place here. But why were they missing from the highway? He left his car and walked back out to the sidewalk. And there he saw it.

It was parked on the opposite side of the street, about fifty yards down the road in the opposite direction from which Carl had come. A big county pickup truck. And there in its cargo area, piled high, were what looked like signs. A group of men, all wearing bright orange vests were pulling up what appeared to be the last of the Everett Diesel signs from the roadway and throwing them unceremoniously into the back of the truck.

Carl was horrified. So horrified that he was tempted to run across the street and weave his way through the oncoming traffic to save the signs. To save democracy.

He took out his cell phone and dialed Scott.

"What is it, Carl? Are you coming in soon? We could sure use you."

"You need to come outside right now. They're taking our signs."

"What are they taking? Who?"

"The signs. All the election signs. I don't know. They are men in bright orange vests."

Just then there was a break in the traffic and Carl ran across the street.

"Stop. Stop", he called, running to the truck. "Put back our signs."

A man jumped out of the truck, holding up his hands. He was wearing a brown sheriff's uniform.

"Stay back, mister," he was saying. "They're just earning their freedom."

"Those signs are for the election," Carl was saying. "You can't just take them away."

The man approached Carl. He was a large individual and walked with the swagger that comes with authority. His badge identified him as Clifton Swinks, Deputy Sheriff.

"We are on a mission," he explained. "These men behind me. They have all…let's just say…have had some encounters with the law. As part of their release program they have been charged to go out into the neighborhoods and remove trash and anything else that detracts from the beauty of our highways."

"What's going on? Why are these signs being taken away?" It was Scott, slightly out of breath, who had arrived just in time to hear the last part of the man's remarks. Mr. Swinks saw Scott's county ID around his neck and that seemed to make an impression. Carl realized at that moment that he had left his ID in his car. Better let Scott handle it.

"The men all agreed that these signs were eyesores," said Deputy Swinks, addressing Scott. "Doesn't everything look nicer with them gone?"

"That may be," said Scott. "But these signs are part of the democratic process and they have the right to be here. You need to put them back." Then to Carl, "Thanks, I've got this covered. We're a bit understaffed inside the center, so if you can get back there, it would be great."

Having done his bit to save the signs, Carl took his leave, happy to have Scott handle the situation.

When he entered the voting room, he quickly understood what Scott had been saying. With Election Day less than a week away, more and more citizens were taking advantage of the in-person absentee option and there was a fair sized line at the check-in table. The assistant supervisor saw Carl and smiled, pointing to one of the empty laptops at the check-in table.

Carl spent the next twenty minutes, checking in voters. Scott returned to the voting room.

"The signs have all been returned to their rightful place," he said. "The thing is, though, the street did look a lot nicer with them gone."

*Perhaps,* thought Carl. *But Democracy by its nature is messy, not pretty.*

# 58

## Wednesday Evening, 9:00 P.M.

"I would really like it if you could be at Carter Run for the opening," said Rosemary Pennington. Her voice had an almost pleading quality.

*Just like Milton said.*

"Rosemary, I will be there if I can and I'm a phone call away if I'm needed. But if you recall, we were together in June and it went well. Just follow the manual like you did then. And make sure they give you an actual room this time. School will be closed that day so there is no reason for us to be stuck in the lobby."

Rosemary agreed and with a few nervous sighs on her part, they ended the call.

The phone rang.

"Hello."

"Hello. Is this Carl Marsden? I'm Patty McGrath, your chief at Happy Acres. I'll tell you what I told the office. We'll need lots of extra signs there. At least sixteen. It's a very complex location with entrances off two main streets. Really they shouldn't be using it for voting. There's a church a mile down the road which is so much better."

For the next fifteen minutes, Ms. McGrath continued to expand on the needs at Happy Acres and the failure of the county to understand. Carl tried to assure her that he would get additional signs from the Government Center on Monday and put them in place.

*At least she seems on top of the situation,* thought Carl, as they completed their call.

Carl looked down at his list. The Chesterbrook, Danby, Hagerman, Pikesville, and Tower chiefs had all been home and they had had good discussions. The Hagerman chief was new but she sounded like she had a good grasp of things. The Tower chief seemed well aware of the challenges there. And of course, he had already talked to the Wallingford chief at the meeting.

On the negative side, neither the Cooper nor either of the Manchester chiefs had been at home and Carl had left each a message. And the phone number for the Seneca Grove chief had resulted in a strange noise coming out of the receiver. He would have to revalidate that number with the Command Center.

It had been a reasonably good evening with eight out of twelve precincts accounted for.

# 59

## Thursday, October 29

***Late Blooming Candidacy Complicates Race***
*By J.C. Styles, Washington Herald*

*The race to fill the empty seat on the county's Soil and Water Commission has become increasingly more complex with every passing day. A write-in effort, apparently spearheaded by students from local colleges, for George Mason teaching assistant and doctoral candidate Howard Morgenstein has been launched and is seemingly gaining traction. The homemade signs that started populating the neighborhoods last week have increasingly been replaced by professional signs that have the same look and quality as those of the other candidates.*

*The seed for Mr. Morgenstein's candidacy apparently came from a statement made by Cynthia Phelps, when she suspended her own campaign for the seat after a weak debate performance. Ms. Phelps at the time had the endorsement of the county Democratic Party, an endorsement that has since been revoked. It has been reported that many person hours have been spent at the county Democratic office, as volunteers have been crossing out her name on all party literature and fliers. There is no way, of course, to recall the countless party fliers that had earlier been distributed at back-to-school nights and other events. Party personnel fear that Phelps, whose name remains on the ballot, might still receive votes from voters who are unaware of the unfolding events.*

*The apparent beneficiary of all this confusion is Republican endorsed candidate Frederick Rawlins, although at this stage no one is really sure. There has been no polling done for this race as it is for a seat that rarely generates much interest and is frequently not contested.*

*"The inability of the Democratic Party to find a credible candidate leaves the public with no choice but to rally around the Rawlins candidacy," said Republican County Chair Lester Miggins. This would seem to be verified by the usually verbose Democratic Party Chairman Brian "Biff" Logan who when asked, simply reiterated the same terse "no endorsement" that had been previously issued.*

*Observers also wonder if this unsettled situation might provide an opening for Independent Green candidate Everett Diesel. Mr. Diesel could not be reached for comment, although he is scheduled this Saturday to be reading selections from his latest treatise on the transcontinental railroad at a local library.*

*Perhaps the most puzzled person of all is Mr. Morgenstein himself, who has indicated repeatedly that he is not a candidate. When pressed however by reporters as to whether he would be willing to serve if elected, he said, "Of course, I would. No one should turn down a call to serve. But it's not something I am campaigning for. It's not something I want. All my students should be aware that there is a mid-term coming up on the 4th and they would be well advised to turn their attention to that rather than some half-baked political activity."*

# 60

## Saturday, October 31, 8:30 a.m.

*So this is it,* thought Carl as he entered the Center Grove Community Center for the final time of the election season. Saturday. Nine to five. The last day of in-person absentee voting.

"I need to spring two things on you," said Scott to Carl, as he arrived. "First of all Mildred is sick. She won't be here today."

"Oh, I'm sorry," said Carl. "I hope it's not anything serious."

"Some intestinal bug. She didn't look all that good yesterday. Anyway I've talked to the Command Center. For today, you are the Assistant Supervisor. Congratulations."

"All right. Is there anything special I need to know now, that I didn't know before?"

"Only that you are now the primary person to handle curbside voters. Ideally I like to have two officers go out to work with them but, as this is the last day, we will be up to our neck in here, so for the most part you'll be working solo."

The polls opened at 9:00 a.m. and for the first hour or so, Carl worked at the table where the voters filled out their applications, checking them for completeness. There were two other officers as well, working the table which was good because Carl had to be ready to go outside, at a moment's notice, to help those who needed assistance outside.

"We have our phone number posted," Scott had said. "But sometimes helpful party poll workers will see someone that needs help and they'll come in and let us know."

It was about 9:45 when the first "helpful poll worker" entered the voting room. It was none other than Cindy, wearing her badges for Valerie and Howard (no longer homemade).

"A lady out front needs help," she called out to Scott, who pointed to Carl. Carl grabbed a clipboard, voter applications, and some *Request for Assistance* forms and followed Cindy out the door.

"Will you be here all day?" he asked.

"Pretty much. We'll get some breaks, which I suspect is more than you will get," said Cindy. "The green Outback, over there," she added, pointing.

Carl proceeded over to the car, where an elderly lady was seated in the front seat. He tapped gently on the car window. She pushed the control and the window opened.

"I'd like to vote," she said. "The young lady said I didn't need to come in."

"No, you don't. You're fine right here," said Carl. "Now let's get you started on your application."

He gave the lady the application mounted on a clipboard and a pen. She seemed like she knew what to do, so Carl remained vigilant but silent.

"Where it says 'reason for absentee ballot,' what should I say?"

"The reason codes are on the back, ma'am."

She turned the form over and started to study the various reasons for voting absentee.

"Well I'm not going away to college. That was a few years ago." She looked up at Carl and giggled.

"Yes, ma'am."

The rules were that Carl was not allowed to prompt the voter in any way. The voter had to come up with the reason by him or herself.

"I'm just not sure," the lady continued. "I might be visiting my daughter. Or she might be visiting me. I'm not sure."

"Where does your daughter live ma'am?"

"She lives in Opal. About a mile south of the shooting range."

"And you might be out of town visiting her?"

"I think so."

"That sounds like personal business outside the county."

"Yes it does. And here, I see it." The lady turned the form, back over and wrote down the correct code. She proceeded to fill in the remaining information and handed it back to Carl.

"And now I need your ID, if you please."

The lady opened her handbag, located her wallet, and removed her driver's license. The photo on the license matched that of the lady.

"I'll be back in a minute," said Carl, taking the application and license.

He hurried back into the community center and got on the line which was beginning to build. When he got to the front, he handed the license and application to the officer behind the desk.

The officer keyed in the information on the laptop and confirmed the voter. She wrote the Congressional district on the application and returned it to Carl. He went over to the ballot table, where the officer there gave him the correct ballot inside a privacy folder.

Now it was back outside with the ballot, privacy folder, clipboard, and pen.

"Thank you, young man," said the lady, putting away her driver's license, as Carl stepped back to respect her privacy.

The lady started marking her ballot. She seemed to know who she wanted to vote for. Then she stopped.

"He isn't on the ballot. The man I want to vote for is not on the ballot. Morganson for Soil and Water. Where is he?"

This was one of those times when Carl had to choose his words very carefully. "This is the correct ballot. You may vote for any of the candidates listed or you may write in a name. That is your choice."

*Please, I can't say any more.*

"Well I guess I'll write it in where it says write-in," said the lady, slowly.

Carl made a point of staring at the rich cloud cover overhead.

"All right, I'm done," said the lady cheerfully. Carl took the ballot in the folder and gave her an "I Voted" sticker. "I have one last request. Please let me go inside and insert the ballot into the scanner. We want to make sure the scanner accepts the ballot before you run off. Can you stay right here for just a minute more?"

The lady indicated her assent and Carl hurried back to the community center. As he passed Cindy, she said, "I just went in to tell your boss. Three other cars out here need curbside."

Carl hurried into the voting room and went to the scanner. It successfully read the ballot.

Scott called over, "Three more cars. Some of them may have multiple occupants."

"I'm on it," said Carl grabbing a supply of clipboards, applications, and pens.

He hurried out of the building and gave a "thumbs up" to the lady. She smiled, nodded, and proceeded to back her car out of her parking place.

"The white minivan at the end, the red car next to it, and the green Buick right over here," said Cindy.

This was just the start of a long day. Some of the voters, like the first lady, were able to mark their ballot without any assistance but others needed help. One after another they came. The elderly and frail, people on chemo, on oxygen, in wheelchairs, people with Alzheimer's. They just kept coming. There was no help from inside the voting room as the volume of able-bodied voters being processed precluded anyone else working curbside. It was just Carl. People would have to be patient. People would have to wait.

It was however, the sort of day that brings out the best in people. The poll workers from both parties helped, to the extent the law permitted, by informing Carl of the next batch of folks who needed assistance. Eventually Scott was able to free up another officer to help. And they just kept coming. No time for a lunch break. No time for the bathroom. Just voter after voter.

Finally around 4:30 p.m., Scott intervened. "You're taking a break. I need you fresh for the close," he ordered. "Sandra will take the last half hour for you."

Carl took his seat over by the corner of the room. To his surprise Milton was there as well. Milton had been serving for the past couple of weeks as rover to the in-person satellite locations, bringing extra supplies and ballots as they ran out.

"Just about at the end of the road," said Milton, as Carl sat down. "In another half hour, in-person absentee will be history and we can focus on next Tuesday."

"How do you like your new route?" asked Carl.

"I like it just fine," said Milton. "At last I have a route close to my home. Everything looking good with you?"

"It took me a few days but I finally reached all my chiefs but one. I've tried three different numbers that the Government Center gave me but I still can't reach the Seneca Grove chief. I'll try again tomorrow and if necessary drive to the guy's house."

"Is that Hazlet?"

"Yes, Millard Hazlet."

"You may have problems with him. He's been known to run off at the mouth."

"Thanks. That will be something to look forward to."

They sat in silence for a few minutes.

"That certainly was a stressful time we had at the warehouse. With all those bad tests," said Carl.

"Yes, it was," agreed Milton. He paused. It sounded like he wanted to say more.

"But I'm glad we cleared it all up. By identifying those bad test decks."

Milton was silent.

"I mean that was it. They all tested good once we got rid of them," Carl repeated. For some reason it had become very important to hear Milton agree with him.

"That Thursday morning," said Milton, quietly, more to himself than Carl. "The scanner I tested that morning. I could have sworn I was using the 'A' test deck."

"No," corrected Carl. "It was the 'E' or the 'F.' Those were the bad decks. You had to have been using one of those."

Milton looked up at Carl. "Really? I suppose it must have been."

"And of course, none of this really matters. I mean, everything out there tested good. In the end, they all tested good." There was a sense of urgency in Carl's voice.

"I suppose you're right," said Milton. "I don't remember things as well as I used to. Well I need to move on. If I don't see you before Tuesday, have a great day."

# 61

## Sunday, November 1, 6:00 p.m.

Cindy had been deeply moved as she watched Carl tend to all those special needs voters.

"You need a little down time before the big crunch," she had told him near the end of the day. "Come over to my place tomorrow evening. I'll fix us dinner."

Carl gave her a curious look. Cooking was not one of Cindy's strengths.

"OK, it will be take out Chinese," she said. "Or pizza or something. Bottom line is that you will be in combat mode Monday and Tuesday, so a couple of hours without elections on your mind will do you good."

It sounded inviting but that conversation had occurred before Milton's doubts had been expressed, so elections were very much on Carl's mind when he arrived at Cindy's apartment.

"I thought you were going to put the election out of your mind," she said, frowning as she looked at Carl's rover election notebook.

Carl grinned sheepishly.

"Yeah, fat chance that was going to happen," she said, ushering Carl in. "What is on your mind now that can't wait a few hours?"

"It's those scanners. I don't think the bad test decks explain all those bad tests."

Cindy looked at Carl skeptically. "Is this based on new information or just old lingering doubts?"

"I'm not sure," said Carl. "I was talking to Milton late yesterday, and his memory of one of the bad tests sort of mirrored my own. He thought he might have been using one of the good test decks but he just wasn't sure."

Cindy considered. "I tell you what. Let's order some pizza. Then do an hour of mindless TV. At that point, with fresh minds, we will examine this whole test situation in as much detail as you want. Is that a deal?"

One hour later found them sitting on the couch, finishing their pizza, and watching a game show. The 'contestants' were a pair of families that seemed to be spending most of their time shouting at each other.

"I apologize for this," said Cindy. "But sometimes drivel like this helps clear my mind."

"That's fine," said Carl. It felt good to be taking a break.

"So what does tomorrow look like?"

"Pretty intense. It starts at 8:00 a.m. when I get to meet the illusive chief from Seneca Grove, one Mr. Millard Hazlet. I finally got to him by way of the assistant chief. It seems that Mr. Hazlet had decided to disconnect his landline to save money, but never got around to sharing his cell phone with the Government Center. Anyway he and the assistant chief will be at the school at eight and I've decided to join them. Milton has some reservations about him and I want to see for myself."

"At nine I'll be at the Pikesville Community Center for a similar conference. Then I need to get over to the Government Center to pick up my supplies, along with some sixteen extra signs for Happy

Acres. This is followed by putting up those same signs. Then it's over to war-torn Manchester where my two chiefs will be trying to sort things out. Then to Hagerman. New chief. Needs handholding. Followed by Wallingford. New, very nervous chief. Lots of handholding. At that point it will be late afternoon. There are a number of precincts that will be setting up then. Cooper. Danby, Tower. Carter Run. I'll just do what I can. I can't do them all.

"Remember that," said Cindy. "You're there to help the chiefs but ultimately they are responsible. They'll muddle through. Just like I did."

What are your next two days like?"

"Busy, but nowhere near what you're doing. Tomorrow, I'll be handing out fliers at the same supermarket where I got my original petition signatures. Then on Tuesday, I'll be setting up card tables with brochures at the three of the smaller precincts but I won't be staying there. Val wants me to mostly split my time between Manchester and Tower. Those are the two largest precincts in this part of the county. Then win-or-lose, there will be a party over at their house, where I intend to get totally plastered. You're invited, by the way."

"Do you really intend to get 'totally plastered' in front of your nephews?"

"No, of course not. Sometimes…I say things I don't really mean."

"I hadn't noticed," said Carl, dryly. "Anyway thanks for the invite, but I need to get to bed as early as practicable Tuesday night. We have canvass at the Government Center the next day. I'm told it could get rather complex. Normally we don't worry about write-ins if they are in small numbers. We just lump them together. But if there are a significant number of write-ins for any one candidate, as we suspect there will be," he gave Cindy a pointed look, "well that makes things more complicated."

Cindy got the message.

"I really have pissed off a whole lot of people this election," she said, starting to giggle. "Who says one person can't make a difference?"

She then rose and took the dirty dishes back to the kitchen.

"All right, let's get serious. Here's the deal," she said, going over to the table in the dining area, on which lay a laptop, pad of paper, and Carl's rover notebook. "We talk this thing through. Completely. What you know. What you surmise. What you guess. Everything. We take as long as it takes. When it's over you'll either have something you can take to your superiors or you drop the whole thing. And I mean drop it." She looked intently at Carl, daring him to disagree. After a moment, he nodded his head.

"OK," said Cindy. "Tell me what you have."

Carl took out his notebook and opened it.

"Well there were these scanners that gave us incorrect vote totals. We compared them to the test decks we used and they were off. Not by a lot but they were off."

"How many machines are we talking about?"

"OK, let's see. There were eleven."

"Tell me about them."

"The first was Monday afternoon. I was testing with Jack right after lunch. The second one was first thing Tuesday morning. I was testing with Brenda. That was the morning when you were there. Then late that same day, Milton had a bad test."

"Stop right here. You had a theory that the Braxton machines were bad."

"Yes, but that theory was pretty well shot to hell. On two counts. One, the vast majority of the Braxton machines tested fine and two, some of the machines that failed were not Braxton. And don't forget, after we uncovered the bad test decks—"

"I'm not interested in the bad test decks. Not yet, anyway. We've got three bad machines so far. Were they all Braxton?"

"The first one was not. The other two were."

Cindy grabbed a pen and notebook paper and started writing things down. Carl's eyes wandered over to the desk in the corner, where there was a framed photo of Valerie, Stan, and the boys. He had never noticed it before.

"And I believe I recall you saying that you think you might have been using a good test deck for the Tuesday morning test."

"Yes. I wish I could be positive, but that's the one."

"OK, that's Tuesday. Let's move on to Wednesday."

"Wednesday, we had three bad machines. One right after lunch. Then two later in the afternoon. I was testing with Brenda on all of them. No wait, the first one I had begun with Jeannette that morning. Then we had that meeting with the registrar and we finished up, right after lunch."

"And the Braxton breakdown."

"The first one was Braxton. The latter two were split. One Braxton. One not."

"Got it. Now to Thursday."

"That's when it hit the fan. We had four bad tests. First thing in the morning, Milton had a bad test. Then—"

"Is that the one he's had second thoughts, concerning the test deck?"

"That's the one. Then later in the day we had three more. One just before lunch. The other two after. All tested by different people. Brenda, Scott, and myself."

"Were any of those Braxton?"

"The first one that Milton tested. The others were not."

"And then on Friday, you found the bad test decks?"

"That's right."

"How were they bad?"

Carl was seeing a side of Cindy that only rarely came out, a side that her looks, personality, and even ambitions frequently concealed. A sharp analytical mind that could direct its focus onto the essence of a situation and a tenacity to stay with something until it was resolved.

"We had stamped 'test ballot' on each of the ballots in the test decks. But we were sloppy and the words from the 'test ballot' stamp overlapped the, for want of a better term, bar code on the side of the ballot. This somehow confused the scanners into misreading the ballot and tabulating incorrect results."

"And how many corrupted test decks were there?"

"Three. Two for the 12th congressional district and one for the 11th. But to be completely accurate, we never were quite sure about the 11th test deck. The stamp went right up to the bar code but we weren't sure if it truly overlapped. But we threw it out anyway using, as they say, an abundance of caution."

"Without ever testing to see if the deck was actually bad?"

"You're right. We should have," said Carl, squirming a bit in his chair.

"I'm not here to judge," said Cindy, with a faint smile. "And by the way, what was the congressional district break down for those bad tests? Were they all from the 12th?"

"Most, but not all. The machine I tested Wednesday after lunch was for the 11th. And also the one that Milton tested on Thursday."

"OK, so then Friday came. You discovered the bad test decks, retested all the machines, they all tested good, you uncorked the champagne, and headed home for the weekend."

Carl laughed. "That's pretty much it."

"And then the following week, everything tested good until…"

"The very last day of testing. It came late in the day. We had started on it earlier, but there was some confusion and Terrence had us load ballots into boxes before he realized that we still had some testing to do. So it was fairly late in the afternoon when we finished testing it. And the results were bad. That machine was replaced. So we don't really need to think about it."

"Was it Braxton?"

"Yes."

"Was it the $12^{th}$?"

"Yes."

"And that's it?"

"That's it. Eleven machines."

"So, let's see what we have," continued Cindy, looking over her notes. "Eleven bad tests. It looks like six machines were Braxton, five were not. Nine were from the $12^{th}$ congressional district, two from the $11^{th}$. Two of the tests came first thing in the morning. Then there was one just before lunch while the others were later in the day. And there were definitely two bad test decks for the $12^{th}$ and maybe one for the $11^{th}$."

"That pretty much says it."

"Plus," said Cindy slowly, "both you and Milton have at least some doubt over whether you were using a bad test deck for one of those tests."

Carl looked down at the floor. "I wish I could be sure."

"And once you got rid of the bad test decks, they all tested good," said Cindy to herself. "They all tested good, except the one on the last day."

"Which we have taken out of service."

"They all tested good," Cindy repeated. "It keeps coming back to that."

There it was. All on the table. Something didn't seem quite right but what was it? Whatever theory they came up with seemed to have exceptions. Things that were not explained. And always they came back to the same undeniable fact that every machine that left the warehouse to go to the precincts had, in the end, tested good. And the vast majority of them had tested good, right from the beginning. Eleven bad machines out of literally hundreds. And even they weren't bad. Not really. Once you got rid of the bad test decks. They all tested good. They all tested good.

By 11:00 p.m. they were both mentally exhausted. Each had been silent for about fifteen minutes, wrapped in their own thoughts. At last Cindy spoke.

"Carl, I want you to do me a favor. I want you to go home and put this out of your mind. You've given it everything you have and you have two grueling days ahead of you."

"You mean, give up?"

"Yes. Give up. Sometimes that happens. It's not worth agonizing over. Focus on what really matters. You helped me do this, a couple of weeks ago. Now I'm helping you. Get the hell out of here and get some sleep."

And that was it. Cindy practically pushed Carl out the door. She was genuinely sorry she had not been able to help him but mostly she was concerned that his obsessive dwelling on this could do him real harm.

"But they all tested good," were his last words, as he left her apartment.

"Yes, sweetheart. They all tested good."

# 62

## Sunday Evening, 11:00 p.m.

*Well those good intentions sure backfired. He's in worse shape now than when he first arrived,* thought Cindy grimly, closing the door.

She returned to the dining room and gazed at the notes she had made.

*I don't know what the hell is going on here but I can't waste any more time with it. I need to get some sleep.*

She went back to the bedroom area to prepare for bed.

Fifteen minutes later, she was back at the table going over those same notes looking for something, anything.

*Carl is the most detail person I know. And when he is zoned in on this election stuff, he is amazing. If he thinks something is wrong, then there is. And Milton too, was uneasy about this.*

"But in the end, they all tested good," she said softy.

*They all tested good.*

The mantra seemed to be mocking her.

But of course that wasn't quite true. The scanner that they tested on the last day. It failed and they took it out of service. No bad test deck here. It just failed. They all assumed it was just one bad apple. She drew a circle around her entry for that machine.

*What about the others? They were all victims of bad test decks. Or were they?*

She studied her notes one more time.

*For the moment, let's assume Carl's right. That Tuesday morning's machine was running with a good test deck…*

Another circle drawn, this time around the Tuesday morning scanner.

*…and the one Milton had doubts about. That's the Thursday morning one…*

Another circle.

Cindy paused. This was going to take a while. She looked over at her handbag.

*No, I've been doing too much of that lately. Maybe the fridge.*

She went back to the kitchen and returned with a glass and bottle of wine. But before she could pour, something else kicked in her mind.

*Carl was never sold that the 11th test deck was bad. Now which ones were from the 11th?*

She studied her notes again. One of the 11th machines was the one Milton tested Thursday morning. Nothing new here. But the other one was the one Carl tested Wednesday, right after lunch. The one he had started with Jeannette and completed with Brenda.

Cindy drew another circle.

So now we have four scanners, for which there was at least a reasonable probability that their failure was caused by something other than a bad test deck.

Then another thought came to mind.

*When in doubt, go to the internet.*

She opened her laptop and turned it on.

*OK, smart girl, what now?*

*Let's try something. Anything.*

She typed "scanners that fail" and pressed the search button.

There was an article, several years old, about a scanner that sometimes accepted multiple ballots that stuck together. The scanner wasn't made by *ElectionPro* and looked nothing like the scanners that the county used.

"That's not it," said Cindy softly, shaking her head. "Why don't I try…?"

"*ElectionPro* scanners." Press search.

The company website came up. The banner proclaimed,

*ElectionPro, committed to providing a worry-free election experience to all.*

Cindy had to laugh, "Yeah, Right."

*Now that I'm here, what do I look for? Perhaps the specs of the machine. Not that I'd really understand what it says.*

She clicked on "products" and quickly found a picture of the scanner that the county used. There was some specs concerning the dimensions of the machine but nothing about its inner workings.

*This is getting me nowhere. Don't be stupid, girl. Go to bed.*

She took a sip of wine and looked back at her notes. What she saw suggested something. She went back to the search engine and typed just "*ElectionPro.*"

The same company website was the top entry, but she started to scroll down, looking at additional articles. Anything that might yield a clue…

Everything she saw indicated that *ElectionPro* was a highly respected company. There were entries from localities in various part of the country that used their equipment, all with high levels of satisfaction. This mirrored her own memory from the three elections she had served. She couldn't recall a single problem.

Still Cindy plodded on, examining article after article. The wine soon ran out and her head was drooping.

*Is it 2:00 a.m. already? Stupid. Stupid.*

There was an article. It looked like it came from some on-line trade publication. It didn't really feature *ElectionPro* but the company was mentioned.

*Wait just a minute…this is…interesting.*

She activated the print button with her mouse. The printer sprang into action.

*All right, so why don't I search on…*

She looked at the search results. An entry about halfway down.

*Why isn't that…haven't I've seen you before?*

Again, the print function.

Cindy's head was no longer drooping. She was wide awake now, scanning the search results for additional items of interest.

*And what do we have here?*

She pulled up the article and read. Line by line. Her eyes darted back to her notes and the four circled entries. Then back to the article.

"Oh my God," she whispered, as she activated the print function one last time.

# 63

## Monday morning, November 2, 2:30 a.m.

"Hello…Hello."

"Carl, this is Cindy. We need to talk."

"What? What—What time is it? Did I oversleep? Who is this?"

"It's Cindy. It's 2:30 a.m. You did not oversleep but we need to talk."

"Is anything wrong? Are you all right?"

"I'm fine, Carl. But I need you to come over here. There is something I have to show you."

"Can't it wait till the morning?"

"No, it can't. Your schedule is full, remember? And you need to see this. I'd drive over to your place but I've been drinking and probably shouldn't drive for a few hours."

"You've been drinking?"

"Yeah, I needed some stimulation and didn't want to smoke and there was this bottle in the fridge—anyway please Carl, it's late, I know it's late. You still need to come over. Trust me on this."

"Ok. I'll get dressed and be right over."

"Thanks. And Carl, you were right all along."

"Right? About what."

"Those Braxton machines. We have to get them out of there."

# 64

## MONDAY, 2.55 A.M.

CARL GOT DRESSED in record time, grabbed his rover election notebook, and started his car. All grogginess instantly disappeared with Cindy's mention of the Braxton machines. The traffic at 2:45 a.m. on a Monday morning was virtually non-existent and in a matter of minutes he was proceeding up the walkway to Cindy's apartment. She must have been looking for him in the window for the door opened before he had a chance to ring the bell.

"Thank you for coming," she said, ushering him in. With her hair disheveled and barefoot in her UVa sweats, she looked the epitome of a college student pulling an all-nighter, which in a sense is what she had been doing.

"I'd offer you some wine but I drank it all," she said as she pulled up a seat at the table and motioned Carl to do the same.

"We need to go through this slowly," she said. "And I need to you to tear apart my reasoning if you see any flaws."

Carl nodded, solemnly. This was clearly her show.

"Part of our problem is that we had too much data. This whole thing about the test decks muddied the water."

"But they were clearly a problem—"

"Yes, they were 'a' problem but not 'the' problem. Now please be quiet and let me explain."

"But you said you wanted me to attack your reasoning if—"

Cindy shot Carl a look that clearly said, "Don't mess with me."

Once she was satisfied that he would remain silent she continued. "First I isolated the bad results that we could at least strongly suspect were not from the bad test decks. There were four. The one on the last day, the pair that you and Milton expressed doubts about, and the Wednesday one for the 11th district. I've circled them on this notebook page, the one I started hours ago. What do they have in common?"

Carl studied the page. "They're all Braxton machines. But that doesn't prove—"

"Exactly," said Cindy. "Now I want you to try and remember. The Tuesday morning machine that failed. That was the morning I was at the warehouse. I arrived about 8:00 a.m. and it had already had failed when I got there."

"That's right."

"So in less than an hour you did everything. Early morning announcements from Terrence. Rolling the carts and scanners to their work stations. Producing the *CreateBallot* cards. All that date and calibration set up. Grab the test deck. Vote the deck. Analyze the results. All in the hour before I got there."

"Well, yes. I mean, no. Not really. We set up the scanner the day before, just before we left for the day. We do that sometimes."

"And you left the scanner on?"

"Yes. That's not a problem. Terrence locks the cage when we leave so no one can get in and disturb anything."

"Is it possible that Milton did the same thing with the Thursday morning machine that failed?"

"I guess so. You'd have to ask him. What are you saying? That Braxton machines don't like the sunrise?"

Cindy ignored his remark. "And the machine that last day. You said something about how you were loading ballots into boxes and that interrupted your testing."

"Yes, Terrence was so excited that the ballots had arrived that he had us all start loading ballots into boxes without realizing that some of us were still testing. Once he realized that we still had testing to do, he sent us back to complete the test."

Cindy seemed to be measuring his every word. "What about the 11th district machine? The one you started with Jeannette and finished with Brenda."

"Yes, that was the day that the registrar came to give us a talk. It lasted quite a while."

"Which came in the middle of your test cycle?"

"Yes. What of it?"

"Stay with me, Sherlock. Now remember back to the evening when I first told you I was running for Soil and Water. You told me then, that none of the Braxton machines had ever been used in an actual election."

"You remember me saying that?" said Carl, in surprise.

"You said it, didn't you?"

"Yes, but I didn't think you really listened when I start rambling on about election stuff."

"Carl, I listen to everything you say."

There was a pause. Carl seemed taken aback by that simple declaration. Cindy continued.

"Don't you see? Each of the machines that I circled was turned on for an extended period of time. More than what normally occurs in the testing cycle."

"Yes," Carl agreed. "But that's what they're designed to do."

"Now let's turn to the internet," said Cindy, once again ignoring Carl's latest remark. "I've learned a fair amount about *ElectionPro* this evening. Did you know that the *ElectionPro* scanner measures 15 inches by 17 inches by 6 inches and weighs 24.7 pounds?"

"Not really. Does that matter?"

"We'll table that question for a moment. But what certainly does matter is that five years ago *ElectionPro* bought out another company called *VoteSmart.* Don't you love those names?" Cindy reached over to the end of the table and took the first of the printed reports that were piled there.

"I'm not sure where you're headed," said Carl. "Companies buy other companies all the time."

"Check out the part that I highlighted."

Carl took the paper and for a few minutes studied it. "Apparently the purchase was motivated by the desire to acquire some technology that *VoteSmart* had developed."

"Exactly. Next I did a search on *VoteSmart.* And this is what I came up with." Cindy reached over and presented Carl with her second finding.

"That's our scanner!"

"Right again. I looks the exactly the same, except for the logo. Same features, everything. It even measures 15 inches by 17 inches by 6 inches and weighs 24.7 pounds."

Cindy was silent for a moment, allowing everything to sink in. At last Carl spoke.

"You obviously have something else to show me."

She reached over and grabbed the third printed report.

Carl went over it carefully. Very carefully.

"This doesn't prove anything," he said slowly.

"No, it doesn't," agreed Cindy.

"Just because there were instances of these machines overheating when left on for extended periods of time—"

"Like during an election—"

"—which resulted in incorrect vote totals being recorded even though everything else seemed to be working fine..."

They both sat in silence contemplating the situation.

"I'm sure that defect has long been corrected," said Carl.

"Absolutely," agreed Cindy. "*ElectionPro* scanners have been out in the field for several years. Everyone raves about them."

"Could it be," said Carl slowly, "that some of these early machines fell through the cracks and were never upgraded to fix the defect? Then they were purchased by Braxton."

"And Braxton tested them but of course they tested fine," continued Cindy. "But they were never used in an actual election. And then we bought them and here we are."

Again they were both silent, deep in thought.

"What do you think?" asked Cindy.

"I think that you are more of an election nerd than you let on."

"We have you to blame for that," she said, smiling.

"To the matter at hand, this explains our results. But that doesn't mean it's true. As impressive as this research is, it's not going to convince Terrence to pull the Braxton scanners from this election."

"Is there any way this theory could be tested?"

"Actually, yes there is. We purchased thirty scanners from Braxton. Twenty-five were assigned to precincts. Twenty-four are at their locations, as we speak. The twenty-fifth, the one that failed the test the last day, was taken out of service. It's already been discredited so we can't use it in a test."

"There are however nine other machines still at the warehouse that could be used in a test, and five of those are Braxton. Each of those was originally going to be a third scanner for the most populated precincts. When the tests started to go bad, Terrence decided to hold them back in reserve. But they were fully tested and primed for the election. All you need to do is turn them on, enter the election code, and you're ready to vote."

"So someone could turn them on tomorrow morning and then return several hours later and run a test," said Cindy. "Are there any precincts out there where both machines are Braxton?"

"I don't think so," said Carl. "Wait a second. I have that list that Michael made." He reached into his notebook and pulled out a paper and studied it for a moment. He had previously penciled in the precinct names next to the serial numbers. Twenty-five serial numbers had a precinct while the other five were labeled "in reserve."

"This confirms it. No precincts have two Braxton machines."

"So if tomorrow's test confirms our theory," said Cindy. "Terrence or somebody would simply instruct those precinct chiefs to use only the good machine and we'd be home free."

"You're exactly right," agreed Carl. "The challenge is to convince Terrence to run that test. I'm not exactly the person he likes to listen to."

"Well he sure as hell isn't going to listen to me," said Cindy. "You have to do it. It's the only way."

Carl nodded. "I have an eight o'clock at Seneca Grove. I'll call Terrence right after that and see if I can convince him."

They looked at each other. "And I think we are done," said Cindy, getting to her feet. "God, what a night. You need to go home and salvage whatever sleep you can."

Carl nodded, suddenly feeling desperately tired, as the adrenaline rush of the past thirty minutes was beginning to wear off. It had truly been an exhausting night and two very full days awaited him.

# 65

## Monday, 8:00 a.m.

"And that entrance over there, that's where the cripples come in," said Millard Hazlet, chief election officer for Seneca Grove, as he pointed to a side door.

Carl saw the assistant chief wince at Mr. Hazlet's choice of words. While Carl was not one to obsess over "political correctness," this was a bit much.

"Yes I see where the *handicapped* voters would use that entrance," said Carl, "seeing how the *handicapped* voter parking spaces are on the curb, directly outside the door."

"Yeah, that's what I said. Anyway we'll set up the check-in table here, and the scanner over here. And, I don't know, the poll watchers can sit wherever."

"I've drawn up a diagram," said the assistant chief. "Perhaps this might be of some use."

Carl looked at the diagram. "The cafeteria opens directly to the outside. If the line gets too long, people will be standing in line outside."

The assistant chief considered. “This is my first time as an assistant chief but I’ve served here as an officer a number of times. We are a small precinct. I’ve never seen the line get that long. Even for the last presidential.”

Carl was thankful for an assistant chief who seemed both conscientious and capable, even if a bit timid. While this was going on, Millard was ordering one of the custodians in a not too gentle fashion, to start bringing the necessary tables and chairs to the cafeteria.

“You gotta be firm,” he said to Carl. “Once we have the table and chairs in here, we can set up. I’ve already taken the signs out of the cart. They’re over on that table. It was a shame they had to redo all those signs to have Spanish as well as English. If they can’t speak English, they shouldn’t be voting.”

That was it.

“Millard,” said Carl in a tone that he hoped was both calm and firm. “I need you to take care in the choice of words that you use. People might take some of the things you’ve been saying the wrong way.”

“Oh, I know all of that. Don’t worry, I watch what I say in front of the voters. Just ask Milton. We got along great.”

*Milton is the one who warned me about you.*

Carl looked at his cell. Almost 9:00 a.m. He was running behind.

“Very well,” said Carl. “I’ll see you tomorrow. Call me if there are any problems.”

“Yeah. Whatever. Don’t worry. We’re fine,” said Millard, with a dismissive wave of the hand.

Carl exited the cafeteria and went back to his car. He was glad he had come here. He felt that the admonition he had given Millard was appropriate, while at the same time he was reassured that this precinct, with a low voter total and good logistics, would not be a major problem. Provided the assistant chief could keep Millard from straying too far.

Once in the car, he checked the time on his cell. No use trying to postpone it. The longer he waited, the shorter the window of opportunity. He went over one more time the things he needed to say and the order in which to say them. He recalled Cindy's words.

*"You have to do it. It's the only way."*

He dialed Terrence's number.

# 66

## Monday, 9:00 a.m.

"No. What you're suggesting is outrageous. Our testing is complete. Everything tested good and we are ready for Election Day. We are not going to revisit this just because of some harebrained theory that you dreamed up."

"But don't you see, that explains the bad test results—"

"We have an explanation. The bad test decks. We don't need to look at things that happened over five years ago to a handful of machines made by a different company. You've allowed this ridiculous Braxton theory to obsess in your brain. Well let me bring you down to earth. We have a very challenging election tomorrow. And you have serious responsibilities and challenges. I know about the construction mess over at Manchester. That high-rise at Tower is always a challenge. You've got three first-time chiefs who need your support. You have a responsibility to the county to focus on the precincts that need your undivided attention and drain that other crap from your mind. Is that understood?"

In the face of such a withering reprimand, Carl felt no choice but to yield.

"Yes, sir," he said meekly.

"Very good. And when this election is behind us, we can discuss whether your continued service as a rover is in our mutual best interest."

*I guess that's it,* he thought after hanging up. He felt bad that Cindy's research had come to naught and he felt bad that there was now a risk that some twenty-four precincts would be tabulating incorrect results. But in one sense, Terrence was right. He had a lot on his plate and he could not afford wasting time revisiting battles that had been fought and lost.

He quickly texted Cindy.

*We lost. Terrence said no.*

Carl started the car. He needed to get to the community center at Pikesville where the chief was presumably setting up.

His cell buzzed.

*McDonalds on Carter Rd. Noon.*

# 67

## Monday, 9:45 a.m.

It was a twenty minute ride over to the community center at Pikesville. With weekday traffic, it was not nearly as easy as it had been the previous Sunday. He might want to reevaluate the way he would drive his route. Carl parked his car and preceded to the front door. The volume of cars in the parking lot indicated that it was a very busy facility. He entered and went to the front desk.

"Where will the election be?" he asked the man at the desk.

"Empire Room," said the man, waving his hand in the direction of a hallway. Carl proceeded down the hallway and easily found the designated room. There was an elderly couple, setting up tables. Carl checked his list to confirm the names.

"Would you be Jessie McComber?" he asked.

"That's me," said the man. "Doris over there, is my wife and assistant chief. Except in real life, she's the chief." He gave Carl a wink.

"How's everything look?"

Jessie walked over to Carl. "Well it's certainly a nicer facility than the Methodist church where we used to run this precinct.

My only concern is that they seem to be determined that we don't impact the routine of the center one little bit. But I suspect we'll be able to work things out. We have an experienced team and it should go well."

Carl nodded and they exchanged a few pleasantries. He primarily meant this to be a token visit so he and Jessie could meet, as he was anxious to get over to the Government Center to pick up his supplies, extra signs for Happy Acres, and maybe, just maybe, have another go with Terrence. It looked like Jessie was doing all the right things so Carl took his leave.

He got into his car and made the drive to the Government Center. Up to the elections office on the third floor. As he entered, Brenda was coming out, pushing a dolly filled with materials for her route.

"Just wait till you see your pile," she said. "You're getting enough signs to guide people to the North Carolina border."

Carl proceeded to the front desk and showed his badge.

"Your things are in the back," said the receptionist, pointing to an aisle that ran off to the right.

"Can you tell me if Terrence is around?" Carl asked.

"He's in a meeting," was the terse response.

Carl went past the reception desk to an area where Michael was distributing the necessary items to the rovers.

"All right, Rover 5. We have for you five packages of extra ballots, sign here please, an iPhone so we can track your every move, two extra EPBs, two extra *CreateBallot* machines, this envelope with extra EPB flash drives, a last minute memo from the board on the care and feeding of poll watchers, and over in that cart are twenty-five extra signs to enable you to somehow bring order out of chaos at Manchester and Happy Acres. Am I forgetting anything?"

"Oh, yes," continued Michael. "Chesterbrook. Both scanners as well at their supporting bins, toppled over when the workmen delivered them. The bins are cracked but probably still useable. The chief has already set up but you and Milton need to go over there sometime this afternoon to confirm that the scanners still work. Here is your test deck. Milton says he can be there at 4:00 p.m. Let him know if that time is not convenient. Now I believe that is everything. Have a nice day and may the election gods be with you."

"Thanks," said Carl, feeling a bit overwhelmed. "Do you have any idea when Terrence will be out of his meeting?"

"No, I do not. But he did leave me a message to deliver to you which was, in his own words, 'suck it up and make it happen.' I'm not sure why he singled you out because that's the basic message we give to everyone."

Even with the aid of a dolly, it took several trips for Carl to get all the items to his car. Many of the items went on his back seat while the signs were all placed in the trunk. He looked at his cell. It was almost 11:00 a.m. He would have just enough time to get over to Happy Acres and plant the sixteen signs that the chief had demanded, before meeting Cindy at McDonalds.

He wondered what she had in mind. Probably some last minute plea to Terrence. At this stage, Carl didn't see the point. There was nothing left to do but hope. Hope that they were wrong and all would be well. And probably it would be. That scenario that had been so convincing in the middle of the night, now seemed to wilt in the light of day. After all, as they had noted countless times,

*They all tested good.*

# 68

## Monday, Noon

"Two quarter pounders, two medium fries, one chocolate shake, one coke, and two cookies. That will be $14.95 please," said the lady behind the counter.

"This one's on me," said Cindy, whipping out a twenty. "Don't argue," she added as Carl began to speak. "I'm the one who's forcing this command appearance on you."

"So how's the morning going so far?" she asked, as they took their seats.

"Reasonably well, other than Terrence shooting me down. I just put up so much signage at Happy Acres that I felt like I was creating a road rally. There's no way anyone is going to get lost over there."

They spent the next few minutes eating their food. Cindy seemed content to let the conversation lag. Carl didn't mind. He had to break for lunch sometime and this was as good a way as any.

"So," said Cindy, breaking the silence. "I gather that Terrence was less than helpful."

"Which means," she continued, thoughtfully, "that we've lost the front part of our time window. There's not enough time for the machines to be turned on and adequately tested by the end of the day. Not enough hours would elapse before a valid test of our hypothesis—"

"Yes, it's done," agreed Carl. "Even if Terrence has a last minute change of heart, we've lost our window. The warehouse closes at 3:30 p.m."

"So what this means," said Cindy, slowly, and obviously deep in thought, "is that the actual test won't occur until tomorrow morning, after the machines are turned on this afternoon."

Carl couldn't believe what he was hearing. "What are you talking about? It's over. There will be no test. Terrence nixed it."

"Yes," Cindy agreed, "but you're just going to have to convince Terrence or someone to run the test tomorrow morning. Once they analyze the results and see the light, they can send word out to the affected precincts. Those precincts would—"

"But how are we—"

"Please Carl, don't interrupt. Those precincts would, at the end of the day, take the ballots from the corrupted scanner and feed them into the good one. It would elongate the close in those twenty-four precincts but that can't be helped. The Government Center would have to issue some sort of press release on this, so the public and political parties realize what's happening. And that should do it. Are you finished with those french fries?"

Cindy reached over and grabbed a fistful of fries from Carl's tray.

"You don't seem satisfied," she said, flashing a bright smile. "And I'll admit, you have the toughest part. Convincing someone to come over here tomorrow, even as the election is taking place, and vote the test deck for those machines. But you have to do it.

We are about to have an election where we know the results will not be accurate and we are not letting that happen." Cindy's demeanor had suddenly turned deadly serious.

"May I speak?" asked Carl.

Cindy nodded, her cheek bulging with french fries.

"You're forgetting the first part. Those machines first have to be turned on, the election passcode entered, and then opened for voting."

"Which reminds me," said Cindy. "You need to give me the passcode."

"You!"

"Yeah, me. Your schedule is completely full this afternoon so I'll have to go over there and turn on the machines."

"But that's impossible. They won't even let you in the warehouse."

"Of course they will. Don't forget that I'm a candidate. I have that piece of paper somewhere in my handbag saying I'm allowed to come to the warehouse anytime up to Election Day to monitor how things are going. It's my prerogative as a candidate, to make sure my candidacy is getting a fair shake."

"But you dropped out, remember?"

"I did not 'drop out' as you put it. I merely *suspended* my campaign. I am still on the ballot and am actually very optimistic about tomorrow's election." Cindy seemed determined to keep a straight face.

"Optimistic about what. That you'll edge out Diesel for third place."

"Well, perhaps not that optimistic. But the point is that I still have a right to be there. That paper will gain me entry. Nothing improper. I'll sign the log at the front desk like I did before. Now as I recall, I don't have to log out."

"No, you don't."

"Good," she said thoughtfully. "That eases things a bit. And you once mentioned that the planned security alarm system hasn't been installed yet."

"I'm sorry but I'm not following you," said Carl. "OK, you're in the warehouse. I'll give you that. You still have to go back to the rear of the building where the election cage is. The fence is some ten feet high. There are two sliding gate entrances and both are locked with padlocks."

"And inside the cage are the nine machines? The ones I need to turn on and prime for voting?"

"As I remember, yes. But I don't see how you're going to get in there. Look, I know you can turn on the charm. I've seen you in action. But there's no way you'll get those workmen to unlock the padlock and slide open the gate just because you flutter your eyelashes at them."

"I wasn't planning on having the workmen help me. And I wasn't planning to slide open the gate, either."

"But then how—"

"Did I ever tell you," said Cindy, her bright smile returning, "that I was in the rock climbing club?"

# 69

## MONDAY, 1:20 P.M.

"CARL, THIS IS Sharon Goldman. Where are you?"

"In what I suppose is the new 'front lobby.' Where are you?"

"In the cafeteria. That's where they're putting us. Both precincts. From where you are, turn to your right, through the double doors, and down the long hallway."

"Got it. I'll see you in a minute."

When the decision was made earlier in the year to split the heavily populated Manchester precinct, the Office of Elections came up with the very unimaginative monikers of "Manchester 1" and "Manchester 2." Sharon Goldman was the chief election officer assigned to Manchester 1 and she along with her Manchester 2 counterpart were scheduled to set up their precincts at the voting location, starting at 1:00 p.m. Carl had agreed to meet them and lend a hand but his lunch with Cindy had run late. Hence, the call from Sharon.

The prolonged lunch had been unavoidable. First it had taken Cindy several tries before she was able to convince Carl that she was completely serious.

"Being a rock climber is one thing. Being a cat burger is another," he said, trying to talk her out of it.

"If you have a better plan, then tell me," was her response. "And 'to do nothing' is not a plan. This matters, Carl. You know this, better than most."

In the end he acquiesced. Part of him was afraid the whole thing would blow up in their faces while the other part was ashamed that she had to talk him into it.

*Well time to temporally let go of the bizarre and get back to the mundane world of election preparation.*

Carl pushed open the double doors. There before him was one of the longest and dreariest hallways he could ever remember. Portions of the ceiling were missing and bare light bulbs, hanging from what Carl surmised were the rafters, provided what little illumination there was. Halfway down the hallway, there was a gap in the tile floor, which was filled by wooden planks.

*It's like Dante's Inferno.*

After what seemed an interminable walk, he reached the end of the hallway where things brightened considerably. To his left was what appeared to be the entrance to the cafeteria. He entered and was relieved to see that it was a large, well-lit space which would be perfectly adequate to handle the two precincts. Provided the voters were able to get there.

"Are you Carl?" a gray haired lady called. She quickly walked over to Carl, followed by a man of Asian descent.

"This is Hai Chen, my assistant chief. What do you think of our digs?"

"The room is great," said Carl. "The access is terrible."

"Isn't it though?" said Sharon. Then she called to a pair of ladies, at the far end of the room. "Mandy. Victoria. The rover is here."

Then back to Carl. "They are our Manchester 2 counterparts."

Once they had all assembled and introductions made, Carl asked the first question that came to mind. "Has anyone served here in the past?"

"I have," said Victoria, who apparently was the Manchester 2 assistant chief. "Back when this was a single precinct. They always put us in the gym which is on the other side of the school, where the parking lot is. We ran things with no problems at all."

"Couldn't we get the gym for this election?" asked Carl.

Victoria laughed. "The gym no longer exists. The bulldozers took it out in mid-July."

"We asked the activities office. No, we begged the activities office to find us something else, but this is all they had to offer," said Mandy.

"I'm concerned about the handicapped voters," said Carl. "That's a long hallway. Plus you need to go up those steps to get into the building. There should be a ramp there. Has anyone asked the custodian about getting one?"

"I did," said Mandy. "They don't have anything."

"How do they suggest the handicapped people get here?"

"On the other side of the school. Through there," said Mandy, pointing to a door at the far end of the cafeteria, leading to the outside.

"Let's take a look," said Carl, walking to the door. Sharon and Mandy followed.

Carl opened the door to what appeared to be an alley. There was an extended curb running the length of the school.

"I guess this would work," said Carl. "We'll need to put up a lot of signs, directing handicapped voters to this side of the school. I'm not crazy about having the entrance for the handicapped folks being so far removed but it still should—"

Carl's train of thoughts was interrupted by a deafening sound as a dump truck filled with stones came rumbling down the alley. It passed them and went on its way toward the front of the school, leaving small pieces of stone on the pavement.

They returned to the cafeteria. Carl didn't want to prolong this any longer than he had to. The chiefs and their assistants had a lot of work before them in setting up the room. Fortunately both chiefs, as well as their assistants, appeared to be on top of things. The precincts were in good hands but they had been dealt a tough hand to play.

"Ok, I'll tell you what. I will put up some extra signs directing handicapped voters to the alley. But also, and this is key, you need to make sure that the signs offering curbside assistance to handicapped voters are prominently displayed at the main entrance. In fact, if you have the manpower, you should probably rotate an election officer out by the main entrance, to offer curbside to anyone who appears to be in need. Does that make sense?"

Sharon and Mandy both nodded.

"Good. I'll leave things with you in here, while I put up the extra signs outside. Can you think of anything else right now?"

"Any suggestions on handling the media?" asked Sharon. "We've been told that Manchester frequently gets the local TV stations for live coverage."

"Just what the manual says," said Carl. "Keep it brief. Don't offer any predictions. Refer anything that sounds the least bit controversial to the Office of Elections. The only bits of hard information you can give them are the number of registered voters and the number of people who have voted."

Carl then left, but not before emphasizing that they could and should call him if anything came up that they were unsure of or just needed support on. Once outside, he removed a number of “handicapped voter” signs from his trunk and placed them in what appeared to be good positions. He wished he had more.

He also checked with the office to see if perhaps the workman could be given the day off tomorrow or at least not run dump trucks in the alley. “We don’t control that,” was the answer. “The renovation schedules are set between the county and the contractor. You’ll need to go through the county bureaucracy to get it changed. We wish we could help you but it’s out of our hands.”

Carl realized that this was going to be a very challenging situation. It was too late to do much now, but he resolved that next time he would actively engage the Office of Elections to come up with a better solution.

*That is, if for me, there will be a next time.*

# 70

## Monday, 3:00 p.m.

"Ben, I need you over here. We need to open the cart and check its contents."

Ben extricated himself from the group that was in the process of creating a snakelike path, delineated by tables and chairs, through which the voters would form their line to the check-in table.

Carl watched as Ben joined his chief at the cart. She was holding her copy of the manual in one hand and a pair of nippers in the other. Beside her was the precinct's "kit."

"All right, Kathy. Let's do it."

Kathy, a woman about Carl's age, knelt down, cut the seal and proceeded to unlock and open the cart door.

"First we take out the EPBs. There are two. Check. 'Peripherals', those EPB accessories. Check. Two *CreateBallot* machines. Check…"

Kathy continued to read out the checklist of items in the precinct cart.

*She's doing everything by the book,* observed Carl approvingly. *I would say Hagerman is in good hands even if she is a first-time chief.*

Carl checked his phone for voice or text messages. There was a voice message from his partner from the June primary, Rosemary Pennington from Carter Run. She had been sending him a series of messages all day long, reporting on her worries and concerns. Most of the time it was needless worry. He pressed "play" and listened.

*"Carl, this is Rosemary Pennington again. The office lady at Carter Run is now saying that we can't set up the gym until 9:00 p.m. tonight. Something about a basketball game that was not on the schedule."*

Carl let out a sigh of exasperation. Most of the schools were cooperative and some even went out of their way. Even at Manchester with all its problems, Carl sensed at least empathy, if not assistance. But the staff at Carter Run Elementary School seemed determined to be as difficult as possible. It had been that way in June and continued to be that way now. Carl made a note to bring it up with Terrence after the election.

He then dialed Rosemary and spent the next twenty minutes listening to her angst. He assured her that he would be at the school at 9:00 p.m. and would monitor and, if necessary, assist her and her team with the setup. That seemed to settle her down, somewhat.

Now what was the time? His cell said 3:30 p.m. Cindy must be at the warehouse now but he was powerless to help her. He was also not needed here as Kathy and associates seemed to have the Hagerman precinct well covered.

Where to now? He had promised Marianne Tomkins at Wallingford that he would try to be there for her setup, but that was before Michael had informed him of the situation at Chesterbrook. He had heard stories from the rovers of the rough treatment that the deliverymen sometimes extended to the equipment but he had assumed that they were "tall tales." Apparently not.

Fortunately Carl's arrival at Chesterbrook exactly coincided with Milton's. Together they obtained admission to the already secured gymnasium. The bins were cracked in several places but the scanners proved to be of sturdier stuff. Both scanners processed the test decks correctly. They reset the counters to zero, and put fresh seals on the scanners. Carl was just exiting the school when his cell rang.

"Carl, this is Daniel Pitcairn over at Tower. We have none of the real estate signs."

"The wire frames should be on the inside of the cart's right door. The plastic sleeves are folded in the upper right shelf, inside the cart. They were all packed at the warehouse."

"I know. The frames are there but not the signs."

Carl gave an inward groan. Packing the real estate signs. That was a Station One job. Somehow they had neglected to pack them. The fact that his Station One assignment had come before, and not during, the setup for this precinct was of scant consolation.

"Is anything else missing?"

"No, everything else looks good. We're just finishing the setup now."

Carl quickly assessed the situation. Those real estate signs were critical in designating the entrance to the voting parking area from the street. He had some extras and he really should get those over to Tower now. The Tower precinct was located in a high-rise, which in turn was located in the most populated area of the county. They were already getting into early rush hour. He didn't want to make the trip over there now but he had no choice. Those other schools would hopefully be able to set up on their own.

"I'm on my way, Daniel. I'll get there as soon as I can."

# 71

## Monday, 4:45 p.m.

And so it continued. A half hour drive over to Tower. Twenty minutes to brainstorm with Daniel as to where best to put the signs. A phone call to Marianne over at Wallingford.

"Yes, I think we're all right. Is there any chance you can be here tomorrow for the opening?"

"I'll try. And always remember that you can call if you need anything."

A phone call from the Cooper chief.

"Why do I need to drive my election materials out to the Government Center tomorrow night after the close? I'll be tired. Can't someone else do it for me?"

Carl tried to explain that everyone would be tired. "This is what you signed up for."

Twenty minutes more to listen to the Cooper chief vent. Emit sympathetic noises where appropriate.

Another call. This one from Patty McGrath at Happy Acres.

"We need more signs."

*Please, tell me you're joking!*

"Patty, I posted sixteen extra signs this morning. I really think you're well covered."

"The voters might make a wrong turn onto that service road."

"You mean the gravel road that dead ends at the tool shed?"

"That's the one."

"In which case, they'll turn around when they get to the shed and come back. I think we can count on the voters being able to figure out that they don't vote in a tool shed at the end of a gravel road. Trust me, Patty. I drove the route this morning when I put up the signs. You're OK."

"All right, if you say so. But I won't be held responsible if the voters make that wrong turn."

"Duly noted. See you tomorrow."

Then as soon as he hung up, there came another, far more cryptic, call.

"The code won't work."

"What did you enter?"

"General113"

*That's not what I told her. She must have scribbled it down wrong.*

"Try General1103"

Another pause.

"It works. I'll get back to you when I'm done."

They completed the call.

Carl then glared at his cell phone, daring it to make a sound.

*You be quiet if you know what's good for you.*

He drove back to his townhouse. He needed to organize things for tomorrow. Once he was home, he went over all the things he needed to take with him, and where in the car they would reside. The things that he had been issued: The manual. The kit. The canvas bag. Two-way radio. iPhone. packs of extra ballots. EPBs. flash drives. *CreateBallot* machines. To that he added a flashlight, stapler, calculator, tape measure (in case disputes arose over the forty foot line). Everything out to the car and packed in such a manner, that it could be retrieved as quickly as possible.

He then went back inside, threw a frozen dinner in the microwave and proceeded to make a couple of sandwiches for the next day. He put the sandwiches, some bottled water, and a few snack items into a cooler. He wasn't hungry but he forced himself to eat his dinner. He then looked at the clock. It said 8:00 p.m. In an hour he would be at Carter Run, watching Rosemary and her team set up their precinct. It wasn't right that she should have to do that so late in the day, but in a way Carl was thankful. It gave him something to do. Something to do besides wait.

His cell phone rang.

"It's done. Just one problem."

"Which is?"

"Only eight machines were there."

"Do you remember which one was missing?"

"Yeah, I wrote it down. Let's see, it's the serial ending in 1702."

Carl looked over his list.

"That's one of the ones we had an eye on. Still this should be sufficient, I would think."

"When will you make the call?"

"Tomorrow morning about eight."

"OK. Well, good luck tomorrow."

"Thanks. You too."

A pause.

"Am I going to jail for this?"

"If you are, I'll probably be in the next cell. We can pass notes back and forth."

They said their goodbyes and hung up. The ball was in his court. Cindy had done her part, and at personal risk. Somehow he would have to convince Terrence. But how? Terrence had made it clear that he was not going to listen to anything Carl said. But if not Terrence, then who? Who was there who would be willing to listen to him and also have sufficient authority to order the test?

That was the question that Carl was mulling over in his head, as he got into his car to drive out for his 9:00 p.m. rendezvous with Rosemary and the Carter Run team. And it was still the question that he was struggling with as he returned to his townhouse an hour and a half later. He was exhausted from the day just ended, apprehensive about the day ahead, and still completely uncertain as to how to bring Cindy's efforts to a successful resolution.

# Part Four

## November Third

# 72

## Tuesday morning, November 3, 3:00 a.m.

This was the part that was always so tough. The night before. Trying to get to sleep when there was so much on his mind. Eventually around 3:00 a.m., he gave up, got dressed, and had some breakfast, a bowl of cereal.

He then contemplated his route. He had sort of promised Marianne that he would start at Wallingford. But where to next? That was a no-brainer. He would try to be at Manchester as close to the 6:00 a.m. opening as he could. Do whatever he can to ease things for Sharon and Mandy. After that it was mostly geography. Seneca Grove, Danby, Chesterbrook, and Cooper were all in that area. But then again, Rosemary would probably be demanding an early appearance at Carter Run. Which means I don't get over to Tower until midday. I don't like that. That leaves Hagerman, Pikesville, and Happy Acres for later in the day. But what was it that Milton said?

*Your planned route is usually shot to hell in the first couple of hours.*

And of course the kicker was to somehow convince Terrence that testing those eight warehouse machines needed to be done. Carl briefly wondered what had become of the ninth machine. Serial ending in 1702.

The minutes ticked by. He turned the pages of his manual, randomly reviewing sections. Finally at around 4:40 a.m., he decided that the time had come. He took the remaining items out to the car, ready to start the day. Fortunately the weather was breaking in his favor. No rain and rather mild. The temperature might reach sixty.

Once in the car, he turned on his iPhone and inserted it into the cigarette lighter. He then turned on the radio which would be his constant companion all through the day. The radio was silent, except for some static. It was still a bit early.

He started the car and pulled out of the townhouse parking area, into the street.

The radio sounded.

*"Base, this is Rover 16. I'm heading over to Precinct 604, Groveton, for the opening."*

*"Copy that 16,"* Carl recognized Terrence's voice. *"Good morning and smooth travels."*

Carl reached over and grabbed the radio. Pressing the transmit button he reported in.

*"Base this is Rover 5. I'm going over to Precinct 310, Wallingford for the opening."*

*"Copy that 5. Good morning and have a great day."*

As Carl drove along the road leading to Wallingford Elementary School, he listened as other rovers from various part of the county, radioed in their initial destinations. It might be still dark out, but Election Day was coming alive.

He pulled into the Wallingford parking lot, a few minutes before 5:00 a.m. A single flood light illuminated the parking lot but the school itself was still dark. Carl sat in his car and waited.

A car pulled into the parking lot. Then another. And another. Shapes could be seen getting out of the respective cars. Shadowy figures began to congregate at the door. Then suddenly a light shone from the window, next to the door. The door was opened and the people entered. It was time.

# 73

## Tuesday, 5:00 a.m.

It had been a conscious decision of Carl's not to enter the school at the same time as the other officers. While he was there to provide whatever support was needed, Marianne, not Carl, was the chief. It was up to her to welcome her team and get things started. Now that it appeared that most of the team had entered the building, Carl got out of his car and proceeded to the front door. Through the front door and down the hallway to the gym, where the sound of voices could be heard.

He entered the gym and saw about seven or eight people, standing in various poses, waiting to be given direction. Marianne and a middle aged man, apparently the assistant chief, were over by one of the tables, studying the manual. Carl looked around at the tables and chairs that had presumably been set up the day before. It appeared to be functional. Carl was able to imagine where the voters would queue up, prior to check-in. Where they would receive their ballots. Where they would mark them. And finally, the scanners over by the second doorway. Yes, Carl could imagine how it would work.

Carl walked over to where Marianne was standing. She saw him and gave an appreciative smile. Carl nodded but said nothing.

"It says that we first swear in the officers," Marianne said. The assistant chief nodded. For a moment she hesitated and looked over at Carl who gave an almost imperceptible nod.

"All right everyone," she called. "I need to swear you all in."

She first had everyone introduce themselves and then had them swear the oath that was on the sheet she had retrieved from her kit. Once given, she had each of them sign the oath sheet.

"Next I need to welcome the poll watchers. There doesn't appear to be any poll watchers, at least not yet, so we'll go to the next item. I need to assign you your jobs. Dave, do you think you could get the Electronic Poll Books up and running? Oh and Elizabeth, why don't you help Dave? Uh...Harold and Sameer, why don't you put up the signs while James and I will get the scanner going."

"What about me?" asked an elderly lady.

"Oh, Doris. You do the signs with Harold. Sameer, on second thought, here is a handout on the *CreateBallot* machines. Why don't you get them set up?"

It was easy to see that Marianne was a first-time chief, new to all this. It was also easy to tell that she had studied the manual and had a plan. Not a perfect plan perhaps, but a plan nonetheless. Carl noted that Dave, who had been Marianne's choice to get the EPBs going, was by far the youngest person on the team, probably still in his twenties. Probably tech savvy. And the two officers who Carl sensed were the "least promising" were put in charge of the signs. That was wise. You could always correct any mistakes in the signage after the polls opened but getting the EPBs and scanners up by 6:00 a.m. was critical.

For most of the following hour, Carl watched as Marianne's team assembled the precinct. The EPBs came up as did the scanner. As the minutes passed and as various check points were accomplished, Marianne's confidence seemed to rise. At one point, Carl was poised to intervene when a poll watcher for the Democratic Party arrived. His presence seemed to throw Marianne off her game for a moment, but she went back to the manual and checked what needed to be done. Take the poll watcher's letter of authorization. Give him a poll watcher's badge. Now get back to what you were doing, in this case getting the privacy booths set up.

It was getting closer to the 6:00 a.m. opening bell and Carl realized it was time to leave. Wallingford was in good shape. Time to get over to Manchester and see how they were doing. He was just ready to take his leave when his cell phone rang.

"This is Millard Hazlet. Seneca Grove. The EPBs won't open."

*And you waited to 5:55 to tell me.*

"What does the screen say?"

"It wants a password."

"Well provide it. It's on a small card inside the small envelope that you were provided."

"Yeah, well I put the card down and someone took it."

Carl thought.

*The EPB passwords are generally "Election" followed by the precinct number. Let's see, Seneca Grove is 306.*

"Try Election306."

A pause.

"Yeah. It seems to work. Bye."

*Your welcome, Millard.*

With that done, Carl gave Marianne a wave and left the gym. He passed a line of voters that extended down the hall and out the door. It was still dark. Sunrise was over an hour away. As he made his way to his car, he could hear Marianne's voice announcing that,

*"The polls are now open."*

# 74

## Tuesday, 6:20 a.m.

*"This is Tracy Miller, WMML news, speaking to you live from Manchester High School, one of the largest polling venues in the county, as voters are literally streaming past me to get to the polls. Here in this cratered parking lot where huge mounds of dirt reside everywhere, the glorious chaos which is democracy marches forward. And now emerging from the school, having just cast her vote is the Democratic Party endorsed candidate for a seat on the school board, Valerie Turner. Ms. Turner, could you spare a moment please? How are things looking on the inside?"*

*"They're looking great. The lines are long but everyone is upbeat. Democracy is alive and well at Manchester."*

*"And how does the race look from your perspective?"*

*"Tracy, we are very optimistic about this race but we're taking nothing for granted. I will be campaigning right up to the 7:00 p.m. close."*

*"And speaking of your campaign, could you please share with our viewers how your campaign has been affected by the very unfortunate breakdown of your sister, Cynthia Phelps, in her ill-fated campaign for a seat on the Soil and Water Commission?"*

*"There was absolutely no 'breakdown' as you call it. My sister came to a reasoned conclusion that her continued candidacy was not in the best interests for all concerned. She has since enthusiastically endorsed another candidate for Soil and Water, and has been actively working on both his and my campaigns."*

*"By 'another candidate,' are you referring to the rather bizarre write-in campaign that has been launched for Howard Morgenstein?"*

*"There is nothing bizarre about a spontaneous, grass roots, effort for an eminently qualified candidate. I support him, I just voted for him, and my campaign workers have been authorized to distribute his literature as well as my own."*

*"And just how has the Democratic establishment reacted to your decision to openly endorse a candidate that they have refused to back."*

*"Tracy, I am a Democrat; I'm proud to have the party's endorsement, but the party does not speak for me. I support whoever I want to, based on my own criteria, not the party's. Now if you'll excuse me, I have some potential voters to meet."*

Valerie quickly walked away before Tracy had a chance to ask any more questions.

"You're getting good at this," said Carl, having paused a moment to watch the interview, before going into the school.

"Am I?" said Valerie. "I suppose that's a good thing. Cindy warned me about getting in front of a camera with…that person. Speaking of which…"

She gave Carl a piercing look.

"Yes?"

"Cindy was supposed to hand out fliers for me yesterday but she bailed at the last minute. Was very apologetic about it. Even got one of her friends to cover for her. Said something came up that she just had to do."

"Really?"

"Yes, really. I'm not upset. She's back in harness this morning, over at Tower handing out campaign lit. I just wondered if you knew what it was yesterday, that just couldn't wait."

"Well, I don't know...I mean Cindy doesn't clear her activities with me..." said Carl, avoiding Valerie's gaze. He shifted his focus to the parking lot. "... and besides I wish there was some way to make things more orderly in this parking lot. I guess it will get better once the sun comes up. And let's see...Signage is good. They have the correct number of 'voter parking' signs. I better go inside and see how it looks. Good talking to you, Valerie. I'd wish you good luck, but I'm not allowed to right now. On duty and all that."

"Yeah, I bet you don't know," said Valerie, with a wry smile. "Be careful, my friend. I've known her a lot longer than you have."

Carl gave quick nod and walked quickly up the steps and into the school. He could feel the energy as he walked down the long passageway. Yes, the lighting was as dreary as ever, but the people made it seem less depressing. These were the early voters, stopping to vote on their way to work. They walked quickly, purposefully. They were also able-bodied. The folks for whom the long walk would not be so easy would come later.

About halfway down the hall, the line began. Actually it was two lines.

"Manchester 1 to my left. Manchester 2 to my right," the election officer called out, every few seconds.

"Which one are we in?" Carl heard a lady ask her husband.

"Beats me," he said.

Others seemed confused as well.

Carl sprinted ahead, making sure his county badge, hanging from the lanyard around his neck, was prominently displayed. With his manual in one hand and radio in the other, he hoped that it was obvious that he was an official and not someone attempting to "cut" the line.

At the entrance was posted a large map of the area, showing the boundaries for the two precincts. This was fine as far as it went but people in the back of the line were getting confused. There should have been two of those signs issued, one in each precinct cart.

He entered the cafeteria and took it all in. This was indeed a "mega" polling site with a combined precinct total well in excess of 5,000 voters. He quickly spotted Sharon, standing by the ballot table.

"Do we have another one of those boundary signs?" he quickly asked. "People at the back of the line are getting confused."

Sharon pointed to a table where a number of signs were placed.

"I'm sorry, we didn't think of that—" she began.

"Don't worry about it. Setup looks good in here. With your permission, I'll take this out to the hallway where your man is directing traffic."

Sharon nodded and Carl grabbed the sign and some tape. He hoped he wasn't being too abrupt. These were two tough precincts and the last thing they needed was a chief obsessing over every little mistake.

He carried the sign down the hall to the officer directing traffic.

"This might help," he said, giving it to the man. "You might want to tape it to the wall."

The officer nodded appreciatively and took the sign and tape. Carl returned to the cafeteria.

Both precincts were operating at full capacity. Each had four EPBs lined up side-by-side at the check-in tables. Each had the customary ballot table, ballot marking area, and two scanners. Everything was fully operational.

Having satisfied himself that these two precincts were functional, Carl started looking for little things that perhaps could be improved upon. One thing he noticed was that Mandy, the Manchester 2 chief, was one of the persons checking in the voters. For the moment this was fine, but ideally chiefs did not assign themselves specific jobs, especially during the early morning rush. Rather they kept themselves in reserve to handle "special" situations.

Carl walked over to where she was checking in a voter. He did not want to intrude on her work, but still felt the need to make a suggestion. But before he could speak, she said,

"We had three no-shows this morning. Two called in sick. The third didn't call at all. We're hanging by a thread. If you can get me someone, it would be great."

"I'll see what I can do," said Carl. He quickly crossed over to the other side and approached Sharon.

"They had three no-shows over there and they need help. Can you spare anyone?"

"I can spare one person," said Sharon. "Sidney," she called to a man at the ballot marking area. "We're sending you to Manchester 2, at least for a little while."

Carl then led Sidney over to the other side.

"Mandy, this is Sidney. He is now part of your team."

Mandy flashed Carl a quick smile of gratitude and then turned to Sidney. "Do you know how to check in voters?"

"I think so. I took the class."

"Then you're on. Here's the manual."

"I'll watch him do the first couple," said Carl quietly to Mandy, as she got up and returned to the chief's table.

Carl watched Sidney as he processed the next couple of voters. He seemed to have it in hand. Just out of curiosity, he took a stroll behind the two check-in tables, seeing how the flow was going. One of the EPBs caught his eye. At the bottom of the screen, the battery icon indicated a 2% charge. That wasn't right. With that amount of juice in the battery, the EPB was about fifteen minutes away from a total shutdown. Looking more closely, he saw the reason. The power light wasn't on. The machine was running purely on battery power.

"You need to plug that machine into the power strip," he said to the lady working the EPB.

"Oh, no," said the lady, cheerfully. "See that cable. It's connected to the EPB next to me. They talk to each other and keep in sync. Isn't it marvelous?"

"Yes, it is marvelous," agreed Carl. "But the power doesn't work that way. We need to plug it in. So with your permission..." He quickly knelt down, found the end of the power cord and plugged it in. The power light went on and Carl breathed easier.

Suddenly, Carl's radio began to sound.

*"Base to Rover 5. Base to Rover 5. You're needed at precinct 317, Pikesville. Please acknowledge and proceed there immediately."*

Carl pressed the transmit button. "Base this is Rover 5. I'm on my way to Pikesville."

Carl left the cafeteria but not before assuring both chiefs that things looked good and their teams were doing a great job. With that, he hurried from the building.

# 75

## Tuesday, 7:10 A.M.

WELL THERE GOES *my planned route,* thought Carl as he got back into his car and carefully navigated his way out of the Manchester parking lot. The Pikesville Community Center was farther from Manchester than any other precinct on his route. Twenty minutes without traffic. Now with rush hour it would be longer.

*What was happening there?* The message had been rather cryptic.

The drive gave Carl the opportunity to think about the phone call he needed to make. He didn't see how he was going to persuade Terrence to send someone over to the warehouse to do the test. He assumed that the entire election staff at the Government Center was fully committed to supporting the people in the field. Phone banks where staff would handle technical questions from chiefs and rovers. Another phone bank to deal with voter registration issues. Was there anyone just sitting around at the Government Center, waiting to take a twenty mile drive over to the warehouse to test an already discredited theory?

It was about a half hour later, with dawn beginning to break, when Carl pulled into the parking lot at Pikesville. Even at this early hour, the large parking lot appeared to be mostly full. He parked a fair distance from the entrance and went as quickly as he could to the front of the building. There, on the front steps, was the chief, Jessie McComber, who was having an intense discussion with a man who appeared to be on the staff of the community center.

"Those 'voter parking signs' have to go," the man was insisting. "Our members are being inconvenienced. We never agreed to your taking our very best parking spaces."

"We need those spots," pleaded Jessie. "The voters can't be forced to walk the full length of the parking lot."

"If you do not remove them, I'm calling the police," said the man. "And then you can start taking down those signs inside the building as well. They are confusing our members. The world doesn't stop just because you're having an election."

"Carl, I'm so glad to see you," said Jessie. "Mr. Rodriguez says we have to take down the 'voter parking' signs."

"And the indoor signs, or else I call the police" chimed in Mr. Rodriguez.

The whole scene had a strange feel as people were coming into the center, some to vote, others to use the pool or exercise room. They were all looking with curiosity at the confrontation. Partisan poll workers also seemed to be following the events intently.

"Mr. Rodriguez, perhaps we may speak in private," said Carl, trying to be both cordial and authoritative at the same time. He also indicated to Jessie that he should get back to his primary mission of running the precinct.

Carl then explained, as best he could, that the community center had made a formal agreement with the county. They had both agreed as to what needed to happen on Election Day and it was a shame that no one had informed Mr. Rodriguez. For the next several minutes Carl allowed himself to be a verbal punching bag as Mr. Rodriguez stormed on about all the various demands that management placed on him and how service to the community center members was his primary focus. In the end, they both agreed that people in charge need to communicate better and that perhaps the police need not be troubled. Carl took a deep breath, entered the center, and proceeded to the Empire Room where Jessie seemed to have everything in order.

Satisfied that the situation was stable, he went back outside to his car. Dawn had broken. It was 7:45 a.m. If he was going to make that call, he would have to do it soon. Real soon. Like now.

# 76

## Tuesday, 7:45 a.m.

Carl sat in his car, trying to plan his call. What could he say to Terrence that hadn't already been said? And what chance did he have of convincing him in the midst of the intensity of Election Day? Was there another way? Perhaps another person he could talk to.

*Well maybe there is one other person who might be able to help.*

Time for action. The number was still in his directory. He placed the call.

"Roger Dellman."

"Roger, it's Carl Marsden. I know you no longer work with the elections but we have a unique situation that you might be able to help us with."

"This wouldn't involve the Braxton scanners by any chance, would it?"

"Oh. Terrence mentioned it?"

"Oh yes. During the dark times when all those machines failed, it was mentioned from time to time. But I thought that was all cleared up when you discovered the bad test decks."

"Well, not really," said Carl. And with that he launched into his narrative. The doubts concerning whether the test decks explained everything. The research that uncovered *ElectionPro*'s history and the issue with scanners that were left on too long.

*At least he's listening.*

"It's an interesting theory," Roger admitted. "But it's still just a theory. A month ago it could have been tested but it's a bit late to do this on Election Day."

"Not really. It can be tested today. Eight scanners are over at the warehouse. They have all been primed and turned on. They are ready to accept ballots at this very moment. Four of them are Braxton machines. All are for the 12$^{th}$ congressional district. They could be tested and certified in under an hour. Possibly as little as a half hour."

"When were these machines turned on?"

"Late yesterday."

"How late?"

"Probably early evening."

"Did you turn them on?"

"No, I had my hands full preparing for today."

"Then who?"

Carl paused. They'd probably figure out it was Cindy from the log sheet but for the moment it was best to keep her name out of this.

"I can't say. But they were turned on."

"By the Election Fairy, I suppose."

There was silence on both sides of the line for almost half a minute. Carl began to be afraid that the connection had been lost. At last Roger spoke.

"Carl, as you know, I no longer work with elections. However I am on loan for the day, to work at the Command Center to help out. But that doesn't give me the authority to override Terrence and call for this test. We are resource constrained right now. Everyone here in the office is committed to supporting the Election Day effort."

*I'll give it one last try.*

"Roger, I've made my case. There is a very real possibility that twenty-four precincts today are going to report incorrect results. There is a way, with minimal staff commitment, to test whether that possibility is an actuality. I've made my pitch to Terrence. I've made it to you. I leave it to your best judgment."

Carl could hear Roger's sigh on the other end of the line.

"I'm promising nothing but I'll think about it."

"Thanks, Roger. I appreciate it."

"So how are you enjoying being a rover?"

"It's the best job ever."

# 77

## Tuesday, 8:10 a.m.

At this point, with no apparent emergencies, it became a matter of geography. The closest precinct was Carter Run. Let's go over and see how Rosemary is doing.

A few minutes later he arrived at the elementary school.

*Signs look good. Poll workers seem to be behaving themselves. Voters entering and exiting the premises with no apparent problems—*

*Wait a minute. What do we have here?*

The sign said, "Support your local Brownie Troop 1130. Cookies 50 cents. Three for $1."

And they were doing a brisk business, too. More voters than not were stopping to sample the delights of Troop 1130. Three of the cutest little girls you would ever want to see were raking in the change, while their proud mothers hovered in the rear. And the cookies looked good too. Far better than anything Carl had packed.

The problem was that the ladies from Troop 1130 had placed their stand well within forty feet from the front entrance. There was no need to even measure. Carl would have to take it up with Rosemary.

He entered the school and followed the signed arrows to the gym.

"Hello, Carl," said Rosemary, in an uncharacteristically upbeat manner. "We're having such a good morning. All the machines work. My officers are great. Everything is perfect."

Carl looked around. Things did indeed look in good order. Milton was right. For all her angst, Rosemary always seemed to pull through.

"It looks great, Rosemary, except for one slight problem."

Rosemary's face fell. "It's the Brownies, isn't it? They were just so adorable, I didn't have the heart to tell them to move."

Carl gave a sigh. "OK, I'll be the bad guy. Don't say I never did anything for you."

Carl retraced his steps to the front of the school, taking his tape measure out of his pocket.

"Would you like to buy a cookie, mister?" one of the girls asked. "We're almost out of chocolate chip but we still have plenty of oatmeal raisin and peanut butter."

Feeling absolutely miserable, Carl addressed the mother who appeared to be in charge.

"I am terribly sorry ma'am. The law says that all fundraising activities need to be at least forty feet away from the polling place entrance. You will have to move your stand."

"I don't understand," said the woman. "The girls have always been allowed to sell their cookies here."

"I'm sorry. We are required to follow the law and the law says forty feet. Now I have a tape measure so I can determine a new location for your stand."

"Mommy, are we breaking the law?" asked one of the girls.

"Certainly not. This is outrageous," said the mother.

Carl went back to the front door of the school. He then started walking backwards, allowing the tape to extend as he went.

"What's happening?" asked another one of the girls.

As Carl continued his backward progression, he realized in horror that he was going to run out of sidewalk before he ran out of tape. When the tape finally reached the forty foot mark, he was several feet removed from the curb.

"So now the girls have to sell their cookies in the middle of the street?" said one of the outraged mothers.

"Mommy, you always tell us not to play in the street."

Carl realized all too well that he was in the midst of what could prove to be a public relations disaster. This was beginning to attract attention from the incoming voters. He had to resolve this as quickly as possible.

"We can trace a forty foot arc from the door," he explained, dragging the tape in such a way that the forty foot radius was maintained. At last he arrived at a point on the sidewalk. It was no longer in the direct path of the entrance, but it was the best he could do. He didn't write the law. He didn't agree with the law. But he was responsible for enforcing the law.

"Good grief. Let the kids sell their cookies," said a passerby.

"They can sell their cookies. They just need to be—"

"This is what's wrong with our country. Government bossing us around."

Fortunately the mothers, while looking daggers at Carl, picked up the table and moved it to the approved location.

"There. Are you satisfied?"

"Yes, thank you ma'am for your cooperation," said Carl. "I agree that it's a silly law but…"

No one seemed inclined to listen to Carl's opinion of the law. In an attempt to smooth things as best he could, he said, "May I buy one of your peanut butter cookies?"

The girls looked up at their mothers.

"It's all right, dear," said one of them.

The awkward exchange was made quickly. Carl gave a polite bow and went back to his car.

# 78

## Tuesday, 9:00 a.m.

Fortified by a tasty peanut butter cookie and a few sips from his water bottle, Carl was ready to soldier on. His cell buzzed. It was the chief over at Cooper.

"A voter needs assistance. But when we got out the *Request for Assistance* forms, we discovered they were all in Spanish. Do you have any English ones?"

After navigating the perils of public relations with the Brownies, Carl reveled in a simple problem he could solve. Yes, he had lots of *Request for Assistance* forms in English.

*Hang in there, Cooper, I'm on the way.*

Fifteen minutes later, he arrived at Cooper Middle School. He parked his car, opened up the canvas bag, and quickly located his supply of *Request for Assistance* forms.

*One pad of the forms in English. That should to it.*

He looked around the parking lot and began to frown. Something was missing. There were no "voter parking" signs. Absolutely none. There were poll workers doing their thing and respecting the forty foot limit. The parking spaces closest to the school, while occupied with cars, had not been designated for the voters. As he looked over the lot, he saw what he presumed to be voters walking from cars parked in various locations. Many of the people seemed to have long distances to walk.

Carl quickly entered the school and proceeded to the cafeteria. He had spoken to Tom Fischer, the chief, a couple of times on the phone. The second time had been that prolonged discussion about the need to return things to the Government Center the night of the election. Tom had been identified as a new chief and Carl had intended to give him a bit of special attention but with the various demands of the last week, it had never happened.

"Thank you," said Tom heartily, as he accepted the pad of forms. "We had our morning rush for a couple of hours but things seem to have eased up a bit."

Carl looked around. The setup was good. There was a small line of voters at the check-in table.

"This is my first election as chief. I was here as an officer in June and I've more-or-less followed the same setup that the chief used back then. Pretty little thing she was, even if a bit headstrong."

"It looks good," said Carl, choosing to ignore Tom's comment about Cindy. "The only issue is outside. There are no designated voter parking spaces."

"Yes, I figured, we'd let them park wherever they want to. I mean, who am I to tell them where they should park?"

Carl realized he needed to be firm. This was far more important than evicting the Brownies.

"We have to set up voter parking spaces," said Carl. "This school is open today for parent-teacher conferences and whatever else. Non-voters are taking the good spots. We can't have people walk the length of that very large lot to get here. It's especially important for the elderly and handicapped."

Tom gave a shrug. "What would you suggest?"

Carl considered. There was no easy solution.

"We go out and identify the spaces we want to allocate. We then have the office make an announcement over the PA, directing the people in those spaces to move their cars. We will give the license plate numbers. In the meantime, one of your people can stake out the lot and when a close-in space becomes vacant, we pounce on it with the appropriate sign."

It was not easy. The people in the office were reluctant to make an announcement and Tom's support was halfhearted at best. But eventually an announcement was made. Not every car was moved, but enough did move so that a number of voter parking spaces could be claimed. A full hour passed before Carl was able to move on. It had been time consuming but Carl felt it had been worth it.

His radio sounded.

*"Base to Rover 5. Base to Rover 5. Proceed immediately to Precinct 325, Tower. Reports of a disturbance involving poll workers. Please investigate and report back ASAP."*

*"Rover 5 to Base. I'm on my way. I'll let you know when it's sorted out."*

Once again, he would have to drive the entire width of his route.

*I do wish they would organize these crises better. It would be nice if they were in adjoining precincts for a change.*

# 79

## Tuesday, 9:55 a.m.

As he sped on his way toward Tower, Carl tried to imagine what sort of "disturbance involving poll workers" he would encounter. Tower was a rather unique precinct. It was a high rise condominium residence and a significant percentage of the voters at the precinct were actual residents. The precinct was in the "party room," situated two levels below the lobby entrance. Because of this, there were actually two designated "polling place entrances." One was from inside the building, a hallway that ran from the elevator to the party room. The outside entrance was at the end of a long sloping walkway, with concrete walls on either side that led from the rear parking lot.

Because of this unique setup, the Electoral Board had granted permission for poll workers to distribute their literature inside the building. They could place themselves in the hallway that led from the elevator to the party room, so long as they were at least forty feet from the door of the party room. Carl suspected that the altercation was probably coming from the entrance inside the building. This was unexplored territory for most poll workers and perhaps some confusion had arisen as to what they were allowed to do.

At the end of the access road were two signs, pointing in opposite directions. One could bear left to the "Main Lobby" or turn right to the "Service Entrance." A "voter parking" sign, also pointing to the right, informed would-be voters of the correct path. Carl however, veered left. He wanted to see how things were, coming off that elevator.

Parking spaces were abundant in the front of the building. Many of the residents were, no doubt, at work. Carl parked his car and hurried up the walkway into the building, armed with his manual and tape measure. He flashed his ID to the security guard and proceeded to the elevator. An elderly couple stood by the door, waiting for it to open. They appeared to be studying a sample ballot.

"And who do we want for Soil and Water Conservation Board, Herb?"

"Say, what?"

"The Soil and Water Conservation Board. Who do we want?"

"We want the Democrats. Which one is the Democrat?"

"It doesn't say. It just lists the names. There is Diesel, Phelps, and Rawlins."

Carl remained scrupulously silent.

"How about Diesel? That sounds like a Democrat."

The door opened.

Carl allowed the couple to precede him. He then walked out into the hall. There were indeed poll workers from both political parties who had set up tables with their fliers and brochures. Close to, but separate from, the Democratic table was a folding chair which had some fliers for Howard Morgenstein. As far as Carl could determine, everyone seemed to be behaving themselves. Although he couldn't be absolutely sure unless he measured it, they appeared to be about forty feet from the party room entrance.

*I'm not sure what the issue is. Better go in and ask the chief.*

He entered the room.

"Please have your ID ready and proceed over to the line," the election officer said.

"Thank you," said Carl. "Is your chief available?"

"I'm not sure," said the man. "We are very busy and—"

"It's all right Norm," came a voice. "He's our rover."

"Well excuse me, Mr. Rover," said the man, even as the chief, Daniel Pitcairn came over to Carl.

"Thank heavens, you're here," he said. "We have a problem."

"So I understand," said Carl. "But the folks in the hall seem to be all right."

"Oh, it's not them," said Daniel. "It's not even the regular party people, the ones I see every election."

Carl remained silent, waiting for Daniel to tell his story.

"Both school board candidates have people out there with their fliers," he said, pointing to the door, opening to the outside of the building. "You know, the Hayes-Turner contest. I'm not sure if you've read about it but there is a lot of emotion regarding that race."

Carl nodded. He was beginning to get a sinking feeling.

"We have a rather unique outside entrance. It's a narrow walkway with a low brick wall on either side. The wall extends past the forty foot limit. It actually runs for fifty-nine feet. I measured it this morning. For years there has been a gentleman's agreement among the poll workers not to campaign in the walkway. They all stand outside before the brick wall begins."

Carl nodded. He was beginning to anticipate what would come next.

"Well anyway, that's how our day began. But a little over an hour ago, the Hayes rep decides he is going to campaign right at the forty foot line. He measured it himself, right before my eyes.

Then the Turner rep followed suit. She said as long as the Hayes rep insisted on being at the forty foot line, she would too."

Carl's sinking feeling became more pronounced.

"Anyway, they've positioned themselves so the voters can get by, but it's very close quarters. And I'll tell you, I'm not happy with this, no matter what the law says."

Carl nodded. "Let me go out and talk to them. Maybe I can get them to see reason."

Daniel looked relieved. "I would appreciate it."

Carl then walked over to the far door, through which three voters had just entered. He passed through the door and emerged onto the walled walkway.

It was as he feared. There was a middle aged man holding some brochures and sporting a large "Hayes for School Board" badge. And to his right was Cindy, wearing her Turner and Morgenstein badges. They were both trying to interest the trickle of voters walking past them in their fliers.

Carl proceeded to walk down the walkway toward them. The Hayes supporter saw him first.

"Good morning sir," he said heartily, extending his hand. "And what a fine morning it is. I am Jeffrey Hudgins, volunteer for the Janet Hayes campaign." They shook hands.

For the briefest of moments, Cindy's face registered surprise at Carl's appearance but she quickly recovered.

"It is indeed a fine morning," she said with her most radiant smile, likewise offering Carl her hand. Then as an afterthought. "Cynthia Phelps, Turner for School Board campaign."

Carl shook it while giving her what he hoped was his sternest expression.

"Really, folks," he said. "This is not helping either of your campaigns. Why don't you both go back to the beginning of the walkway where the other party reps are? No one will have an advantage and the voters can come to the door unimpeded."

"Sir," said Mr. Hudgins. "I have the upmost respect for all the hard work that you and your associates put in to make this day a success. But I do insist on my legal right to campaign up to the forty foot line and I will not be intimidated by either you or my most worthy advisory." He nodded in Cindy's direction.

"As long as he stays, I'm here," said Cindy, grimly.

"You know what you're both doing is illegal?" said Carl.

"Show me your evidence if you have any... No, I didn't think so," declared the Hayes volunteer solemnly.

Cindy simply folded her arms and gave Carl that determined look, he recognized all too well.

Carl's cell phone buzzed.

"Carl, it's Patty McGrath over at Happy Acres. One of the *CreateBallot* machines is broken. It....well it's hard to explain but it's broken. We have so many handicapped and elderly folks here and so many of them want to use those machines to create their ballot. We're down to one machine and the line is growing. Do you, by any chance, have an extra?"

"Yes, I do," said Carl. "I'll get one over to you as quickly as I can."

"Thanks Carl. You're the best."

"You're welcome. See you soon."

*That is, as soon as I finish refereeing the children's hour.*

Carl considered the situation carefully. As much as he wanted to scream at both of them, he suspected it would accomplish nothing beyond giving him the opportunity to vent. The Hayes supporter was obviously determined to exercise his "rights," and he knew all too well Cindy's tenacity.

"I'm disappointed in both of you," he said, speaking to both, but mostly to Cindy. "You have allowed yourselves to sink into a petty little turf war which will do nothing for the candidates you claim to support. That call was from the chief at the Happy Acres precinct. A machine over there has failed and I need to bring over a replacement. But I can't do that until we resolve our little dispute. I am reasonably certain that what you are doing is in violation of some statute or another and I am going back inside and the chief and I will comb the law book in search of the appropriate law. When we find it, I will return to remove both of you to where the other poll workers are. In the meantime, you can take satisfaction in knowing that instead of helping the voters at Happy Acres, I shall be spending however long it takes to resolve this senseless dispute."

"You can make all the pious proclamations you want but I'm not moving unless and until you show me the rule that says I shouldn't be here," declared Mr. Hudgins.

Cindy glared at the man for a moment. Then as Carl turned to go back inside, she said, "May I have a moment, sir?"

Carl nodded and motioned toward the area at the top of the walkway. Together they walked to a point where they could talk in private.

"OK, you've appropriately shamed me," said Cindy. "But he made me so mad. He was one of those jerks at the debate who kept yelling catcalls at Valerie."

"The day is young and we both need to be at our best," said Carl. "It would be a personal favor to me if you would move back to the fifty-nine foot line."

Cindy shook her head and smiled. "You don't have to play the 'personal favor' card. I'll move back. It's the right thing. You need to get to Happy Acres."

"Thank you."

"On a different note, how did your call to Terrence work out?"

"I didn't call Terrence. I talked to Roger instead."

"And..."

"He says he'll think about it."

"I guess that's progress. He better not think too long though."

"I've got it! I've got it!" shouted Daniel Pitcairn, as he came running out through the door and up to where the Hayes supporter stood. "It's in the manual. '§ 24.2-604. Campaigners cannot hinder or delay a person from entering or leaving a polling place.' That supersedes anything to do with the forty foot limit." He opened the manual and allowed both Cindy and Mr. Hudgins to look at the appropriate section.

Daniel continued, "In my judgment as chief election officer of this precinct, you are both hindering and delaying voters from entering the polling place and as chief I am instructing you to retreat to the fifty-nine foot line. If you wish to lodge a protest with the Government Center that is your right. In the meantime you are legally required to leave."

Cindy looked over to Mr. Hudgins. "That would appear to settle it," she said. "As Valerie Turner believes deeply in the rule of law, we will abide with this decision, however much we may disagree with it." She gave Carl a wink.

"Janet Hayes bows to no one when it comes to law and order. We are glad that our campaign has contributed to a better understanding of the law and we will happily relocate to the top of the walkway," declared Mr. Hudgins.

The two adversaries gave each other a solemn bow and together they walked to the top of the walkway.

"Score one for the rule of law," said Daniel.

"So it appears," agreed Carl. "Well done, sir."

# 80

## Tuesday, 10:45 A.M.

*Well at least we got something right,* thought Carl, as he drove through the Happy Acres complex, at the required 20 mph speed limit. The extra signs, planted every few yards it seemed, appeared to have done the trick. They marked a clear, unambiguous path to the administration building, where the voting was taking place.

While some of the precinct's voters lived outside the complex, a significant portion were residents of the retirement community. These residents took justifiable pride in the precinct's percentage of voter participation, which was one of the highest in the county.

Carl had a soft spot for those seniors who took their voting responsibilities seriously and helping the handicapped exercise their franchise was one of his primary motivations for participating in the election process. And here before him, both entering and exiting, was a steady stream of voters. Some walked unassisted while others had aids to accompany them. Others used walkers or were in wheelchairs. One was on oxygen. But they all wanted to vote and it was Carl's job to make it as easy for them as he could.

Carl opened the rear door of his car and pulled out one of his *CreateBallot* machines. These were the machines that were used by folks who otherwise would experience difficulty in marking the preprinted ballots. This might include people with visual problems or just shaky hands. The *CreateBallot* device allowed the voter to mark his/her selections on a series of touch screens where their choices were prominently displayed for easy selection. At the end of the session the machine would print a ballot which could then be inserted into the scanner.

Carl carried the machine through the front door and into a spacious lobby where the voting was taking place. There was a short line of people getting processed at the check-in table. He could see a number of folks seated at the voter marking area, marking their preprinted ballots. Others could be seen inserting their ballot into the scanner and receiving the highly coveted "I Voted" sticker. It all looked quite normal except…

There was a single voter seated in front of the *CreateBallot* machine, creating her ballot. Then to her right, back a respectable distance, was the beginning of a line of perhaps fifteen people, all waiting patiently for their turn.

"Pretty amazing, isn't it?" said a voice behind him.

Carl turned around. It was Patty. "We could help them mark the preprinted ballot, of course. Just fill out the *Request for Assistance* form and bingo, they would be out of here in a flash. But these folks want to do it themselves, and that machine is the way to accomplish that. Anyway, follow me and I'll show you the problem."

Patty led Carl over to the corner of the lobby where a *CreateBallot* machine had been placed on the floor. Its entire front panel stuck out at a weird angle.

"One of my officers thought it would be interesting to open the machine to see how the card mechanism works. Needless to say that officer has been permanently reassigned to handing out "I Voted" stickers. We can't get the panel to close. Why don't you try it?"

Carl knelt down and pushed down on the panel. It would not budge. He knelt even lower to inspect the mechanism but was unable to determine the cause. He stood up and shook his head.

"We'll have to do an exchange. I'll start by writing up the necessary paperwork."

Carl took the appropriate form and entered the required information, including the serial numbers of both machines involved in the exchange.

"Here, sign both copies…Good…Now let's get the replacement up and running."

First Carl unlocked the side door of the broken machine and took out its flash drive which was then inserted into a similar slot in the replacement machine. That done, he lifted the new machine and took it over to a table, near the already functioning *CreateBallot.* Now it was just a matter of connecting the cords to power and flipping a switch.

"Now we wait, and hope," he said cheerfully to Patty.

The warm-up phase for the *CreateBallot* took a couple of minutes during which the screen flashed all sorts of messages, assuring the user that things were going well.

"How is everything else going?" Carl asked, as they waited for the machine to complete its warm up.

"Quite well, actually."

"No one has taken the wrong turn down the gravel road to the tool shed?"

Patty's face seem to turn a slight shade of red. "No, but the day is young."

At last the "open for voting" message appeared on the screen.

"I think you're in business," said Carl.

Patty signaled for one of her officers, who had been in the ballot marking area, to come over and help with the *CreateBallot* station. While this was going on, Carl looked around. Everything else seemed to be working fine. With a farewell wave to Patty, he scooped up the broken machine and returned to his car.

# 81

## Tuesday, 11:45 a.m.

Jack Vincent was the senior citizen among the rovers, having served for close to twenty years. Although he occasionally helped with Station Two testing, his warehouse specialty was managing the precinct carts and scanners for the 240 precincts in the county. Jack seemed to have internalized where each of these items belonged in the warehouse and during testing he was the one who ensured the precincts were being processed in the correct order.

Jack no longer had a rover route. Rather he worked Election Day at the Government Center, helping to process the absentee ballots that needed to be tabulated. In this effort, Jack generally took a "late shift" which officially began at 2:00 p.m.

It was shortly before noon when he arrived at the Government Center. His plan was to eat lunch in the cafeteria and then report upstairs where he would help out doing whatever until his shift began. Election Day at the Government Center was always exciting. There was so much going on. He rushed through lunch and headed upstairs to the elections office.

"Anything for me to do?" he asked the lady at the reception desk.

"Go on back and ask," she said.

Jack walked back to the cubicle area, looking for familiar faces. At one of the desks was his old boss, Roger Dellman. Roger now worked for the tax department, but apparently he was being borrowed for the day.

"Hi Jack," he called. "I'm looking up problem voters on the state registration system. It's an 'all hands on deck' day."

"Anything I can do?" asked Jack, sitting in the chair next to Roger's desk.

"I think we're covered here. You might want to check with Terrence," said Roger, studying the screen. He then spoke into his phone.

"All right, I have this person on the screen. She is registered at 15 Edgewater Drive. Hagerman precinct. If she moved in July, she can go back there and vote…That's right but tell her, after she votes, to fill out a C*hange of Address* form… All right...You're welcome. Bye."

"OK, I'll look for Terrence," said Jack, getting up.

He started to walk away.

"No, wait…"

Jack turned around. Roger seemed undecided about something.

"Is there something I can do?"

Silence. Roger seemed to be considering something carefully. Very carefully.

"Yes, there is," he said slowly. "How would you like to take a ride over to the warehouse?"

# 82

## Tuesday, 12:15 P.M.

"You can't have people parking in the fire lane."

"And what am I supposed to do? The tree trimmers are taking up half the spots in the parking lot. The good spaces, too. The ones closet to the entrance."

The Danby chief had a point. Apparently someone had decided that with school not in session, it would be a good time to do some tree trimming at Danby Elementary School. The crew had arrived at 10:00 a.m. and started by claiming the portion of the parking lot closest to the front entrance. The chief had tried to get them to leave, or failing that, at least determine how long they would stay. Apparently some language issues had exacerbated the problem. Finally in frustration she had given up and moved some of the voter parking signs to the area right in front of the school door, which happened to be labeled as a "fire lane." It was the only issue in this otherwise, well run precinct.

Carl looked over at the tree trimmers who were seated on the lawn taking their lunch break. He walked over to see if something could be worked out.

"How long will you be working here?" he asked the first person he reached. The man, of a Hispanic appearance, looked up at Carl with a puzzled expression.

"How long will you be working?" asked Carl again, more slowly this time, regretting that he hadn't retained more from his academic exploits in high school Spanish.

The man pointed to another, who apparently was the foreman. Carl went over and asked the same question.

The man listened. "Two hours, here. Two hours there," he said, with a heavy Spanish accent, pointing at the far end of the lot where some more trees were clustered.

"Muchas gracias," said Carl, trying to sound authentic. The man laughed, realizing correctly that these were probably the only Spanish words that Carl knew.

Carl returned to the front of the school. There was a trickle of voters coming in and out of the building, all of whom seemed to have parked in the fire lane directly in front of the school. The chief was there, waiting for him, with a "what do you propose now?" look on her face.

"They are going to be here for the next two hours. After that they will move further away and you won't be affected, so we just need to think of something that will get us to 3:00 p.m. or thereabouts," he said. He very much wanted the chief to be part of the solution.

"They can't park in the close-in parking spots because of the trimmers," said the chief. "If you insist they can't park in the fire lane, that only leaves the spots at the end of the lot, where they haven't started working. But that will be a pain for everyone and worse for the handicapped folks who just can't or shouldn't walk that distance."

"Which is why we need to have that curbside sign posted by the front door. The one that gives them the cell phone number of one of your officers. You'll then have someone go out, direct them to one of the parking spots, and process them curbside."

The chief shook her head. "That's too involved. It will never work."

"I agree it's complicated," said Carl, "but it's only for a couple of hours at a relatively quiet part of the day. Look, I can't order you to do anything. I can only point out the law and the correct procedures. And the fact that what is happening now is a safety risk."

Slowly the chief nodded her head. "OK."

"Then you'll do as I propose?"

"I said, OK."

Carl wasn't sure the chief bought it. This was the one that Milton claimed pretty much ignored everything the rover said. But he had no choice, He couldn't hover over the chief all afternoon.

"Thank you for your help on this," he said, hoping rather than believing that the chief would comply.

# 83

## Tuesday, 1:00 p.m.

"So here I am at the warehouse," mumbled Jack, as he walked up the ramp to the front door. It was his own fault. Going around asking everyone if he could do something. Not for the first time, he wondered if this was just some busywork that Roger had given him, just to keep him occupied. He could not imagine anything as useless as testing voting machines on Election Day. The testing had been completed weeks ago. And these machines were not even being used today.

He wrote his name on the log at the welcome desk and proceeded to the rear of the warehouse where the "cage" was. The enclosure, secured by the chain-link fence, was where all the election related items were stored. The last time he had been here, all the carts and scanners had been in their proper places. Ready to go out to the precincts. Now it was empty. Well almost. He walked to the far end of the cage where the padlock was. He inserted the key that Roger had given him, opened the lock, and slid open the gate, gaining admittance.

There they were. Eight scanners, four in each row. Just like Roger said.

Jack examined each scanner carefully. Public count zero. Zero report has been printed. Screen says "insert ballot." Yup, these babies were ready to go. Jack went over to the workbench on the far left where the test decks had been kept. Those decks had caused so much trouble but they had finally gotten rid of the bad ones. He picked up a deck for the 12th congressional district. Roger had said they were all from the 12th congressional district. Add to that a set of *CreateBallot* cards that had previously been created. And the "cheat sheet" which had the anticipated result.

*All right. The sooner I get this wasted exercise done, the sooner I can get back to the Government Center and do some real work.*

Jack went to the first scanner and started inserting ballots. He would position the ballot, give it a little nudge, and the scanner would do the rest, sucking it in. An hourglass symbol would rotate on the screen for a few seconds, the counts on the screen would kick up by one, and the machine was ready for the next one. Within a few minutes the entire deck had been "voted." Jack then pressed the "close poll" button, and then pressed "confirm." He knelt down to open the bin and retrieved the voted ballots. Within a few seconds the printer started to generate its report, but Jack did not concern himself with that. Not for a while, anyway. There was seven more machines to be voted.

It was boring, tedious work but Jack soldiered on. Seven scanners to go, then six, then five. By now several printers were going at once, even as the first couple of machines were in "pause mode" as they were preparing to print out the write-ins. "Don't worry about the write-in report," Roger had said. "Just the numbers on the main report. Those are the ones that need to be verified."

At last all eight machines were fully voted. Jack gathered up the ballots from the eighth machine and returned them to the workbench. Now it was time to verify the printouts.

*First machine...looks good, second machine...looks good, what a waste of time, third machine...looks good, fourth machine...*

It was all methodical. No real thought. Just verify the stream of numbers.

*Wait a minute. That's not quite right. No, it's not. Let's see, this is machine number five.*

Jack checked machines six, seven, and eight, and now with an increased sense of focus. They were definitely off. He went back to the earlier machines. No, they were OK. It was just scanners five through eight that were off.

He dialed his cell.

"Roger. It's Jack over at the warehouse. And it's the damnedest thing..."

# 84

## Tuesday, 1:30 p.m.

Carl had just completed his visit to the Hagerman precinct and was well pleased. Even though Kathy was a rookie chief, Carl had sensed the day before that the precinct was in good hands. And this indeed was proving to be the case. The signs were correctly posted, the team members all seemed diligent in performing their duties, and the voters were being processed both efficiently and cordially. It really isn't difficult, just so long as you follow the manual. With a touch of common sense and good humor thrown in. Carl had to admit that sometimes he had difficulty with the common sense part.

He considered what to do next. The only two precincts he had not yet visited were Chesterbrook and Seneca Grove. He was completely comfortable with Chesterbrook. Nancy Jordan had been his assistant for several years and Carl had great respect for her abilities. Many of the other officers there had worked with Carl as well. Seneca Grove however was in the hands of that "politically incorrect" chief who had waited until 5:55 this morning to phone in his EPB problems. Not much choice here. Visit Seneca Grove next. Chesterbrook could wait.

Suddenly his radio sounded.

*"Base to Rover 5. Base to Rover 5. Go immediately to precinct 306, Chesterbrook. They are almost out of ballots. I repeat. Go immediately to Chesterbook."*

Carl was dumbfounded. That wasn't right. Precincts don't run out of ballots at 1:30 in the afternoon. He picked up his radio.

*"Rover 5 to Base. Are you sure about this? Are you sure that Chesterbrook is short on ballots. It seems a bit early for that."*

Almost immediately,

*"Base to Rover 5. They need ballots at Chesterbrook. The situation is dire. Go there immediately."*

There it was, as strange as it seemed.

*"Rover 5 to Base. I'm on my way."*

Carl had the upmost empathy for the stress that a chief felt when the ballot supply ran low. He remembered the angst that Cindy and he had experienced last January, when they realized that they were running out.

*But that wasn't at one-thirty in the afternoon.*

Ten minutes later he arrived at the Chesterbook parking lot. He grabbed a pack of ballots and the necessary forms and quickly walked to the school, experiencing feelings of nostalgia as he went. He went in the front door, following two other voters, walked down the familiar hall, and made a left turn into the gym.

"Carl!" shouted Nancy, almost the moment he came in. She immediately got up from the chief's table and engulfed Carl in a big hug.

"I'm so happy they made you a rover. You really earned it," she said, beaming at Carl. "Of course we miss Milton but they told me he has a route closer to his home. Everything is going great here. I've got such a good team. But of course, you trained most of us."

Carl looked around. So many of the officers here were folks that Carl had worked with over the years. Pam and Jerry Blevens. Theodore McDougald. Millicent LaGrande. He looked forward to personally greeting each one of them.

But suddenly he remembered.

"I've got those extra ballots you requested. You must be having a busy day."

Nancy frowned. "Yes, we are having a busy day. It was unusually heavy around eleven this morning. But we're nowhere close to running out. We started with eighteen packs of a hundred each. We just opened our ninth pack. We'll keep close tabs on it but I think we'll be good for the day."

Now Carl was truly puzzled. The directive from rover radio had been so explicit. Had they mixed up the precincts?

"We are having a bit of a problem with both scanners," continued Nancy. "They read the ballots fine but the feeder mechanism that directs the ballots into the bin is a bit balky. We have to jiggle it from time-to-time to get the ballot to drop into the bin. We can deal with it but it's annoying and it's gotten worse as the day wears on."

This was apparently the result of the bins been toppled during the delivery. Before Carl could respond however, his cell phone buzzed.

"Carl, this is Milton."

"Hi Milton. Funny you should call. I'm over at Chesterbrook and everyone is saying how much they miss you."

He could hear Milton laugh. "Well tell everyone thanks. Actually though Carl, I'm calling on a matter that may interest you on a personal level. At least I think, maybe, but I'm not quite sure and I don't want to presume something that is none of my business…"

Carl was taken aback by Milton's tone. He sounded a bit flustered, which was very unusual for Milton. He was usually so calm in his unassuming, capable way.

"What is it?"

"I just got this strange request from the Command Center. They wanted to know if I had the cell phone number for Cindy Phelps." There was a pause, as Milton apparently wanted to give Carl a moment to digest what he had just said. He then continued.

"They knew that I had been her rover in the June primary as well as last January and they thought I might still have her cell number. Actually I do not. I always erase all my chiefs' numbers from my cell after an election. But I know she's not a chief today since she's a candidate. Or at least, was a candidate. I can't imagine why they would want to talk to her. Anyway I hope I'm not being presumptuous, but I thought you might be interested…"

"I appreciate that, Milton. Thanks."

"OK, I'll let you get back to things. Have a good afternoon."

"Thanks. You too."

Immediately upon hanging up, Carl dialed Cindy.

"They're on to us. Or at least to you. Milton just got a call asking for your cell. He didn't have it but it's only a matter of time."

"Well they can't catch me if they can't find me," said Cindy, with a dramatic flourish. "Actually I'm having a great time here at Tower. It turns out that Mr. Hudgins is a good guy. His daughter is a senior at Manchester High and has applied for early admission at UVa. I've been telling him about all the good campus hangouts in Charlottesville—"

"Cindy—"

Carl could hear her sigh.

"Yeah, I know. We wanted to get noticed and now we're being noticed."

They were both silent for a few moments.

"I'll deal with it," she said, at last. "And whatever happens, I am absolutely certain we did the right thing."

"Me, too. See you at the finish line."

# 85

## Tuesday, 2:15 P.M.

*"This is Tracy Miller, WMML news, with our continuing Election Day coverage of all the local races. I'm here at Carter Run Elementary School where we will examine one of the darker sides of our county's electoral process. With me is Sissy Congleton of Brownie Troop 1130 and her mother, Mrs. Congleton, who will share with us their sobering tale. Sissy could you tell us, in your own words, what happened at this very spot this morning?"*

*"Yes, we were here to sell our cookies. We had chocolate chip, and oatmeal raisin, and peanut butter. And we sold most of the chocolate chip but not so much of the oatmeal—"*

*"Please, Sissy dear. Tell Miss Miller about the man."*

*"Yes, there was this man. He said we had to leave. We were breaking the law. And he had this measuring stick and said we had to go back into the street to sell our cookies and we were being bad and that's what he said."*

*"Tell us about this man. Did he have any authority?"*

*"I'm not sure. He said he was from the Elections and he was a Martian and—"*

*"No Sissy. We went over this. He wasn't a Martian. His name was Marsden. Carl Marsden from the Office of Elections. And he told the children they would have to move their stand, even though they had sold their cookies in the exact same place last year."*

*"And then he bought a peanut butter cookie and—"*

*"Thank you Sissy and Mrs. Congleton for sharing your story. And there you have it, ladies and gentlemen. It would appear that there is no place on Election Day for the Brownies of Troop 1130. Not at least in the eyes of Carl Marsden and the county Office of Elections. Indeed a sad moment for the citizens of our county and for cookie lovers everywhere."*

*"On a different note, we have just been advised of a piece of fast breaking news. It has been learned that there will be a special emergency meeting of the county Board of Elections, this afternoon at 3:30 p.m. What makes this meeting especially intriguing is that it will not be held in its usual location at the Government Center. Rather it will be held at the county warehouse facility in Springdale. It is not known what the subject of that meeting will be. One can only hope that somewhere on the agenda will be a call for justice for Sissy Congleton and the Brownies of Troop 1130."*

*"This is Tracy Miller. Keep your dial on WMML for all the day's election news."*

# 86

## TUESDAY, 2:30 P.M.

WELL IT COULD *have been worse,* thought Carl, as he exited Seneca Grove Elementary School. He had intended to visit this precinct earlier, to see how this aging, crusty chief was faring, but various "situations" had postponed his visit. But finally the time had come. It was the last precinct on his route to be visited and it was actually running fairly well. It was a small precinct and the number of voters had indeed been modest. The setup, while not the greatest, had been adequate, the equipment was working, and the chief had apparently kept his abrasive comments to himself.

*Now that I've visited every precinct once, where to now?*

There was only one answer. In the absence of any mandatory claims on his attention, he needed to return to Manchester and see how the two beleaguered teams of election officers were holding up.

Rush hour traffic had not yet begun and Carl made the uneventful trip over to Manchester, pulling into the parking lot for what he hoped would be the last time. Unlike some of the smaller precincts that were in an afternoon lull, a steady stream of voters could be seen, both coming in and going out of the school's entrance. As he parked his car, he caught sight of a dump truck rumbling down the lane that ran from the opposite side of the school. He got out of his car and proceeded to the sidewalk in front of the entrance. Poll workers for the various candidates were actively working the crowd. Many had set up folding tables upon which their campaign material rested. Carl recognized some of them from his earlier visit.

"Morgenstein for Soil and Water," said a young man, probably a college student, as he thrust a flier into Carl's hands. Besides listing his qualifications, the paper showed exactly how a voter could cast a write-in ballot.

"Vote for my mom. Vote for my mom."

One of Valerie sons was holding up a poster while Stan was handing out brochures.

"Hi Carl," he said. "Val's over at Happy Acres, working the senior vote. But since you're here, let me share something with you."

"I'm listening," said Carl. Stan's tone suggested that it might be serious.

Stan motioned for Carl to move in close. He apparently didn't want to be overheard.

"This location is really hurting. It's OK for the able-bodied folks but the handicapped people are having a rough time. A lot of them are struggling to get up the stairs and then there's that long walk. The officers inside are doing the best they can, but it's tough. There's a lady from some organization that promotes 'ease of voting' issues who has been walking around taking notes. I believe she is inside the polling place right now. She will probably want to talk to you."

Carl nodded, taking it all in. He was somewhat relieved to see one of the election officers standing next to the curbside voting sign. Carl thanked Stan and went over to the officer.

"Are you getting much business?" he asked.

"Some," he said. "But there are people who, because of pride or whatever, simply don't choose to get curbside service. It hurts that they don't have a handicapped entrance near the main door. To enter the building, they have to drive around to the other side of the school and most folks don't want to go to that trouble. Especially with those dump trucks coming through on a regular basis."

Carl nodded sympathetically. "Well just do the best you can to promote curbside to anyone who seems to be struggling."

The officer nodded.

*Well I better go inside and see how it looks,* he thought grimly.

The hallway did not look any more inviting than it had at 6:00 a.m. There was however one major difference and not for the better. Earlier, the people walking the long, dim hallway had been able-bodied folks on their way to work. They had taken the walk briskly and in stride, anxious to do their civic thing and get on with the day. Now many of the people were folks, who while not exactly handicapped, were making the walk much more slowly. A few used walkers while with others, it was a cane. Still others walked unaided, but very slowly, like it was taking a lot of effort. Carl did note with approval, that a few chairs had been placed at a number of spots along the route. An elderly lady was seated in one of them.

He reached the end of the hall and made the turn into the cafeteria. It was still very much a beehive of activity. All the EPBs were in use and short lines of voters could be seen at the various voting stations.

"Excuse me, are you with the county?"

It was an earnest looking lady, wearing a badge that read "Poll Watcher, Republican Party."

Carl nodded his head. He sensed that this would not be pleasant.

"Besides being a poll watcher, I am with the 'Virginians for Fair Voting.' We are a non-partisan watchdog group, and I must say that this location is sadly lacking in a number of ways."

For the next forty-five minutes the woman unloaded on Carl, making many of the same points that Stan had made, but with a dramatic flair. She wondered how many seniors might have given up, in the face of the obstacles they confronted. It was simply unacceptable that the county had provided such a poor voting location. She did not blame the election officers who were obviously doing their best. Neither did she blame the school. Obviously the project had to be done. As she went down her list of people she did not blame, Carl noted that he did not seem to be on that list. Every so often she would stop to catch her breath. At that point Carl would start to say something, but she would cut him off and start speaking some more.

It was a painful session, especially since Carl recognized the validity of the woman's observations.

"I fully appreciate everything you said and I will do everything I can to make sure it does not happen again."

That was the mantra that Carl repeated whenever there was a break in the woman's monologue.

Eventually the woman nodded and went back to her poll watchers table.

Having been thoroughly grilled and feeling exhausted, Carl looked for the two chiefs. Sharon was sitting at the chief's table doing some paperwork. Carl went over to her, sitting down.

"I'm writing some of my observations in the *Chiefs Notes*," she said. "If you're looking for Mandy, she's out in back, calling in a voter ID to the registrar's office. Besides our other problems, the cell phone reception in here sucks."

She smiled grimly and continued. "I see our poll watcher has told you at great length many of our imperfections. We've really done the best we could. We put chairs in the hall for people who get tired. Always an officer outside with the curb-side sign. If there is anything else we can do, I'd sure like to know it."

"I can't think of anything," said Carl. "Are many handicapped voters coming around to the back?"

"A few, but the dump truck brigade kind of discourages that."

At that point, Mandy entered the room by the back door. Seeing Carl and Sharon, she walked over to join them.

"I've never seen anything like this," she said, sitting down.

For a few minutes the three of them sat there, lost in their own thoughts.

"I can't think of anything else to say or suggest," Carl said at last, breaking the silence. "Except that you're both doing an exceptional job under horrendous conditions. And next time, I will make sure to engage the school earlier and we'll make sure this never happens again."

"At least the worst is over in terms of numbers," said Sharon.

"Speaking of which, how are you fixed for ballots?"

"I think we're OK but it will be close," said Sharon.

"We're roughly the same," agreed Mandy. "With all that has happened though, I'd feel better with another pack."

It was the least he could do. "Wait right here."

"We're not going anywhere," said Sharon, laughing. "Except to jump off a bridge."

Carl made the roundtrip to his car and signed over an extra pack of ballots to each of them. He was learning a lot this day. Not every voting location was as supportive as his own Chesterbook had been. And as Milton had pointed out, not every chief was as experienced as he was, or as quick a learner as Cindy had been. But somehow they were all managing to muddle thorough. And they would all do better next time. Of this he was determined.

Carl returned to his car. The immediate question before him was where to next? Since there didn't seem to be anything pressing right now, it might be a good time to get the earlier misunderstanding at Chesterbrook resolved, or at least brought to people's attention.

He took out his phone and dialed the command center.

"Command Center. Betty Mitchell speaking."

Carl was surprised. All day long it had been Terrence manning the phone. Betty was the head of outreach and had supervised him at the new citizens event back in September.

"Betty, this is Carl Marsden. Terrence is not there?"

"No, he was called away. I'm pinch hitting for him. What can I do for you?"

"It's not so much what you can do for me, but I need to report something. A while back, I was informed by the office that it was urgent that I go over to Chesterbrook because they were running out of ballots. When I got there, they were fine. Not even halfway through their allocation. Just thought I should pass that along."

"Well I'll certainly make note of that for Terrence when he comes back but I can't really tell you why it happened. Sorry."

They concluded their call. Carl was contemplating what to do next when his cell buzzed.

"Carl, this is Jessie over at Pikesville. I wanted to catch you before we got into the teeth of rush hour. We've done some projections, and we're going to need another pack of ballots before this thing is over. Can you get that to us?"

"Absolutely. I'm at Manchester now, so it should be about twenty minutes but I'll get over there as quickly as I can."

They said their goodbyes and concluded their call.

*First Manchester, then Pikesville. At this rate I'm going to be delivering a lot of ballots in these last few hours.*

# 87

## Tuesday, 3:30 p.m.

"This special meeting of the county Board of Elections will come to order. Present are the following board members: Kate McGowan, chairman, Gerald Sinclair, vice-chairman, Gilda St. Orange, secretary. Also in attendance are Gordon Carruthers, General Registrar, Terrence Bucholtz, machine coordinator, Roger Dellman, former machine coordinator, and… just who are you, sir?"

"Kate, he's Jack Vincent, seasonal employee," said Roger.

"Right, and Jack Vincent, seasonal employee. The time is 3:30 p.m. and this meeting is now in session. Well, it's quite a merry little band we have assembled here this afternoon," said Kate, looking around the table, located in the rear of the warehouse, the exact table where the rovers assembled every day during testing. "Perhaps our registrar will enlighten us all on why we are here, especially when there is so much to do back at the Government Center."

"Thank you, Kate," said Gordon Carruthers. "At about 1:30 this afternoon, Roger informed me of a development that throws into question whether all the scanners which have been deployed into the field are operating correctly."

"And by 'in the field,' you are referring to scanners currently in use in the precincts, even as we are speaking?"

"I would like to go on record by saying that all machines currently in use have been thoroughly tested and were found to be in perfect working order," said Terrence.

"Do you dispute that, Roger?"

"I don't dispute that they were thoroughly tested, but recent developments have put into question, at least in my mind, whether certain scanners in the field are about to fail."

"Do we know specifically which ones or does this doubt cover our entire inventory?"

"It is very specific. In twenty-four of our precincts, one of the two scanners in use is from the allotment that was purchased from Braxton County—"

"Oh come on," interrupted Terrence. "Not that again. Did Marsden put you up to this?"

"Who?"

"Marsden. Carl Marsden. He's one of our rovers. At least for now, he is. He's had this ridiculous theory that the thirty machines we purchased from Braxton County earlier this year are bad. The whole thing is absurd. Every one of those machines has been thoroughly tested. They were tested by Braxton. They were tested by us, when we accepted them back in August. And they were tested again in October. From the beginning, Marsden has been bad mouthing them. He just won't let it drop." Terrence had gone red in the face from his frustration concerning the topic that never seemed to die.

"Do you have anything to support Marsden's theory?" Kate asked Roger. "And why are you even involved in this."

"Carl called me this morning. He claimed the machines were suspect, due to an old manufacturer's defect that slipped through the cracks. He said he had some documentation describing this defect, but more to the immediate point, he said that a simple test existed that could test his theory."

Terrence started to say something but Kate cut him off. "Let's hear what Roger has to say."

"Carl said that there were eight scanners in the warehouse area ready to be tested. Powered on. Passcode already entered. Ready to be voted with our test—"

"Did you leave the scanners in the test area, in this condition?" Kate asked Terrence, effectively ignoring her own admonition to allow Roger to tell his story uninterrupted.

"Certainly not," said Terrence. "Those machines were originally slated to be in the field and were thoroughly tested. We subsequently decided that they were not needed so they were left in the warehouse with the power off and their screens dark."

"If that is the case," said Kate, turning her attention back to Roger, "then who powered up the machines?"

"Carl refused to say. All he said was that they had been on all night and if we ran the test, we could see if the Braxton machines worked. Four of the machines we are talking about were from Braxton. His theory was that these machines will overheat if left on for an extended period of time and will subsequently record the wrong results."

"We'll table the question of who turned on the machines for the moment," said Kate. "Was the test that Marsden requested performed?"

"Yes, it was," said Roger. "At my request, Jack here went over to the warehouse. Jack why don't you tell the rest."

"Not much to tell," said Jack, who in truth was itching to get back to the Government Center and do some real work. "The scanners were all there, ready to be tested. I fed the test decks into each one and printed the results. Four machines gave good results. Four did not. These are the tapes." He put the tapes on the table. For a few minutes there was silence as the tapes were passed around and inspected."

"Very interesting," said Kate, studying the tapes. "And rather disturbing. And we have no idea who came in earlier to power up those machines?"

"There is a possibility," said Roger. "We examined the visitor's log from yesterday. There were three entries. Two were from the morning. They were county truckers who were picking up equipment from the warehouse to be taken to a number of fire stations."

"And the third?"

"It came about 2:30 p.m. The name listed was Cynthia Phelps."

"That name sounds familiar," said Kate.

"She was the chief that the board almost fired during last January's primary."

"Ah yes. Now I remember. And later that night she helped track down that chief who went missing. Sort of a one day celebrity. Is she a chief this time around?"

"No," said Terrence. "She is a candidate for Soil and Water. Or was. She dropped out a couple of weeks ago. But her candidate status would have allowed her entry into the warehouse."

"I remember her," said Gilda. "She was the candidate who had the meltdown in the debate."

"We've made some attempts to locate her, but so far have been unsuccessful," said Roger.

"But even if she was allowed in the warehouse, she would not have received admission to enter the cage. So how did she get in?" said Kate. "That is a question I would like to see answered.

I would also like to see that documentation that Marsden claims to have about the machines."

"I believe I can shed light on both those questions."

So intent were they on the matter at hand, that they had failed to notice the newcomer's entrance.

"And who are you?" asked Kate.

"I am Cynthia Phelps, your post-meltdown candidate for Soil and Water. And I am here to beg you to please take those twenty-four Braxton machines out of circulation."

# 88

## Tuesday, 4:30 p.m.

*All it takes is a fender bender and two malfunctioning traffic lights to turn a twenty minute drive into an hour,* thought Carl as he rushed up the walkway to the Pikesville Community Center. He had been happy to see that the "voter parking" signs were still in place. Apparently his earlier chat with Mr. Rodriguez had been sufficient. Carl also noted a steady stream of voters both coming and going. Pikesville was a large precinct, second in size only to Tower and Manchester, and the large number of cars in the parking lot reflected that.

"I had almost given up hope," cried Jessie, as Carl entered the Empire Room.

"Traffic was bad," said Carl. "I'm glad you anticipated this before things got critical. How has the day been?"

"Really good," said Jessie. "Once we got past that misunderstanding with Mr. Rodriguez. This is a much nicer facility than the Methodist church was."

Carl was in the process of signing over the ballots to Jessie when his radio sounded. It was Betty's voice. Terrence was apparently still away.

*"Base to Rover 5. Base to Rover 5. The Tower precinct needs more ballots. Please go there immediately."*

Carl looked skeptically at the radio, thinking back to the Chesterbrook false alarm. He was about to enquire about the source of the request when the radio sounded again.

*"This is for real, Carl. The chief called it in."*

"Sounds like you guys are having a fun day," said Jessie.

"Something like that," said Carl, even as he was pressing the transmit button on the radio.

*"Rover 5 to Base. I'm on my way to Tower with the ballots."*

All this crisscrossing of his route was taking time. Valuable time. Was anything happening with respect to those Braxton scanners? He had been so hopeful after Milton's earlier call. They were looking for Cindy. That along with his earlier conversation with Roger. Surely they realized that something was wrong with those scanners. He would check with Cindy when he got to Tower. Perhaps she would have an update on what was happening.

Another half hour eaten up on the clock, as Carl pulled into the rear Tower parking lot. Mr. Hudgins was still at his station, promoting the Hayes candidacy.

"You certainly are loyal to your calling," remarked Carl.

"Absolutely. We've got a great candidate. Janet Hayes is a winner and will help get the school board back on track."

"I don't see your rival anywhere."

"No, she left a while back."

"Did she tell you where she was going?"

"I assume to some other precinct but I can't be sure. We're not exactly close confidants."

Carl nodded and proceeded down the walkway into the precinct where he was greeted by an appreciative chief.

"We're halfway through our last pack. We might have made it to the end but I wasn't sure. We have almost two hours to go."

Once again, the paperwork was completed and the ballots turned over. Carl returned to his car. What was happening? Was anything happening? Nine hours since he had spoken to Roger. Three since he had spoken to Cindy. He needed to know. He dialed Cindy.

Three rings followed by,

*"Hi, this is Cindy. I'm out and about right now so just leave a message and I'll get back to you. Have a great day."*

"Cindy, what's happening? Is anything happening? I'm completely in the dark. Call when you get a chance."

What to do now? The mega precincts at Manchester, Pikesville, and Tower had all received their extra ballots. Perhaps he could turn his attention to the smaller precincts, some of whom had first-time chiefs. He would head over to Wallingford where he had started the day twelve hours earlier. Help Marianne prepare for the close.

He was halfway down the road to Wallingford when his cell buzzed. He pulled into a shopping center.

"Carl, this is Cindy. I'm at the warehouse. The Board has been meeting since 3:30 p.m. I showed them everything. All that internet stuff I printed for you. And then Jack Vincent showed them tapes from the test he ran earlier. It was just like we thought. The four Braxton scanners printed bad results. Jack's a great guy, by the way. The stories he has to tell—"

"Cindy, I'm glad you're making friends everywhere but has the board made a decision about those Braxton scanners?"

"Not yet. Right now, they're debating a motion to install barbed wire on top of the fence. They were rather mystified that I was able to climb it. I offered to give them a demo."

"Cindy, the polls close in less than two hours. At that point twenty-four machines will start printing out bad results. They need to issue a directive not to record any of the votes coming from those machines and feed the ballots into the good scanner. Surely Roger, and by now even Terrence, realizes that."

"I think they all realize it. But they've gotten themselves sidetracked. Some of those board members love to talk. By the way, I found out why you were sent to Chesterbrook on a false alarm to deliver those ballots that they didn't need. It seems that there have been cases of poll watchers jumping to their own conclusions and calling their favorite board member to get more ballots delivered. The chief is not even consulted. Terrence and Roger have put a stop to that."

"Interesting. Well just do whatever you can to nudge them along on those Braxton scanners. I'd hate to see it come to nothing after all this."

"I don't know how this will play out," said Cindy, solemnly. "But I promise you, it will not come to nothing."

# 89

## Tuesday, 5:45 p.m.

"So now if you just remove these sections from the manual," said Carl, "you can delegate tasks to your officers. You can then concentrate on tallying the results on the scanner and working on the SOR."

"I've been studying the 'Close Polls' section for the past hour," said Marianne. "I think I know who will do the various things. So far everything has worked, just as they said it would. The EPBs, the scanners, the *CreateBallot.* My team has been great. And I appreciate everything you've done for me."

"Which was precious little. You've done it yourself."

Carl then allowed his mind to drift back to the first time he had been a chief election officer and the feeling of intense satisfaction he had felt at the end of the day. He sensed that Marianne would feel the same way in a couple of hours.

He headed back to his car. The radio was silent. His cell was silent. A little over an hour to go. Where to next? Carter Run? Cooper? Hagerman? They all had relatively inexperienced chiefs. Maybe he'd squeeze in a quick visit to each…

*"Base to all Rovers. Base to all Rovers. In a matter of minutes, there will be a major announcement. Keep your radio on this frequency and turned on at all times. I repeat, in a matter of minutes, there will be a major announcement."*

# 90

## Tuesday, 6:00 p.m.

"Now let's go over again what we want to say," said Kate. "We want to be sure we have accurate results but we also want to be able to measure the degree to which the Braxton machines are failing. So all scanners will close and print their results. However the results from the Braxton machines will not be entered into the Statement of Results. Those tapes will be placed in the 1B envelope, the envelope we normally use for provisional ballots that are cast after 7:00 p.m. Since there is no indication that Richmond will extend voting hours, that envelope will be empty anyway. Then when the results of the good machines are fully tabulated and printed, we rip out the tape and remove the bin that contains those ballots."

"Then," continued Roger, "We empty out the ballots from the bin under the bad scanner. We then insert that now empty bin under the good scanner, reopen the polls, enter the 'supersede' password, zero out the counters, print a fresh zero report, and feed the ballots from the bad machine into the good machine. When that's all done we tally those results which becomes the second entry of the SOR. The rovers do this all the time in the warehouse."

"This plan only works because we have a good scanner in each of those precincts. Thank God there aren't any precincts where both scanners are Braxton," added Kate.

"This is giving me a headache," said Gilda. "How much time are we adding to the close by doing all this?"

"Quite a bit," said Roger. "It's going to take quite a while for the machines to print all those images of the write-in votes. Remember it's not just going to be a few 'Mickey Mouse' write-ins. There's going to be a whole ton of write-in votes in the Soil and Water race."

"For which we have our esteemed guest to thank," said Kate, with a sour expression on her face.

For the briefest of moments, all eyes in the warehouse shifted to Cindy who smiled weakly.

"Now what do we want to do as far as spinning this?" said Gilda. "Do we really want to admit that our testing was insufficient?"

An uncomfortable silence engulfed the room.

"There is no spin. We simply relate what happened and what needs to be done," said Terrence, breaking the silence. "This lapse reflects on me more than anyone else. Heaven knows, Carl Marsden alerted me to the potential problem weeks ago. We recognize our mistakes, learn from them, and resolve to do better."

"That's probably the best course," agreed Kate. Slowly the others nodded.

"I'll call this in to Betty Mitchell so she can transmit it to the rovers. We need to get those affected chiefs on board ASAP," said Gordon, who went to the phone on a side table to make his call.

For the first time in a couple of hours the people at the table began to relax, just a bit. The next few hours were going to be painful, especially for the chiefs involved. In addition, they would have to explain it all to the parties and well as the public. But at least they had a handle on what was to be done.

"And I think we owe a debt of gratitude to you Ms. Phelps for—what is it?" said Kate, looking at Cindy, who had tentatively raised her hand.

"There is still, as I see it, one unresolved issue," said Cindy.

That brief moment of calm vanished instantly. The board members looked at each other apprehensively. No one wanted to ask the question.

At last Terrence spoke. "And that issue is…?"

"There were thirty scanners purchased from Braxton. Is that correct?"

"It is."

"Twenty-five of them were assigned to the precincts. Twenty-four are out there at this very moment. The twenty-fifth failed on the last day of testing and was taken out of service."

"That's correct. I have the list of precincts here. It will be part of the announcement to the rovers."

"Twenty-four plus the one," repeated Cindy. "And then there are four more here in the warehouse." She pointed to the row of scanners on the other side of the fence.

Cindy fell silent, shifting her gaze from person to person. Slowly they began to understand.

"So, where is the thirtieth scanner?"

For a few moments everyone was silent. Each one hoped that someone else had the answer. But no answer came.

"Oh shit," said Kate.

# 91

## Tuesday, 6:30 p.m.

*"That is the process that each of the twenty-four precincts must execute. This is the same process that rovers use in the warehouse. You will need to explain it to the chiefs for the involved precincts. The Office of Elections is issuing a statement to the parties and the media. Allow the poll watchers to observe as always but don't get involved giving long explanations. Now here is the list of affected precincts. For Rover 1: Carson, Danvers, For Rover 2:..."*

Carl already had a copy of the list but had not committed it to memory. He was pretty sure some of his precincts were impacted. Hopefully, none of the larger ones.

*"...For Rover 5: Pikesville, Tower, Manchester 1, Manchester 2, Hagerman, and Chesterbrook, For Rover 6..."*

*All the heavy hitters,* thought Carl grimly. With just thirty minutes to go, Carl realized that it would be impossible to talk each of the chiefs through the process before the polls closed. However since it would take a certain amount of time for the scanners to tabulate and print the results, they did not actually need to know exactly at 7:00 p.m. Still it was a daunting task, complicated by the poor cell phone reception at Manchester. Carl would have to drive over there in rush hour to deliver the instructions in person. As he made the trip, he would talk to as many of the other chiefs as possible on his cell speakerphone.

He started with the Tower precinct. Dan, the chief, had seemed like a pretty sharp guy and this would be a good way to start things off. He made the connection and explained the situation and the remedy, making sure that Dan also had his speakerphone on so the assistant chief could listen in. This proved to be a bit of a challenge as the assistant chief had to have things repeated a number of times, but they finally seemed to be on board with the process, just as the Manchester parking lot came into view.

It was ten minutes to seven when he pulled into the parking lot. There were still a number of voters entering the school.

His cell phone buzzed.

"Carl, its Milton. I had only one precinct impacted, so I've been redeployed to help you. Who can I contact?"

"I've done Tower and I'm just entering Manchester. If you could do Pikesville and Hagerman, that would be great. Then we'll finish up at Chesterbrook."

"You got it. And congratulations. You were right all along about Braxton."

No sooner had they completed the call, when Carl's phone buzzed again.

"Carl, its Cindy. The board asked me to call you to see if you had any idea where the missing scanner might be? You know the 1702 serial."

"The board asked *you* to talk to me."

"Well, yeah. Since we're partners in crime and all. The database listed the machine as 'in reserve' so we've spent the past half hour searching the entire warehouse, hoping to find it. You can't imagine all the stuff in here. Do you know that there are dumpsters of perfectly good books that are going to be shredded?"

"But why do they think I might know where the missing machine is?"

"Because they're desperate. We all are. Right from the beginning you were the one person who was fixated on those machines. They're hoping you noticed something that we all missed."

As much as Carl wanted to get into the Manchester precinct to talk to the chiefs, he realized that locating the missing scanner was imperative. Scanners don't just disappear. If it was not in the warehouse, it had to be in one of the precincts. Which meant it was swapped in for another machine, but they forgot to log it into the system. *But there were just the eleven. The eleven machines that he and Cindy had agonized over in such excruciating detail. That was all there was...*

But then Carl remembered.

That last day. There had actually been two scanners that had failed. He had completely forgotten about the first one, the scanner that had simply failed to turn on. The second one, of course, had been the one that had printed bad results later in the day. And he remembered insisting that it be replaced by a non-Braxton machine. So it had to be the first machine. It was obvious. How had he missed it?

"Cindy, there were two failed machines from the testing on the last day. They must be somewhere in the warehouse."

We did find two scanners, tucked away in a corner, but neither was 1702."

"Yes, but I think one of those might have been replaced by 1702. It's the one that won't turn on at all. Find which one it is and then locate it in the database. Whatever precinct it is assigned to, is probably the one that currently has 1702."

"Got it. Thanks."

With the call completed, Carl got out of the car just in time to hear Mandy announce,

*"The Polls are now closed."*

# 92

## Tuesday, 7:10 p.m.

"Just shoot me now," said Sharon, not for the first time since Carl had begun explaining the drill.

"Just remember, 'suspersede1' is the password," repeated Carl. "I would recommend you start closing down your scanners right away."

"And which one is the bad scanner?" asked Mandy.

"Let's see," said Carl. "It's this one, over here." He showed her the list of serial numbers on his sheet, pointing to the one that was labeled "Manchester 2."

"Just shoot me now," repeated Sharon.

"The sooner you close the polls, the sooner you'll get out of here," said Carl.

Both chiefs nodded and, along with their assistant chiefs, went back to where their respective scanners were located. Other officers were in the process of taking down the EPBs, *CreateBallot* machines, and signs. Sharon and Mandy and their teams had done well. Now they were dead tired and wanted to go home. They all did.

Carl walked over to Sharon.

"You've done great today. Just hang in there a little bit longer."

Sharon pressed the necessary buttons and the machines went in to "think mode." And then they started printing out the results.

As an election official, Carl's entire disposition was to ensure that the process worked. The next day he might read with interest, the actual results. However for a few seconds he allowed his curiosity to get the better of him and looked at one of the tapes being produced. Manchester was known as a heavily Democratic precinct and the results being generated seemed to reflect that. The Democrats were winning in the races for US Senate and House of Representatives by wide margins. Then came the local races:

School Board, Hayes 462, Turner 545, Write-ins 5.

Soil and Water, Diesel 105, Phelps 102, Rawlins 319, Write-ins 298.

Bond issue, Yes 659, No 356

"Don't put too much stock in those," said Sharon, who noticed Carl's interest. "That's one of the bad machines."

"Right," said Carl, getting back into focus. He had to leave anyhow, now that he was assured that Manchester was under control. With few parting words of encouragement, he left the precinct.

# 93

## Tuesday, 7:30 p.m.

Carl returned to his car intending to drive to…he wasn't sure.

I better check with Milton to see if he's finished with Pikesville yet.

He took out his phone and saw that there was a message, just a few minutes old. He pressed the appropriate buttons.

*Damn it, Carl! Pick up the friggin phone! It's Cindy. Call me. Now!*

Carl did as directed.

"Where were you? In a cave?"

"I might just as well have been. The cell phone reception in Manchester High is spotty at best and—"

"Yeah, you'll have to tell me about it some time. We found the dead scanner and ran the serial through Michael's database. It's listed as being at the Chesterbrook precinct."

"That can't be. Chesterbrook already has one Braxton machine."

"Well guess what. Now they have two. They won the lottery. We need you to get over to Chesterbook ASAP. In the meantime call Nancy Jordan. She's the chief over there."

"Yes, I know who Nancy Jordan is. I've known her since you were in high school."

"Right. Anyway confirm with her that 1702 is indeed there. Then get back to me. We were about to call her ourselves."

"What happens if 1702 is indeed there?"

"Don't know. We're working on it. We'll get back to you."

"OK, but there is something else you should know. The black bins, on which each of the scanners rest, were knocked over by the workmen during the delivery. I've verified that the scanners are working but the feeder that runs from the scanner to the bin is messed up. They've been struggling with them all day."

"Which means that just swapping scanners won't be enough. They'll have to bring in a whole new unit. Damn it. We'll need a truck for that."

"Cindy, excuse me for asking. You're not on the board; you're not an employee; you haven't even been sworn in. How come you're in the middle of all this?"

"I'm not really sure. It started as a formal meeting some four hours ago but we're pretty much freeform right now. It's like I've become an honorary member of the board. For tonight anyway."

"Right. Well I'll call Nancy. In the meantime, just let your fellow board members know we do need a plan and sooner would be better than later."

# 94

## Tuesday, 7:35 P.M.

*"This is Tracy Miller with the early returns from our local contests. With 15% of county precincts reporting, it would appear that Schuyler Elementary School might be getting that renovation after all, as the school bond issue seems to have the early lead by about a 2 to 1 margin.*

*"Our other races are, at this time, 'too close to call.' For school board, Republican Janet Hayes is holding a razor-thin edge over Democrat Valerie Turner. Turner was an outspoken advocate for the bond issue so it appears to be quite possible that voters accepted the message, but not the messenger.*

*"Meanwhile there is an intense battle for Soil and Water Conservation Board between Republican Frederick Rawlins and, would you believe it, 'Write-ins.' It is believed that a substantial portion of those write-in votes may have been cast for George Mason Teaching Assistant Howard Morgenstein, but this will need to be confirmed in the coming days. Lagging behind are Independent Green Everett Diesel and Democrat dropout Cynthia Phelps.*

*"Overshadowing these early returns is the bizarre statement, just issued from the county Board of Elections, indicating that returns will*

*be significantly delayed in twenty-four key precincts, which includes the Democratic strongholds of Tower and the two Manchester precincts.*

*"Analysts are still deciphering the rather complex announcement, but it would appear that some of the scanners used in these precincts might have been corrupted. This, of course, opens up the public imagination to all sorts of scenarios.*

*"So the only thing that's clear is that you need to keep your dial on WMML for all the fast breaking election news."*

# 95

## Tuesday, 7:40 p.m.

As Carl was preparing to call Nancy Jordan, his cell buzzed. "It's Milton. I talked to the chiefs at Hagerman and Pikesville. The chief at Hagerman is Kathy, the rookie. She is sharp. Picked it up right away. She'll be OK. Not so with Jessie, here at Pikesville. He sort of glazed over when I described the process. Same thing with the assistant chief, who I believe is his wife. I think I better stay here and work with him until it gets done. Which leaves you with Chesterbrook. I'll head on over there when Pikesville is done but Chesterbrook shouldn't be a problem with Nancy Jordan in charge."

"Sounds good. Thanks, Milton."

They completed the call but before Carl could call Nancy, his cell buzzed again.

"This is the night custodian at Happy Acres. Who's going to take down all these damn signs?"

"Sir, I will get to it sometime this evening."

"We like to keep our grounds neat. No solicitors. No advertisements. Nothing that detracts from the grounds. It's my job to make sure—"

"Right. I will be there, sometime before dawn. Bye."

Finally his phone was not buzzing. He dialed Nancy.

"Nancy, this is Carl. How far are you into the process?"

"Both scanners are printing, Carl. We should be out of here in record time."

*I don't think so, Nancy.*

"I'm afraid I have some bad news. At least one of your scanners in defective. Possibly both. Once the printing stops, do not do anything until you hear from me. Right now, I need the last four digits of the serial numbers for both machines."

"You're breaking my heart, Carl. I'll get those numbers."

There was silence for about thirty seconds. Carl wondered how long his cell phone battery was going to last.

"Carl, the numbers are 1697 and 1702."

It was as he feared.

"Remember what we said before? About not doing anything after the printing stops until you hear from me?"

"Absolutely."

"Well that goes double. We think both of those machines are bad. I'm not sure what the board is coming up with. They're working on it now. I'll be there is a few minutes."

Carl dialed Cindy.

"I just talked to Nancy. They have 1702. Both machines are Braxton."

"Which is what we thought. Get over to Chesterbrook right away. Keep her from doing anything rash. Like going home."

"Will do. I just talked to Milton and he's heading over there too, once he's done helping at Pikesville. Do you have a plan yet?"

"It's evolving, but I don't have time to talk and neither do you. Just get your ass over to Chesterbook."

On that note, Cindy disconnected and Carl started his car. As he pulled out of the Manchester parking lot, his thoughts drifted back to an earlier election where he and Cindy had confronted a whole different set of last minute crises. This was becoming a habit.

# 96

## Tuesday, 8:15 p.m.

"County dispatch, we need a truck."

"And a driver."

"...And a driver...No, this is not a medical emergency but... No, next Friday is not acceptable, we need it...No, next Thursday is no good either...We need it now...Immediately...Don't tell me to have a good day...And don't hang up..."

"They hung up," said Kate, sadly.

"Hopefully Terrence is having better luck," said Roger. "He's up front using the in-house phone to call the warehouse supervisor. There are the county trucks in the parking lot. All we need is a driver with the key and we're in business."

"So here is the plan," he continued. "When the truck arrives, we load two of those four good machines. They'll be driven over to the Chesterbrook precinct. They're printing the results on the two bad machines right now, but those numbers will not be entered in the SOR and the chief and her team will remain on site until the truck arrives."

"Does the chief know this?" asked Gordon.

"She knows," said Cindy.

"Good. When the truck arrives and the scanners are wheeled in, the rover will remove the precinct flash drives from the bad machines and put them in the replacements. He will then turn on the replacements, reopen the polls, enter the supersede password, zero out the counters, print the zero report, and start feeding ballots into the machine. When all are fed in, they close the polls and print the results."

"And how long will that take?"

"Probably about an hour," said Cindy. "The maximum throughput is about one ballot every five seconds. If you figure 600 ballots are being fed into each machine, divided by 3600 seconds per hour, you get about .83 hours. But it's tough for anyone to keep the 'ballot every five seconds' rate going for an extended period, so that leaves us with about an hour."

"That's about right," agreed Roger.

"How do you know all this?" asked Kate, directing her gaze at Cindy.

"My boyfriend's a rover."

Oops. Cindy hadn't meant to say that and her red faced countenance said as much. It had just slipped out. There was a brief, awkward silence.

"So our secret is out," said Jack, flashing a roguish grin in Cindy's direction. Others at the table smiled in amusement at her discomfort.

"Anyway, to finish up," said Roger, getting things back on track. "Once these results are tabulated, it's pretty much business as usual. The chief leads the team in all the reporting and closing activities and their day is done. One additional thing though. The rover is the one who reopens those machines. For the integrity of the process, there should be a second rover working with him."

"Milton will be there as soon as he's finished helping out at Pikesville," said Cindy, regaining her poise.

"Are we all agreed, that this is the plan?" asked Kate, looking around the room.

Everyone nodded.

"Good. Now all we need is a truck," said Kate.

"He's coming! He's coming!" shouted Terrence. "The driver is on the way. He should be here in ten minutes."

A feeling of relief swept the gathering.

"In that case," said Kate, "The chair will entertain a motion that this meeting, convened some four and a half hours ago, be adjourned."

"I so move," shouted Gilda.

"I second," called out the vice chairman.

"All in favor say—"

"Aye!" shouted everyone at the table, whether they were board members or not.

# 97

## Tuesday, 8:30 p.m.

*"Meanwhile in that school board race, with 90% of the precincts reporting, Democrat Valerie Turner has taken a narrow lead over Republican Janet Hayes. Our exact numbers are Turner, 92,380, Hayes, 89,826 but with several major precincts left to report, anything can happen here.*

*"Meanwhile in that very strange race for Soil and Water Conservation Board, the race remains extremely tight as Frederick Rawlins continues to maintain an ever-so slim lead over what is believed to be a write-in campaign for Howard Morgenstein. Rawlins has the endorsement of the Republican Party while Morgenstein, who is not an active candidate, doesn't really have the endorsement of anyone. Right now the vote totals are Rawlins 60,312, Write-in 59,842. It must be cautioned however, that it may be several days before it is verified just how many of those write-in votes were actually cast for Morgenstein as most elections see at least a handful of votes thrown away for the likes of Mickey Mouse and 'None of the above.'*

*"Completing the Soil and Water picture are Independent Green candidate Everett Diesel with 31,112 votes and Democratic Party reject Cynthia Phelps with 26,805. Mr. Diesel has just issued a concession statement in*

*which he 'congratulates the winner, whomever that may be, and urges all Virginians to think "more trains, less traffic."'*

*"Of course, all eyes turn now to those twenty-four precincts whose faulty voting equipment has resulted in an extended amount of time required to report the results. These include the heavily populated precincts of Pikesville, Tower, and the two Manchester precincts, which is why we are stationed right here in the now deserted parking lot of Manchester High School, where we were when it all began some fourteen and a half hours ago.*

*"And even as we speak, we've been handed an unconfirmed report that additional equipment is being dispatched to the Chesterbrook precinct where apparently things are very dire indeed.*

*"So election night is far from over and rest assured that station WMML will keep you apprised right to the very end. This is Tracy Miller reporting."*

# 98

## Tuesday, 8:50 p.m.

"And everything worked just as we said?...Great...And you're heading out to the Government Center now... Wonderful...Well get a good night's sleep, Kathy, you've earned it."

They completed the call.

"Hagerman is done," Carl said happily, walking over to the group of Chesterbook election officers who were sitting together waiting for something to happen. Everything that could be put away had been put away. The two scanners were silent. The tapes had been cut and placed in the 1B envelope as directed. A few minutes earlier, Cindy had called with the status update. All they could do now was wait. Wait for the scanners that they were told would be arriving.

Carl had taken the opportunity to call as many of his chiefs as possible to see how they were doing. One after another they had reported completion. First it was Danby. Then Cooper. Happy Acres. Carter Run. Wallingford. Seneca Grove. And now Hagerman, the first of the precincts that needed "special handling" was done.

Milton came through the door.

"Pikesville is done," he called out. "What's happening here?"

"Not much," said Nancy Jordan. "Have a seat. We are all just waiting."

...and waiting...and waiting...

# 99

## Tuesday, 9:20 p.m.

"Did someone call for a truck?"

"Yes!" they all sounded in unison.

"Hi. I'm Maurice. What do you need loaded?"

"Two scanners, from that group over there," said Terrence, pointing to the row.

The man went over and started to roll one of them toward the door.

"Isn't that one of the Braxton scanners?" asked Cindy.

"Yes, it is. Hold on, Maurice," said Roger, going over to the scanners. "Let's be sure. This one...and this one," he said, pulling two of the scanners out of line.

"They all look the same to me," said Maurice.

That simple statement resulted in uncontrollable laughter from the table.

"Trust me, they are not," said Roger.

"Whatever you say," said Maurice. "I'm getting holiday pay for this little adventure."

"Well, I'm outta here," said Gilda. Others nodded in unison.

Cindy dialed Carl.

"They're loading the truck right now. It's a ten mile drive so you should have it within a half hour."

"Thanks. We'll be waiting."

"Cindy, we're closing down," said Terrence, who then added in a voice just above a whisper, "and whatever happens tonight, and whatever happens to me in the coming days, you and Carl should be very proud of what you have done today."

Cindy nodded in appreciation as they all headed for the exit. Outside Maurice was rolling the second of the two scanners up the ramp into the truck. Various cars were pulling out of the parking lot, as he pulled up the ramp and closed the rear door.

He then walked around to the driver's side of the truck and climbed into the cab.

"Excuse me, miss?" he called over to Cindy. "Where am I taking this to?"

No one had thought to inform the driver of the destination. Cindy looked in amazement at the cars disappearing down the road. It was probably her lack of sleep that caused her to think that this was unbelievably hilarious and she started to laugh.

"My word. You folks sure find a lot of things funny."

"Yes, we do," said Cindy, regaining her composure. "Those scanners need to go to Chesterbrook Elementary School. And they need to get there right away."

"I don't know where that is," said Maurice, taking out his handheld device. "I'll need to use this GPS. What's the address? This may take a few minutes."

"No time for that," said Cindy as she ran around to the passenger side, opened the door, and climbed in.

"I'm your GPS, Maurice. Let's get this mother on the road."

# 100

## TUESDAY, 9:30 P.M.

"AND NOW WITH *the Manchester precincts reporting in, adding their numbers to those that came from Tower a few minutes ago, WMML is prepared to declare Valerie Turner the winner in the school board...*"

"Yes, yes!" cried Cindy.

"Well, you're the happy one," said Maurice. "Turner? I think I voted for her. I usually vote with the Democrats."

"*...while the race for Soil and Water remains too close to call. Republican Frederick Rawlins' lead over 'write-ins' has shrunk to a mere twenty-five votes. And it all comes down to one last precinct. For the past two hours while other precincts have been churning out their results, the precinct at Chesterbrook Elementary School has been stymied by malfunctioning equipment...*"

"Hey, that's where we're going," said Maurice.

"*...while the two remaining candidates, Everett Diesel and Cynthia Phelps, lag far behind...*"

"Uh-oh," said Maurice.

Cindy looked up. Up ahead of her, she could see cars with their brake lights on. At first they slowed but still kept moving.

They passed a sign, announcing an exit in one mile. The cars ahead came to a stop.

"Damn," she said.

The cars started moving again, albeit slowly. Then another complete stop.

"Maurice, we're getting off at the next exit."

"Are you familiar with these side roads, miss?"

"This one I am," said Cindy, as the truck inched passed the sign that said, "Duncan Hill Road, half mile."

# 101

## Tuesday, 10:05 p.m.

The waiting continued. Cindy had said a half hour. It was now going on forty-five minutes. Carl was aware that the WMML camera crew had recently arrived and was poised outside. This meant that at least one of the races was close. It was all so unsettling.

But nothing was more unsettling than the call he had received from Cindy about fifteen minutes ago.

"...yeah, we're on Duncan Hill Road. We had to. The interstate was blocked."

"Cindy, I don't think trucks are allowed on Duncan Hill Road."

"What's that, I can't make you out... Weak signal... We're just passing the point where Julia ran off the road... Whoa, slow down Maurice... Wow, that was hairy... OK Carl, we should be there in a few minutes. That is if... all right, easy does it...Gotta run, see you in a bit."

And still they waited. Carl was tempted to go outside and keep vigil out there but he did not want to face the camera crew.

And suddenly it was happening. A loud banging on the side door. Everyone in the Chesterbrook precinct sprung to life. Carl ran to the door and threw it open. The light from the TV cameras was blinding so he could only make out the shadow of a big hulking figure before him.

"Are you Marsden?"

"Yes, I am."

"I have a delivery of two scanners. Sign here please."

# 102

## Tuesday, 10:25 P.M.

Whenever Cindy looked back on that remarkable day, she pondered on how much of it was a complete blur while other portions could be recalled with crystal clarity. The thrill she felt as she rolled the second scanner through the door of the school, even as Carl and Milton were starting to work on the one Maurice had brought in a few minutes earlier. She remembered hugging each of the election officers from the Chesterbrook precinct, the people she had worked with in that special election the previous January. And she remembered practically collapsing into one of the chairs on the side of the gym.

*I just want to savor this moment*, she thought to herself, over and over again.

And then she remembered something that Mildred Purvis had said, earlier that year during the fundraising event.

*But passion is so important. To believe in something that matters. Something beyond yourself.*

Was this her passion? In the last forty-eight hours, she had pulled a virtual all-nighter, scaled a ten foot fence in total darkness, and crashed a board meeting, all because she felt that it was terribly important that every citizen's vote should be counted correctly. What Howard had found in the county's dirt and streams and Valerie in its schools, she seemed to have discovered in the simple democratic process of voting. She looked over at Carl who was beginning to feed the ballots into the scanner. This was going to take a while. But that was all right. She was where she belonged.

# 103

## Tuesday, 11:30 p.m.

"Yes I realize there will probably be a recount but I don't think that will change matters much…well, you earned it. You ran a good campaign and certainly showed me a thing or two during that debate…not at all, you said what needed to be said, and I'm the better for it…well thank you and good luck to you too."

Cindy looked up at Carl, who had just exited the gym.

"Just making my concession call to Frederick Rawlins. Probably the only time I'll ever get to do that."

"So Howard didn't make it?"

"Lost by sixteen votes. And probably by a few more, once all the 'Mickey Mouse' throwaways are deleted. Still, he's in an excellent position should he want to run next year for a full term. Are you all done in there?"

"We are officially done. Nancy finished the SOR and called it in."

Cindy looked at her cell. "Just for the record, when I ran this precinct we were done by 9:00 p.m."

Carl gave her a sour look.

"Just saying. By the way, did you really make those Brownies sell their cookies in the street?"

Carl laughed but chose not to comment.

"So are you off to Valerie's party?" he asked.

"You bet. It's in high gear. I need to get over there and give my sister a big hug."

"Well enjoy. I am beat. I going home for a deep sleep. I've got that canvass tomorrow."

"Well, that's good Carl, but I have a bit of a problem. You see, Maurice needed help in navigating, so my car is still at the warehouse."

"Oh," said Carl, realizing the implications. "So I suppose I need to drive you to the party. And when you're done there, take you back to the warehouse?"

Cindy gave what she hoped was her most engaging smile. "That would be nice," she said.

"Oh, and I just remembered. I promised to pick up all those signs at Happy Acres."

"So the night is young. Speaking of which…"

She reached out and took Carl by the hand.

"…we need to talk. I said something at the board meeting tonight that I probably should have run by you first."

"What was that?"

"We'll talk about it in the car," she said, giving Carl's hand an extra squeeze.

"You know my life was so much simpler before I met you."

"Yeah, but not nearly as much fun."

And together they walked down the path to the parking lot.

## GLOSSARY

The terms included in this glossary refer to items that may be referred to in the narrative. They are included here to aid the reader in following the story and are not intended to represent the specifics of any real life voting locality.

**Election Officers** are one day volunteers who serve on Election Day. They receive a small stipend for their service and are required to take an oath that they will conduct the election "according to law and the best of their ability."

**Chief Election Officer** is the election officer who is ultimately responsible for the running of the precinct. He/she directs and assigns the other officers and handles all the non-routine situations. In Virginia, the chief election officer is generally of the same party as the sitting governor.

**Assistant Chief Election Officer** is "second in command." He/she must be of the opposite political party from the chief. If the chief becomes unable to perform his duties, the assistant chief takes over.

**Rovers** are seasonal employees, generally former chiefs, who on Election Day drive a preassigned "route" of precincts. They provide the chiefs on an "as needed" basis with extra supplies, technical assistance, advice, and/or encouragement. Prior to Election Day, they prepare and test the equipment that will be used at the precincts.

**Board of Elections** – Three person body which has the ultimate responsibility for the electoral process within a county.

**Registrar** – individual selected by the Board to run the day-to-day operations of the Office of Elections.

**"The cart"** is a metallic crate on wheels that contains the electronic poll books, boxes of ballots, privacy booths, privacy folders, handicapped ballot marking machines, signs, posters, extension cords, and additional supplies. It is delivered to the precinct, locked and sealed, from the county warehouse several days before an election.

**Canvas bag** – contains many of the generic signs, posters, and forms that are used in every election. The canvas bag is generally stored in the cart.

**"The kit"** is a suitcase on wheels that is issued to the chief at the pre-election meeting. It contains many of the forms and signs that are specific to the current election (as opposed to the more generic signs that are in the canvas bag) along with other supplies.

**Poll watchers** are representatives of the political parties who are authorized by the parties to be inside the polling place on Election Day. They are required to present their authorization to the chief upon entering the polls. They may observe but not hinder the activities inside the polling place.

**Poll workers** are partisans who hand out literature for the candidates. They require no authorization and must conduct their activities at least forty feet from the entrance to the polling place.

**Pollbook** is the listing of the registered voters in a precinct. Until recently most precincts used **paper pollbooks** which consisted of binders that contained a line entry for each voter. Voters were "checked in" using the paper pollbook.

In recent years many localities have gone to **electronic poll books (EPBs)** which are computer laptops that contain the same data that used to be in the paper pollbooks. Looking up voters in the EPBs is a lot faster than with the paper pollbooks but most localities still issue the chief a paper pollbook as backup in case there are technical problems with the EPBs.

**Privacy folder** is a plain manila folder. Individual ballots are placed in the folder before being given to the voter. This allows the voter to maximize his sense of privacy.

**Privacy Booth** – three sided cardboard structures which are placed on tables. The voter sits down at the table and works on his ballot which rests within the perimeter of the booth, thereby maximizing his privacy.

**Provisional ballots** are cast in situations when a voter cannot be confirmed as being a registered voter in the precinct. A provisional ballot is placed in a special envelope and is not scanned or in any way counted on Election Day. Generally a phone call is made to the Government Center to attempt to resolve a voter's situation before a provisional ballot is issued. Three days after the election, the Electoral Board meets and determines whether each of the provisional ballots will be counted.

**Scanner** is the voting machine of choice in many localities. The ballot is fed into the scanner which records its vote internally, even as the ballot drops into a bin under the scanner. At the end of the day a tape prints out the result. In the narrative, the scanners are manufactured by a company called ***ElectionPro*** (fictitious name). Also in the narrative, the terms "scanner" and "machine" are often used interchangeably.

**Public count** – number of votes that have been cast on a scanner in the current election.

**Protective count** – number of votes that have been cast on a scanner during its "lifetime."

**Flash Drive** - a portable storage device that is inserted into the scanner. It communicates to the scanner the specifics of the election/ballot and is updated with the election results.

***"Create Ballot"*** (fictitious brand name) is a touch screen ballot creation device that allows a voter to mark his/her selections by touching the desired candidate's name on the screen. This machine is primarily for handicapped voters who might experience difficulty in marking a preprinted ballot. The session is initiated by an election officer inserting a blank card into the machine. After the choices are confirmed the machine returns the card with the selections made. That card is then inserted into the scanner which recognizes it as a completed ballot.

**Zero tape** is printed by the scanner at the start of the day. It confirms that no votes have been cast and that each candidate has zero votes.

**Results tape** is printed at the end of the day with the number of votes for each candidate. Generally, three copies of the results tape are printed which are affixed to different documents.

**Auxiliary Bin** is a bin where ballots are placed that for some reason cannot be scanned at the time they are cast. At the end of the day they are scanned (if possible) or otherwise counted by hand.

**Statement of Results** form **("SOR")** is the official document of the election. It contains the final results of the election as well as other relevant counts such as the number of ballots issued to the precinct, the number of unused ballots at the end of the day, the number of ballots spoiled, number of provisional ballots cast, etc.

**Call sheet** is a form where the results of the election are written down. The numbers from the call sheet are called into the Government Center on election night and those numbers are released to the press as the unofficial results. The sheet is then posted on the door of the polling place for the general public to see.

**The warehouse** is a massive storage facility that houses equipment and supplies owned by the county. Within this facility is a relatively small space which is reserved for use by the Office of Elections.

The **"cage"** is an area, roughly 100 feet by 80 feet, located against a rear wall of the warehouse. It is delineated by a 10 foot high chain-link fence. Its two entrances are sliding gates which are secured during the off-hours by padlocks. Inside are stored the precinct carts, scanners, ballots, and other election related supplies.

**Testing** is the process that takes place at the warehouse in the weeks leading up to an election. Each *ElectionPro* scanner and *CreateBallot* device is loaded with the correct election/precinct information and tested to ensure that it is working properly and producing accurate results. In addition, each of the precinct carts is packed with the supplies and equipment necessary to conduct the election. Representatives from the candidates and political parties are invited to witness the testing.

The different ballots that are used in a locality are sometime referred to as **ballot styles**. The number of different ballot styles used in a county-wide election is determined by the various government boundaries that exist within the county.

**Test Deck** is a set of ballots for an upcoming election that have already been marked in a predetermined way. The deck is used in testing the scanners in the warehouse and is created so that each candidate will receive a vote total that differs from his/her opponents.

During the pre-election testing at the warehouse, the precinct carts and scanners move through an assembly line process. This process begins at **Station One** where the necessary paperwork for the precinct is initiated and the cart is loaded with the correct supplies. The database is updated to match the precinct with the serial number(s) for its assigned scanner(s).

The cart/scanner(s) then proceeds to **Station Two**, where the scanner(s) and *CreateBallot* devices are fully tested. The ballots from the test deck as well as those ballots generated by the *CreateBallot* device are inserted ("voted") into each scanner. The results are then printed. If the printed result matches what is anticipated, the scanner has "passed" the test and will be used in the upcoming election (once the votes are erased and the counters reset to zero).

Any equipment defects are identified and the equipment is either repaired or replaced. All machine produced tapes are saved as part of the historical record. The precinct paperwork is updated to reflect the results of the test.

Only after a precinct "passes" the testing at Station Two, does it move on to **Station Three.** All tapes and paperwork are examined and verified as well as the contents of the precinct cart. The cart and scanners are then returned to their proper place inside the cage where they will stay until it is time for them to be delivered to the precincts.

# About the Author

Bill Lewers was raised on Long Island in the 1950s and has been a political junkie for as long as he can remember. He holds B.A. degrees from Rutgers (mathematics) and the University of Maryland (history) and a M.A.T. degree from Harvard (mathematics education). After teaching high school mathematics for a few years, he commenced a career as a computer professional with IBM. He lives in McLean, Virginia with his wife, Mary.

Bill is a lifelong fan of the Boston Red Sox and this passion is reflected in his first book, *Six Decades of Baseball: A Personal Narrative.* This was followed by *A Voter's Journey* which is one citizen's sixty year romp through the American political system.

Bill began serving as a Fairfax County election officer in 1994. Two decades later he wrote *The Gatekeepers of Democracy,* which was dedicated to the women and men who volunteer to serve on Election Day. *The Gatekeepers of Democracy* has been described as the novel that defined the genre of "election officer fiction." That genre continues with *November Third.*

Made in the USA
Middletown, DE
26 September 2017